FAT CAT

A SHIFTERS NOVEL

RACHEL VINCENT

Dear Reader,

THE QUESTION I get most often from readers is some variation of "When will you write Shifters again?" and for a long time, I thought I probably wouldn't. That I'd exhausted all the stories I had to tell in that world.

But then I realized that new characters would bring new stories with them, and I decided to use this new corner of the first fictional world I ever played in to explore a few tropes I've always wanted to write. The supernatural bar/hangout. Sisters—SISTERS!—in the Shifters world. And a rock-solid bromance. I love these new characters, and I hope they find a place in your heart as well. If they do, feel free to drop me a note online or leave a review!

Thanks again for reading!
Rachel Vincent

ONE

"Charley!" Grinning broadly at me, Doug Myers slid onto his favorite barstool with the familiar creak of well-worn leather. I rinsed lime juice from my hands and grabbed a clean towel, then I headed toward him from the service side of the bar. I could smell smoke on his clothes before I even got close. Wood smoke, not cigarettes. Doug had a small cabin in the Lakeshore complex, deep in the woods outside of town, and though he had electricity and running water, like most of the other Lakeshore residents, he both cooked and heated with wood.

I'd always found the scent to be comfortably nostalgic.

"Whiskey!" His shout was half request, half expletive, and I grabbed a bottle of middle shelf on my way. And for the millionth time I wondered what Doug, or any of my other regulars, was like before he was infected.

My gut—from being a bartender, or a shifter, or maybe both—told me he was an alcoholic. Not a social drinker. Not a weekend binger. My best guess was that before Doug Myers found himself on the wrong end of a set of claws, he was a liver-damaged, chronically dehydrated, perpetually inebriated drunkard. Possibly a bit of a legend in whatever small southern town he hailed from, but also consistently around three shots of whiskey away from falling over dead.

These days, though, his color was good—no sign of jaundice—and like most of my patrons, he hung out in the bar not to get drunk, but because this was his spot. The place where he belonged.

I'd worked hard to make sure they could all count on that.

"Caught a couple of new scents in the woods today," Doug said as I set a shot glass on the worn-smooth bar in front of him and poured.

"Oh yeah?" I lifted one brow as he threw the shot back, but I didn't bother to close the bottle. Doug was in his early 40s—a decade too young to be my father—and like most werecats, he had a hard time getting drunk.

Shifter metabolism foils the effort; our bodies process alcohol too quickly for us to feel its effects, short of guzzling straight from the bottle.

But like most werecats, Doug never gave up trying. Which was why the Fat Cat Bar and Grille, the only shifter-friendly bar in the territory, enjoyed a steady stream of regular customers, most of whom ran up large tabs.

Without spouses or kids, they had little else to spend their money on anyway. May as well spend it at my place.

"Yeah." Doug tapped the bar, and I poured him another. "Out in the common run." The large, heavily wooded acreage behind the Lakeshore cabin complex, which was open to shifters around the clock as a recreational area and hunting grounds.

Our Pride owned the land through the magic of shell corporations and limited liability companies, though I could never claim to understand exactly how all that worked. What mattered was that it *did* work. That the "private property" signs kept humans away and out of danger.

Mostly.

"Well, the common run is called that for a reason. All shifters are welcome." Whether or not they lived at Lakeshore. I visited the common run myself, regularly.

"I know, but I thought you'd be interested." He threw back his second shot, and I poured one more.

Interested? Yes, because it was my job to keep tabs on how many and which shifters live in the zone. Concerned? No. Our territory attracted newcomers regularly. Some were just passing through, out of curiosity. Others decided to stay. "Thanks, Doug. Let me know if you catch their names or figure out where I can find them."

"Will do, boss!" he called as I walked back to my tub of uncut limes.

I was not Doug Myers's boss, but like many members of our Pride, he was a little fuzzy on the meaning of my title.

My position—Marshal of the northern zone of the Mississippi Valley Pride—had existed for less than three years. Our Alpha, Titus Alexander, had created the job around six months after our Pride was officially recognized, when he'd realized that though ours was geographically the smallest territory in the US, we had the largest population by far. Which meant we also had the *densest* population.

All but two members of our Pride were strays. All but four were men. Basically, we were all sitting on a powder keg of testosterone and newly minted shifter strength and speed, neither of which came with any instructions or any truly helpful instinct.

"Doug, you want anything to eat?" I asked as I sliced the last lime. He'd been munching from the peanut bowl but hadn't touched his third shot yet.

"Um… Is Davey cooking?"

"No, we've officially removed food prep from her job description," I told him. "Billy's at the grill."

"Billy the Kid!" Doug grinned. "Thank God."

"I heard that." My sister pushed through the swinging door from the kitchen carrying a plastic rack of clean tumblers, her human arms straining beneath the weight. "And for the record, I never wanted to be in the kitchen in the first place." She stuck her tongue out at Doug, and as she turned on her square-toed boot heel to set the rack on the counter, one blond pigtail swung over her shoulder to trail down her back, beneath her cowboy hat.

"No offense, Davey," Doug called from his barstool. "You're great on this side of that swingin' door."

"None taken, hon." She set two still-steaming glasses on a shelf beneath the bar. "So, you want a burger or somethin'?"

"Steak, if you got it. Rare. Fries on the side."

"You hear that, Billy?" Davey shouted toward the swinging doors.

"Got it," he said from the kitchen, but it was clear from her frown that she couldn't hear him.

"He's on it," I told her with a smile.

"Shifters, with their freaky hearing," she grumbled.

"You're just jealous," I said as I grabbed a couple of glasses to help her finish off the rack.

"Of course, I'm jealous. You think I like being the token human in this place?"

I winked at Doug as Davey lifted the empty crate. "I think you thrive on it."

"Oh, come on, you know we love you, Davey," Nolan Blake called from the other end of the bar, where he was finishing his third beer.

Other customers whooped in agreement from various

tables, and Davey tipped her hat at them. "Love you guys, too."

A little too much, maybe.

Normally, a shifter bar would be the last place you'd expect to find a human female bartender/waitress/bookkeeper. Especially considering that it was against shifter law to reveal our existence to a human. To *any* human. But Davey had found out about shifters accidentally, and that couldn't be taken back.

And the truth was that the closer I kept her, the less I worried about her safety among the dense population of male strays in the Mississippi Valley.

Davey brushed by Vance Cooper on her way into the kitchen. Vance was one of six enforcers under my supervision, two of whom also worked as both security and jacks-of-all-trades at the Fat Cat. The other four enforcers lived spread throughout our zone: the western third of Tennessee and the western tip of Kentucky.

"Hey Davey," Vance said as he held the swinging door for my sister. "You closin' tonight?"

"Is this a day that ends in Y?" She smiled up at him. *Way* up. Vance was six foot five, barefoot, which made him a good thirteen inches taller than my baby sister.

Who—she constantly reminded me—was no longer a baby at all.

The door swung shut behind her, and Vance headed my way. "Hey, boss."

I really was *his* boss.

"Hey. You just back from patrol?" I asked as I pulled another beer for Nolan, at his signal from down the bar.

Vance nodded. "All's well in town."

"Town" would be Buford, Tennessee, about fifty miles northeast of Memphis, off a largely unkept length of state highway 18. Buford had around four thousand residents, including—unbeknownst to most of them—the largest concentration of shifters in the state. All strays.

All men, except for me.

There was no easy way to get to Buford. But once you found it, if you were willing to drive deeper into Hardeman County, you'd find the Fat Cat Bar and Grille. Though few people were ever willing to drive that far. Few human people, anyway.

Most shifters—even those who lived in town—were used to being out in the boonies. That was where we hunted, both alone and as a community. Where we congregated. It was where many of us lived.

"Doug's just reported a couple of new scents out in the common run," I told Vance as he helped himself to a beer from the tap.

He gave me an amused look. "Good work, Doug." Vance drank from his mug while I stared out at the front room of the bar. There were only a handful of customers this early, most of whom had stopped in for a beer and a burger before working a night shift.

Vance turned to me as Davey came out of the kitchen carrying Doug's dinner. "A *couple* of scents? Together? Or two separate scents?"

"Good question. Doug?" He'd heard us, of course. It's difficult to avoid eavesdropping, as a shifter.

"How the hell would I know if they were together?" Doug asked around a juicy bite of his steak. It was perfectly rare and clearly well-seasoned. Billy was really getting good on the grill.

"Were both scents in the same place?" I asked Doug.

"Yeah." He gulped from his glass as Vance and I moved closer. Everyone in the bar was listening now. Including

Davey, who'd started drying glasses that weren't even wet, for an excuse to stay near. "Smelled them on my run this morning. Several places, in fact. Always together. Overlapping, kind of."

"Well, that seems definitive, if odd," Vance said. "Strays traveling together."

Making a stray is illegal—comes with an automatic death sentence—so most strays are made by accident and born into our world in trauma. It's disorienting, to say the least. Isolating, usually. Those who survive learn to keep to themselves, at least until they find a safe haven, like the Fat Cat.

"*Maybe* they were together." I shrugged. "Or maybe one was following the other, and that's why the scents overlapped."

Davey tossed the towel over her shoulder. "Cats can't track by scent."

"I am aware," I said with a smile. My sister was very proud of every nugget of shifter knowledge she'd accumulated. "But we can stalk each other, just like a human would." Only much more effectively, with hyper-functional vision and hearing. "We won't know what's going on until I get a chance to talk to them. Doug, you let me know if you smell them again, okay?"

"Will do, boss."

The late afternoon lull set in, and I stared out the window as the sun began to set, shining on trees across the highway, heavy with vibrant fall leaves. I wiped down the bar and confirmed the week's liquor order with Davey, pausing to nod to customer after customer as the afternoon crowd headed out the door one by one, most of them on their way to pick up a night shift at the elevator factory or one of two local correctional facilities.

Shifters make *really* effective prison guards.

Every last one of them called out, "Bye, Davey!" as they pushed through the door, making the little bell overhead jingle.

The night crowd arrived in fits and starts, keeping Davey, Vance, and me busy pouring shots, pulling drafts, and serving burgers. I smiled as I listened to the regulars greeting one another. As I watched them share well-worn booths and sit together at the bar. It wasn't like this, at first.

Back when Titus assigned me the northern zone to run, this place was more like the wild west: every man for himself. Strays naturally found it hard to trust, and asking them to fall in line under a woman, when most of them had never even met a female stray, seemed like a Herculean task. But Vance was with me from the beginning—actually, he was here *before* I got the job—and Tucker, my other local enforcer, came along shortly after that. In the beginning, Titus lent me several of his men from the south zone of the territory, but I sent them back after less than a week when I realized that I needed the citizens of the north zone to trust *me*, not a series of temps who didn't know the area. Who could never love it or its residents like I did.

It took a while. But eventually, the Fat Cat became known as a sanctuary for strays in the area. Slowly, a real community began to form.

Still, no community is without its challenges.

Tucker arrived just after eight, and he took over behind the bar so Vance could go on his break. "All's well up north," he assured me. Tucker had spent the past day and a half in Kentucky, checking in with our two northernmost enforcers, updating our citizen roster—an electronic census database— and making sure our guys up there had everything they needed.

All of that could be done over the phone, but I'd learned

quickly that face-to-face interaction was the best way to gauge my enforcers' states of mind. And to maintain a positive relationship with them.

That, and Tucker liked the occasional isolation of a long drive, after a couple of weeks tending bar and busting the odd head. It gave him a chance to think.

"They managed to track down the new guy?" I asked.

Tucker nodded, his short, light brown hair catching the glow from the overhead fixture. "Turns out he's new to the area, but he was infected more than a decade ago, so he doesn't need to be debriefed. I added him to the database and emailed you his particulars."

"Thanks." I hadn't checked my email in a few hours. Because I *hated* email. "I'll take a look and forward it to Titus."

"Everything quiet here?" Tucker asked.

"So far, so good. Though Doug Myers reported a couple of new scents. A pair of them, most likely."

"That's interesting. New guys usually wander into the territory alone."

"Yeah. We're keeping an eye out."

The bell over the door rang again, and I looked up as Cam Senet shuffled toward the bar. Though he was one of our younger regulars, he was walking like an old man that night, frowning, kind of hunched over. Looked like he'd just been kicked in the gut.

"Cam? How's it going?" I asked while Tucker moved to the other end of the bar to pull a couple of drafts.

"Been better." Cam slid onto a bar stool in front of me, running one hand through short-cropped brown hair, briefly exposing an old scar snaking over his scalp. "Tracy dumped me."

"Well, shit. I'm sorry." I pulled a shot glass from beneath the counter and turned to my sister. "Davey—"

"On it." She was already tapping on her phone, her blue eyes narrowed at the screen.

The song playing on the jukebox in the corner ended abruptly, and a shout echoed from the other side of the room. "Hey! I paid for—"

The opening beats of "Another One Bites The Dust" began to play, and the shouter's mouth snapped shut. "Sorry," he said, his gaze finding Cam. "That sucks man. Been there."

They'd all been there.

"Raise your fuckin' glasses!" Davey shouted as I poured a shot on the house for Cam.

A dozen hands went up around the bar, each holding a pint mug or a lowball glass. "Another one bites the dust!" Davey called out, and they all echoed the familiar toast. Then they drank.

And ordered another round.

Yes, this is a sanctuary. It's also a business.

Cam threw back his shot and gestured for another. "She said I was 'emotionally unavailable.'"

And the truth was that Tracy, whom I'd never met, was probably right about that.

Natural-born female werecats were few and far-between, and female strays—infected, rather than born as shifters— were so rare that most male strays would live their entire lives without ever seeing one. I was the only one most of my regulars had ever met. Which meant strays had virtually no chance of ever dating or marrying a member of their own species. Of conceiving natural-born shifter babies.

And yet, it was very, very difficult—nearly impossible— for a male shifter to maintain a long-term relationship with a human woman, because one of our most important rules is

11

that we may not, under any circumstances, reveal our existence to the rest of the world.

Davey was the only human I'd ever met who knew about us, and part of the reason I kept her so close was that Titus had admitted when he'd named me Marshal that he could not be sure what would happen if his fellow Territorial Council members found out how much she knows.

So she was our little secret, out here in Hardeman County, in a middle-of-nowhere bar off a cracked two-lane highway. And for her part, Davey *did* seem to enjoy being the Fat Cat's "token human." No matter what she claimed.

She listened to Cam narrate the end of his two-month courtship of a human woman named Tracy—his third romantic failure this year—and I went back to placing orders and pouring drinks as the Friday night crowd grew.

Until an unfamiliar scent drew my gaze to an equally unfamiliar form, as he walked through the door.

I couldn't remember the name of every stray in the northern zone, but my cat brain never forgot a scent. If I couldn't place this man's, it was because we'd never met.

"Tucker." I tugged him to the far side of the bar and whispered so softly that I was barely speaking, counting on my very low volume and the blasting of the jukebox to cover my voice. "Do we know the guy who just walked through the door? Gray-on-gray canvas jacket over sweater. Tan hiking boots."

Tucker studied the newcomer's face and took a subtle sniff in his direction. "I don't." He turned to Vance, as my right-hand man pushed his way through the swinging door from the kitchen. "Got an ID on the gray jacket?" he whispered. "Guy with a short beard and blue eyes?"

The new guy *did* have blue eyes, and they were *gorgeous*.

Vance shook his head. "Want me to make an introduction?"

"With any luck, he'll come to us," I said. "Tucker, you start clearing tables near the door. Vance, you loiter near the restrooms." Because the rear exit was back there. "I'll see if Doug recognizes his scent."

I didn't really expect the new guy to run; he probably wouldn't have come in if he had anything to fear from a bar full of shifters. But it was always good to have my bases covered. And a shy stray would be less intimidated by Davey and me than by Tucker and Vance, so I needed them to vacate the service area.

I watched subtly as the stranger hovered in the doorway, taking the place in. He'd likely never seen this many shifters in one place, and he probably wasn't close enough yet to realize I was a one of them. It never occurred to most guys to check my scent; they just assumed any woman they met was human.

After a couple of minutes, he made his way toward the bar, and I leaned over to whisper to Doug. "There's a guy in a gray jacket heading our way. When he sits, I need you to take a whiff and give me a signal if he's one of the strangers you smelled in the common run."

Doug nodded, his eyes wide at my request. He was always eager to help. Even when no help was required.

"Welcome to the Fat Cat. What can I get you?" I said, as the stranger sat on a stool two down from Doug.

Doug inhaled through his nose, then he nodded at me, a gesture that was more enthusiastic than subtle. This was one of the cats he'd scented. The other one, though, was still in the wind.

"Whatever's on draft." The stranger took in my scent,

evidently unaware that I'd just been investigating his, and his eyes widened.

That's always a fun moment.

He sniffed in Davey's direction, and his mouth snapped shut, cutting off whatever he'd been about to say upon discovering that there was, in fact, a human in the room.

"Don't worry," I leaned across the bar to mock whisper. "She knows."

"She does?"

"I am fully in the know about the feline nature of the majority of our clientele," Davey assured him with a grin as she slid a bowl of peanuts toward us. "The cat is out of the bag, you might say. But let's not spread the word about that, okay?"

He gave her a solemn nod, promising to keep her secret, then he twisted to look around the room again. "I thought this place was a rumor." He turned back to the bar, his dark brows arched, evidently impressed. "In fact, I bet on it. Which means I'm out fifty bucks."

I smiled as I set a beer in front of him.

The stranger sipped from his glass, still looking around. "You know where I can find Eamon? I need a word."

The entire bar went quiet. Seriously, you could have heard the ends split on a single strand of my hair.

"Eamon MacLean is no longer a member of the Mississippi Valley Pride," I said in as neutral a tone as I could muster. "If you have business with the Marshal, you'll want Charley Studebaker."

He frowned, clearly put out by the news. "Well, can you point me in his direction?"

Brows arched, I extended my hand for him to shake. "Charlene Studebaker. Marshal of the northern zone."

"*You're…?*"

Davey laughed. "She is."

"But you're—" His mouth snapped shut.

"A bartender? Yeah. I can also whistle all of *Bohemian Rhapsody*. I am a woman of many talents."

He had the decency not to admit that the word tripping him up was *woman*. "What happened to Eamon?"

Before I could decide how to answer a question most people would never have the nerve to ask, the bell over the door jingled again, and four women in their mid-twenties came in, giggling. I could tell from the glazed eyes and easy laughter that three of them were already half-drunk.

The tone in the bar changed immediately. The awkward silence surrounding the Eamon question morphed into the buzz of casual conversation and the clink of ice in glasses as the ladies made their way to the bar, but beneath that I could feel a tension that was the natural result of both a secret that must be kept and genuine excitement over the opportunity for a bunch of mostly straight men to drink with the female of the species.

Well, the female of *a* species, anyway.

I arched a brow at the newcomer, and he nodded to let me know he understood what had just happened.

We don't get many humans at the Fat Cat, but they aren't entirely unexpected on the weekends. And they're almost always women; human men rarely make it over the threshold. It's something hormonal. Something in the scent of a bunch of male werecats that they find subconsciously threatening.

Women, though… Any human woman looking for a strong, confident, capable, employed man will find what she wants at the Fat Cat. It's my job to make sure that she *only* finds what she *actually* wants.

So far, that hasn't been a problem. Ours is a good crowd, by and large.

"You got this?" I asked Tucker. He nodded, while Davey started taking the women's orders.

"Nope, no margaritas," my sister said with a shake of her head. "No mojitos. No daiquiris. No cocktails of any kind. But I can throw a cherry on top of a Jack and Coke, if you want."

"Perfect," declared a woman with a pink blouse tucked into her boot-cut jeans. "This place is *adorable*," she whispered to her friends. "So rustic."

That's us. *So* rustic.

I made eye contact with the newcomer. "Let's go have a chat."

He stood, beer in hand, and I motioned for him to follow me. Vance fell into step with him as I led them through the kitchen to my office.

"Am I in some kind of trouble?" the stranger asked as I held the door open for him.

"Have you done something wrong?"

"No. I just heard that if you visit the northern zone, you should check in with the Marshal at the Fat Cat."

"But you didn't hear that Eamon hasn't been the Marshal in more than a year and a half?" Vance asked as he closed the office door behind us.

The stranger shrugged. "I guess my information is a bit dated."

"Well then," I said as I sank into my desk chair, gesturing for him to have a seat in one of the guest chairs. "Consider this your check-in. Welcome to the northern zone of the Mississippi Valley Territory. I have just a few questions for you."

"Okay." He gave me a solemn nod as he sat. "Fire away."

How cute that he thought I needed permission.

"First of all, what's your name?" I asked as Vance leaned

against the door at the stranger's back, arms crossed over his broad chest.

"Austin Graham."

"Mr. Graham, when were you infected?"

"Just over four years ago. I'm a Tennessee native. Though this was the free zone, back then."

So it was. We had many shifters who pre-dated the recognition of our Pride.

I leaned back in my chair, holding his gaze. "Do you plan to stay in the territory?"

He crossed his arms over the front of his gray jacket. "Am I obligated to divulge my plans?"

The question raised my hackles, but I reminded myself that it was not unusual for strays—or humans—to feel protective of their privacy. "No. Though we try to keep our census updated, so if you leave, we'd appreciate a heads up."

"Fair enough."

"As I said, I'm Charley Studebaker. I hold Titus's authority and I operate in his name everywhere in the territory north of the Tennessee state line."

For a while, Titus had tried to do it all himself. Educate all the strays on the rules and obligations that came with our new citizenship. Track down all the newly infected members and teach them the basics of instinct, shifting, hunting, loyalty, and the pecking order. He'd tried to be father, brother, priest, and king to every werecat in the Mississippi Valley, and burnout came hard and fast, even with Robyn Sheffield at his side and Jace Hammond at his back.

Dividing the territory into zones was Titus's first major decision as an honest-to-god Alpha, and from what I've heard, he didn't have much trouble getting approval for that from the Territorial Council. Some of the other Alphas truly didn't care what went on in the "stray Pride." Some actually had faith in him. Others were hoping to give him just enough rope to hang himself with. Regardless, within six months of the Mississippi Valley Territory's inception. Titus had divided it into three zones and appointed two Marshals to run the day-to-day operations of the middle and northern zones.

Titus oversees the southern zone himself, from his house an hour north of Jackson, Mississippi, and as an Alpha in his own right, Jace was the obvious choice to run the middle zone.

I was not Titus's first choice to take charge of the north. In fact, I wasn't even infected yet, when he created the zone. But how Eamon MacLean screwed things up and I got his job a year later was a whole 'nother story.

"The gentleman behind you is Vance Cooper, my second-in-command," I said. "The gentleman behind the bar is Tucker, another of my enforcers."

"And the woman?"

"Davey. My sister." I watched him closely for any sign of interest, but I saw none; Austin Graham appeared to be all business. Still, *everyone* got my standard warning. "The fastest way to get yourself escorted out of the northern zone in the trunk of my car is to make trouble for her. That means you can talk to her while you're here. Politely, obviously. You can order food and drinks from her. But the moment you leave the bar, you will forget she exists until the next time you come in. Understood?"

"Of course." Another nod.

"You will not seek her out, outside of this bar. You will not ask her personal questions. You will not speak to anyone else about her. Everyone in the northern zone knows those rules, so if anyone asks you a single question about Davey, you will immediately report that to me or to one of my enforcers. Do you understand?"

"Ms. Studebaker, I have nothing but respect for your efforts to protect your sister. More than you could possibly know." Graham's brows furrowed over those deep blue eyes. "Is she in some kind of danger?"

"That's unclear. As I hope you know, exposing our existence to a human carries the death penalty for a shifter, all over the world. But guidelines for what to do with humans who already know about us are rather vague. So we take every necessary precaution with Davey. With Titus's blessing."

"That is very good to hear." He seemed to truly mean that, and my curiosity about him swelled. But he'd already declined once to give us any personal information beyond his name, and I was starting to believe he had real reasons for that.

"Good. Now, we don't have any official citizenship process—everyone is welcome—but those who live in the territory are expected to follow the rules at all times. Breaking any one of them is grounds for immediate expulsion not just from the northern zone, but from the entire territory. Are you familiar with all of the rules and expectations that come with citizenship in the Mississippi Valley Pride?"

"I suspect I am. I'm not exactly newly—"

Shouting echoed toward us from the front of the bar, and I spun in my chair to face the north wall of my office. It was a cacophony of sound. A sudden burst of voices, all of them outraged.

"Charley!" Davey cried, a second before something collided with the other side of my office door.

Vance spun around and pulled it open to reveal my sister, her blue eyes wide. "Something's going down outside. Some new guy confronted Nolan Blake and they're fighting, out in the front parking lot. Tucker's trying to break it up, but—"

Vance pushed past her on his way out the door.

"Shit," Austin Graham swore, already on his feet to follow.

I grabbed the rifle mounted on the wall behind my desk and ran after them.

My zone. My rules. Anyone who doubted that was welcome to fuck around and find out.

TWO

I raced through the bar, my rifle aimed at the floor. The dining room was eerily deserted, plates and glasses sitting abandoned on every table, but through the grimy front windows, I could see a crowd of regulars with their backs to the building, gathered around the fight like kids on a playground. And I could still hear shouting.

"Hey!" Vance roared as he burst through the front door ahead of me. "Break it up! Now!" If he'd been in cat form, that would have worked. He had one of the most impressively deep and loud roars I'd ever heard. It echoed with power and authority.

But there was no time for either of us to shift, and his human voice, strong though it was, made little impression beyond a few of the strays at the back of the crowd. Those few turned to make way for him, and Vance, in turn, opened a path for me.

Instead of yelling, I planted my feet wide apart and fired my rifle into the air, from the middle of the crowd.

The boom echoed, and shocked silence descended all

around me. Everyone turned to stare, many of them covering very sensitive werecat ears.

Guns were *heavily* frowned upon in the majority of the shifter world. It was considered much more noble to solve inter-cat squabbles with claws and canines. But this was Tennessee, and I didn't have an air-horn, so...

"Okay, that's enough!" My gaze narrowed on the stranger, our second in a day. Behind him, Doug Meyers was gesturing frantically at me to indicate that this was the source of the second scent he'd caught in the woods.

Which I'd figured out for myself.

Like Austin Graham, this second stranger was tall and broadly built, but he had deep brown eyes and only a day's chin stubble, dark enough to stand out starkly, even against deeply tanned skin. He wore a casual red wool button-up and rubber-soled waterproof hiking boots.

But even though he'd started this, the man in the red shirt wasn't my immediate concern.

"Holy shit!" a female voice whispered from my left. "Holy *shit*! I've never seen anyone move that fast. Swear to god, their fists blurred in the air."

"That was a fucking brawl!" her friend—a skinny woman in glittery pink heels—added.

Great.

"Davey, pour these ladies each a drink on the house," I said, and my sister nodded. I watched, silently imposing calm and quiet upon the crowd as Davey led the human women back into the bar.

As soon as the door closed behind them, I turned to the man who'd started all this, only to find Austin Graham at his side, clearly furious. "What the hell are you doing? This wasn't the plan," he growled.

"Fuck the plan," his friend—clearly—in the red shirt snapped. "I saw an opportunity, and I took it."

"You two." My gaze flicked between them. "This is Vance. You do *not* want to fuck with him. Follow him to my office and wait for me there."

"Who the hell are—" Red Wool demanded, but I cut him off, my rifle still aimed at the sky.

"You might notice that you're outnumbered." I gestured with my free arm at two dozen mostly large shifters ready to back me up in defense of their community.

Strangers were welcome. Aggressors were not.

Soft growls echoed from all around me, aimed at them both.

"Come on, Bishop," Austin mumbled. Then he turned a fierce glare on Nolan Blake as he passed, dragging his friend along. "We're not done with you," he growled.

Tucker snarled. "That's for Charley to decide."

As Vance and Tucker disappeared into the bar, flanking Austin Graham and his friend, Bishop, I turned back to the crowd. "Nolan, stay put. Everyone else, please go back inside and enjoy your evening."

As one, they headed into the bar, grumbling beneath their breath about the antagonistic new strangers.

"Nolan?" He had my full attention, with everyone else gone. "What's going on?"

"I swear, Charley, I have no idea. I was just drinkin' my beer, eatin' my nachos, when that asshole sat down next to me and 'suggested' we go have a talk in the parking lot." He used air quotes.

My brows dipped. "Why would you go outside with someone you've never met?"

He hesitated for longer than he should have. And finally,

Nolan shrugged. "I didn't say I'd never met him. I said he was an asshole. They both are. Bishop *and* Austin."

"I'm gonna need more than that, if you expect me to keep them out of your face." A face which was already a patchwork of black and blue bruises, surrounding a newly crooked and bloody nose.

"Okay, look, I had a few run-ins with them, back in Covington—"

"They're from Covington?" A small town about an hour west of here.

"Yup. I am too, though I don't live there now. I stumbled into them when they were newly infected and offered to show them the ropes, and they acted like I'd just pissed in their faces. Needless to say, we didn't get together for sleepovers and bake sales." His nervous shrug told me that wasn't the whole story. As did the sour scent of his sweat.

"They were newly infected. Were they sick?" Strays still in the grip of scratch fever weren't able to process much, as they struggled with a barrage of overwhelming new senses and cravings. Needs and inexplicable instincts. Not to mention the fever itself.

I was out of my mind for a solid week, when I was infected.

"No, no," Nolan insisted. "They were fully recovered. Just still new."

"So, why would they attack you? Did they follow you here?"

"I have no idea, Charley. I swear. I didn't know they were in town. I haven't seen 'em in months, at least." He ran one hand through his hair, staring down at me, and the scent of his sweat grew stronger. "This is totally random. Swear to god."

"Okay. Go have a beer. But do *not* leave until you hear from me."

I patted a few shoulders and smiled at everyone on my way through the front room. Mostly because the human women were still drinking at their corner booth, with a couple of the regulars, and the Fat Cat needed to feel like a normal bar where patrons might get into a fight in the parking lot, but they certainly do not grow fur and claws. Where there was definitely not a basement level full of steel-barred cells and emergency medical equipment.

"Charley!" Doug Myers slid off his barstool and fell into step with me as I rounded the bar. "It's them. They're the two strangers I smelled in the common run."

"Thanks, Doug. I caught that." I turned him by the shoulders and pointed him back at his stool, then I lowered the bar into place behind me and headed through the kitchen into my office. Where I nearly choked on the cloud of testosterone hanging in the air.

Austin and Bishop sat in the pair of matching chairs in front of my desks, with their backs to me. Neither of them turned as I closed the door and rounded the side of my desk.

"Gentlemen," I said as I sank into my chair. Though so far, one of them had *utterly* failed to earn that title. I focused on Bishop. "My name is Charley Studebaker, and I am Marshal of the northern zone of the Mississippi Valley Pride."

"So I heard." He crossed thick arms over the front of his red wool button up.

"Okay, that's a good start." Once, a newcomer had refused to say a single word. "Now, why don't you tell me why you attacked one of my patrons?"

"Patrons?" Bishop frowned. "Are you a cop or a bartender?"

"Neither. As I said, I'm the local Marshal in charge of this zone. I also own and run this bar. And you are…?"

"Bishop Mattheson," he grumbled.

Behind them, Tucker began typing silently on his phone, Googling both of them.

"And you're both from Covington?"

Austin shifted in his chair. "Not originally. But that's where we currently live."

"And what is your business with Nolan Blake?"

"What did he say?" Austin asked.

"Doesn't matter," Bishop insisted. "We don't owe her any information."

Vance rounded Bishop's chair, stepping into their line of sight. "That's where you're wrong."

"I report directly to Titus Alexander. You can explain the assault you just committed to me, or you can deal with him." I frowned when I got no reaction. "Do you know who that is?"

"Alpha of the territory," Austin said. "I assure you we're neither green nor anarchists, no matter what Nolan Blake told you."

"Yet you live in my zone, and we've never met." As uncommon as that was, it was not unheard of. Many, many strays lived in the zone before our Pride was officially recognized, and despite all of our outreach efforts, we had no way of knowing that we'd actually found them all. Though once we did find them, we added them to the census, both to help form a better snapshot of the community and to help estimate our operational budget for the next quarter.

Titus was a businessman. He was generous with the necessary funds, but requests had to be officially submitted and properly formatted. Which meant there was way more paperwork involved in running a shifter zone than I'd anticipated.

"I wasn't aware we were required to check in," Austin said.

"We aren't," Bishop snapped.

"That's true." I nodded. "You aren't. But you also aren't allowed to attack people in the parking lot of the only shifter-friendly bar in the country. This is a safe place for strays, and I can't let an incident like this disturb the peace and make people feel threatened." Or rile up any territorial instincts among the locals. "So, let's hear it. Why were you beating up Nolan Blake in my parking lot?"

Austin may not have thrown a punch, but they'd clearly come here together with a mutual goal.

When neither of them spoke, I shrugged and set my cell phone on my desk. "Or I can call Titus."

Bishop and Austin looked at each other. Bishop shrugged. They turned back to me, and though neither seemed truly intimidated by the idea of meeting Titus Alexander, they did seem inconvenienced by it. As if they hadn't allowed for the kind of time that would take, in whatever strategy they were executing.

"We didn't come here to beat up Blake," Austin finally said.

"We came here to kill him," Bishop added, and it was the somber, dead-serious quality of his voice, as much as what he'd said, that shot chills up my spine.

I glanced at Vance, and he moved back in front of the door, just in case.

Both Bishop and Austin stiffened as their escape was blocked, but that could also be because of the double threat stationed at their backs. Out of their line of sight. But to their credit, as abrupt and matter-of-fact as Bishop was, neither of them seemed to have any particular bone to pick with me.

"I'm not sure how much you know about shifter justice, but just as in the human legal system, murder is against the law," I began.

"No one said anything about murder." Austin's cadence was smooth and deliberate. He sat absolutely still, as if he were afraid that any movement might spook me and trigger violence from the men at his back. Which told me he'd been a shifter long enough to understand how instinct works. "We're here to *execute* Blake, for crimes committed." He glanced at Bishop in irritation before turning back to me. "But none of that was supposed to happen in your bar. This was just supposed to be recon."

"Okay. Couple of points." I held up one hand and ticked them off on my fingers as I spoke. "Nolan Blake hasn't been charged with or convicted of any crimes that I know of." Cats running from the local Marshal don't typically take up residence on a stool at her bar. "And even if he had been, you're not authorized to carry out sentencing."

"We're not operating on legal grounds," Austin admitted. "This is more of a...moral imperative."

"I see." That was a first. Usually, shifter murders in my zone were crimes of passion. Tempers that couldn't be restrained. And they were almost always committed by recently infected strays who hadn't yet learned to control newly powerful bodies and newly chaotic emotions and impulses.

Austin and Bishop didn't fit that mold. Parking lot brawl aside, they seemed rational and coherent, if recalcitrant. They were calm. Honest. And *absolutely* determined to carry out their violent...imperative.

"Well, if you have a criminal complaint, we can certainly handle that. But I can't let you just murder—"

Bishop opened his mouth to object, and I rephrased.

"Excuse me, *execute* a citizen of this territory without authorization. Nolan has the right to a trial, by virtue of his membership in the Mississippi Valley Pride."

"We're not interested in some kind of prolonged political circus," Bishop insisted. "All we need is for him to admit what he did. Then he can pay for his crimes."

"Be that as it may…" I waved Tucker forward, and he opened the recording app on his phone without being asked. "Tucker is going to take your statement, and we'll forward it to Titus. I can't promise you that the process will be fast, but if there's any legitimacy to your complaint, Nolan will be taken into custody for the duration of the investigation and trial. And if he's found guilty, you *will* get justice."

"Fuck this. Let's go." Bishop stood, and Tucker suddenly seemed to swell with what can only be described as defensive aggression. He suddenly *felt* bigger, as every muscle in his body tensed. As he prepared to launch into action.

To stop them from leaving.

"Bishop. Sit," Austin said softly.

"This isn't what we came here for," Bishop insisted.

Austin ran one hand over his beard. He was looking at me, rather than at his friend. Or brother. Or…partner?

No, their connection didn't feel sexual. But it did feel personal. And deep.

"We can at least hear them out," Austin said. "It never hurts to listen."

"This is bullshit," Bishop grumbled. But he sank back into his chair.

Tucker tapped the record button on his phone, still lying in the middle of my desk blotter, then he stepped back.

"I understand you want to lodge a criminal complaint against Nolan Blake, a citizen of the Mississippi Valley Pride. Please state your names for the record."

Austin's brows rose. "Are you also a cop?"

"No. Again, I hold no legal authority in the human justice

29

system," I said. He smiled, but not really *at* me. More to himself. And suddenly I understood. "Are *you* a cop?"

"My name is Austin Graham," he said for the record. "I'm on extended personal leave from the Covington Police Department."

"He's a detective," Bishop added.

Which explained why he was the one willing to at least humor our process.

I glanced at Vance and found him frowning deeply. He seemed as frustrated as I was to realize we'd been unknowingly squandering a very valuable asset: one of our own with access to police resources.

"And you?" I glanced at Bishop.

"Bishop Mattheson." He glanced at Tucker's phone as he spoke. "I work in construction."

"And what crime would you like to report?"

"The infection and murder of Yvette Graham," Austin said. "By Nolan Blake."

I leaned back in my chair. Obviously, that was a very, very serious accusation. A fact which was clearly not lost on them. "Yvette Graham. Your wife?" I asked Austin.

"My baby sister," he said.

"*My* wife," Bishop growled, gripping his chair hard enough to make the arms creak. "And her name was Yvette Graham-*Mattheson*."

And there it was. Their connection. That inexplicable bond that was personal, but not sexual. Shared grief of one man's sister, the other's wife.

"Well, shit," Vance swore from behind them.

I exhaled slowly as I met his gaze. Then I turned back to the men seated in front of me. "Okay. Tell me what happened."

THREE

"Bishop found her." Austin's voice cracked. His beard had a reddish cast to it, despite the deep brown of his hair, and he tugged on it briefly as he spoke. The gesture felt...anguished. An unconscious attempt at self-comfort. "He called me at work and told me to come home. Immediately."

"You live together?"

Austin nodded. "We've been roommates for three years. That's how Yvie and Bishop met."

"I found her on the couch." Bishop took over the narrative as if he hadn't heard my question. Or Austin's answer. "I came home from work, and she was just lying there, eyes closed. But she wasn't really sleeping. She was breathing weird—shallow and fast—and her face was bright red. She was burning up. There was a bandage on her arm, right here." He touched the underside of his left forearm. "And there was a bunch of first aid stuff on the coffee table. Hydrogen peroxide. Cotton balls. Gauze. And medical tape."

"Scratch fever," I whispered. "She was infected."

"Yeah." Bishop nodded. "And she'd tried to tend the wound herself."

"I had six missed calls," Austin said. "My ringer was off, because I was on a case. In an interview. I called back when I got a chance, but she didn't answer. Bishop called me two minutes later."

"She called me too," Bishop said. "Eight times. I didn't hear the phone because I was working the jackhammer, chewing up some concrete on a big renovation job. When she didn't answer, I left work. I had a bad feeling. Yvie *always* answered her phone."

"So, someone bit her?" I stood and started pacing behind my desk because moving always seemed to make my thoughts flow more freely. "In cat form, most likely."

It *was* possible to infect someone while in human form—in mostly-human form, anyway—but most strays didn't know how to shift just their teeth or claws. Many didn't even know that was possible. That wasn't one of the things we taught newly infected strays, for obvious reasons.

"Tell me about the crime scene," I said, still pacing. "Could you smell the attacker? Any residual scent?"

"No." Austin looked a little insulted by my question. "Because our living room wasn't the crime scene. There was no sign that anyone else had been there. Ever. We never had guests, for obvious reasons. Our front porch camera caught Yvie's car on the way into the garage that afternoon, and the footage showed no one in the passenger seat. There were no other scents on the upholstery, either in her car or in our house. No unknown footprints. No broken glass or busted locks. Nothing out of the ordinary at all."

Bishop shrugged. "As far as we can tell, she came home injured—infected and already sick—and tried to treat the wound herself."

"Wait. She was attacked by a big black cat, but she didn't

go to the hospital. She didn't call the police or animal control. She called *you*. Both of you." There could only be one reason for that. I eyed them each in turn from behind my desk. "She knew about you. That you're shifters."

Bishop was the first to look away.

"Yes," Austin said at last. "There's just no way to keep a secret like that from a member of your own household."

I should've busted their balls. They clearly knew the rules: if you can't keep the secret from someone you're living with, then move out. There are no excuses. No exceptions. But even if I were heartless enough to make that point to two grieving men, I wouldn't do it with my sister serving drinks twenty feet away.

My human sister. In a shifter bar.

That would make me the world's biggest hypocrite.

"There's no way someone just randomly happened to infect the wife and sister of two shifters," Bishop said. "No way that was an accident."

"In a criminal investigation, there's no such thing as a coincidence," Austin added. "She was targeted." The determination in his tone told me they'd discussed this. They *believed* this conclusion.

So did I.

"Okay." I sank into my desk chair again as my gaze found Vance. He exhaled slowly. Tucker nodded. They both understood the gravity of what we were hearing. "Let's back up a bit. I assume you saw the injuries. Was she scratched or bitten?"

Austin leaned forward in his chair, and I could see that he knew what I was getting at. "It wasn't self-defense, Ms. Studebaker."

"Call me Charley. Everyone does. And you don't know it

wasn't self-defense. She could have stumbled upon some-thing. Caught someone unaware—"

"It was a bite," Bishop said. "*One* bite. No scratches. No bruising."

"And it was clean." Austin leaned back in his chair again, letting that sink in. "Even swollen and infected, you could see each individual puncture. The shape of each tooth. There was no tearing. She wasn't acting in self-defense, and she didn't fight back. Which means someone held her still. Carefully. She was infected on purpose. Whatever else happened to her, the *point* of it was to infect her."

A sick feeling began to churn in the pit of my stomach. "But then he let her go." And it *was* a he. More than ninety-nine percent of werecats worldwide were men. The percentage was even higher if you counted only strays.

Austin nodded. "He identified her, took her or cornered her somewhere private, held her still, bit her—once, neatly—then let her go."

Suddenly the room seemed to be narrowing on me, the walls slanting inward. I tried to suck in a breath, but my throat wouldn't open. My lungs were paralyzed.

I gripped the desk, my fingers pale from the tension.

"Charley." Vance appeared at my side, one hand on my shoulder. It was a comforting touch, but it was also a warning.

I could not show weakness in public. Or in front of any of my territory members. Most especially, I could *not* show weakness in front of two strangers who'd just admitted they came into my zone to kill someone.

"Ms. Studebaker?" Austin leaned forward in his chair. His reddish beard caught the light, and my gaze fixed on it.

My throat relaxed just a little, and air leaked in. "It's Charley."

He nodded, and for a second, I was certain he could see more than I wanted him to. As if I were the one being questioned. "Charley."

"I need a minute to confer with my second." I stood, still gripping the desk, and with any luck that looked like a power move, rather than an attempt to remain upright. "Tucker, please get them each a beer on the house. And keep them *away* from Nolan Blake."

Tucker ushered Austin Graham and Bishop Mattheson out of my office. I heard their fading footsteps. The soft rustle of fabric. I processed the fading of their scents. But I didn't really see them go.

The door clicked shut, and I sank into my chair. Someone pried my hands from the edge of the desk and my chair swiveled. Vance's face took up my entire field of view: brown skin, tight, short-cropped curls, and the kindest, darkest eyes I'd ever seen. "Charley." He squeezed both my hands. "Breathe."

"It's the same." My words carried almost no sound, but he heard them.

"It's not the same." His thumbs traced circles on the backs of my hands, over and over, and I tried to feel that. To feel only that. To hear only the barest whisper of his skin brushing mine.

To push everything else away.

"It is. It's him." I sucked in another breath, and logic finally began to beat back my fear. My panic. "But that isn't possible," I admitted softly. "Silas is dead."

"Very, very dead," Vance confirmed. "Buried and rotting. So, it can't be him. Which means it isn't the same. It was some other woman—"

"Yvette Graham-Mattheson."

"—and she was attacked by some other man."

"And she didn't survive."

Vance nodded. "She didn't survive."

Women almost never survive scratch fever. I am a very rare, very lonely exception.

"What happened to her was terrible, and her loved ones deserve closure. They deserve justice. And you can't give that to them while you're reliving your personal trauma. While you're conflating what happened to you with what happened to her. It isn't the same."

"It's not the same," I repeated, staring into Vance's eyes. "It isn't Silas."

He nodded, and finally he let go of my hands. "You okay?"

"Yeah. I'm fine."

Vance stood, then he leaned with one thigh against the edge of my desk. "I can take over, if you want. Continue their statements and write up a report for Titus."

"No. Thanks, but no. That's my responsibility."

"But if it's triggering—"

"Then it's triggering." I stood, rolling my chair back with the motion. "It isn't the same, but it's very similar, and ignoring those similarities would be just as reckless as ignoring the dissimilarities. Pour me a shot, please, and bring them back in here."

With a quiet smile, Vance rolled open my bottom desk drawer. While I wiped my sweaty palms on my jeans, he pulled out a bottle of very expensive tequila and my personal shot glass. It was clear, shaped like the skull of a saber tooth tiger—a gift from Titus, when he gave me this position. Vance poured a shot, then he disappeared into the kitchen.

I threw the drink back and took a deep breath while I listened to his steps fade into the cacophony from the front room. Relishing the clean burn of good tequila. I poured myself one more shot and downed it, then I put the bottle and the glass away.

By the time Austin Graham and Bishop Mattheson re-entered my office, followed by both Vance and Tucker, my hands had stopped shaking. I looked past the trauma of my own infection, focusing not just on the present, but on the immediate future. On what I had to do in the next few minutes. The next few days. I'd gotten good at that over the past year and a half, this latest slip-up notwithstanding.

"Have a seat." I gestured toward the guest chairs.

"Are you okay?" Austin asked as he sank into the right-hand seat.

"I should be asking both of you that question." I sat behind the desk as Tucker started the voice recorder on his phone again and set it on my blotter.

"No," Bishop growled. "We are not fucking okay."

"I get that, and I'm sorrier for your loss than you can likely understand." I exhaled slowly and folded my hands on the blotter, clasping them just a little too hard. "I can't bring Yvette back, but I can help you get justice."

Bishop huffed. "We can get our own justice."

"I'll rephrase: I can help you get the kind of justice that won't end with you buried next to whoever killed your wife and sister. Which is the penalty for murder, in every US shifter territory."

"We know who killed her," Bishop insisted. "And we don't give a shit about your laws and consequences. We don't recognize your authority."

"Oh really?" I glanced at Austin and found him frowning. Staring at his lap. "Well, that won't stop our laws and conse-quences from applying to you." I leaned over my desk, pinning Bishop with my focus. "I'm trying to save your life, Mr. Mattheson."

"I don't give a shit about my life," he growled, and his response came so quickly that there couldn't possibly have been any real thought behind it. He was a hothead, to be sure. A man who spoke and acted before he thought. But he was also mired in deep, dark pain.

I nodded. "Fair enough. But do you care about *his* life?" I asked with a glance at Austin. "You two are close, right? You live together. You married his sister. I'm guessing it was a tight little family." And that with Yvette gone and the human world at arm's length, the two of them probably felt like they had nothing left but each other. "You're like brothers, right?"

Austin nodded. Bishop's jaw clenched so hard I could hear his bones creak.

"So, are you willing to get your brother killed in your quest for revenge? Because I'm offering you an alternative. Justice for Yvette. Execution for her murderer. And a chance for both of you to heal and, eventually, to move on."

Bishop glared at me across the desktop. "We don't want to move on."

"Of course, you don't. Not yet. But I know from experience that there's only so long a person can exist in this heightened state of rage and pain. It isn't sustainable, because whether you want it to or not, time blunts every impact. It blurs memories and eases pain, and eventually, while you'll never forget Yvette, you *will* begin to remember yourselves. To live again. And that isn't a betrayal of her." I glanced at Austin again, then my gaze resettled on Bishop. "In fact, I'm guessing that's what she'd want for both of you."

Tucker gave me a small head shake from behind them, silently advising me that they weren't ready to hear this yet.

And he was right. No one in the grip of grief wants to hear that their pain will fade. That they will someday choose to move on.

"Let me help you," I said, switching gears. "Let me put my resources to work for you and keep you on Titus's good side. On the Territorial Council's good side."

"We don't give a shit about—"

"Bishop," Austin said. And I could tell from his tone alone that I was right about him. That a man who'd dedicated his career to working within the legal system for justice would respect that same process on the shifter side of things.

At least, as long as it worked in his favor.

Austin turned back to me. "You're not going to sideline us."

I shook my head. "Wouldn't dream of it. In fact, I'm assuming you have resources that we don't. My suggestion is that we pool our respective resources to the benefit of us all. We have a vested interest in finding Yvette's killer as well."

"Obviously, we can't have someone like that on the loose in our territory," Vance said.

"Then hand Nolan Blake over to us," Bishop growled. "And we'll solve all your problems."

"There's a process," Austin said.

"Fuck their process."

I exhaled, fighting for patience. "If you live in this territory, it's your process too."

"I don't recognize your auth—"

"Irrelevant," I snapped. "Those who don't recognize the authority of the US government are still expected to follow the law. To pay taxes. It's the same for us. If you don't want to follow our rules, leave our territory. That's the last time I'm going to say that. The next time you even hint that you intend to break our laws, I'll have you escorted straight to the border. If you're lucky."

"If you're not, we'll hand you over to Titus," Tucker added. "Good luck hunting your wife's killer from a cell in his basement."

Bishop's brows furrowed as he glared at me. But he kept his mouth shut.

I leaned back in my chair. "Well, if that's settled, I have a few more questions before we submit our official report."

Austin nodded. "Go ahead."

"First of all, when did this happen?" I asked as I pulled a notebook and pen from my top desk drawer.

"About three months ago," Bishop said.

"She was bitten on July thirtieth." Austin's voice cracked. "She died two days later. August first."

I scribbled as he spoke, writing for myself, even though Tucker was still recording on his phone.

"Did you take her to a hospital?"

Austin shook his head.

"We knew better," Bishop said. "There was nothing they could do for her that we couldn't."

"IV hydration? Antibiotics? Monitor her pulse and her fever?" A human hospital didn't have to know what was wrong with her to treat the symptoms.

"We did all that ourselves," Bishop said. "We keep serious first aid stuff on hand, for obvious reasons."

As did most shifters, because going to a doctor would bring the risk of something odd being noticed in a blood test. I just wasn't sure if two strays who'd eschewed our community would be aware of that. Or would care.

"You did the right thing," I assured them. "And the outcome likely would have been no different in a hospital."

"We did call an ambulance when she died, though," Austin said. "They did an autopsy. Officially, Yvette died of an unidentified bacterial infection. The CDC was briefly involved, but since she tested negative for everything they know to test for, they bowed out and let us bury her."

That was a risk we wouldn't have taken, but I was glad, for their sake, that they had a grave to visit.

"If you're ever in that position again, make a religious objection to the autopsy. If there's no sign of violence or contagion, they'll respect that."

Austin nodded. Bishop stared, his gaze unfocused, at my desk blotter. He'd gone oddly quiet, now that his immediate anger had faded. Now that getting his hands around Nolan's neck was no longer an imminent possibility.

Speaking of which...

"What makes you think that Nolan Blake was involved?"

Austin's sigh warned me to settle in for a story. "We didn't, at first. We've spent several weeks tracking down every shifter we've ever met, demanding proof of an alibi."

"Whoa, wait." Vance rounded Bishop's chair, leaving Tucker at their back, guarding the door. "We would have heard about that. Someone would have reported being harassed by the two of you."

Bishop shrugged. "I assure you, they would not."

I exhaled. "You threatened them."

Austin glanced at his lap again, clutching the arms of his chair. Bishop stared right at me, answering me with eye contact, though his mouth remained shut.

Their threats wouldn't have worked on the average shifter, in the average territory. But the Mississippi Valley Territory was anything but average, and the same was true for our members. They hadn't grown up with an Alpha. With a council to turn to for help. With an innate sense of their position in a distinct and meaningful hierarchy. They'd grown up human, and at best, they now lived with a forever-dueling mindset wherein human habits and tradition battled with largely inscrutable feline instincts and new rules that often felt arbitrary.

Finally, Austin shrugged. "Most of the cats we know exist outside of your community." Shifters who hadn't yet made themselves known to us. "So, they wouldn't have contacted you anyway."

"And you ruled them out?" Tucker asked.

Bishop twisted in his chair to nod at him. "All of them. But Nolan Blake wasn't even on our radar until we saw the footage."

"What footage?" I asked, as he turned back to me.

Austin pressed his lips together. "There's one part we haven't told you yet."

An uneasy feeling churned in my gut.

"The day she was bitten, Yvette withdrew ten thousand dollars from her personal savings account," Bishop said. "In cash. That was nearly every dime she had."

Holy shit. I could feel Vance staring at me. I could practically hear what he was pointedly not saying.

It's not the same.

"That can't be a coincidence," Bishop said.

Austin nodded grimly. "There are no coincidences in a murder investigation."

"He robbed her," Tucker said, and though neither of our guests turned, they both nodded. "The bastard made her withdraw a bunch of money, then he bit her."

"Or, he bit her to scare her, then made her withdraw the money," Bishop said, but I was already shaking my head.

Vance shrugged. "Or, he just happened to see her withdraw ten thousand dollars for some other reason, and he robbed and bit her."

"There's no way any of those things happened unless he bit her in human form. And most strays don't even know that's possible." I could tell from the looks on their faces that neither Bishop nor Austin had known.

"We've been assuming there were two of them," Austin said, confirming my suspicion. "Likely one in cat form."

"That's why you haven't killed Nolan Blake." Suddenly, accosting him in a public bar made more sense.

"We were trying to get him to come with us. For interrogation," Bishop said. "We want him dead, but not before we know who else was involved."

Austin sat straighter in his chair. "Though, you're saying it's possible that *no one* else was involved?" He turned to Bishop before I could reply. "We would never have known that without their help."

"I'm also saying it's possible Nolan has nothing to do with this." I'd only known him for a few months, and only as a bar patron, but I couldn't imagine him biting and robbing a human woman. Especially a woman he knew to be related to the two vengeful gentlemen sitting in front of me, practically baying for his blood. "What footage are we talking about? What did it show?"

"Security footage," Austin said. "I couldn't get the bank's footage without a warrant, and obviously no judge would issue a warrant based on a woman who died two days later of an infection apparently unrelated to her bank withdrawal. But the convenience store across the street had two cameras, and the night manager was more than willing to let me watch their footage when I caught him selling beer to a minor. One of their cameras showed Yvette entering the bank, then leaving ten minutes later."

"And Nolan was with her?" Surely they would have led with that, if it were true.

"No. But two minutes before she arrived, an old blue Chevy pickup drove slowly past the bank. The same blue Chevy that's sitting in your parking lot right now. One guess who it belongs to."

FOUR

"Holy shit," Vance whispered as the door clicked shut behind him. He sank into the guest chair Austin had just vacated, running one hand over his scalp. "*Holy shit.*"

"Yeah." I pulled my bottom desk drawer open again and grabbed the tequila.

"We've investigated infection and murder before," Vance said as I poured myself a shot. "But this…"

"Yeah." I threw the drink back and slid the bottle and the glass toward him.

"It doesn't make any sense," he said as he poured one for himself.

"Not one bit."

"Robbery at gunpoint?" He threw the shot back. "Sure. But at incisor-point? That seems complicated to pull off, and…unlikely."

"And Nolan Blake?" I shook my head. "He's not a thief."

"And he's certainly not a killer."

"So then, why was he at the bank when Yvette withdrew ten grand?" I shrugged. "Maybe there *is* such a thing as coincidence in a murder investigation."

"Or it wasn't his truck. Surely Chevy made more than one blue truck." Vance closed the bottle and pushed it back toward me. "We need to see that footage. To verify the model and year. And the license plate, with any luck."

I nodded. "Titus will want to see it too."

"And we need to talk to Nolan again." Vance stood. "Want me to write up the report for Titus?"

"Yes, please." He knew how much I hated paperwork. "But I'm going to go ahead and call him."

"Now? You know you could just email him."

I gave him a look.

Vance rolled his eyes. "Yeah, I heard what I said."

"Can you keep everything calm for a few minutes?"

"Of course."

"And take Nolan downstairs? But stress that it's just for an interview." The prison-style cells tend to make people nervous.

"I'm on it. What do you want me to do with Austin and Bishop?"

"Um… Have Tucker find them a place at Pine Cove. Short-term. We'll start with a month." *Surely I can solve a murder in a month.* "If Stuart has a problem with it, have him call me."

"Will do." Vance closed the door as he left.

I took a deep breath and stowed the tequila. Then I picked up my phone. The "favorites" list in my contacts had nine people in it. Six of them were my enforcers. The seventh and eighth were Titus and Jace. Davey was at the top of the list.

I tapped on Titus's name, and the phone began ringing in my ear. There was only a fifty percent chance that he'd answer, because he thought that if he didn't, I'd just send him an email.

He was wrong.

The call went to voicemail, and I hung up without leaving a message. If there was anything I hated more than email, it was voice mail.

I called back immediately, which I wouldn't do if this weren't an emergency. Titus answered on the second ring. "Two calls in twenty-seven seconds. What's wrong?"

"And a good evening to you, too."

He sighed. "Charley, it's Friday night, and I'm still in my home office. Robyn is making her irritated face at me from the doorway, and—"

"This is not my irritated face. This is my patient face," Robyn said from across a room I couldn't see. "But if you *want* to see my irritated face..."

"—and my brother is waiting on the other line," Titus continued. "So please just get to the point."

"Fine." If Titus could be considered a representative sample, billionaires never have time for pleasantries. "Vance is working on the formal report, but I wanted to call to give you a heads up."

"I'm listening."

But he was also typing. And sipping coffee. And probably approving graphic designs and budgets for various investment properties and office spaces.

I was supposed to know what he did for a living. What the business he'd inherited from his father and vastly expanded—the one that funded most of the Mississippi Valley Pride's expenses—was, but every time he started talking about it, I zoned out around four words in.

It was all *very* boring.

"Two previously unknown strays came into the bar tonight and accused one of our regulars of robbery and murder by infection."

"Okay." Another hurried sigh. "I'm sorry you're having a

rough night. Just let me know what you need from me. In an *email*, Charley."

"No, Titus, don't hang up." He wasn't disinterested. He wasn't callous. He was just very, very busy. And he'd delegated this responsibility to me for a reason. While he wanted to be kept in the loop, he didn't truly want to be bothered until and unless that became absolutely necessary. And I couldn't blame him. "The victim was a human woman."

Titus exhaled, long and slow. The typing stopped. He took another sip of his coffee, then I heard the light thump of him setting the mug down. "Robyn, Knox, may I have the room?" he said, speaking to his wife and one of his enforcers.

Over the line, I heard footsteps and another soft click. "Give me the details," Titus said.

I told him what I knew about Yvette Graham-Mattheson. About her husband and brother. About Nolan Blake and the blue Chevy truck. About the missing ten thousand dollars.

"But the human police aren't suspicious? They aren't…involved?"

"No. Well, no one other than Austin, the brother."

"It would be good to have a cop in our census," Titus said.

"Agreed." What went unspoken between us was that Austin would never join the Pride if we failed to get justice for Yvette.

"What's your gut, regarding this Blake guy?"

"Nolan's not a murderer. He'd defend himself, if he were threatened—"

"Any shifter would."

"—but it doesn't sound like Yvette was much of a threat, and it doesn't sound like her bite was the result of a struggle. Obviously, I didn't see the wound, but Bishop and Austin said it was clean. No tears in the flesh. No sign of a struggle."

"Any reason to believe they're lying?"

"They're angry and hurting, of course, but I heard no unusual elevations in their pulse." Shifters can't smell a lie, exactly. But those of us who are trained can hear the signs, at least when circumstances are favorable. "And I don't see any obvious reason for them to lie."

"So, you think she was unconscious when she was bitten? Asleep? Or restrained?"

"That's the only thing I've come up with so far."

A heavy silence settled over the line. "It's not him, Charley."

"I know."

"Silas is dead. We buried him."

"I *know*." And Titus meant that "we" literally. He'd personally helped me bury the bastard who bit me. That was the only time I'd ever seen him get his suit dirty. "But it doesn't sound like whoever bit Yvette Graham-Mattheson was working alone. And if that was the case when I was bitten…"

"Then we missed something." Another sigh. "We missed some*one*."

"Exactly. And if that's true, then he's at it again. Whoever he is."

"It's been *years*, Charley. You think Silas's partner—if there even *was* a partner—just started up again, after all this time? Why? Why *now*?"

"I don't know. And I don't know that that's the case. Maybe he moved. Or got better at hiding what he was doing."

"You think he never stopped."

"I don't know. But that's why I'm calling."

"Okay." Titus's chair creaked as he leaned back. "Dig into it. Look for other cases that went unreported. Unnoticed. And keep me updated."

"I will. And like I said, Vance is sending you the report. But...do I need to spell out the complication inherent in that?"

"You'll need information from the other territories, but you can't actually ask for it without telling them why you need it."

"Exactly." And we damn well knew better than to tell the Territorial Council that there may be a stray on the loose infecting and killing human women.

"I'll call Faythe. She'll help without sounding the alarm, though she'll probably only have access to information from the South-Central Pride." Faythe Sanders was the world's only female Alpha, and Titus's closest political ally. I'd never met her, but he had assured me that someday, I would.

"Thanks. And we'll see what we can find out elsewhere, without drawing attention."

"What do you need from me?"

"Nothing, at the moment," I said. "We still have funds in the budget, and with Austin and Bishop, we have two extra sets of hands."

"No, what do *you* need? Personally? How are you doing with this?"

"I'm fine."

"*Charley...*?" Disbelief dripped from both syllables of my name.

"I had a bad moment, but it's passed. The best way to get over something is to barge straight through it, right?"

"Sometimes."

"I want to find the bastard, Titus."

"Okay." I could practically hear him nod. "Go do it. I'm transferring some extra funds for you, just in case. This is a priority. I want it solved fast, because I can't keep it from the council forever, and I don't want to take them an unsolved human murder."

"Understood. I'll be in touch when I have more information."

I WOULD NEVER HAVE GUESSED, based on the vibe in the front of the bar, that one of my regular patrons had just been accused of murder. Darts were being thrown, pool being played, food and drinks consumed as if this were just any other Friday night. And for most people, I guess it was.

Fights were not entirely unheard of in country bars, and as far as most of the customers were concerned, that's all that had happened. Thanks in large part to Davey, Tucker, and Vance.

I lifted the bar flap, headed into the dining area, and Tucker tossed his head toward the back of the building, where stairs led up to my private quarters, and, alternately, down into the basement, silently telling me that Vance had taken Nolan Blake downstairs as requested.

I nodded my acknowledgement.

Davey arched her brows at me as she set a plate of Buffalo wings on a table across the room, but I could only give her a subtle shake of my head. I wasn't in the position to indulge her with an update at the moment, and thanks to her human hearing, she probably knew less about what was going on than anyone in the building, other than the human women still laughing and drinking at their booth.

On my way across the room, I grabbed an unused chair, which I set at the end of the booth where Austin Graham and Bishop Mattheson were silently sipping from tall, frosty mugs of draft beer. I sat backward on the chair, folding my arms across its spine, and glanced from one man to the other.

But before I could speak, Bishop tossed his head in Davey's direction as she headed back to the bar.

"You got a human waitress in a shifter bar?" He looked distinctly disapproving. And knowing how his wife had died, I could totally understand. "Austin said she's your sister?"

"Yes. Davey. And this is the safest place for her." Considering that she'd refused to leave the territory. Her home. "I hope it goes without saying that she's off limits."

Bishop scowled. "I'm not interested in your sister. I *just* lost my wife."

"I know. But everyone gets the warning. No exceptions."

He seemed to approve of the policy, the only common ground Bishop and I had found so far. "Your names are Charley and Davey?" His head canted at an angle that might have meant he was amused. "So, what, your folks really wanted sons?"

"Never gets old." I cleared my throat and glanced at Austin to draw him into the conversation. "I just got off the phone with Titus Alexander," I said as softly as I could, well aware that anyone who could eavesdrop on us would be. "He's up to date on your case, and Vance is filing a formal report as we speak." From the computer in the basement. "We're finding housing for you—"

My phone buzzed, and when I dug it from my pocket, I saw Stuart's name on the screen. "Speaking of which…" I sent the call to voicemail; I'd call him back when half the bar wasn't trying to listen in. "So, you two are welcome to hang out here—beer's on the house—until I have a key for you, and—"

"We're not staying," Bishop said. "Though I would take another beer."

I counted to five before responding. It's this thing Davey talked me into, to help me keep my temper. Ten is the goal, but I've never made it past eight. "We agreed to work together on this investigation," I whispered. "To share our respective resources. For that to work, you'll have to be here. You don't have to stay at Pine Cove, but—"

"We have a house."

"In Covington," I pointed out. "That's a drive. It'd be much easier if you were sort of…on hand."

"What is Pine Cove?" Austin asked.

"It's a shifter-friendly apartment complex in town. Five different two-story buildings, four units each."

Bishop scowled. "And by shifter-friendly, you mean…?"

"All the tenants are shifters. All Pride members. As is the manager, Stuart Jones." Rejecting human tenants wouldn't be legal, of course, but since the change in management a couple of years ago, Pine Cove hadn't had a single application from a human, because those who came to tour decided, universally, that they didn't like the vibe. Though they couldn't *quite* put their finger on a reason they didn't feel safe in a neighborhood with no crime to speak of. "We're arranging for a short-term occupancy. At the Pride's expense, of course."

I glanced around, worried that if that part were overheard, people would start to catch on that this was about more than just a bar fight.

"You're going to put us up? For free?" Bishop looked and sounded beyond suspicious. "Why would you do that?"

"Because they need us," Austin told him.

"Because we need each other. And because we have a somewhat generous operating budget for this investigation, considering the potential it has for making our Pride—and our Alpha—look very, very bad to the Territorial Council."

Austin nodded slowly. "You don't want them to know that a human woman was murdered in your territory."

"We don't want them to know until we have a perpetrator to hand over," I admitted as softly as possible.

"You have a perpetrator," Bishop growled.

"We have a *suspect*," I corrected him. "But the council isn't just going to take your word that he's guilty." Even if the Alphas gave a shit about Nolan Blake's civil rights—and most of them did not—they weren't willing to risk letting the real killer go unidentified. Uncaught. Especially if he turned out to have been involved in my infection, a case we'd assured them was solved years before. "We need evidence and a very, very solid narrative. And you need justice. We can all get what we want out of this if we work together. And that will be easier if you stay close by."

The two men stared at each other across the table, evidently having a silent conversation. Rather, an argument, based on Bishop's scowl.

"Come on." I stood and swung my chair back into place at the table behind me. "I'll show you the apartment, and you can—"

"You don't have a key yet," Austin pointed out, instead of standing.

"Stuart lives on-site. He has the keys."

"I appreciate the offer." Bishop paused to sip from his mug. "But I'm not sleeping on an air mattress in an empty apartment when I have a perfectly good bed of my own in—"

"The apartment's furnished," I growled softly. And if it wasn't, it could be, within a matter of hours.

"Let's just look," Austin insisted, finally standing.

Bishop growled again. But then he gulped the last of his beer and they both followed me out to the parking lot.

.   .   .

So, I wasn't *quite* being truthful when I told them only shifters lived at Pine Cove. My sister lived there too. The only place safer for Davey than in the unit upstairs from Tucker and next door to Vance would have been with me, and she'd moved out of the Fat Cat a year before, over my strenuous objection.

Bishop's ten-year-old white 4Runner pulled into the gravel spot next to mine as I climbed out of my truck. Instead of getting out, though, he continued whatever argument he was having with Austin, which I couldn't hear over the loud music obviously intended as a smokescreen. So, I jogged across the gravel parking area toward Stuart Jones's door, which he opened before I got close enough to knock.

"Hey, Charley," he said as he stepped out holding a large ring of keys. In his mid-sixties, Stuart had been managing Pine Cove since long before I was infected. Possibly before I was born. If he had any family, I'd never met them, and if he'd ever lived anywhere else, I'd never heard about it. His entire life was wrapped up in these twenty rental units, which was both a pro and a con.

His gaze traveled past me to the 4Runner. "Short term lease, huh? That's against policy, you know."

"Titus approved it, and he's paying, so…" I shrugged. No need to remind the manager that Titus owned the entire complex and paid Stuart's generous salary. "How many units are available?"

"Three, at the moment."

"Any of them furnished?"

Stuart rolled his eyes. "Does this look like the Ritz to you?"

"Had a feeling. I may need you and a friend to help move some stuff in, from my storage unit." My parents had left most of their furniture when they'd moved to Florida three years before. "There's dinner and a few beers in it for you both, at the Fat Cat."

"Dinner?" Stuart looked distinctly unimpressed.

"That, and my undying appreciation."

He gave me a crooked smile as he rubbed the gray scruff on his chin. "Well, how could I say no to that? So, who are the new guys?" he asked as he stepped toward the 4Runner.

I put one hand on his chest to stop him. "I'll give the tour, if you don't mind."

His unruly left brow rose. "Since when do the Marshal's duties include showing apartments to mysterious new Pride members?"

"Need-to-know, Stuart."

"Fine." He handed me the keys. "Show 'em 2A. But I'm gonna 'need to know' names, if they're going to be tenants. Even short-term."

I nodded. "I'll let you know on my way out."

Stuart went back into his apartment, and the blinds at his front window twitched as he pulled one of the slats down, watching while I made my way across the gravel lot. Bishop and Austin got out of the 4Runner as I approached, and I led them to the lower left unit of the building we'd parked in front of. "Stuart lives across the parking lot," I said as I slid the key marked 2A into the front door. "He's nosy, but he keeps things up and running, so let him know if you need anything."

Bishop huffed. "We haven't—"

"*If* you decide to stay," I added as I opened the door. "There's only one bedroom, so you'll have to take turns sleeping on the couch, and—"

"What couch?" Bishop scowled at the empty apartment.

I set the key ring on the small, tiled breakfast bar. "Stuart will bring in furniture. If you stay."

"We'll stay," Austin said.

"I'm not going to—" Bishop began, but Austin cut him off.

"Fine. *I'll* stay. You can go home, if you want. I can do this without you."

Bishop narrowed his eyes at his brother-in-law, but there was true consideration behind the glare. "You're not going to cut me out of this. She's—she *was*—my wife."

"And my sister," Austin snapped. "I'm not going to argue with you over who loved Yvette more. What I *am* going to do is find her killers. And Charley's right; we're best equipped to do that here, with the assistance and budget of the entire Pride behind us. So you can stay and help, or you can strike off on your own, and I'll let you know when we've got him."

"*Asshole*," Bishop muttered. But I recognized defeat in his tone.

"We'll get the furniture in ASAP. Tonight," I promised as I crossed the room to push open the bedroom door. "Bathroom's through there. The fridge is unplugged, but functional. I suggest you go grab some groceries, and with any luck, by the time you get back, there will be a couch and a bed here, at the very least."

I glanced at the clock on my phone's lock screen. Eight minutes after ten pm. "Grocery store's closed, but the gas station on Pierce has the basics. If you want dinner, burgers are on me at the Fat Cat. I have to go talk to Nolan Blake, but I'll give you an update in the morning. Okay?"

Austin nodded.

"Any questions?"

"Can we get the key?" Bishop asked.

I took the 2A key from the big ring and set it on the counter. "I'll have Stuart leave an extra with the furniture. Write down your numbers for me please." I handed Austin my pen and notebook, open to a fresh page. "I'll send you my contact info, as well as Tucker's and Vance's. They both live in the building to the east."

Austin scribbled in the book, then handed it back to me.

"Call me if anything goes wrong with the furniture. Otherwise, I'll text you tomorrow."

I updated Stuart on my way out, and it was nearly ten-thirty by the time I made it back to the Fat Cat. I parked out back and went in through the kitchen, where I nodded to Billy as he dropped a basket of fries into the deep frier. "Kitchen closes at eleven," I reminded him. After that, it was just drinks and snack mix at the bar.

"Counting down the minutes," he assured me with a toss of his head, which would have swung chin-length brown hair out of his eyes, if it weren't secured in his hair net.

"You know, you're getting pretty good at that," I said with a nod at the grill.

Billy snorted. "Only if you're comparing me to your sister."

I stuck my head out front and waved at Davey to let her know I was back, then I headed through the kitchen and downstairs, where Vance was still babysitting Nolan Blake.

"'Bout damn time." Nolan popped up from a folding metal chair as I jogged down the last few steps into sight. "Charley, will you please tell me what the hell is going on here? I left a beer on the bar upstairs, and this fucker just keeps saying you'll explain when you get here."

"Vance is only doing his job, Nolan."

"And I was just trying to have a beer and a burger on a Friday night, but now that's all shot to hell." He plucked a bloody tissue from the folding card table he'd been sitting in front of and showed it to me. "So I want you to tell me how it is that I got assaulted—I'm the victim of a *crime*—yet I'm down here staring at a set of steel bars..." He waved at the cells behind him. "...and they're up there drinking on the house."

"Sit down, and we'll figure all that out." I grabbed a wire trash can from the corner and held it toward him. Nolan swiped at his nose, though it had long since stopped bleeding, then he tossed the tissue into the can. But he didn't sink back into his chair until I pulled one up across from him and took a seat myself, with Vance at my back. "This night has been a shitshow for all of us, and the sooner we can get it sorted out, the sooner we can all go to bed. So I need you to tell me everything you know about Austin Graham and Bishop Mattheson. Starting with whether or not you ever met the woman they had in common: Yvette Graham-Mattheson."

FIVE

I exhaled as Vance locked the front door of the Fat Cat and turned off the neon sign.

"Good god, what a long day." Davey turned to lean back against the bar, propping her elbows on the worn-smooth wood. Her laptop stood open behind her, most of the screen taken up by an inventory spreadsheet, which she'd started working on around one a.m., when the crowd started to thin.

Last call was at one-thirty on Friday and Saturday nights, and tonight, that final half-hour of business really seemed to drag on. "You have no idea," I told her as I started stacking chairs on tables.

"Well, whose fault is that?" She closed her laptop and began wiping down the bar.

"It's not like I could fill you in with ten sets of shifter ears sitting a few feet away."

"Well, now we're alone," she said as Billy backed through the swinging door from the kitchen, pulling the mop bucket, his hair finally free, now that he was done cooking. I glanced at him pointedly, and Davey rolled her eyes. "Billy doesn't count. He knows everything that goes on around here."

Billy did *not* know everything that went on in the Fat Cat. But she had a point; it would be impossible to keep our basement guest a secret from the short order cook.

"Did Nolan Blake kill that guy's wife?" my sister asked.

"Which guy?" I inverted the last chair onto its table and turned back to the bar.

Davey set her cowboy hat on her laptop and glared dramatically at me. "Whichever guy lost his wife."

She'd been talking to Vance. Or Tucker. Clearly it was time for another reminder to my enforcers that despite her omnipresence at the bar, my sister was *not* an employee of the northern zone.

"It's complicated," I finally said, as Davey began counting down the cash register. "But I don't think so. Stay out of the basement, though, just in case."

Her hands stilled, one clutching a stack of twenties. "You're holding him, even though you think he's innocent?"

"Technically, he's a guest of the zone, for his own protection. I took him a mattress topper and a spare set of sheets. My good set."

"Cell C is practically a spare bedroom, at this point," Vance added. "Charley took him a fucking plant."

"It's plastic," I clarified, as Davey blinked at me. "And to be clear, I'm pretty conflicted about locking him up. I don't think Nolan did it, but I can't prove that, and his statement was less than helpful." He'd admitted to having met Yvette, but insisted it was total coincidence that he drove by the bank that day. He gave us access to his bank account, where we could see that he'd made no large deposits. But until Tucker had time to dig into his finances, we couldn't assume that he didn't have other accounts. Until we searched his place, we couldn't verify he wasn't holding onto the cash. And none of that would prove that he didn't have a partner who'd kept the money.

He seemed to have no motive, but if there was even a possibility I was wrong—that he was a threat to Davey or any other human woman—I had to keep him in a cell until we knew for certain.

"And I can't swear that if I let him walk out of here, the grieving widower won't try to rip his head off. Speaking of which…"

"You put them up at Pine Cove?" Davey guessed. She shrugged when I gave her a look. "I heard Tucker on the phone with Stuart."

"They're in 2A. Stay away from them."

"You know I will."

"I know no such thing." She only followed around half of the instructions I gave her about running the bar and even less of my life advice.

Davey rolled her eyes. "So then, why don't you just tell Vance to spy on me?"

I dipped a rag in bleach solution and began wiping down the beer taps.

"Oh my god, you already did!" She turned to glare at Vance, who was cleaning the soda gun holsters. "You're—?" She shoved him, and he backed away from her, both hands up to protest his innocence.

"Don't blame him. He's only following orders." I exhaled slowly as Vance motioned for Billy to clear out of the front room and give us some privacy. A moment later, the kitchen door swung shut behind them both. That was just for show, though. A courtesy. They'd still be able to hear everything we said.

"Davey, I'm just trying to protect you."

"I don't need you to—"

"Yes, you do."

Davey's blue-eyed gaze hardened. "I'm a grown woman."

"You're a grown *human* woman with a fraction of the speed, strength, and hearing that the men around you have."

She glared at me, but there was a wound behind the hard shell of her anger. "So, I'm prey. You think I'm *prey*."

I nodded slowly. "Just like I was."

"Oh my god."

"Davey—"

"I'm not *you*, Charley! My life isn't about you! I'm as sorry as I can be about what happened to you, but that's not going to happen to me, because I understand the threat. I know how to watch my back. In large part because of you." She huffed, and the sound carried a bitter note. "And it's not like it hasn't all worked out for you, anyway." She gestured with one out-flung arm at the bar. "This place is *ours*, in case you've forgotten. Not yours. Mom and Dad put you in charge, but they signed it over to *both* of us."

True, but our circumstances had changed since then, as had ownership of the bar. When he'd named me marshal, Titus had bought thirty percent of the Fat Cat just to help me out, and his minority share had been the only thing keeping us in the black until word spread through the shifter community. Until business picked up.

Our parents wouldn't even recognize the clientele, if they were to drop by for a visit.

"It was your decision to turn this place into a shifter sanctuary, but the truth is that I was here long before any of your zone members. I *belong* here," Davey snapped. "So you can't run me out. Not even to protect me."

"I'm not trying to run you out. I *want* you here."

"But only on your terms."

"They aren't *my* terms. They're logical terms." A familiar nausea churned deep in my gut. Rising toward my throat. "*Safe* terms. I know you don't want to think about it—maybe you don't even think it's possible—but it happened to me. It happened to Yvette Graham-Mattheson, and who knows how many others. And I'm the exception, Davey."

"I know."

"You don't, though." I sighed as I sank onto one of the barstools. "You don't *really* understand."

"I understand that you survived scratch fever, and now you have superpowers. Now you have this whole community. All these friends who'd basically take a bullet for you."

"That's not..." *Entirely* inaccurate. "That's not the whole story."

"It is, though. And it's the same for Robyn." Titus's wife. "If you two survived, I could."

"You could. But you probably *wouldn't*. The cold, hard truth is that for every human woman who survives infection..." And I'd only ever heard of three, including myself. "...there could be a hundred who died. Surviving is very rare. And I'm not going to risk you—"

Davey rolled her eyes again. "But that's just it. I'm not taking risks. It's not like I'm standing in the middle of the street naked, daring some asshole to bite me. I'm just living my life. Trying to, anyway. And I don't need you to order your enforcers to watch me. I'm not going to go near the psycho widower or that other guy. The brother?"

I nodded.

"I don't need you to tell me that, because I'm not an idiot. Nor am I suicidal. So why don't you just...back off." With that, she scooped up her hat and her laptop and stomped through the kitchen, boots echoing across the floor. A second later, the back door squealed open, and a moment after that, I heard her car door slam and her engine rev to life. Then Davey was gone.

I resisted the urge to track her phone. To make sure she went straight home. Because she was right. She was an adult. And this *was* as much her bar as it was mine.

"She'll be fine," Vance said, and I looked up to realize he was standing six feet away, holding a fresh rag. Ready to resume cleaning the soda guns. Shifters could move nearly silently when they wanted, but Vance was *really* proficient at stealth. "No matter what she says when she's mad, she knows you're just worried about her. That it comes from a place of love."

"I hope you're right. But you're still going to keep an eye on her."

He nodded. "As always."

TUCKER KNOCKED on my door at ten-thirty a.m. I recognized his distinctive double rap, and by the time I'd stumbled out of my bedroom into the small living room, I could smell the aromas of fresh coffee and a small assortment of pastries.

"Hey," I said as I opened the door to find him on the landing, the stairs behind him descending into the Fat Cat's kitchen.

"Hey." Tucker took in my bare legs and lack of bra with the same disinterested amusement he gave my disheveled hair.

"Thanks." I plucked the coffee from his grip as I stepped back to let him in. "Don't you dare laugh. I didn't get to bed until three am."

"That's why I brought Danishes." He'd been out the door by eleven last night and probably in bed by midnight, since he wasn't closing.

I gulped from the steaming cup, then set it down and grabbed a cheese Danish from the bag. "You're the best."

"I really am. Though, you may change your mind in a minute."

"Why? What's wrong?" Still chewing, I set my pastry on a napkin and headed back into my bedroom, where I pulled on last night's jeans without bothering to close the door. I was not Tucker's type.

He'd never actually *said* he had a guy up north, but he always volunteered for the Kentucky leg of the enforcer check-in, so I'd drawn my own conclusion.

I was still tugging a clean tee into place over a fresh bra when I rejoined him at the short breakfast bar.

"Nothing's wrong," he assured me. "But nothing's particularly right, either. I dug into Nolan Blake's finances this morning, and it turns out he *does* have another bank account. It's more than a decade old and has never had a balance above five thousand dollars."

"Do I want to know how you got access?"

"Probably not."

"Fair enough. His apartment?"

"I stopped by on my way here and did a search. Which would have been much easier if he lived in Pine Cove."

"Nosy neighbors?"

"Probably." Tucker set Nolan's keys on the counter. "Want me to return these?"

"I'll do it. What'd you find?"

"Nothing, other than an embarrassing collection of porn."

"Embarrassing, how?"

"The man still watches DVDs. And his taste is super straight and boring."

I laughed as I bit into my Danish. "Nothing else?" I asked with my mouth full.

"Nope. No other scents. If he's ever had company, I couldn't tell it. He had fifty bucks in ones and tens hidden in the freezer—idiot—but no other cash. Nothing suspicious on his hard drive. Not even anything interesting. Either he works very hard to hide criminal activity, or—"

"Or he hasn't committed any."

"Exactly. You go through his phone?"

"Yeah." I licked Danish glaze from my fingers. "Most of his incoming calls look like spam. He texts regularly with five or six people. One of them is his mother, and a couple are Fat Cat regulars. The others appear to be coworkers. Nothing suspicious in any of the texts. Nor in his photos, including the recently deleted, but not *really* deleted category. You print out his bank statements?"

"Yeah, along with his one credit card. I'll go through them in detail today, but at a glance, there's nothing there. No storage units. No large expenses. No recurring payments, other than utilities and rent. If he has a second phone, it's a burner—nothing he pays monthly."

"So, no sign that he's in debt or desperate for money. I don't think it's him," I said.

"I don't either." Tucker reached into the grease-stained bag and pulled out a bear claw. "Which means—"

"We need to explore other options. Other suspects."

"But first, let me recommend a shower."

"Yup. As soon as I finish my coffee." I took another long sip.

He nodded. "Hear anything from the husband or brother this morning?"

"No, but they'll be here in an hour, and I promised them lunch. Feel like flipping burgers?"

"No, but I'm not going to leave you alone with them."

I rolled my eyes. "I can handle myself."

"Which is why *they're* the ones I'm worried about."

"Thanks. I'll be down in half an hour."

Tucker snorted on his way out of the apartment. "I'll believe that when I see it."

I slammed the door in his face, and he chuckled all the way down the stairs.

"So, you don't think Nolan Blake is guilty because he didn't leave big piles of cash on the coffee table for you to find?" Bishop snapped, his fist clenched so tightly around his soda that I worried he'd break the glass. "Because there was no confession written in blood on his bathroom mirror?"

"I don't think that's a fair way to characterize the evidence," I informed him as calmly as I could. "Or the lack thereof. The fact is that while he admitted to having met Yvette on one, possibly two occasions, he swears he hasn't even seen her in months, and unless you're holding out on me, we have no evidence to the contrary. He still has family in Covington and an account at that bank, which is why he was there that day."

Bishop huffed. "Or so he says."

"His bank statement verifies that. He made a cash deposit of three hundred dollars within minutes of the moment his truck drove past the camera. It was payment for an odd job he did for his mother's elderly neighbor."

Austin exhaled. "And you believe all of that?"

"At this point, I can see no reason not to."

"Okay, one habanero pimento cheeseburger and one turkey club." Tucker said as he set a plate in front of each of them. "Both with fries. Boss, your jalapeño bacon cheese-burger is coming up."

"Thank you." I moved the bottle of ketchup to the center of the table. "Please bring your plate too, and join us."

"So, can you prove Nolan Blake didn't kill my wife?" Bishop demanded, as Austin swiped one of his fries through a glob of pimento cheese dripping from his burger.

"Doesn't work that way," Austin said. "The justice system doesn't prove innocence. It tries to prove guilt, but even that isn't real proof. It's a jury's best guess. In theory, that's beyond a reasonable doubt, but in reality, the jury tends to agree with whichever side puts on a better show in court."

"Wait, seriously? You can't prove someone innocent?"

Austin frowned at him. "We don't even try. The government charges criminals and tries to prove they're guilty."

"Obviously he's talking about the human justice system," I said, as Austin dumped ketchup onto his plate. "We operate under a different burden of proof. But we still can't prove innocence. It's virtually impossible to prove that someone *didn't* do something."

"So then, how does anything ever get done in your line of work?"

I ignored Bishop's question and turned back to Austin. "We're going to keep Nolan Blake in custody for a few days, just in case, but honestly, that's mostly to keep you two from killing a man we have no reason to believe is guilty."

Bishop huffed around a bite of his club. Nothing blunts a shifter's appetite. Not grief. Not frustration. Especially not murderous rage.

"So—" I glanced up as Tucker reappeared at our table holding two more plates, then I scooted in to let him sit.

"Jalapeño bacon cheeseburger," he said, setting my lunch in front of me. His own plate held only a massive pile of chicken strips and a gravy boat full of honey mustard. No fries. No salad.

"Thanks." I turned back to Austin and Bishop. "I want you both to know that Yvette's case is our top priority. Mine, and Titus's."

"Everyone's," Tucker added, dunking his first strip into the gravy boat.

"In fact, we're about to expand the scope…significantly."

"What does that mean?" Bishop asked.

"It means they're worried that Yvette may not have been the only victim." Austin glanced from Tucker to me. "Based on what?"

I exhaled slowly. "There was a case a few years back that had some similarities. Some differences too, but enough similarities that we can't ignore the possibility that they're related."

"That one went unsolved?" Austin seemed to have forgotten that he was still holding the last quarter of his burger.

"No," Tucker said. "They put that fucker *in the ground*. It was before my time as an enforcer, but…" He shrugged with a glance at me. Waiting for me to take the lead on how much to tell them.

"We considered it solved at the time," I confirmed. "But if we're looking for two men in Yvette's case, then—"

"Then there could have been two involved in that other case," Austin concluded. "But you only put one in the ground."

"Exactly."

Bishop washed his bite down with a big gulp of soda. "Which means what? You think whoever got away back then has a new partner? And those are the motherfuckers who bit Yvette? Who took her money?"

"The cash is an outlier." Tucker turned to me, both brows arched. "Right? There was no robbery in that other case?"

"That's right." I swirled a fry in my ketchup, worried that if I made eye contact with either of them, they'd see the truth. They'd know whose case we were really talking about. "It's possible the MO has changed. It's also possible that Yvette's withdrawal had nothing to do with what happened to her."

"That seems unlikely," Austin said.

"She'd been saving for four years," Bishop added. "If she'd decided to spend that money, she would have said something. To *both* of us."

"Okay. I hear you. But we have to explore all the options, and one of those is that her withdrawal was unrelated to her infection. But we will *also* look into the money."

"You don't have access to any police database, do you?" Austin asked.

"No. And I'll be honest, there have been times when your help in that regard would have been *truly* appreciated. And we may still need it, in this case. What we really need right now, though, is access to hospital records. Unfortunately, we don't have that."

Bishop scowled. "No Pride members who're doctors?"

"Titus has an enforcer who's a nurse," Tucker said. "He can get into the records where he works, and possibly at other hospitals in that network. But that won't help us if other victims were treated or died at other hospital networks. Or if they died at home."

"So then, what's the plan?"

"We do the work." Austin shoved the last of his burger into his mouth. "The tedious deep dive into piles of largely useless information that makes up the majority of detective work."

I nodded. Tucker snorted. But Bishop looked lost. "Which is what, exactly?" he asked.

"We'll start with the obituaries." I took a bite of my burger and motioned for Tucker to continue.

"There's no national or even state-wide database of obituaries. For the most part, you have to scroll through them online, either on individual funeral home websites or in local online newspapers, where those still exist. We should be able to narrow the search results by age range and gender—looking for women in their twenties and early thirties—but even then... Well, obituaries rarely list a cause of death. So, if we find a name that looks promising, we'll hit social media, looking for posts from family members, or even the deceased herself. People post about long or unexpected illnesses. About loved ones' deaths."

"That does sound tedious," Bishop said.

I nodded. "It's also depressing. But it's our only option, at the moment. Tucker is going to head that up for us. I'll have my other enforcers looking online too, when they're not patrolling."

"Or flipping burgers?" Austin glanced at my plate.

"This was a favor," Tucker said. "Manning the grill is not in my job description."

"Maybe it should be." For the first time since I'd met him, Bishop's expression looked...less than stormy. "Hell of a turkey club, man." Maybe it was the food, but more likely, it was knowing that we were all dedicated to his wife's case. Seeing a path forward, even if it was longer and bumpier than he'd imagined.

People liked—many of us *needed*—to have a solid plan in place. I totally got that.

SIX

"— C an't imagine what you're going through…"

My sister's words floated toward me the moment I stepped out of my apartment. As it always had, her voice seemed to rise above the din of the bar—the clink of glass, water running in the kitchen, and voices overlapping in sometimes boisterous conversation.

"Worst day of my life," Bishop Mattheson answered, his deep voice rumbling through me like a roll of thunder.

I took the stairs two at a time. Three long strides got me across one corner of the kitchen to the swinging door, which I shoved open on my way through.

Davey stood behind the bar, her laptop pushed to one side. She was sipping from a short glass of straight whiskey. Bishop sat across the bar from her, a bowl of snack mix between them. Next to his glass stood a half-empty bottle of Jack Daniels.

His eyes were rimmed in red. His words were slurred.

"He's shitfaced," I whispered to Vance at the other end of the bar. "How'd that happen?" I couldn't remember seeing a *truly* drunk patron in years. Not a shifter patron, anyway.

"He bought the bottle," Vance whispered back. "Both that one, and the one before."

So, the grieving widower was good for business.

With a sigh, I grabbed a rag and cleaned my way down the bar toward them. "Last call was ten minutes ago," I said, lifting the bowl of snack mix to wipe the surface beneath it.

"Which is precisely when he bought that bottle," Davey informed me.

Ah. A loophole.

"Well, you have about twenty minutes to finish it," I told Bishop. "The Fat Cat closes at midnight on Sundays, and we're not allowed to let you leave with a drink purchased here."

"Violation of the local liquor laws?" he guessed.

"Exactly."

"And Charley *never* breaks rules..." Davey said as she closed her laptop.

"Sarcasm?" Bishop frowned. "I can't tell whether that means she's no fun, or she's *lots* of fun."

"No fun," Davey and I said in unison.

Bishop actually cracked a smile, though it faded quickly as he upended the bottle into his glass. "Yvette was a lot of fun."

Davey cleared her throat. "Mr. Mattheson was telling me about his wife."

"She lit up the room, you know?" He glanced from me to her, then back. "Like flipping a switch. People say that all the time, I know, but it was true with Yvie. People couldn't take their eyes off her. She just...glowed." Bishop turned up his glass and drained it in several gulps.

"Where's Austin?" I asked, subtly removing the empty bottle. "Close out his tab," I whispered to Davey.

"He's at home. At the..." Bishop shook his head, struggling to focus. "The apartment. Been reading obituaries since before the sun came up. Don't think he's eaten since breakfast."

Well, that's not good.

"Okay, why don't I give you a ride home?"

"S'not my home," Bishop slurred.

"I know. Give me just a minute." The bar was empty except for two of our regulars, who were arguing in the corner booth. "Closing up early, guys," I called to them as I crossed the bar to flip the sign on the door. "Vance, hit the neon. And ask Billy to drop some fries and make a burger to-go, please. Something quick and easy."

"Kitchen's closed!" Billy called out. "I've already cleaned up."

"Just make me a damn burger!" I snapped. "Then you can go. I'll clean it up myself, when I get back."

Billy grumbled a series of expletives from behind the swinging door. But then I heard the walk-in fridge squeal as he opened it.

"Can you two close up?" I asked Vance, tossing a glance at Davey to include her in the question.

Vance nodded.

"Already on it," Davey piped up without pausing as she counted down the register drawer. A surprising number of our regulars still paid with cash. "Did you know that I own thirty-five percent of this place?" she said to Bishop. "It used to be fifty percent, but we have a silent partner, now, so—"

I headed into the kitchen and prepped the bun and burger toppings for Billy, who was still grumbling beneath his breath. A minute later, Davey came in with the soda spouts soaking in a clear tub of bleach solution. I opened my mouth, but she started talking before I could get a word out.

"Before you say it, I was *not* ignoring your instructions. I did not seek Bishop Mattheson out or ask for information about the case. He came to the bar. What was I supposed to do, refuse to serve him?"

"Once he was drunk? Yes. It is illegal in the state of Tennessee to serve alcohol to anyone who is visibly inebriated." Which she damn well knew.

Davey rolled her eyes. "In a normal bar, that would qualify as a joke."

"She's not wrong," Vance said as he pushed his way through the door, and I wasn't sure which of us he was talking to.

"The man's in pain," my sister insisted. "He wanted to be drunk enough to talk about it with people who could understand. And this is just about the only place around where that's the case."

Another loophole in my instruction for my sister to stay away from the homicidal grieving widower.

"I get it. But my orders stand. I'll see you both tomorrow," I added as I pulled the fries from the deep frier and salted them. "Thanks for closing."

I piled a double order into the to-go box, next to the burger Billy had just assembled. "Thanks. You're the best." I patted him on the back as he hung up his apron, then I double-checked all the stove and griddle knobs on my way out, to make sure nothing was still running.

As I bagged up the food and added a couple of sodas from the cooler, Vance helped Bishop into my passenger seat and got him buckled.

"I feel so useless," Bishop slurred as I drove around the building into the front parking lot, then onto the road.

"Because you're drunk?"

He shook his head. "I'm not useless because I'm drunk, I'm drunk because I'm useless. Austin's spent the past two days on that damn computer, staring at the screen until his fuckin' eyes bleed. Tryin' to help. Using detective skills I just don't have. If it isn't posted on Facebook or searchable on Google, I don't have any idea what I'm doing, online."

Most of the information Austin was looking for *was* on Facebook or Google, but I lacked the patience to explain that to a drunkard. So I kept quiet.

"Meanwhile I just pace around behind him, asking if he's making any progress, until he basically orders me out of the house. I bet that's what you've been doing all day too. Searching obituaries? Looking for more murder victims?"

"Not *all* day." The zone still had to be run, even with a murder case on my plate. As did the Fat Cat. But yes, I'd spent several hours scanning obituaries from the past twelve months, in my assigned Tennessee and Mississippi counties.

We'd divvied up the work, to make sure we weren't duplicating our efforts.

"Well, all I could think to do was call Yvie's friends. The ones I had numbers for, anyway."

"Her friends? Humans, I assume?"

"Yeah. All of them. But I figured that if she wasn't robbed —if she really had plans for that money—she might have told one of them."

I turned to look at him while my car idled at a red light. "Bishop, that was a *great* idea." And so simple I hadn't even thought of it.

"Wish I'd thought to do that sooner. But we just assumed she was robbed when she was attacked."

"Did her friends know anything?"

He shook his head. "Not one of them. Her old college roommate, though, said she didn't think Yvie would have spent all that cash at once. She'd been saving for years, and everything other than what she spent on her wedding dress—

Yvie and Austin's parents are dead, so they were no help with the wedding—she had earmarked as a down payment on a bigger house. We were hoping to get one of our own. To stop paying rent, you know? And Yvie's old roommate said she wanted one with a nursery. That she was hoping to get pregnant, in a couple of years."

Bishop broke down into the kind of full body wrenching sobs that can tear a man apart. They shook my whole car.

I had no idea how to react. How to comfort him.

I'm not good with emotion. Not the kind you can see, anyway.

Fortunately, by then we were pulling into the Pine Cove parking lot.

I parked in front of 2A and flashed my brights through the window. As I was helping Bishop out of the car, Austin opened the door. "Help me get him into bed," I said as I looped Bishop's arm around my shoulder.

"How the hell did he get that drunk?" Austin took his brother-in-law from me, effortlessly supporting the man's weight. Practically carrying him toward the door as I ducked into the back seat for the food.

"My sister may be the most generous bartender on the planet." I followed him inside and set the food on the breakfast bar, then I trailed him into the bedroom.

Where I stopped in the doorway, suddenly struggling to breathe.

Ben.

Somehow, the furniture still held his scent. The sheets were new—I'd bought them myself—as was the mattress topper. And the pillows. But the mattress... The headboard. The dresser and nightstand. They all somehow still smelled like my brother, years after he'd died.

Or maybe they didn't. Maybe because I *knew* this stuff

was his, my brain was supplying the scent it believed should be here.

Grief was a strange, fierce beast.

"You okay?" Austin asked as he lowered Bishop onto the bed. Onto a rumpled comforter that still smelled like the plastic it had come in, and kind of like Austin himself.

Evidently Bishop had been taking the couch.

"Yeah. Sorry. I just…all this stuff was my brother's. I'd assumed Stuart would bring furniture from my parents' old guest room, but…" I shrugged. "He probably had no idea what was what." He'd never met Ben. Or my parents.

"This is *your* stuff?" Austin glanced around the room as he pulled Bishop's shoes off and let them thunk onto the floor.

"My mom and dad moved to Florida a few years ago. They gave the bar to me and Davey, and they sold their house so they'd have enough to retire on. And their condo came furnished, so…" I shrugged.

"So you stored all their stuff, instead of selling it?"

"Yeah. I mean, I took some of it for my apartment, and Davey took what she wanted. But my dad's old office couch didn't make the cut," I added with a glance through the doorway into the living room.

"That would explain the cigar scent."

"Sorry. Are you allergic?"

"No. My grandpa smoked them, so it's like nostalgia for me. Your scent isn't in the upholstery, though."

"Yeah, we weren't allowed in Dad's office. It was kind of his personal space."

Austin dropped Bishop's second boot on the floor. "I had no idea you'd furnished this place with your own stuff. That was very kind, and if I'd realized, I would have thanked you sooner."

"No need."

Austin huffed. "I feel like donating your own furniture is above and beyond the duties of the average zone Marshal, so…thank you."

I'd never been good at accepting thanks graciously, so I just nodded, as Bishop snorted in his sleep and rolled over.

"That's my fault." Austin glanced at the bed as he followed me out of the room. "I told him to get lost for a while."

"Yeah, he mentioned that. He'll be fine in an hour." It was a miracle he'd managed to get drunk, and that certainly wouldn't last long. "He said you hadn't eaten, so I brought you a burger. Though I'll understand if you're tired of them."

"Not gonna lie, if I'd known you were taking requests, I would have asked for pizza." Grinning, he reached for the bag.

I pulled it out of his range, one brow arched. "Have you heard the one about beggars and choosers?"

His blue-eyed gaze suddenly intensified, one corner of his mouth ticking up in a quiet smile. "So, you're going to make me beg?"

The bag crinkled in my grip. I blinked at him, my pulse suddenly a bit unsteady.

"I apologize." Austin took two steps back. "That was completely out of line."

"No, it's fine." A few of the regulars at work flirted with me occasionally, but none of them meant it. As hard-up as some of them were for female companionship, most of the guys thought of me as an authority figure—a ball-buster—rather than as someone they actually had a chance with. Or *wanted* a chance with.

Many men—especially shifters—had no personal interest in a woman who outranked them. And for the most part, that was fine with me. I needed to preserve my authority more than I needed to get laid.

At least, that's what I told myself...

"No, it isn't okay," Austin insisted. "I just... Nothing has felt normal for the past three months." He sat and ran one hand through his thick brown waves. "Yvette wasn't just my sister. She was my roommate. My *friend*. Nothing feels the same without her here to tell me how I'm fucking everything up." He sank onto the couch. "But you..."

"Me?" I could see his pain. I could *feel* it, just watching him. But I wasn't sure what I had to do with any of that.

"You didn't know Yvette. You never met her. You exist outside of my life before all this, and for just a second there, having a normal social interaction with a normal person made things feel, well, normal. I felt like the man I used to be, before...all this." He exhaled slowly, finally looking up at me again. "Which is just my whiny, bullshit way of saying I didn't mean to hit on you. I just...reacted."

"Really. It's fine." In fact, that was probably the healthiest reaction I'd seen from either him or Bishop in two days. "Heads up." I tossed the bag, and Austin caught it in one hand.

A southpaw. *Interesting...*

"Thanks for this," he said as he set the paper to-go container on the coffee table next to his laptop. "I really do appreciate it."

"No problem." I dropped into the old leather armchair, which used to be in the guest room at my mom's house, and leaned forward to snatch a fry. "So, any progress?" I asked with a glance at his screen.

"Not a lot," he admitted as he plucked a pickle slice from the bottom of the food container. "It turns out that women don't routinely die in their twenties and early thirties."

"Thank god."

"I did find a couple though. Their causes of death weren't listed, so I had to cyber-stalk them, and I eventually ruled them both out. One was a car wreck. The other was ovarian cancer in a thirty-four-year-old." He lifted his burger from the container. "What about you? Any luck?"

"None. I only searched three counties though. And I only went back twelve months. I'll widen that search tomorrow. And Titus has promised us an update from his enforcer who's a nurse. Turns out he works for the largest hospital network in the state of Mississippi, and he has access to all of those files. Might take him a while, though."

"And if we find nothing?" Austin's knee bounced against the edge of the coffee table. "If it's just Yvette?"

I stole another fry instead of answering.

His leg went still. "You don't believe that, do you?"

"It's just a gut feeling. Nothing I can quantify. Nothing I can even justify. But if there are other victims out there, I have to find them." I had to know. "And I *will* put the guilty party in the ground. You have my word."

"You'll have to fight Bishop for the honor." His voice lowered into a soft but intense growl. "And me."

Something twisted deep in my gut as I looked at him. As he looked back. I found my grief and trauma mirrored in his gaze, and beneath that, I saw a desperate, unacknowledged, and embarrassingly familiar need for…something. For just *one* moment free from—

I popped up from my chair, shattering the sudden intensity of the moment. "Do you have beer? Tell me you went shopping."

"Yeah. Second shelf."

The refrigerator door opened with the soft sound of broken suction, and the cold air felt good on my overheated skin. I closed my eyes, and Austin's face hovered there behind my eyelids. There was something about him. Something compelling in the quiet intensity of his pain and his drive for justice.

"Find them?" he called.

"Yeah." I grabbed two bottles and popped the tops off on the countertop on my way back to the living room.

Austin thanked me when I set a bottle in front of him, wiping a smear of ketchup from his lower lip with a paper napkin. He chewed for several seconds, taking his time, and I realized that was intentional. Either he didn't want to answer my questions, or he was trying to figure out how to ask one of his own. Finally, he washed his bite down with a swig of beer, then he turned that intense gaze on me again. "So... why didn't you tell us your sister lives here? In the complex."

"Oh, I'm sorry. Did you need a list of all the residents?" I crossed my arms over my chest. "Should I ask Stuart for a directory?"

He chewed slowly, making me wait for his response. "Sarcasm is your tell," he said at last. "If I were you, I wouldn't play poker." He smiled, and somehow that lightened the weight of his gaze.

"And what did my 'tell' tell you?"

"It's a shield. You use it when you feel threatened."

I snorted. "I'm *not* afraid of you."

Silence. More chewing. Then, "I know. You're not afraid of much, are you?"

No reason to dignify *that* with an answer.

"But you're afraid *for* Davey." Another slow bite. "I swear to you that we're not a threat to her. Or to anyone who didn't kill my sister."

"I know. But she's here in this world because of me, and I

kind of feel like that gives me the right to be over-protective. To withhold trust until it's earned, on her behalf."

Austin nodded slowly. "I felt the same way. In fact, I kept Bishop at arm's length for six months, trying to keep him away from Yvette."

"Why stop after six months?"

He chuckled, then took another sip of his beer. "I found out they were sleeping together. And going to extraordinary lengths to keep that from me."

"You're a fucking shifter." I blinked at him. "How the hell did they keep that from you?" He should have been able to smell his friend's scent on his sister's clothes, and vice versa.

Austin shrugged. "Where there's a will, there's a way." He took the last bite of his burger and passed the fries toward me as he chewed. "So…if you're worried about her, why keep her here? Why not send her to live near your parents? Or at least find her an apartment where she won't be surrounded by shifters?"

"It's…complicated. Mostly by the fact that she's an adult and, as she puts it, I am not the boss of her. Also, she has an equal stake in the bar, and she won't sell it to me. It took me months to convince her to sell fifteen percent of her stake to Titus, just to keep us afloat in the beginning."

"Oh. Wow. I didn't realize."

"Yeah. And if I *could* convince her to move to Florida, that would just mean I'd basically never see her. It's not like I can fly down there whenever I want."

His brows rose. "The territorial boundary restriction?"

"Yeah." Werecats could only travel into another territory with permission from that territory's Alpha, and most of those Alphas were reluctant to have strays on their land. Even stray Pride members, who've vowed to follow the rules.

"Really? I wouldn't have thought that would be much of a

problem for you, considering how short our society is on female shifters."

I shrugged. "I *might* have appeared to the council during a 'congratulations on surviving scratch fever' video call and sworn in a profanity-laden rant that I would *not* be marrying one of their sons and producing their grandchildren. Ever." I crunched into his last fry, then spoke around it. "And since that gives them no use for me, I'm basically grounded from leaving the territory. Unless I want to find a direct flight into one of the free zones." And I certainly did *not* want that.

"Ouch."

"Yeah. I rarely see my parents as it is, because traveling gets harder for them every year. Losing my sister too doesn't seem like much of a solution to anything. And since I can't keep her away from the bar, considering she's part-owner, I figured the best way to keep her safe is to put her next door to my most trusted enforcers."

"So...you're spying on her."

"I'm protecting her."

Austin huffed. "How's that different?"

"I don't ask for updates on her activities. I acknowledge that it's none of my business what she does, as long as she's safe while she's doing it."

"So, you're basically the mom handing out condoms to her teenagers."

"No! No condoms. This is not a condom-relevant scenario."

Austin laughed. I laughed.

We were still laughing when Bishop stumbled out of the bedroom, wiping his chin on his sleeve. "Sorry man," he mumbled, his unfocused gaze trained on the back of Austin's head. "I think I puked on your shoes."

SEVEN

"Seriously, nine a.m. is an hour that shouldn't exist." I slid into the corner booth across from Vance just as the swinging door squealed open behind me.

"Maybe this will help." Tucker appeared next to our table with a plate in his right hand and two more balanced on his left arm. All three were piled high with chicken strips and waffles, with sides of butter, syrup, and peppered white gravy.

"Oh my *god*, you're the best." I took the plate he handed me and I'd already devoured half of one giant chicken strip before he could settle into the booth on Vance's other side. "You're going to make some lucky young man very happy, some day."

"Damn right I am. And that has nothing to do with my cooking."

"I don't know," Vance teased. "I think you missed your true calling."

"Fuck off. I only cook for you assholes, and that's only because I know no one else is going to."

"Though, to be fair," Vance said as he dunked a quarter

section of a Belgian waffle into his syrup. "He who habitually works the early shift basically owes the closers breakfast."

Tucker rolled his eyes. "I think the phrase you're looking for is 'Thank you, Tucker.'"

"Thank you, Tucker," Vance and I said in unison, as I opened my notebook and pulled my pen free from the spine. "Okay. Updates?"

"Wait!" Tucker popped up from his seat, headed toward the bar. A moment later, he was back, carrying three tall Bloody Marys garnished with celery, olives, cherry tomatoes, and one wedge of avocado each. "I almost forgot the healthy part."

Vance snorted. "That's the healthy part?"

"Do you not see the celery?" Tucker demanded. "The avocado? They're both green."

"As is the olive." I plucked mine from the end of its toothpick and ate it. "Okay. Take two. Updates?"

"The new census app is up and running, in beta," Tucker said. "Titus wants us to make a list of trusted Pride members to invite, to try it out. We're really hoping this'll make it much easier for new members to register, and for us to keep up with changing addresses and phone numbers. You can set personal details to completely private, or to be shared only with Pride leadership. Members have to have an invitation to join, and they have to be confirmed by the admin before they can actually use the app. For obvious security purposes."

"Awesome." Vance tapped on his phone as he chewed, checking out the app's updates.

"Yeah. Great," I added. "And I am *really* going to find a moment to download that. I swear."

"Charley, I promise it's much more efficient than keeping a list of phone numbers in a notebook in your purse."

"Joke's on you," I informed Vance. "I don't carry a

purse." But I did have an address book full of scratched out and replaced phone numbers. "Fine. I'll download the app." That was *kind of* part of my job as Marshal. "What else?"

"Rob and Gael have sent their weekly reports," Tucker said, referencing my two northernmost enforcers, whom he'd visited in person earlier in the week. "The printouts are on your desk, but they're also in your inbox, should you decide to log into your email. Ever."

"Funny. What about Logan and Elias?"

"They promised we'd have their reports by five," Vance said. "I can print those too, if you want."

"Both of you can fuck right off. I know how to work my email."

"She *is* a little young for a technophobe," Tucker stage whispered as he dunked a chicken strip into his gravy.

"I'm not too young for a damn thing," I informed them as the familiar growl of my sister's engine rumbled from the front parking lot. I mentally tracked the sound as it circled the building to the employee lot out back. "What about the obit search? Tell me you guys had more luck than I did."

"I found one possibility," Vance said.

"Me too. But just the one." Tucker dribbled melted butter onto the last half of his waffle. "I haven't heard from Austin yet, but I was going to give him a call after this, for an update."

"No need," Davey said as she pushed her way through the swinging doors into the front of the bar. "Charley was over there 'til nearly two in the morning. I'm sure she can give you both the inside scoop."

Tucker's brows rose as his gaze slid toward me.

"Don't," I snapped. "Davey helped Bishop get shitfaced, so I took him home."

"She also took dinner to Austin," my sister added. I

twisted in my seat to glare at her as she set up her laptop at the bar and began opening the register.

Davey gave me a sugar-sweet smile. Evidently that was my comeuppance for sticking my nose in her business.

"Austin Graham is hyper-competent, even-tempered, and he has access to police resources," I said, sitting straighter as I leaned into my professional voice. "Titus agrees that he'd make a valuable addition to the Pride, and he's made a budget line addition specifically for that recruitment effort. So while our top priority is obviously finding Yvette's killer or killers, we are also officially pursuing Austin Graham as an employee of the zone."

Davey snorted. "Yeah. All potential bosses take their hot male prospects dinner in the middle of the night. Nothing at all to do with those eyes…"

Tucker chuckled. "She's not wrong about the eyes."

I ignored them both. "But to answer the original question, no, Austin didn't have any luck. And I'm betting if we don't find anything today, he'll be done with our 'multiple victims' theory." A cop needed evidence to build a case, and if we couldn't give him any, I was worried that he'd revert to his original suspect. Who was snoring in my basement at that very moment. "So…what'd you find?"

Tucker reached into his back pocket, then he slid a folded piece of printer paper across the table toward me. "Emily Forrester. She was twenty-six when she died almost three years ago, of a non-specific infection. I found an old Facebook post from her mother, saying Emily had died within hours of developing a high fever out of the blue. By the time they got her to the hospital, she was non-responsive. She never woke up. She left behind a twenty-seven-year-old husband, but no kids."

"The husband…?" I asked around my last bite of chicken.

"Human, as far as I know. He's not registered with the Pride, nor does he appear in any of our records as a known rogue."

There was an awful lot of paperwork involved in running the first stray Pride. *Maybe I should download that damn app.*

"Any record of her withdrawing cash?"

"No idea," Tucker said. "Nor am I sure how to find out, without either hacking into her bank or becoming a cop in that jurisdiction and applying for a warrant."

"Or interviewing her friends and family," Davey piped up from behind me.

"And it may come to that," I acknowledged. "Okay, Vance, what did you find?"

"Brittany Walsh. She was thirty-two when she died last year, so on the upper end of the age range. Similar symptoms, according to a sister who set up a crowd-source page to help pay for her treatment. Which wound up paying for her funeral. She was in the hospital for three days, though, before she died. It was a rural hospital in eastern Tennessee. They never figured out what she had."

Eastern Tennessee. "That's not our Pride, Vance."

He shrugged. "I expanded the search. If we're looking for some kind of serial offender, what are the chances that he—or they—would stick to one territory?"

"Slim to none," Davey said, before I could even open my mouth. "Concentrating his victims in one spot would make him more likely to get caught."

"Davey!" I snapped. "You have a stake in the bar, not in the Pride!"

Vance shrugged. "She's not wrong."

"I *know* she's not wrong. But she doesn't work for Titus, and she isn't supposed to know about any of this. And we don't have access to information from the Appalachian Pride."

"Wasn't that Jace's territory?" Davey lifted the bar flap and came into the dining area. "Before he joined this one? Or...he founded this Pride, right? With Titus?"

"Someone's done her homework," Vance said with a smile.

I growled softly. "This is *not* her homework."

Davey pulled a chair up to the end of our booth and snatched the last chicken strip from Tucker's plate with a grin. "I'm right though. Right? So, Jace might still have contacts he can ask?"

Vance nodded. "He might—"

"He *does*," I interrupted. "But if he uses those contacts, then his brother-in-law, who's the Appalachian Alpha, will want to know why we need information about dead human women with infection-like symptoms. Which means the entire territorial council will know. And that's exactly what we're trying to avoid. At least until we have a bad guy to hand over."

"You're going to hand him over?" Davey asked with her mouth full. "Because I think Bishop Mattheson will object to that."

"We won't literally hand him over," I conceded. "We'll just be handing over a name or names, assuming we find the aforementioned bad guy or guys in our territory."

"But we'll be *really* fucked if he's moved on," Tucker added.

I leaned around Vance to glare at my sister. "Now, will you *please* go open the bar and let us get done here?"

Davey stood with a groan, which only grew louder when I handed her my dirty plate.

"Okay, anything else I should know about this Brittany Walsh?" I asked, as Davey took my plate into the kitchen.

Vance slid a sheet of paper toward me. "Not that I know of. She was married with one child. A four-year old. No sign that her husband was a shifter, but Jace may know more about that."

"Okay, I'll ask him if any of his former Pride members are named Walsh. It's highly unlikely that her husband was a stray, since they're rarely allowed to join Prides."

"Except this one!" Davey announced as the kitchen doors swung open again behind me.

"Except this one." Vance smiled.

"Okay, if that's it for now, I'll check in with Austin and call Jace, and someone should—"

"Was that Emily *Blake* Forrester?" Davey asked, as I stood from the booth. I turned to see her at the bar again, staring at her computer screen. She looked past me at Tucker, and I turned back to him.

"Um...I'm not sure," he admitted, crossing the dining area with his own plate and glass. "I assume Forrester was her married name, but I don't remember whether or not the obit listed her maiden name."

"It did," I said with a glance at the paper he'd given me. "Emily *Blake* Forrester. Who left behind her husband, Martin, her parents, Bobby and Anne, and two brothers. Carey and—"

"Nolan *fucking* Blake!" Davey cried, spinning her laptop around to face us. "He's right there on her Facebook profile, listed as her brother."

I turned to Tucker with both brows raised.

"I'm so sorry," he said. "I've looked at hundreds of obituaries in the past two days, and they all started running together."

"So, wait." Davey closed her laptop. "Austin and Bishop accused Nolan Blake of killing Yvette, but it turns out Nolan's sister might actually have been a victim too? Did he kill his own *sister*?"

"Let's not jump to conclusions." Vance was looking at Davey, but he was actually talking to me. Because if Nolan was somehow involved in Emily and Yvette's deaths, then he could also have been involved in—

Tucker cleared his throat. "I'll go through them again and make sure I didn't miss anything else."

"Let's put that on hold," I said, as the first customer pulled into our lot. "The bar opens in ten minutes, and I have to go talk to Nolan. So— *Shit*," I swore with a glance through the front window at the white 4Runner. "It's Austin and Bishop. If they ask for me, tell them I'll be with them as soon as I can. Do *not* tell them about any of this." I waved the folded obituaries for emphasis. "And keep them out of the basement."

MY MIND RACED as I headed downstairs. I could hear Vance unlocking the front doors, and when I focused, consciously blocking everything else out, I could hear Bishop cursing beneath his breath about being hungry. He was probably standing on the welcome mat, right in front of the door, beneath the neon sign.

I couldn't afford to think about the brother and widower right now. This moment wasn't about them. It wasn't even truly about Yvette and Emily. Not entirely anyway.

I stepped into the basement and bolted the door behind me. Then I dropped the bar, an old-fashioned two-by-four slab of iron fitted into two brackets, intended to hold the door shut, medieval-style.

That wouldn't keep Austin and Bishop out, if they decided they really wanted in. A couple of good hits from a shifter shoulder, and the brackets would pull loose from the wall. But the bar would give me several seconds of warning.

"Charley?" Nolan Blake sat up from the twin-sized bunk in his cell, rubbing his eyes. He'd tossed around in his sleep overnight, and the mattress pad and ill-fitting sheet had slid half out from under him. "Breakfast time already?"

"It's damn near lunch time." I tried to keep hostility out of my voice, and I think I mostly succeeded. Under the circumstances, that was a fucking miracle. "Someone will bring food down in a minute. First, though, I have some follow-up questions for you." I grabbed a bottle of water from a half-empty case on the floor and slid it through the bars toward him. There was a toilet in his cell—an upgrade I was glad Titus had been willing to pay for.

Otherwise, we'd have to let prisoners out to use the restroom. Or we'd have to empty buckets.

Startled, I realized I was now thinking of Nolan as a prisoner, though until that moment, I'd thought of the cell as protection for him.

I sank into a chair several feet from the bars.

"What's going on?" Nolan asked. "You mind if I get dressed before…whatever this is?" A pile of clean, folded clothes sat in one corner of the cell. Tucker had brought them, after he'd searched Nolan's apartment.

"Let's get this over with first." I leaned forward, resting my elbows on my knees. "Tell me about Emily."

"Emily? You mean my sister?" Nolan shook his head, clearly confused. "What about her?"

"How did she die?"

"I don't— What is this about, Charley? Why are you… Why are you digging into my family?"

"We weren't. Her name came up in a search of human women who died of infection-like symptoms. So...how did she die?"

"I don't know, really. I wasn't there." He ran one hand through brown sleep-tousled hair. "All I know is that one day my mom called to say she was sick. Then she called back a few hours later and said Em had died. It was crazy-sudden. My mom was out of her mind with grief. I could hardly understand a word she said, so my brother had to take the phone from her. All he said was that Emily had gotten sick while her husband was at work. By the time he found her, she was unconscious, and there was nothing the hospital could do."

Foreboding swelled in the pit of my stomach. "Sick with what?"

"I don't know. Mom said the hospital never figured it out, but they didn't think it was...communicable."

"What did her husband say? Your parents? Your brother? What did people tell you about your sister's death, Nolan?"

"Nothing!" he shouted, and suddenly he was on his feet, pacing, his cheeks bright red. Anger? Resurfaced grief? "None of them told me a damn thing. They just wanted to know when my flight would get in. When I could be there for the funeral. And I—"

His voice broke.

Nolan cleared his throat and looked right at me. He *glared* at me. "And I had to tell my family—my *mother*—that I couldn't come to my own sister's funeral. She lived out east, you know? Near Knoxville. That's the goddamn Appalachian Pride, and they don't let strays in."

Which meant that Tucker had expanded his search beyond our zone too. I spared a moment to be proud of my guys for going above and beyond what I'd asked of them.

"Did you apply for travel?" I asked Nolan.

"Hell yes, I applied. And back then, I didn't know what the hell I was doing. Or how to get help. It took me hours just to figure out who to call. And all they'd say was that it would take a month or more to process my application. A goddamn month!"

He sank onto his bunk, his head cradled in both hands. "Emily had been in the ground for nearly six weeks when I got an email telling me my application to cross the territorial line had been denied."

Good god.

"I didn't get to say goodbye. I've never even seen her headstone. And my family won't speak to me. I had to tell them I couldn't get off work for my own sister's funeral, and now not one of them will even take my calls. I have to stalk my brother's fucking Facebook page for pictures of my niece and nephew."

Anger swelled within me on his behalf. "I'm so sorry." And I was. I was really, really sorry. And…I believed him. I believed his grief, anyway. That kind of pain couldn't be faked.

But that didn't make him innocent. And that didn't rule out anything he may have done afterward, out of some twisted need for revenge. Or to process his loss.

I'd seen weirder, in my time as Marshal.

"I am sorry. But I still have questions."

"About Emily?"

"About how she died."

"I told you, I don't *know*!" Nolan sat up straight on the bunk, meeting my gaze as if he had nothing to hide. Baring his soul.

"Okay, then, when was the last time you saw her? That

week, maybe? I know you couldn't go to the Appalachian territory, but had she come to see you?"

"No, not in more than a year. Why—?" Nolan's mouth snapped shut. "You think she died of scratch-fever. That's what this is about. And you think that *I*...? You think I killed my own *sister*?"

"No," I told him. "I don't think that." And by then, I really didn't. "But I still need to hear you say it. For the record. Did you see your sister at all in the days before her death?"

"No. Like I said. It had been a year or so since she came out this way."

"Did she know you're a shifter? Did she know we exist?"

"No. And *no*! None of them knew. I wouldn't have had to lie to them if they'd known!" Nolan's expression crumpled. "Look, you have to understand what you're doing, right now. You're telling me, in one breath, that you think my sister was murdered, fuckin' three years ago, out of nowhere, and you think I did it. Can you see how that might be unearthin' some trauma for me?"

"Yes. I can." Of course I could.

"Do you *know* that? That she was infected? Or are you just guessing? Trying to make puzzle pieces fit?"

"We're still investigating. Following all the leads." Trying to *unearth* leads, so they could be followed. "And it would be helpful if you could get some information for us, from your family."

"What kind of information?"

"About her illness. What she was doing in the day or so before she got sick. Who she saw. Where she went."

"I can try. But I'm telling you, Charley, they're not speaking to me. Not for years. That's what happens when you skip your own sister's funeral."

I wanted to believe that things were different now. That in the years since Titus and Jace had formed Mississippi Valley Pride, we'd gained some standing in the eyes of the greater shifter community. That if Davey did move out to Florida, and—god forbid—she died, I'd be allowed into the Southeast Territory for her funeral. To grieve with and comfort my parents.

But I couldn't swear that was true.

"I'll see that you get your phone back, so you can try to contact your parents. I have just one more question, then I'll make sure that you get some food, too."

"Go on," he snapped. "There's nothin' stopping you."

"Did Emily know any of your shifter friends? Did she meet any of them, when she visited you the year before she died?"

"No. *God* no. She was here with her husband. We hung out doing touristy things. Touring local parks and caves and shit. Not hanging out with my friends. Not that I really had many shifter friends, back then."

"You're sure?"

"Yeah, I'm sure. Do you really think she was infected? That someone, what? Bit her? Scratched her?"

"I don't know," I told him. "But I think it's a possibility."

"You think it was some kind of accident? Like maybe she startled someone in cat form? I mean, you don't really think it was murder, right? I mean there are easier ways to kill someone."

"Yes, there are. And no, I don't think killing her was the point. Assuming she *was* killed." I stood and moved my chair back to its position against the wall. I wasn't prepared yet to answer the rest of his questions. "Hey Nolan, do you know, or have you ever heard of a woman named Brittany Walsh?"

"No. I knew a Brittany Edison a few years back. Can't say I've ever known a Walsh, though."

"What about…" I pulled the folded obituaries from my pocket and scanned Brittany's until I found her maiden name. "Brittany Heller? Ever meet her?"

"No. The only Heller I ever met was old man Heller. Grouchy old dude who used to hunt on the common run, years ago. He told me once that he was an alcoholic for the first forty years of his life, and he only quit drinkin' after he was infected, because it cost him too damn much, then, to get drunk. And he never could stay drunk anyway."

I managed a smile.

"He was definitely a dude, though. Not a Brittany."

"Okay. Thanks. I'll have some lunch sent down."

"Charley, when am I getting out of here?"

"I'm working on that," I assured him as I turned back from the doorway to face him.

"But I didn't do it. I didn't kill Yvette Mattheson, and I sure as hell didn't kill my own sister. You've got the wrong guy locked up."

"That may be true. But it's as much for your protection as anything." I wasn't sure what else to tell him. I truly didn't believe he'd killed Emily. But I couldn't tell how much to believe of everything else he'd told us. And I still couldn't be sure Bishop wouldn't kill him on sight.

"Isn't that my choice, though? Shouldn't I get to decide whether or not I need protection? I could just leave for a while. Head to one of the free zones."

"Not while you're still a person of interest. I'm sorry, Nolan." Then I left before his grief could influence my objectivity.

EIGHT

A fragrant carpet of moldering leaves and pine needles sank beneath my paws as I ran, my claws digging for purchase in the slick spots. The air was clean, clear, and a more than a little chilly that late at night, and though it was pitch black out, thanks to the clouds covering the sliver of moon already riding low on the horizon, I could see very well. My feline eyes were perfectly suited to take advantage of light humans wouldn't even be able to register.

In the northern zone, the two places shifters were most likely to gather were the common run and the Fat Cat, which made it difficult for me to indulge in solitude during normal-people hours. But at three am, I had the common run to myself, as near as I could tell.

Wind ruffled my fur as I ran. My breath puffed up in little white clouds. My lungs—and my legs—gloried in the blissful burn of exertion.

I ran as far and as fast as I could, and when I could go no farther, no longer, I collapsed in a pile of leaves and rolled around in it, huffing in indignation when an entire family of mice fled squealing from my invasion of their territory.

Fortunately for them, I wasn't hungry.

I blinked up at the sky, watching as clouds rolled slowly across it, briefly revealing that silver of a moon. Tiny, bright flashes of starlight seemed to swell as I stared at them, oblivious, on a cosmic scale, to my petty human—and shifter —troubles.

The sky always felt so serene out here. A velvet expanse of peace and quiet from my perspective, even though I knew the reality, if I could travel out there, might feel much different.

I mean, how peaceful could giant balls of flaming gas really be, up close?

There was an analogy in that, somewhere. Something about the nature of my role as a zone Marshal, and how important it was to project a sense of calm, even when I felt like the whole thing was a blazing ball of gas hurtling through space.

Or maybe I was just feeling a bit dramatic.

Finally, blissfully exhausted, I rolled onto my stomach again, my legs folded beneath me, and—

A startled yip leaked from my throat.

Austin Graham stood beneath an arch formed by the branches of two trees. Stark naked. His pale skin practically glowed, dense musculature highlighted by another brief flash of moonlight between drifting clouds.

His eyes were cobalt lasers, shining right into my soul.

I growled, exhibiting my irritation not just with him, but with myself. I hadn't heard him. To be fair, I hadn't been listening for him, but he shouldn't have been able to sneak up on me like that, much less reclaim his human shape without me even noticing.

Because there was no way he'd hiked this far out into the woods naked and on two legs.

Fighting embarrassment, I shifted back into human form as fast as I could, struggling through the gristly pops and groans from my body as bones elongated and joints re-formed. As my fur receded, my canines and claws shrinking into their human equivalents. There is no vocabulary adequate to express how badly a shift hurts, in the moment. It's torture. As a fledgling stray, I swore after that first time, when my body compelled its own change, that I would never do that voluntarily.

But as it turned out, the joy of running in cat form was worth the temporary agony. Not that there was really any choice; if a shifter stayed in human form for too long, his body would command the change on its own. With more than the usual amount of pain, and likely at a very inopportune time.

In my original skin again, I stood, shivering without fur to keep me warm. Austin seemed unbothered by the cold. In every…respect.

Natural-born shifters, I'd been told, don't equate nudity with sex, especially when that nudity was associated with a recent shift. For them, being naked was just part of everyday life. Abby Wade, the only natural-born tabby in the territory, told me once that because of that, shifter men actually find lingerie more erotic than nudity, because it's *supposed* to look sexy. It's an intentional request for attention, of the carnal variety.

Strays, though…

Well, several years into my life as a shifter, it was still difficult for me to look at a naked man and not…glance down. Which was why I was almost insulted that Austin's gaze remained firmly trained on my eyes.

I didn't like thinking that he had more self-control than I did. Or that he was simply disinterested.

"What are you doing here?" I clenched my jaw to keep my teeth from chattering. A shifter's body temperature typically runs warmer than a human's, but without fur, the cold still bothered me.

Austin swung a small bag from his shoulder and pulled the drawstring closure open. "My understanding is that the common run is open to everyone."

"So, I'm supposed to believe this is a coincidence? You weren't looking for me?"

He shrugged as he pulled a bundle of plaid cloth from the bag and tossed it to me. "Am I supposed to believe you haven't been avoiding Bishop and me all day?"

Fair enough.

"What's this?" I shook out the cloth. Clearly it was his shirt, considering that it smelled just like him, but—

"You're cold."

"Thanks," I said as I shrugged into the material. It would be a long walk to my car in human form, and I hadn't brought clothes, because I hadn't intended to shift back in the middle of the woods.

Austin nodded as he pulled a pair of pants from the bag and stepped into them.

"You followed me?" I asked as I fastened the first button.

"No, I found you. You must have really been focused on your run, because I made no effort to be quiet. I didn't want to startle you."

"How'd you know where to look?"

"Davey said you come out here when you need to think."

Thanks, sis.

I nodded, though the truth was that I came out here—I shifted and ran—when I *didn't* want to think. When I needed the blissful oblivion of my paws pounding against the earth, my body moving too fast for my thoughts to keep up.

There was no human-form equivalent, though I'd always thought the exhilaration of race car driving might come close. Not that I'd ever tried it.

I crossed my arm over my chest, holding his gaze. Waiting for him to ask about Yvette's case. To ask why I'd snuck out the back door of the bar after I'd spoken to Nolan Blake, then avoided him all day.

"So...who is that?" Austin said instead, and I didn't understand what he was asking until I turned to follow his gaze, which was focused on the ground behind me. On a narrow rectangular outline barely visible in the dirt, beneath an old, half-rotten tree.

Shit.

"That's a grave, right?"

"Um...yeah." But not the kind of grave you visit or put a headstone on. It was the middle-of-the-woods, hope-no one-ever-finds-it kind of grave. One that had been there for years and had been refilled twice, because of natural sinking.

One I hadn't intended to show him.

It was a grave I'd had no idea I was headed toward, as I'd run through the woods with no conscious destination. My subconscious, though, was a real bitch, and this was not the first time she'd fulfilled some need I wasn't even aware of feeling.

In this case, the need to make sure that monster was still six feet down, his grave undiscovered, his eternal damnation uninterrupted.

"So, whose is it?" Austin was looking at me rather than the grave, and again I wondered just how good he was in an interrogation room. All I could tell for sure was that I wanted him on my side of the table.

"No one's. No one worth mentioning, anyway."

"Well, it must be important, if you came all the way out here to—"

"Just ask me," I snapped, my tongue so thick I had to concentrate on the words. "Just ask what you came out here to ask."

Austin glanced at the grave again, then his focus returned to me. "You have very loyal friends. Employees, I mean. And a very loyal sister. None of them will tell me a damn thing without your approval. So...what are you hiding, Charley? What did you find out from Nolan this morning?"

"Nothing useful." I started walking in the direction of my car and, his footsteps followed, crunching through dead leaves and fallen branches. "Nolan's sister died a few years ago, of symptoms that could be scratch fever."

"*Could* be?"

"She was in another territory, and he wasn't able to see her. Or go to the funeral."

"And you think he had nothing to do with it."

I glanced at him as we walked, twigs biting into the soles of my feet. "He's not that good a liar, Austin. No one is."

"Okay, but that doesn't mean—"

"That he didn't kill Yvette? I know. But you're the one who says there are no coincidences in a murder investigation."

"You're saying it would be coincidence if his sister was murdered in the same manner he murdered *my* sister, if those aren't related?"

I nodded, stepping over a rotting log.

"But it isn't coincidence if they *are* related. If he committed both murders, or he killed Yvette as some kind of copycat. Or to get some kind of twisted revenge for his sister."

I stopped walking and suddenly he was so close, I had to

look up. "So then, show me how they're related. Does Nolan Blake have some reason to want your sister dead, the same way his died? Did you kill his sister? Did Bishop?"

"No. Of course not."

"Then he had no reason, that you know of, to kill Yvette?"

Austin frowned. He pressed his lips together.

"You're the cop. If you can find a connection, I'll listen. But until then, don't you think the most likely scenario is that his sister was a victim of the same crime, by the same perpetrator?"

Austin started walking again, and I found myself rushing to catch up, to my own irritation. "Are there any others?" he asked without looking back.

"Possibly," I hedged. "We're looking into another death with similar symptoms. And my guys are still reading obits. We haven't heard from Spencer, Titus's enforcer yet, but I expect to very soon."

"When?" Austin stopped and turned so suddenly I almost collided with him. "When do you expect to hear?"

"I don't—" I took a step back so I could focus on his face. "Whenever he gets the information we're looking for. Or reaches a dead end. And I can't tell you when that will be—"

"Charley—"

"—but I can tell you I'm expecting an update. I left my phone in my truck, though, so if you'd like to—"

"Yes. Thank you." He took the lead again, which meant he knew exactly where I'd parked.

We walked in silence, while I tried to ignore the frigid draft wafting beneath the shirt he'd lent me.

My truck stood alone in a gravel lot at the edge of the woods, just beyond the last cabin in the Lakeshore complex. About five hundred feet from the lake in question, where shifters in cat form loved to splash around on warm summer evenings.

Titus had spent a lot of money to help build our little community, but the common run was among the most effective of his purchases.

"Where's your car?" I glanced toward the lake, then up the dirt road leading to the lot.

"I caught a ride from the bar with Doug Myers. He said he lives in one of these cabins?"

"Yeah. That little one-room, over there." I pointed through the dark toward a small structure to the west, where smoke rose steadily from a crumbling stone chimney. "He's a good guy, if a little nosy." I pulled a pair of pants from the gym bag in the back seat of my crew cab and stepped into them. "Get in the truck." In the drivers' seat, I picked my phone up, still connected to the charger. "Damn it." I tapped the darkened screen, and nothing happened. "It's dead."

Austin buckled his seatbelt. "The charger doesn't work when the car's not running."

"I know that, smartass. But it was plugged in during the whole drive over here."

"And that might have been helpful," he said, one corner of his mouth twitching. "If it had actually been connected to your truck." He lifted the cord from the center console, demonstrating that it was not, in fact, attached to the USB port in my dashboard.

I growled, pointedly ignoring him as I started the engine and headed down the dirt road toward what passed, in these parts, for civilization.

. . .

THE FAT CAT was completely dark when I pulled into the parking lot, then circled around to the rear entrance. Davey, Vance, and Billy had closed up nearly two hours earlier.

In my office, I pulled on the rest of my clothes and returned Austin's shirt, then I settled into my desk chair while my computer booted up with groans akin to an aging rocket trying to blast off.

"It shouldn't take that long to load, you know." Austin leaned forward in the left-hand guest chair to peer at my screen. "You need a new one."

"No one *needs* a new computer. People just like to say they have the latest bells and whistles. But most things function just fine with neither bells nor whistles."

I considered myself to be a prime example.

He gave me an amused look. "So, we're defining bells and whistles as a processor manufactured in this century?"

"Funny. My desktop is fine."

"Your desktop is slow as—"

"Ha! It's up." I pointed at the monitor.

"Your mouse creaks like my grandfather's hip. Is that a *mechanical* mouse? Is there a little *ball* rolling around inside?"

"You missed your calling. Why are you not on stage, making fun of people for a living?" I asked as I opened my email. I stifled a groan as new messages appeared, seventy percent of them spam. "Why is email even a thing? Who thought it was a good idea to trade paper junk mail for electronic crap?"

"The trees. The entire world's population of trees thought that was a good idea," Austin said while I deleted the unsolicited messages one at a time, to be sure I didn't miss anything important.

"No, I do not want to try a new shampoo or open a new bank account." *Click. Click.* "I don't care what faces the British royal children made during some parade last week." *Click.* "And I don't intend to donate to— Oh, Titus wrote back. I clicked on the message. "He's forwarded an email from Spencer Cole, one of his enforcers, who's also an ER triage nurse. Can't imagine he has much time to go on patrol..." I mumbled as I scrolled down to Spencer's message. I'd met him once and found him both genuinely nice and easy to talk to. I suspected he had a great bedside manner.

"Okay, so it turns out that the hospital Spencer works for, in addition to being part of the largest network of providers in Tennessee, is also sister-network to a system with facilities in four other states, all of which were accessible to some degree from Spencer's intake desk at work. He apologizes for the delay, saying he had to wait until they had a really slow night, in order to search the records without being seen. And he's included a—"

My gasp echoed through the office.

"What?" Austin popped up from his chair and circled my desk, where he started reading over my shoulder. "That's a list. He sent you a list of names. Of victims."

"Of *potential* victims." Listed with ages, dates, and locations. "Women in the right age range who came to a hospital in that network with symptoms similar to Yvette's. And the letter D in parentheses next to some of them—most of them —means—"

"Deceased," Austin finished for me.

"Yeah."

"How many is that?"

I counted the names. "Twelve. In the past...three years."

"Plus Yvette, and Nolan's sister."

"And the other woman we're looking into," I added, when I'd realized Brittany Walsh wasn't on the list either.

"And if their names aren't here, it's possible there could be more."

"Yes, but we don't know all of these women had scratch fever," I pointed out. "We don't know that *any* of them were actually infected. We need to dig in and find out what we can about them. Where they were in the days before they got sick. Whether or not any of them knew Yvette or Nolan's sister, or had any connection to the shifter community. Or to each other. If any of them *are* victims, it's possible they knew their killer. Or met him somewhere they may have in common with each other."

Austin snorted. "I'm pretty familiar with how an investigation works, Marshal."

"Of course. Sorry."

"I'm calling Bishop."

"I'll call Vance and Tucker. Titus says to let him know if we need additional resources, but I think we should wait on that until we have the list narrowed down. Then, if we need it, we can ask for help digging into their lives."

"Agreed." Austin's phone was pressed to his ear, already ringing. "Where are you going?" he asked as I headed out of my office.

"My cell's dead. I'm going to use the bar phone." And start a *big* pot of coffee.

NINE

"Wait, so what does all this mean?" Bishop asked, scanning the list of names I'd printed. "You think all these women were killed by whoever killed Yvette? And you don't think that was Nolan after all?"

"To be fair, we were never sure he was guilty," Tucker pointed out.

"And we're not sure all of these women are even dead, much less that they're murder victims," I added, sliding into the corner booth next to Tucker. I set the full coffee pot on a folded rag on the table, and Bishop snatched it immediately to refill his mug.

"So, you don't know much of anything, yet?" he said as he ripped open three sugar packets at once, spraying tiny crystals all over the table.

"That's true." I filled my own mug. "We're including you on the ground floor of this as a courtesy. But if you'd rather just get updates when we have more information, you're welcome to go back to bed." I was pretty proud of the *mostly* professional tone I managed to maintain.

"Bishop." Austin settled into the booth next to him. "Give them a break. Charley just got the list an hour ago."

"But she's known about Nolan's sister and that other dead chick for nearly twenty hours."

"Yes, and I would have told you sooner if I thought I could trust you not to kill him."

Bishop grumbled, but he didn't argue the point.

"Okay, let's take a look." Vance pulled a chair up to the end of the booth and handed out extra copies of the list. "Bishop, Austin, let us know if any of the names stand out to you. If you or Yvette knew any of the women or ever traveled to any of those towns."

"None of the names are familiar, but—"

"Seriously?" Bishop snapped, interrupting his brother-in-law. "Nashville? Yes, I've been to Nashville. I'm sure we've all been to the fucking state capitol. Atlanta, check. Chicago, yes. If we're looking for a killer based on who's been to several major US cities, I'd say we're screwed."

"Focus on the names then," Tucker said. "Do you recognize any of them?" His laptop sat open in front of him, his mug steaming next to it as he Googled one of the women on the list, who had no D in parentheses next to her name. He was trying to determine whether or not she was still alive.

"I've never met any of these women," Austin said. "At least, I don't know the names. But it's possible that Yvette met some of them? She did travel for work, occasionally."

"But if they were all infected in different places, over a span of several years, what makes us think they'd be connected to Yvette? Couldn't their connection be to the killer?" Bishop asked.

I nodded, privately impressed. "In fact, I'd say that's probable. But we're trying to cross all our Ts."

Austin sipped from his mug. "There isn't enough information here for me to know much. But, since we're crossing Ts, as well as confronting coincidence in a murder investigation, is there any chance that Megan Myers is related to Doug Myers? The guy who gave me a ride tonight?"

"Surely not…" I breathed.

"On it." Tucker's fingers flew over the keyboard, and a social media page appeared on his screen, with Doug Myers's face smiling out at me awkwardly from the user profile. He clicked on the family section, where a mother, two sisters, and four cousins were listed. "Um…can we confirm that Megan Myers was a resident of Macon, Georgia when she died? And that she was twenty-eight years old?"

"I can confirm that she died in a hospital in Macon," I said, with a glance at the printout on the table in front of me. "And that she was not quite twenty-nine," I added, after a second for some mental math.

"Then yes, there's a good chance she was the Megan Myers listed here as Doug Myers's youngest sister. Her page has been memorialized, which means someone has submitted proof of her death to the site."

"Oh my god." I dropped the list, and it drifted onto the table.

"Austin's sister Yvette. Nolan's sister Emily. Doug's sister Megan." Vance counted them off on his fingers. "That's more than coincidence."

"And that may not be the end of it," I told them. "Nolan said he didn't know Brittany Heller, but that he used to know an 'old man Heller' who ran on the common grounds years ago."

"Just a second." Tucker started typing again, and Brittany's profile came up quickly, because he'd been on it recently. He clicked on her pictures and scrolled through them until he found a four-year-old image of an old man with a grizzly gray beard and a prominent scar over his left eye. He swung the laptop around so the others could see it. "That could be an 'old man Heller,' right? It's from a post she wrote when her dad died a few years ago."

"Oh my *god*." My hands shook. I stood and set my coffee down so I couldn't drop it. "Tucker, go wake Nolan up and show him that picture. Find out if it's the old man he remembers. Everyone else, get out your phones and laptops. Find out how many of these women are—or were—related to shifters. Cross reference every single contact on any of their socials with any name in the census, for all three zones of the Mississippi Valley Pride. I'll ask Titus for a list of all the natural born shifter families he knows of. And I'll…make more coffee."

Instead, I headed straight for my office. I closed the door and sank into my chair, where I stared at the wall until my hands stopped shaking. Then I pulled open my bottom desk drawer and took several gulps straight from the tequila bottle. When my insides were almost as steady as my hands, I plucked my phone from the charger and dialed Titus.

He answered on the first ring, probably because I never called him before five in the morning.

"FROM TITUS." I slapped a purple sticky note onto the table. On it were written the surnames of every natural-born werecat he could think of: all of the US Alphas and their various progeny. There were fewer than I'd expected.

Because very few female werecats are born, the population never really increases. Titus joked privately to me once that they must keep very careful genealogy records, to make sure no cats too closely related were…mingling. And Jace once told me that every couple of decades, there's some sort

114

of shuffling of eligible bachelors between the US and Canada, in an attempt to keep the gene pool fresh.

I've always found the entire concept—the shifter population conundrum—both terrifying and sad. But the bright side was that we only had a handful of names to add to our search.

Tucker took the sticky note and began comparing it with the names on the list from Spencer. "No matches," he said.

I shrugged as I sank into the chair Vance had vacated in order to cook breakfast. "That's not terribly surprising." I was proud of how steady my voice sounded. How normal I suspected I looked, despite the cacophony of terror and dread pelting me from within my own head. "Those guys—" I pointed at the note. "—are born shifters. Very few of them marry and start families, because there aren't enough shifter women to go around. The occasional child conceived accidentally with a human woman would almost certainly take the mother's surname. Which means it'll be much harder for us to know if any of their relatives are among the victims."

"Wait, I don't get it," Bishop said. "What does that mean?"

I sighed. Strays had a very uneven knowledge base about shifter science and social structure, because most of us had been infected by accident. "We really have to start an orientation class, to teach people the basics," I said with a glance at Tucker.

"You know I agree!" Vance called from the kitchen, above the sizzle of bacon on the griddle. "But unless you make attendance mandatory, it won't do much good."

"What the hell are they talking about?" Bishop demanded with a glance at Austin.

He shrugged. "No idea."

"The quick version is this," I said. "And keep in mind, I'm not a scientist, and if I ever heard the proper scientific terms for any of this, they went in one ear and out the other. But basically, all of us—every stray in the world—has a pure-bred werecat ancestor somewhere down the line. Often way, way back. We have to, or scratch fever would kill us."

Sometimes it did anyway, even for men.

"Wait, seriously?" Austin's eyes were wide.

"Yeah. Humans who get bitten but don't have that gene can't become shifters. They just die of the infection. But if you have a dormant werecat gene and you get scratched or bitten, that gene basically gets activated, and if you survive scratch fever, bam! You're one of us."

"So…" Bishop frowned as he glanced from face to face. "All of us, like, in the whole stray territory, we're basically the result of some purebred, natural-born tomcat sleeping around?"

I nodded. "Somewhere down the line of your family tree, yes."

"But it isn't the same for women," Austin said, and I could tell what he was about to say from the way he was clutching the list of hospitalized women. "That's why there are so few female strays, right? Unless you're saying Yvette and I weren't really full-siblings? Like, you think my mom cheated on my dad?"

"Probably not," Tucker told him. Then he reconsidered with a shrug. "I'm not qualified to say that. I have no idea what your parents got up to. But that's probably not why Yvette died. You're right; it's different for women."

"Different, how?" Bishop asked.

"Again, I don't really understand the science," I said as Tucker went back to typing. "For some reason, human women are much, much less likely to survive scratch fever than men are, even with that necessary gene."

"Charley's the only female stray I've ever met," Tucker added, without looking up from his screen.

"I've met Robyn," Vance said on his way in from the kitchen carrying a tray loaded with food. "Titus's wife," he added, in response to a confused look from Bishop.

"We're the only two I know of," I said as I cleared off the table to make room for the tray. "Though there's a rumor that one more of us married into one of the purebred families."

Vance set the tray on our table and passed out empty plates. "I hope family style is okay. I'm not exactly a gourmet plater."

"It's fine, thanks," I told him as I scooped a large helping of scrambled eggs onto my plate. Bishop and Austin helped themselves to bacon and sausage, while Tucker started with a slice of thickly buttered Texas toast.

"But you all three had that gene," Bishop said around half a strip of bacon. "So at least you had a chance, when you were infected." He frowned, staring at his still half-empty plate. "At least Yvette had a chance."

"Yeah," I agreed. "And there's a theory, according to Titus, that more human women would survive scratch fever with proper medical care. That the infection hits them harder, which makes them less likely to recover without treatment, but that more might live if they were being cared for by people who knew *why* they were ill."

"Do you think…" Austin cleared his throat. "Do you think that's true?"

"I don't know," I told him. "But what I do know is that you did everything you possibly could have for Yvette. It's not your fault she didn't make it. It sounds like she was already very sick by the time you found her."

Bishop stood, pushing the table toward Tucker and me as

he leapt over the back of his booth and jogged toward the bathroom, his jaw clenched.

"He thinks it's his fault, for not getting to her sooner," Austin explained. "For not hearing his phone ring when she called."

And I'd just amplified his guilt by saying that quicker medical care might have helped her. *Damn it.*

We chewed in silence for several minutes, except for the tapping at Tucker's keyboard, and Austin filled Bishop's plate to make sure we didn't eat everything while he was gone. "So," I said as I stacked my used plate on top of the cheese-smeared empty egg platter. "Do we have a number yet?"

"Yeah." Tucker closed his laptop and handed me the paper he'd been making notes on. "Five from Spencer's list. Who knows how many more who never made it to the hospital, or who went to a hospital that wasn't in this system. Over a three-year span."

I glanced over the names he'd circled, reading them aloud under my breath. "Galloway. McGowan. Cooke. Baez. And Muniz." I sighed. "I only know two of these. Cooke and Muniz."

"Yeah. Jenna McGowan and Crystal Baez are both sisters of Pride members a few hours north of here. Elias knows them both. And Grace Galloway is the daughter of a man named Kenneth Galloway, who died not far from here a few years ago. He was shot by hunters in the woods, then he limped home and bled out without ever retaking human form. You probably knew him as Kenny G." Vance shrugged. "Bit of a joke, because he played the saxophone. Badly."

"Oh god, I do remember him. I didn't realize he had kids, though."

"Just the one daughter," Tucker said. "His wife left him

and took the kid when she was little. He was infected a few years later, if memory serves."

Bishop appeared again from the bathroom, his eyes slightly swollen. "Wait, so you've found five more victims—"

"*Potential* victims," I corrected.

"—who're related to members of your Pride?"

"Six," Tucker said. "Maria Bruce was the daughter of Curtis White, one of our regulars. She used her mother's surname. She died in June of last year, in a hospital on the outskirts of Memphis."

"And there are probably others," Vance reminded us.

"So, we think someone is targeting female relatives— sisters and daughters—of stray Pride members?" Bishop said, sliding into the booth again."

"I don't think we're ready to draw that conclusion yet," Austin said as he slid Bishop's plate full of now-cold food toward him. "Because we don't yet know that the other women on the list—the ones not related to shifters—weren't also targeted. It's possible that it's just coincidence that several of these women are related to shifters, if the others aren't."

"Actually, that's looking less and less likely." Tucker nudged me, and I slid out of the booth to let him up. "Three of those other women appear to have died of previously undi-agnosed medical conditions, at least according to social media posts by family members. The infections that took them to the hospital were secondary to that." Tucker refilled his mug from a fresh pot behind the bar. "And a fourth was diagnosed with meningitis posthumously."

A deeply unsettling feeling sank through me. Half of the women on Spencer's list were either sisters or daughters of Pride members, and we could add Yvette as well as Nolan's sister Emily to that list. Of the six who were not related to shifters, four had other verified causes of death.

"So, he *is* targeting our sisters," Austin growled, and his anger rolled through me, triggering an echoing growl of outrage from deep in my throat. "Our daughters."

"Why?" Bishop gripped his fork so tightly it was cutting into his fingers. "He's obviously one of us. So what the hell does he gain from killing our female relatives?"

"He isn't trying to kill them." My voice was so soft it would have been inaudible to a human. "He's trying to infect them. He's trying to create female strays from women he knows are carrying the genes that make that possible, in theory at least. Sisters and daughters of known strays."

Stunned silence followed my declaration. There were no dissenting opinions.

I stood and grabbed the empty tray, because I needed something to do with my hands to keep them from trembling. Bishop stared at his plate, but I could feel Austin watching me as I crossed the front of the bar and backed through the swinging door into the kitchen, where I set the tray down and began filling the commercial-size sink with scalding water and dish soap.

The swinging door creaked behind me, and I caught Vance's scent even as I recognized the cadence of his steps. "You okay?"

"Just doing dishes."

"You're the boss. The boss doesn't have to do dishes."

I flicked soap suds at him, and Vance patiently wiped them from his face.

"We had a chance to stop him," I whispered low enough that the running water would shield my voice from everyone out front. "We should have stopped him."

"We thought we had," he whispered back, standing so

close that his arm brushed mine. Vance had been my best friend and most trusted ally for nearly three years. Everything about him was a comfort—his scent, his size, and his voice. The way he always knew not just that I was upset, but *why* I was upset.

But this time…

"We were wrong. We were fucking *wrong*, and that cost lives. We let our people down. We got their sisters and daughters and wives killed."

"No." Vance turned me by both shoulders, his voice so soft I could hardly hear him. "*He* did that. Whoever he is. And we're going to figure that out."

"How is this *possible*?" I hissed, struggling not to let despair leak into my words. Fighting to stay mad, as sudsy water dripped on my boots. Anger was much more productive than fear. Than despair. "We killed Silas. We put him in the ground. How could we not know he wasn't acting alone?"

But the answer to that was even more traumatic for me than the question itself. *I* was the reason we hadn't known. I was the reason we'd buried Silas and moved on, assuming we'd done what needed to be done.

"There was a lot we didn't know back then, Charley." Vance shrugged.

But that was my point.

"This is my fault. None of these cases pre-date mine. I was the first victim, and I said Silas was the only one. How could I not know he had a partner?" We'd put the case to rest based entirely on my testimony to Titus. To the council. I had a chance to be not just the first victim, but the *last* victim, and I blew it.

"You were sick. You were traumatized. You'd just been attacked, and you had no idea what was going on. Who we were, or who *you* were, in this new world. It isn't your fault if your memory was compromised by all that. Or if you were too sick to process what you saw and heard."

"Vance—"

"And it's entirely possible that you never saw anyone else. That you had no reason to know Silas was working with someone."

He was right. I knew that. Still…

"If we'd gotten both of them in the first place, all those women would still be alive. Austin would still have his sister. Bishop would still have his wife."

Vance sighed. "That's on the rest of us, but not on you. Back then, you were the victim, not the Marshal. Not the investigator, the enforcer, the Alpha, or the Council. If anything, we failed *you*."

If I were in his position, talking to a victim, I would say the same thing. And yet, I still felt responsible. I knew, deep in my heart, that I'd had a chance to prevent all of this, and I'd failed.

Vance took a breath, and I could see him thinking through words not yet said. "Do Austin and Bishop know? About your connection to this?"

"No. But I swear I'll tell them if and when it becomes relevant to the investigation."

"And do you anticipate that moment coming soon?"

I nodded slowly. "If we're really looking for an unknown accomplice of Silas's, I think it's going to come pretty fucking quick."

As the sun rose, shining through the back door we'd left open to cool off the kitchen, I washed the dishes, and Vance dried. And he didn't point out even once that we had a commercial dishwasher intended for that very purpose.

. . .

"OKAY, you guys go get some sleep," I said as Vance and I returned to the front room, our hands wrinkled from the hot water. I felt calmer from the mindless work. Ready to move forward. "Davey and Mitch—" Our other short order cook. "—will be here in a couple of hours, and we can open the bar on our own. I'm going to give Titus an update, then nap until nine-thirty, myself. I'm hoping Titus will be willing to send us some extra manpower, ASAP, because this is the most populous Pride in the country, which means our suspect list is basically enormous, so..." My voice faded into silence when I realized Tucker, Bishop, and Austin were all staring at me.

"Um, so the thing is that we can narrow that list of suspects down by, well..." Tucker shrugged. "Possibly quite a bit."

"He's one of yours," Bishop blurted, and Austin turned to glare at him.

My pulse stuttered. "What do you mean, *mine*?"

"All of the shifters who're related to the potential victims we've identified so far," Tucker said. "They're not just from the Mississippi Valley Pride. They're from the northern zone, specifically. *All* of them. They're all men we know, which means they're probably all men the killer knows. We're looking for one of *our guys*, Charley."

TEN

"What is with you today?" Davey asked as she shimmied past me behind the bar, carrying two empty beer pitchers. "Your head is not in the game."

My head was very much in the game. But that game was finding a serial killer, not tending bar.

"I didn't get much sleep."

"Also, there are no enforcers here today," she whispered. "Isn't that a breach of some kind of protocol?"

"Vance, Tucker, and I were up all night working on Yvette's case, so I gave them the morning off. They'll be here in half an hour." Just in time for the lunch rush.

"Hey," Billy said as he pushed through the swinging door from the kitchen, his hair secured in its net. "You wanted to see me out here?"

"Yeah. We're short-handed this morning, and it's slow, so I thought it'd be a good time to try you out behind the bar."

His brows rose, excitement shining behind his eyes. "For real?"

"Yeah. You're old enough." Since I'd filed the proper application, and he was supervised.

"Hey, can I get a beer?" Doug Myers asked as he slid onto a stool at the other end of the bar, and a tide of guilt flooded me at the thought of what I was not telling him. But until we had proof about how his sister had died, saying something to Doug or any of the others would just be compromising the investigation and creating a panic.

So I kept my mouth shut as I nodded at Billy.

"Sure! What kind?" He grabbed a pint mug and pulled a draft just like I'd shown him on a slow night at least a year before. Then he glanced at me with his brows raised, silently asking how he'd done.

I gave him another nod and a smile. He'd become a great short-order cook, but it was good to know he could be pulled up front when we needed him, and the nearly-dead ten am hour was a perfect testing ground. We only had three customers.

"Good job, Billy the Kid," Doug said. "Too bad you can't pull one for yourself, huh?"

"Oh, leave him alone and drink your beer," I scolded Doug as I wiped down the bar, and he seemed more than eager to oblige.

"When do you turn twenty-one, anyway?" Davey glanced at Billy as she stacked clean glasses beneath the bar.

He made an exasperated sound. "Be a while. I *just* turned twenty."

"Damn. How old were you when you were infected?"

"Davey!" I snapped. "For some people, that's personal!" All strays had an infection story. Some, like mine, were traumatic, and asking someone to relive that trauma to satisfy her curiosity just wasn't fair. "If he wants to share his story, he'll do it without being prompted."

Billy tugged the net from his hair and shoved it into his

back pocket, relieved of the requirement while he wasn't preparing food. "I don't mind."

"See?" Davey stuck her tongue out at me. "He doesn't mind. Still," she added with another glance at him. "I didn't mean any offense."

"None taken," he said. "I was fourteen and a half. Went fishin' in the woods and ran into a big black cat." Billy shrugged. "I mean, I'd heard things. People talk, and there had been some…sightings. But I didn't take that any more serious than Bigfoot, 'n shit. 'Till I saw one. I musta caught him by surprise, because he swatted at me. Got me pretty good, too." Billy pushed up his sleeve to show a set of four claw marks curving around his right forearm. "But then I started shouting, kinda swinging my fishing pole at him, and he ran off."

"It was too late for you, though, right?" Doug said, lifting his glass.

"Yeah. I tied my shirt around the wound and headed home."

"You didn't go the hospital?" Davey asked.

"Nah." Billy waved off the question as he scooped up a handful of peanuts from the community bowl. "My mom believed hospitals were where you go to die. She sewed me up, then slathered my arm with Neosporin. In the middle of the night, I got a high fever, so she put me in the tub, packed in ice from the gas station up the road. The fever broke, but then I started twitching, and…well, you know. I grew *fur*, 'n shit."

"So, she knows?" Davey looked so hopeful that I almost cut Billy off, to keep him from telling her the rest of the story. "Your mom *knows*?"

"She did, yeah," he said. "This was before we knew about any Pride. Before there was one here, I guess." Billy tilted his head in my direction. "What's it been, three years since Titus took over?"

"Three and a half, since the founding of the Mississippi Valley Pride. Before that, it was the free zone. No support system. No shifter law. It was basically the wild west."

"Your mom must have been so freaked out!" Davey breathed.

"Yeah, I guess." Billy shrugged. "But, I mean, she'd heard the same stories I had. They had similar ones in the hills in West Virginia, where she was from. Legends, she called them. Until I became one. She kept it a secret without even knowing that was the rule, because she was paranoid that if anyone found out, the government would do experiments on me." Billy grinned. "I think she watched too much late night sci-fi."

Personally, I didn't think his mom was far from the truth, about government experimentation.

"She died a couple of years later," Billy added.

"Is that when my parents hired you?" Davey asked as she refilled the snack bowls. "I remember you were pretty young."

"Um…about a year after that. I stayed with family for a while, but it didn't really work out. Too many secrets."

Doug snorted. "I bet. Furry, snarly secrets."

"Pretty much." Billy turned back to Davey. "It was actually Charley that hired me, though. I met her through Eamon."

I nodded. That was before I was infected, back when Eamon was just a friend of my brother's and a regular at the bar my parents owned. I'd had no idea that shifters existed, or that Ben was one. Or that Eamon and the teenager he'd taken in were anything other than human.

"I brought him on to bus tables, at first," I told Davey.

"But then Dad took Billy under his wing and taught him about the grill, and the rest was history! You were the best damn seventeen-year-old fry cook in the state!" I added, shifting my focus to Billy.

He beamed at me. "Speaking of which, I better go prep some burgers."

"He's only three years younger than me," Davey whispered as the kitchen door swung shut behind him. "How is it that he seems so much younger?"

Doug Myers snorted. "That's what happens when you lose your mom young." He sipped from his mug, then seemed to reconsider. "'Course, that's also what happens when you *never* lose your mom, and she won't let you grow up."

"Personal experience?" I teased.

Doug flipped me off as he slid his empty mug toward me.

The bell over the door rang while I was getting him another beer, and as I turned to hand it to him, a familiar scent surrounded me, swept in on a breeze through the open door.

Titus.

His gray-eyed gaze fixed on me instantly, and anyone unfamiliar with him might have assumed that he'd registered nothing else in the room.

I knew better. Titus Alexander had catalogued every scent and counted every body in the room before the door even swung closed behind him.

"Charley," he said, and every shifter in the bar froze. Heads swiveled in his direction. Pulses echoed rapidly all over the room, like fingertips tapping at the back of my mind. There was something about Titus's voice—about his presence —that demanded respect and screamed "authority." It was a strength. A gravity. An Alpha-ness that I couldn't put into better words, but I could feel every time I was in the room with him.

Even Davey could feel the change. The sudden tension in the bar, which would remain until Titus—as Alpha—made it clear why he had come, and that he meant no harm.

Of course, Davey already knew him.

"Titus. Come in," I said, lifting the bar flap.

"Oh, shit," Doug mumbled, but he didn't truly seem surprised to realize he was looking at our Alpha. Whom he'd clearly never met.

"Titus!" My sister dashed around me and into the dining area, where she threw her arms around the Alpha like an older brother home from college. Which no one else who wasn't related to him by blood or marriage would have *dared* to do. "It's been so long!"

She'd never once greeted me with that kind of enthusiasm.

"Hey, Davey." He returned her hug, patting her back, and over his shoulder I saw a large, gorgeous gentleman with a blond man-bun leaning against a black Mercedes SUV in the parking lot, both arms crossed over his jacket.

Lochlan Hayes, one of Titus's enforcers.

"Are you staying for lunch?" Davey backed toward the bar again. "I can have Billy make—"

"Not this time," Titus said. "Your sister and I have some business to take care of."

Davey spun to scowl at me, silently scolding me for not telling her that he was coming. "I can send a couple of burgers to your office?"

"Thanks, but we're actually going to be in the field today," Titus said, his gaze still trained on me. "In a manner of speaking." The man could say more with a single look than

I usually managed in ten minutes of conversation. "I'll have your sister back to you in an hour, though."

"Just a second." I leaned over the bar to pluck my cell phone from the charger cord. "Vance and Tucker will be here any minute." I couldn't leave Davey alone in a bar full of shifters.

"Loch will stay with her, as well." Titus turned to rap one knuckle on the window, beckoning the enforcer with a wave.

"*God*, he's pretty..." Davey breathed as she watched him approach through the glass door.

"Everyone in here can hear you," I teased. "Hell, they can practically hear your thoughts."

Davey flipped me off, just as Loch pushed the door open.

"I need you to hang with Davey and keep an eye on the place until we get back," Titus said.

"Of course." Lochlan pulled his man bun loose, and I swear to god, he shook his hair out like there was a goddamn spotlight shining on him. I thought Davey was going to melt right into the floor, and I couldn't really blame her.

"Don't forget to call the beef distributer," I said as I backed toward the door.

"Beef. On it..." Davey mumbled, still staring at Loch.

Titus chuckled as he held the door open for me.

"That is not funny," I snapped as it swung shut behind us.

"The hell it's not. Also, it happens everywhere he goes."

"Yeah, well, Davey needs to think shifter men are the kind who belch their beer breath at her from across the bar, not the kind that just stepped off the catwalk. No pun intended. Next time, can you bring someone...uglier?"

Titus gave me an amused look, his shoes crunching on gravel. "Who would you suggest?"

Fair point. All his enforcers were attractive.

"What are you doing here, anyway? When I asked for

backup, I assumed you'd send Jace. He lives, like, two hours closer."

Titus pulled open the passenger side door of an SUV that cost more than my net worth, but he didn't answer my question until he'd settled behind the wheel. "Jace and Abby are at my house for the party."

"What party?"

"Kaci's turning twenty-two, and she has family in town for a few days," Titus explained as he turned left out of the parking lot. I could hardly feel the potholes, in his fancy billionaire-mobile, and there was no road noise to speak of. "They're basically Jace's family too, so…"

Kaci was one of the Pride's four female shifters, and she was married to Titus's little brother, Justus. And while Jace wasn't on great terms with his actual relatives, since he'd been exiled from his birth Pride, he'd been an enforcer in Kaci's home territory for years. In fact, there were rumors of a wildly torrid affair he supposedly had with Faythe Sanders, the world's only female Alpha, before she got married. Though no one ever mentioned that in front of Abby, Jace's girlfriend and Faythe's cousin.

"So, basically, you have a house full of shifter dignitaries, while I have a murderer on the loose, and you don't want the former to know about the latter?"

"Faythe, Marc—" Her husband and co-Alpha. "—and Jace know. Out of necessity. But we're not planning to make any further announcements until we can say we got the bastard."

"Well, thanks for coming. I *really* need an objective eye to back me up on this one." I owed it to the rest of the Pride not to let my own potential bias blind me to evidence during this particularly sensitive part of the investigation.

Titus nodded. "Why don't you lay the killer's profile out for me, one more time."

"Okay." But why? Was he saying this was unnecessary? Trying to help me draw that conclusion for myself? If so, why had he driven all this way, when he could have said that over the phone? "Our killer is likely male," I began. "Not because a woman couldn't or wouldn't have done this, but because there are no female shifters here, other than me."

I paused, shifting in my seat to look at him. "*I* know I'm not guilty, but how can you be sure I'm not the one carrying on in Silas's footsteps? I mean, like Davey says, I know better than anyone that it *is* possible for a woman to survive."

"I'm sure because I know you." The glance he aimed at me was as reassuring as his words. "You would never put another woman through what you went through. You would never risk a life. You would never take that choice—the choice to *stay human*—from her."

He was right. And the fact that he knew me well enough to believe that was the one bright spot in this whole thing.

"This is your case, Charley, and I'm not taking it from you. Right now, you're the *only* shifter in the northern zone I'm sure I can trust."

I took a deep breath, then continued with the profile. "We're looking for a man who's been around for more than three years." Since before we executed Silas. "Who knows the locals. Someone people would trust with information about their families. Their sisters and daughters."

Titus nodded.

"Someone who understands werecat infection methods, including the genetic component. People talk, so in theory, anyone could have heard about dormant genes. But there's a certain circle of people who *definitely* know about that.

People who have reason to understand and discuss that fact, as a part of their job."

Another nod.

"We're also looking for someone who had the opportunity to travel." Because though those women all had connections to our territory, they were not all infected in our territory. "And, lastly, we're looking for someone who knew Silas. Or at least knew enough about what he did to have picked up the theory and run with it." Because we were either looking for Silas's previously unknown partner or for a copycat.

"So, to recap, we're looking for a man who's been around a while and is trusted by the locals. Who knew about Silas's crimes. And who has opportunities to travel, possibly for work." Titus met my gaze while we were stopped at a red light. Less than a block from the Pine Cove apartments.

"So, you think I'm doing the right thing?" I asked.

"If I didn't, I wouldn't have come to help. But before we start, *you* need to be sure of that too. We have to rule them out, in order to be able to work with them. To trust them. We really have no choice."

And *that* was why he'd made me lay the facts out, for the millionth time. To justify, aloud, what we were about to do. "I'm sure." But I still felt like an asshole.

Titus pulled into the parking lot, past the building where Bishop and Austin were probably still in bed, after our late night. He parked in front of the unit where my sister lived. Her car was gone, of course, as were both Tucker's and Vance's, because they'd already left for the bar. "Apartments 3B and 3C, right?"

I nodded. "Vance is in 3C, upstairs. Next to Davey."

"You have keys?"

"No. Stuart does, but he's a gossip," I said as Titus opened his door and got out of the car. I followed him across the gravel lot. "This still feels really shitty," I whispered at his back.

"It'll feel even worse if one of them is guilty, and we never looked into them. If another woman dies in our territory because we weren't thorough enough to investigate your enforcers, even though they fit the profile to a motherfucking T." Titus rapped three times, firmly, on Stuart's door.

"He could be out," I said. "Fixing a water heater or—"

Stuart opened the door. "Hey, Charley. And Titus!" His face lit up. Stuart was a big fan of our Alpha, who gave him free rent, plus a salary.

"Hi Stuart. I'm going to need to borrow your key ring, please." Titus's voice was commanding, but polite.

"The whole ring?"

"Yes."

"Sure thing. One second." Stuart disappeared into his dimly lit apartment, where I could hear a gameshow playing on the television. The scent wafting toward us in his absence was mostly day-old pizza and beer. And sweat.

Two seconds later, he was back, thick key ring in hand. "They're marked," he said as he set the whole thing in Titus's waiting palm. "Can I ask what you need 'em for?"

"No. And you're going to need to keep this confidential," Titus said. "It's a matter of Pride security."

"Of course." Stuart nodded several times, rapidly. Eager to please. But that didn't mean he wouldn't talk about this to anyone who would listen. It wasn't every day the Alpha of the entire Pride dropped by out of the blue to search a couple of apartments.

Not that that mattered. Vance and Tucker would know we'd been in their homes. They'd be able to smell our scents on everything we touched.

"Thank you." Titus waited with a quiet, expectant smile

until Stuart nodded and closed the door.

When we turned to cross the lot, I heard the soft clatter of plastic as Stuart pulled down his mini-blinds to peek through them.

Titus headed straight for the external staircase on one side of building three, sorting through the keys as he took the steps two at a time. I jogged up after him, nerves crawling like ants across my skin.

"This could backfire," I whispered, as he slid a key into Vance's front door. "We could lose the confidence and trust of my best men."

"Or you could gain even more respect from them for turning over every stone. For being vigilant." The door swung open, and Titus shoved the keys into his pocket, where they left a large, oddly shaped bulge. "The bottom line is that we have no choice."

"I'm not even sure what we're looking for," I admitted, closing the door at my back.

"Anything that connects Vance to any of the victims."

"Other than the research I asked him to do, you mean?" I picked up a yellow legal pad to show him a list of the victim's names, along with several other pages of notes from our meeting the night before.

"Yes, other than that. Of course."

We went through Vance's drawers and cabinets. Through his closets and his desk. I looked under his bed while Titus felt around for false drawer bottoms and evidence taped to the under-side of every surface imaginable. We pulled the clothes from his dryer—his hamper was empty—and rifled through the food in his fridge. We squeezed couch cushions and bed pillows, and even examined the seams in both his mattress and his comforter. But we found nothing.

Vance was neat and organized, and he kept a spotless

apartment—no dirt on the floor and no mildew in the shower. But I felt dirty as I stood on the second-floor landing, next to my sister's apartment, while Titus locked up. Like I'd seen things my best friend and most trusted enforcer hadn't intended to show me. Like I'd violated his privacy and his trust.

We went downstairs and repeated the process at Tucker's place, which was directly below Davey's. His apartment was messier, but no more incriminating than Vance's had been, and this time when we were finished, I felt as much relief as guilt.

"This doesn't entirely clear them," Titus reminded me as he locked Tucker's door. "It's entirely possible that if one of them *is* involved, they're smart enough to keep the evidence somewhere else."

"But they aren't involved," I said as we headed across the lot to return Stuart's keys.

Titus pulled up short, gravel shifting beneath his loafers. His gray eyes seemed to bore right through me. "You don't know that."

"I do." I stared up at him, unflinching. "I *do*. My gut says they want to find this guy as badly as I do, and you're the one who told me that sometimes, in this job, you have to trust your gut."

"Okay. I hear you," Titus said. "Still, I'm going to leave Lochlan here, and maybe send one more of my guys. An outsider's perspective never hurts, and they don't fit the profile, because they don't know your zone members. So you know you can trust them."

"Don't do that. Please," I whispered, worried that Stuart was watching through his blinds. That he'd cracked the window open so he could hear. "That will undercut Vance and Tucker's authority, as well as mine. And it'll make them think

I don't trust them. We're may have to interview the family members, Titus. Men who'll be finding out their daughters and sisters died solely because of their common genes. Because of who they are. And they don't know your men. They don't trust your men. But they do trust Vance and Tucker. We did our due diligence. We looked for evidence of their guilt and we found none, so now I need them, not just at my side, but at my back. All of us here need to be able to trust them."

Titus blinked at me, and I could practically see the gears grinding behind his eyes as he considered my words. My tone. My bearing and the speed of my pulse, which conveyed my confidence in my position.

"Okay," he finally said. "I'll take Loch back with me. But you call me if anything changes. If you need anything else. And you keep me updated. Okay? Regularly."

"Done. Of course."

His gaze narrowed on me. "How are you doing with all this?"

"With the news that Silas was basically resurrected, just to haunt me?"

"That's an interesting characterization," he said with a small smile. "But yes."

"I'm fine. It helps, having something to investigate. Something to focus on."

"Well, I'm here if you need to talk."

"Thanks. But I think what I really need is an opportunity just to…punch someone in the face." I pulled my arm back, fist formed, miming the blow. "To just really let someone have it."

Titus laughed, a deep, pleasant sound that set me at ease, on basically a cellular level. "When we catch this guy, you're going to get exactly what you want."

ELEVEN

"You know, it would be good for morale if you made a personal appearance—and had a beer—at the bar," I said as Titus turned his SUV back into the parking lot of the Fat Cat. "I mean, everyone's gonna know you're here, so…"

"What do they know about all this?" He shifted into park, staring through the windshield at the front of the building, where the neon cowboy hat sat atilt over the F in Fat Cat. "Your regulars."

"Very little, so far. They know that Austin Graham and Bishop Mattheson accused Nolan Blake of murdering Yvette, but that's about it. Speaking of which…" I shrugged.

"Yes, I think it's time to let Nolan go. If you're sure they won't go after him."

"I know exactly how to prevent that," I assured him. "But when I release, Nolan, everyone will know the killer is still out there. And the killer will know we're still looking for him. And once we start talking to the relatives…"

"Okay." Titus cleared his throat and straightened his tie. "I'll make an appearance." He pressed a button to turn off the engine, then he got out of the car with clear purpose and speed. Before I could give him any advice about how best to mingle with the locals.

I had to jog to catch up with Titus as he pushed the door open, to the off-key tinkling of the bell.

The lunch rush had begun, and the place was about two-thirds full. Probably due in part to word that Titus was in town, from the three regulars who'd seen him arrive. Knowing that, anyone who *could* come in for lunch would.

"Titus!" Davey called. "Come on over here!" She set a beer on the counter. "On the house!"

A chorus of greetings rang out from every corner of the bar. Titus accepted the beer with gregarious thanks, but I noticed that as he carried it from table to table, shaking hands and greeting people, he hardly sipped from it. He was a whiskey drinker. A very, very expensive whiskey drinker. Which explained the quietly amused look on Lochlan's face, where he stood talking with Tucker in one corner.

Vance was stationed behind the bar, watching the jovial ruckus with a small smile—until his gaze met mine. I exhaled, and when I started toward him, he dropped his bar rag on the counter and pushed his way through the swinging doors into the kitchen.

Davey noticed the silent interaction. She gave me a look that was somehow both puzzled and scolding, as if she wasn't sure what had happened, but she *was* sure it was my fault. Then she went after him, leaving me to take her spot behind the bar.

Titus stayed for around twenty minutes, during which he managed to swallow about half of his beer. Despite his money, and his suit, and his utter unfamiliarity with both boots and cowboy hats, he effortlessly charmed everyone he'd never met and re-connected with those he had. It didn't hurt that he never forgot a name, or that he genuinely wanted to connect with people. To aid and support his fellow shifters.

That's why he'd lobbied so hard, and for so long, to get the Mississippi Valley Pride acknowledged by the Territorial Council.

I walked Titus and Lochlan out roughly an hour and a half after they'd first pulled into the parking lot.

"Do you want me to take Nolan back with me? We can put him up somewhere down south until this all blows over, if you think he's in any danger," Titus said as he unlocked his car.

"Thanks, but I don't think he'd want to leave the area," I said.

"Yeah," Lochlan agreed, pulling his shoulder-length blond hair back into its customary bun. "They'll see that as running away, and they'll see running away as guilt."

By "they," he meant all the Pride members who were about to hear through a very efficient grapevine that we had not yet caught Yvette's killer.

"Yes, of course," Titus said. "But the offer stands, should anything change."

"Thank you. I'll pass that along."

As Titus and Loch pulled out of the parking lot, footsteps crunched into the gravel behind me. I spun around to find Vance standing in the shadows at the corner of the building. He had both hands in his pockets, but the tension in his posture belied the casual pose.

"Hey," I said as I headed toward him, stuffing my hands in my pockets to warm them.

"So? Have you crossed me off your suspect list, or do you need to search me for weapons and evidence?" He spread his arms, practically daring me to pat him down.

"Stuart called?" I guessed.

"You had to know he would."

"I did. And I'd have told you, if he hadn't. I wasn't trying to keep secrets. I was just doing my job." As unpleasant as that could be, when it involved my personal friends.

"I take it I fit the profile?"

"You had to know that," I said, echoing his words.

"I did." But he said it without a smile. "I understand that you did what you had to do. And I understand why that was necessary. But that doesn't mean I have to like it."

"Of course not."

"It might take a bit for me to be okay with this."

"Sure." I nodded up at him. "I'd be pissed if you'd gone through my stuff."

Finally, he grinned. "What makes you think I haven't?"

I rolled my eyes.

"Find anything interesting?" he asked.

"You're very neat and clean. I honestly didn't expect that."

His brows rose. "Should I be insulted?"

"It's a compliment. But the Spiderman boxers?"

Vance burst into laughter. "Did you notice they were brand new? Still smelled like the factory they were made in?"

"No! Because I did not sniff your underwear." I scowled up at him. "You planted those!"

He shrugged, his shoulders still shaking with quiet laughter. "I knew I fit the profile, and that you'd eventually have to search my place. The least I could do was make it fun for you."

"Cute…" I mumbled. "So, then Tucker's bedside draw—"

"Nope!" Vance covered his ears and squeezed his eyes shut, like a giant child in denial. "If he knew this was coming, he didn't say anything to me, and I do *not* want to hear what you found in his bedside drawer." He opened one eye and stared down at me. "He knows you were there today, though. He took Stuart's call."

I sighed. "Great." I really would have preferred to tell them both myself.

"You know things will never be the same between us now, right?" Vance grinned down at me. "Not since you've seen my Spidey underwear."

"Funny. So we're good?"

"Always and forever," he assured me. "Go make peace with Tucker."

We headed back into the bar, but all I could think about as I watched Vance lift the bar flap on his way into the kitchen was that he'd known I was coming. He'd left me a gag gift, for god's sake, and he'd clearly cleaned the apartment in advance of my search.

Which meant that if he *was* involved with the murders, he'd had every possible opportunity to remove—or destroy—the evidence.

"HEY. THANKS FOR COMING," I said as Bishop and Austin filed into my office. "Close the door please."

Bishop pushed the door shut, then he sank into one of the guest chairs in front of my desk, next to Austin. "Is this about Nolan?" he asked. "You're letting him go?"

"Yeah. I guess you knew this was coming?"

"We picked up on that this morning," he confirmed.

"So when you called us down here, we figured it was that, or you wanted to get us out of the apartment so you could search it," Austin finished with a grin. "Or both."

"Ha, ha. I'm not searching your apartment. Or your house in Covington. You two are not suspects."

"Why not?" Bishop asked.

"Because the killer knew a zone member related to each of the victims, and the only one we knew was Nolan," Austin explained.

"And because we believe your grief is real. Also…you'd have to be idiots to accuse him of killing your wife—" I turned to Austin. "—and your sister, if you'd actually killed *his* sister. We knew nothing about this until you brought it to our attention. Well," I amended with a frown. "We didn't *know* we knew anything about this until then."

"And you're *sure* it isn't Nolan?" Bishop asked. "I mean, doesn't he fit the profile?"

"He *does* fit the profile. But we don't believe he'd kill his own sister, just like we don't believe you guys killed Yvette."

Bishop shrugged. "So maybe he didn't. Maybe all the other victims are somehow in revenge for Emily's murder."

"Except that he didn't know his sister was murdered. And Emily wasn't the first victim."

"Oh," Bishop said.

Austin's gaze narrowed on me, and my pulse spiked. That admission may have been a tactical error.

"What I need to know from you guys…" I said, determinedly pressing on, "…is that you're not going to be a problem when I release Nolan." I glanced at my wrist, even though I'd never in my life worn a watch. "In about ten minutes."

Bishop leaned forward in his chair, looking straight into my eyes. "If you're sure he's not the guy..?"

"I'm sure he didn't kill his sister, and he'd have no reason to avenge her death before she even died. Or if he didn't know she was murdered." I could only shrug. "There's no evidence against him, and the timeline doesn't line up."

"She's not wrong," Austin said.

"Okay then." Bishop rapped on my desk with the

knuckles of his right hand, evidently putting the issue to bed. "I have no beef with him." He stood and backed around his chair, headed for my office door. "Let him go."

I glanced at Austin, who nodded, but remained seated. "Have a beer," he called over his shoulder to Bishop. "I'll be there in a minute."

"Make it quick," Bishop returned. "We still have a killer to find."

Austin nodded, and the door closed at his back.

I exhaled and rolled my chair closer to my desk. "I take it you have questions."

"Nolan's sister was not the first victim?"

I nodded slowly. "We have reason to believe there was at least one before that."

His knee began to bounce. I could feel his question coming like a storm on the horizon, and I tensed before he even opened his mouth. "Who's buried out there, Charley? Deep in the common run. Whose grave did you go visit that night?"

"No one's. That was a grave, but I wasn't visiting it."

Austin exhaled slowly. "I'm guessing that grave is around three years old?" I blinked at him, but he held my gaze. "I'm further guessing that you were infected around three years ago? Not long before Emily Blake Forrester was murdered?"

I folded my hands together, pressing them into the surface of my desk. "I don't owe you my personal history."

"Of course not," he conceded. "But you do owe me any information relevant to my sister's case." He gave me a moment to consider that. "Who's buried out there, Charley?"

I exhaled, fighting the urge to pull open my bottom drawer. To dive into that bottle of tequila and live there for a while. "His name was Silas Morelock. We don't know much about him, except that he was already a stray when the Pride was formed. I was not."

"But you were local?" he asked, gently prompting me to continue.

I nodded. "I was born in Buford. My parents bought this bar when I was in the third grade. I basically grew up here. Davey and I did our homework in this very room, though it was my parents' office, back then. We weren't allowed to sit at the bar, of course, but we often ate dinner with our parents at the corner booth. I've been here my whole life. I felt safe here."

"Until…"

"Until one day, not long after my parents moved to Florida, I left after closing for the night, and while I was unlocking my car, some asshole hit me in the back of the head. Hard. I have no idea what happened after that until I woke up cuffed to one corner of a bed in some shitty little cabin. There was a window, and I could see trees through it. In one corner, there was one of those old-fashioned wood stoves, vented through a rough hole cut into the wall, and it was burning bright, but I was shivering. Shaking. Covered from head to toe in both goosebumps and a cold sweat. I ached all over. In every joint. Even my goddamn toes. I'd been kidnapped *and* caught the flu." I huffed. "Worst luck in history, right?"

Austin nodded, but he said nothing. He just listened.

"After a few minutes—I think. I was raging with fever, and I suspect my perception of time was distorted. Anyway, at some point a man came in, and I started screaming. I feared the worst, obviously. But he didn't try to touch me. He just brought me water to drink through a straw. He set it where I could reach it, and he left.

"I couldn't get out. I could move around with just one

arm cuffed, but I couldn't get to the door. He just… He left me there with a big jug of water and an empty bucket."

"So, what did you do?"

"Nothing. That's the only thing I could do. I lay there for what felt like an eternity, delirious with fever. Sipping water. Trying to remain calm and rational. Eventually I realized there was a bite on my arm. It was too swollen for me to tell much about it, but later, after that was all over, Eamon said it was a remarkably clean bite. No tears in the skin. Because I was unconscious when Silas bit me."

Austin nodded slowly. "Yvette's bite was clean."

"I know. Unfortunately, we don't have information about any of the other victims' wounds. But based on the fact that none of the hospital records mention them, I'm guessing they were so minor as to have gone unnoticed. Unassociated with the symptoms they presented."

Another nod. "So, how did you get out of the cabin?"

"I didn't. I *couldn't*. Until I shifted." I finally forced my fingers to unlock, then I ran my sweaty palms across my thighs over and over. "I thought I was dying. It felt like my body was trying to pull itself apart. It didn't feel real. I couldn't process the…the reality of it. I didn't have the concept. The ability to understand what was happening. All I knew was that suddenly the pain had ended, but the entire world looked different. *I* looked different."

"And I'm guessing your paw slid right out of the handcuff?"

"Yeah. Though I didn't process that at the time, either."

"How'd you get out of the cabin, without hands to open the door?"

"The window." I swiped my palms down my jeans-clad thighs one more time, then I parted my hair and showed him the jagged scar running across my scalp for an inch and a half. "I crashed through the glass, with no idea what I was doing. I just kind of…leapt. Then I ran.

"I have no clue how long or how far I ran. I was terrified, and for the first time in my life, I wasn't thinking in an entirely human way. I'm sure you remember your first shift. If you were alone then, you remember that terror and confusion."

Austin nodded, but again, he said nothing.

"Eventually, I collapsed. I don't think it took too long, considering that I was still recovering from the fever and was utterly exhausted. I just kind of fell down on the ground in the woods, sort of…seizing. Paralyzed by pain. Until I was human again. But I was too tired to move. And that's how Eamon found me."

"Eamon?" Austin's brows rose at the new information. "The previous Marshal?"

"Yeah. He was a regular at the bar, even before my parents moved. And a friend of my brother's. He'd been on a run in the woods when he caught my scent and recognized the change in it. Evidently, I'd been thrashing through the under-brush, leaving a trail of blood, so…"

"So he chased you."

"Yes. But not for any nefarious reason. He'd never seen a female stray, and he knew me, so… He approached cautiously and gave me his shirt." Just like Austin had, that night in the woods. "I recognized him. I knew him. But suddenly I could *smell* him. Even in human form, I could smell him, and I could see things like I'd never seen them before.

"He had food in his pack, and he gave me that too. And water. And when he'd calmed me down, promising he had all the answers I needed, he drove me straight to Titus."

"All the way to Jackson?"

I shook my head, leaning back in my chair. Trying to force my frame to relax. "Titus met us somewhere. A hotel. Someplace nice, with room service. They ordered me rare steaks and let me stuff myself while they explained everything. Eamon sewed up my scalp. He even helped me wash my hair, without taking any advantage. He had sent someone back to the bar for the stuff I'd dropped in the parking lot, and that guy showed up with my purse and keys."

"Vance?" Austin guessed.

"Yeah. That was how I met him. They talked me through texting my sister, explaining why I couldn't just tell her what really happened. But I had to tell her something, because I'd disappeared on her for more than a day. So I told her I'd gone home with someone after I closed the Fat Cat. Then I…" I shrugged. "I parted my hair on the other side to hide the wound, and I went on about my life."

"Just like that?"

I shrugged. "What else was I supposed to do?" Though perhaps I was overselling the ease of my adjustment a *tiny* bit. "What did you do, after you were infected?"

Austin mimicked my shrug. "The same, I guess. Though I didn't have access to the northern zone Marshal. That position didn't exist back then. Nor did the rest of this." He spread his arms to take in my entire world. "But I'm glad you did. I suspect you needed all this worse than I did."

I had, at first. Badly. Until I'd learned to defend myself, I would have been very vulnerable on my own, as a woman in a man's world.

"So, how did Silas wind up in that grave?"

"We found him." My voice dropped in pitch until I was practically growling. "Eamon wanted me to let him, Jace, and Titus handle it, but Titus thought it would be good for me to confront my assailant myself. To play a role—the most important role—in seizing my own justice. Like very proactive therapy. Jace agreed. *I* agreed. So they took me out to the woods where Eamon had found me, and we searched until we found the cabin. Titus did some digging and identified the owner as Silas Morelock. He evidently used the place as a hunting and fishing retreat, mostly on the weekends. Titus tracked him down, and they brought him in. And—"

My mouth snapped shut.

"And…" Austin prompted.

"And…he admitted what he'd done—not that he could deny it. They could smell him in my scent. I'll carry a trace of him with me forever, just like you carry a trace of whoever infected you. Just like we all do. Those of us who survive long enough to shift, anyway."

"Who killed him?" Austin asked.

"Titus pronounced his sentence, and it was all very official. But I executed him. They decided that was my right, as the victim." I'd ripped his throat out, and I hadn't missed a single moment of sleep over it.

Until last Friday, when I'd learned about Yvette.

"We want the same right," Austin said. "Bishop and I. We want to be there. We want to watch the light drain from this bastard's eyes, when we find him."

"I have no problem with that," I assured him. "But I'm sure you understand that there are other surviving relatives who could make the same claim."

Austin nodded. "Just as I'm sure Titus will make the right call."

I planted my hands on the edge of the desk and rolled my chair back, assuming this was over. Signaling an end to a debriefing that had felt more like a confession. But Austin didn't stand.

"Why didn't you tell us?" His gaze remained trained on

mine with a relentless steadiness I'd come to associate with both Austin-the-police-detective and with Austin-the-grieving-brother. "I assume we're looking for either an associate of this Silas or for a copycat, and you've known that all along, but you didn't tell us. Why not?"

"Because I didn't know that all along. You came in here ready to kill Nolan Blake, and while I knew that my own case was similar to Yvette's, I also knew there were differences. She wasn't kidnapped. I didn't make any large cash withdrawals."

"But your brother *was* a shifter. So anyone who knew about that dormant gene could assume you had it."

I blinked, considering my next words carefully. "Yes." But I wasn't ready to talk about Ben, and maybe he could feel that. "However, we didn't know that was a victim commonality at first, either. There were too many differences between my case and Yvette's for me to rationally assume they were related. Until we connected the other victims."

"But even then, you didn't tell us."

I exhaled slowly. "Things have happened quickly since then. I was about to tell you."

Austin blinked at me.

"It's personal, okay?" I relented. "My personal trauma. I didn't tell you before because I don't like to talk about it, and because it wouldn't have been helpful before we knew most of what we know now. And because I didn't want to blur the line on my role in this investigation. Give you a reason to doubt my judgement."

Austin stared at me for a second, and I could see him thinking. Weighing the obvious betrayal he felt, that I'd kept information from him, with what appeared to be sympathy for the position I was in. For the merging of my trauma with his. With this investigation.

"I understand," he said at last. "Thank you for telling me."

I stood, and this time he stood with me. "I have to go downstairs. Why don't you take Bishop back to your apartment and fill him in on all of this, and we'll meet again tonight to start looking for connections between the victims— or their relatives—and Silas. Okay?"

Austin nodded. But he hesitated with one hand on the doorknob. "I'm sorry, Charley. For what happened to you. For the fact that we're dredging it all up again. I understand that that isn't fair to you."

"This isn't fair to anyone," I assured him. "But we're going to catch this asshole, whoever he is. And Silas Morelock is going to get a new roommate in hell."

TWELVE

"Nolan Blake," I said as I opened the door at the bottom of the steps, jingling my key ring. "You are hereby free to go."

"Great." He stood, already shoving his stuff into the duffle bag Tucker had brought from his apartment several days before. "And exactly how soon after I step out of this cage will Bishop Mattheson murder me?"

"That's not going to happen. Bishop understands that your sister was likely one of the victims. He's as interested as we all are in catching the *actual* murderer. Please don't leave town, though, until you hear from me or one of my enforcers that we have completed the investigation. Should you feel like you are in danger, let me know. Titus has extended an invitation for you to stay in Jackson for a while, if you like."

"No, thanks. I'm going home to order a pizza. I don't care if I never see another burger again."

"Fair enough. Sorry for the inconvenience."

"Then I'll call my boss and let him know I'm over the 'flu,'" he added, using air quotes as I unlocked his cell.

"I hope there are no hard feelings."

"Hard feelings? No. Firm feelings, maybe. Slightly rigid feelings. Al dente, I think, is how I would describe my feelings. But not truly hard."

"Great. Glad to hear it. Don't change your number or address without letting us know," I added as I followed him up the stairs.

The bar went quiet as we emerged from the kitchen. As I walked Nolan to the door. He said hi to several friends, who returned his greetings quietly.

"What do they know?" I whispered to Davey, watching through the window as Nolan got into his car. "About why he was locked up."

She shrugged. "They all saw the fight in the parking lot. They assume he had something to do with Yvette Graham-Mattheson's death." She lowered her voice, as the buzz of conversation picked up. "But to my knowledge, they don't know about any of the rest of it."

"That's about to change," I warned her. Davey nodded. Then I turned to face the dining area and cleared my throat. "We're closing early tonight, guys!" I called out, to a chorus of groans. "Sorry. Can't be helped. Last call will be at eleven-thirty. Doors close at midnight."

"SERIOUSLY?" Davey practically squealed. "I can stay?"

"Yes." I dropped the cloth cash deposit bag into the safe in the floor of my office, then I lowered the top and twisted the handle, sliding three one-inch-thick hidden bolts into place.

"Okay, I know you're only saying that because there's a killer on the loose and you don't want me to go home unless there's an enforcer next door to listen for trouble through the wall, but I'll take it!"

She was *mostly* right. I didn't want her to go home until Tucker was free to be in his apartment below hers.

While I was virtually positive it meant nothing that Vance had cleaned his place when he realized I'd be searching it, I couldn't take that risk. If he *had* gotten rid of evidence of his involvement in infecting Yvette and the others, I could no longer trust him with Davey. Maybe I should *never* have trusted him with my sister's safety. Yes, he'd have to be an idiot to strike so close to home—to strike someone I'd specifically put under his care—but I wasn't willing to take that chance.

I would be keeping Vance very close at hand until I knew for sure that I could trust him, no matter how badly it stung that I still had to consider my best friend a suspect.

"You want me to get some snacks for you guys?" Davey asked. "Chips and salsa? Or I could have Billy make a giant platter of nachos."

"Chips and salsa sound great. Let Billy finish up in the kitchen, please." It was Thursday, the night he cleaned all the grease traps in preparation for the longer weekend hours. "And I know you've already cleaned the beer taps, but—"

"I'll put one back together and pull pints for everyone."

"Thanks."

She headed into the kitchen, and I moved past her, through the swinging doors into the front of the bar, where Vance was almost done sweeping and Tucker was cleaning the last of the front windows. "Thanks guys," I said.

Austin and Bishop were already seated at the large corner booth.

Billy went home, and Vance and Tucker put away their cleaning supplies, while Davey set up a tray of snacks behind the bar.

"Just so everyone's on the same page," I said, standing at

the end of the booth. "We have one possible new lens to look through, as we narrow down our suspect pool."

"You're talking about this Silas Moreland?" Bishop said.

"Morelock," Vance corrected him.

"Yes," I said. "Well, not him specifically. He's dead. But it's possible that we're looking for someone who either knew him or knew about what he did and has decided to carry on that…work. For lack of a better term."

"Criminal endeavor," Davey supplied as she set a large tray of chips and salsa on the table. "I think the appropriate term is 'criminal endeavor.'"

"Yes. So it is," I acknowledged.

She practically beamed at me as she slid into the booth behind Vance and Tucker, sitting sideways so she could see all of us.

"Okay, so what do we know about this Silas Morelock?" Bishop asked.

"I've already run a background check, and other than a couple of speeding tickets, he has no record," Austin said. "He maintained fishing and hunting licenses until three years ago, but there was no property in his name. Not even that cabin you mentioned."

"Oh!" Davey popped up out of her booth and dashed toward the bar. "I forgot the beer."

"The cabin doesn't officially exist," Vance said. "It was built decades ago, probably by one of his relatives, on state property. Unauthorized, of course. If anyone ever finds it, they'll either tear it down or repurpose it."

Austin frowned. "Someone built a private cabin on state land?"

"It's not unheard of out here," Tucker said. "There are some folks in rural areas who don't recognize land taken in imminent domain for state parks as no longer being theirs. It's kind of a private feud with the state. And like Vance said, this was decades ago. There could be a dozen similar buildings out there that no one's even noticed, other than the families who built them and still use them."

"That's still good information, though, that he had no property in his own name," I said. "Eamon told me back then that Silas basically subsisted on odd jobs, and that he lived with a girlfriend with most of the time." I shrugged as Davey returned with a tray of beer. "That's about all I know."

Other than *precisely* where he's buried.

"Girlfriend's name?" Austin had the notepad open on his phone, his thumbs poised over the keyboard.

"I don't know. Cammie, maybe? I can…" I exhaled and took a step back, so I could sit on the edge of the nearest table. "I can find out." Not in any *pleasant* way, but I *could* find out.

"So, wait." Bishop dipped a corn chip into the communal bowl of salsa. "This Silas dude lived nowhere, squatted on state land, at some point was infected, then just…what? Decided to kidnap Charley and bite her? Out of nowhere? Why? What the hell gave him that idea?" He crunched into the chip, then spoke around it. "I mean, people don't just wake up psychotic one day, do they?"

I had no answer for that.

"It's a valid question," Austin said. "He clearly had a plan when he took Charley, and it sounds like it actually went pretty well for him. Which means there's every possibility in the world that he tried this before he took her. And maybe it didn't go so well that time. I'm going to look for previous kidnappings with a similar MO. Hopefully we'll find one where the victim got away and can be interviewed." He closed the notepad on his phone and pulled a laptop from a bag beneath the table.

"What about his family?" I aimed my question at Tucker, who had his own laptop open. "Not the girlfriend, but blood relatives."

"I'm looking," Tucker said. "But this is probably going to be a deep dive. He wasn't on any socials, so that information is likely locked behind a pay-wall. I'll have to search for birth certificates."

"Got your business expense card?" I asked.

He nodded without looking up from the keyboard. "Had the numbers memorized for years…"

"Okay, do your thing. I have an idea of my own." I picked up an untouched beer and took a big gulp. "Gonna need a couple more of these, though," I said as I stood.

"I'll bring them to your office," Davey offered.

"Don't bother. I've got the good stuff upstairs. Can you guys lock up?" I added, when I remembered that Billy had already gone home.

"Of course," Vance called after me.

I'd finished my beer before I got halfway up the stairs.

I STARED at the phone for twenty minutes before I managed to pick it up. It took another five before I could make myself open the list of contacts.

I'd considered deleting Eamon's phone number at least a hundred times. I'd memorized it years ago, so that would have been a symbolic gesture, at best, but I'd almost made that gesture more times than I could count.

Yet the number was still in my phone, and it was still emblazoned upon my brain as if it had been burned in with a cattle brand. Try as I might, I couldn't get rid of him. Even with him living all the way across the country.

I tapped on his name, and the ringing began on the other

end of the line, but I didn't pick the phone up until he answered. On the fifth ring. One more, and it would have gone to voicemail.

"Charley?" His voice sent pain through my chest, like he'd just shoved his hand between my ribs and given my heart a good squeeze.

That wasn't nostalgia, nor any other kind of affection. He'd killed everything that was between us long ago. He'd murdered our love and cremated the corpse, and what was left —what hurt me at the sound of his voice—was the memory of what once was. It was the ghost of my first love, haunting me from beyond the grave.

"Charley? Is that really you?"

He hadn't deleted my contact information either. Or maybe he still had my number memorized.

"Yeah." To my utter relief, I sounded perfectly normal.

"I didn't expect to hear from you…ever, actually."

"Yeah, well, there are pigs taking flight right outside my office window at the moment, so…"

He laughed, and I wanted to stab the sound right out of him, because it hadn't changed. *Everything* in my life changed when he left, yet he could still laugh exactly the same way he used to. As if losing me meant nothing.

"What can I do for you, Charley?"

"It's about Silas Morelock."

Silence descended over the line, like a blanket smothering us both.

Finally, Eamon cleared his throat. "What about him?"

"Where are you?"

"Montana," he said, taking my apparent change of subject in stride. "There aren't many places I'm allowed to be, as you may recall." Because the US Prides recognized only two remaining free zones.

I wished I had some way to verify his claim, because as I sat there, trying to decide how little I could say and still get the information I needed from him, it occurred to me that he fit the killer's profile perfectly. He'd been around longer than three years, and he knew the community well even before there was a real Pride. Before Titus had named him Marshal. People had trusted Eamon. Told him about their lives and families.

He knew about the genetic component necessary in order to survive infection. And he *certainly* knew about Silas Morelock and his crimes.

"And you haven't left the Montana free zone in the past twenty months?"

"Not since the day I arrived. Why?" he said, and I could practically picture his frown. That asymmetrical dip of just one brow, tugging on the scar that bisected it. "What's going on?"

"We have a situation. And I have to warn you," I added, leaning hard on the professional tone in my voice. "We will have to verify that you haven't been in the Mississippi Valley territory since you left."

"Fine. Verify away." But there was a slightly cooler note to his voice now. "Just tell me what's going on. What you need from me. We can still be friends, can't we Charley?"

No. No we could not.

"We've got a serial."

"*What*? A serial *killer*?" Springs creaked over the line as he sank onto a piece of furniture I had no mental image of. He'd left most of his shit here, so I had no idea what his home looked like. How he'd furnished it.

"We don't think murder is actually his goal. Just like with Silas. We think it's either a copycat or someone who worked with him originally. Someone who's carrying on what he started."

"And I fit your profile, because I knew about Silas."

I nodded, though he couldn't see that. "Not many people do. But there's more. The victims are blood relatives of members of the northern zone. *All* the victims."

"Which means it's one of our guys."

"*My* guys," I snapped, without meaning to. He was pushing my buttons. He'd always been good at that. "They're *my* guys, Eamon. But you knew them well enough to know about their families. Which means you do, in fact, fit the profile."

"Okay. Do what you've got to do to verify that I haven't left Montana. But in the meantime, let me help. What do you need?"

"Information. Our working theory is that we're looking for someone connected to Silas, but we can't find much about him." We hadn't thought we needed to know much about him before, other than how to find him, then where to bury him. "He never owned any property or registered a car in his own name, and—"

"I didn't know that, but it makes sense. Silas was a bit of a…conspiracy theorist, I guess, where the government was concerned. He wouldn't have registered anything with the state."

"We also haven't found any family members. Tucker's looking for birth certificates, though, so—"

"Don't bother. His parents are dead, and Silas was an only child."

"No kids of his own?"

"He had a son," Eamon said, and a jolt of possibility shot through me like a bolt of lightning. Every hair on my body stood on end. "At least, he claimed the kid was his son. Boy named Denny. But Silas wasn't married to the mom, so I have no idea whether his name was on the boy's birth certificate. Nor do I know the kid's last name. He'd be twenty-two or so, now."

"Is he a shifter?"

More silence, and I could practically see Eamon sitting there with his eyes closed, trying to figure out how to say something that was going to thoroughly piss me off.

It wouldn't be the first time.

"Eamon!"

"Yes! Okay? He and Silas were infected at the same time. In the same incident."

"And you didn't think that was relevant information, back when we were hunting Silas?"

"No." Eamon's shields were up. His sword was the sharp edge in his voice. "*You* told us there was only one bad guy. So we hunted one bad guy, and it didn't seem fair of me to throw an innocent kid under the bus, just because his dad was a criminal. They'd have buried him right next to his father, Charley. On suspicion alone. Guilt by association."

"That wouldn't have happened."

"Yes, it would have! You *know* it would have. Titus was out for blood, to prove to the fucking council that he could handle his shit. He was worried that if they thought there was someone out there killing human women, they'd use that as an excuse to take the Pride away from him. He was one vote away from losing the whole goddamn territory."

"He was *not* out for blood." But I couldn't argue with the rest, because it was still true. And Titus's fear was not unreasonable. There *were* members of the council who'd use any excuse to strip him of his position and impose the werecat version of martial law in our territory, to control the "stray population." Jace had told me that himself.

But I could *not* believe that Titus would have executed an innocent boy.

"What I do know…" I said, my voice deep with anger as I paced across my living room floor, "…is that you kept information to yourself. Information that was relevant to what happened to me, both personally and professionally, and might have prevented what's happening now."

"And you've never kept a secret?" he demanded, his voice so soft, so angry, that I could hardly hear it.

"I've never put an investigation at risk."

"That isn't what I asked."

"You lost the right to ask me personal questions," I growled. "This isn't about me."

"Really? You don't feel like this is about you? Not even a little bit?"

My teeth ground together so hard that I could hear my jaw creak. He'd always been able to do that. To flip the switch so that his charming laugh became biting sarcasm in an instant.

"Is there anything else you know about Silas Morelock that could be helpful for us?" The question ground like grit between my teeth. "Any other relatives or close friends? Someone he might have confided in? Anything you know about his son, Denny?"

"Not that I—"

"What was the mother's name?"

"I don't know. I never met her."

"Think!" I practically shouted into the phone. "You told me back then that Silas used to stay with his girlfriend. Was that Denny's mother?"

"No. I don't think so. The way I remember it, he wasn't on good terms with the boy's mom."

"Okay, so what was her name? The one he stayed with. Cammie? Something like that?"

"Connie," Eamon said. "Don't remember her last name. That won't help you, though. She died several years back. Before all this. Before he took you. I think that's maybe what set him off. What kind of...unmoored him from commonly accepted...limits."

"Okay. Thanks." I took a deep breath, trying to slow my pulse. To calm myself. "Anything else? Seriously, the smallest detail might help."

Eamon sighed. "I can't think of anything else I can say or do to help you, Char. We were just following your lead. Even back then."

My temper spiked. "You're saying this is my fault?"

"No. Not in the least. What I'm saying is that you're coming to me with questions and accusations about kid I had —and still have—every reason to believe was innocent, and it's *almost* like you're doing that to avoid questioning the one witness you still have. The person who survived Silas More-lock and might still have details of the attack locked away in memories she's afraid to examine..."

"Fuck. You." Rage simmered inside me, roiling along the surface of a deep dark well of fear and anger. "You want me to relive the most traumatic moment of my life, *just in case* there's something I didn't remember when that trauma was fresh?" My words were short and sharp. I was practically firing them at him like bullets, because that was the only way I could get them out. "Because memories *always* get sharper as they age, right?"

"More pain is the last thing I want for you, Charley. I want nothing but the best for you."

"Fuck off." There was no better, more professional way to respond. "Just fucking fuck you and this awful fucking job. If you were so good at it—if you know everything—then why the hell are you in Montana right now?"

Eamon chuckled again, and again, the sound went straight through my chest. But this time it seemed less like a brutal squeeze of my heart and more like a gentle hug.

I hated that even more.

"I'm sorry. For everything."

"Fuck you. I'm hanging up."

"I mean it. I'm sorry. About Benny, most of all."

I hung the phone up and threw it across the room.

THIRTEEN

"The thing is, he's not wrong," I mumbled, turning up the last bottle from a six pack as I paced the entire length of my apartment. The beer was still cold, because I'd had all six bottles in under twenty minutes—a skill a shifter learned to master if she wanted to pack on any kind of buzz at all. Even knowing it would fade almost as quickly as it built.

"He's an asshole, but he's not wrong." I *was* the only witness left to question.

Unfortunately, my memories of being kidnapped by Silas Morelock were not an endless cave of information ripe for mining. I'd never seen whoever hit me on the back of the head; if that was an accomplice of Silas's, I had no way of knowing. I'd woken up alone in the cabin already raging with fever and delirious.

I had gone over those memories time and time again in the aftermath of my escape, and since then, I'd never uncovered a single new detail. Not for lack of trying.

I drained the last beer bottle and dropped it into the carton, where it clattered against two other empties. But that clattering continued, after the bottles had gone still.

"The fuck…?" I mumbled, turning toward the source of the new sound. It was coming from…beneath me. From outside, kind of. From—

I grabbed the baseball bat from my coat closet on my way out the door and raced downstairs with it held at the ready. The kitchen was dark and quiet, the back door still closed, and as I pushed through the swinging door into the front room, moonlight shining through the windows temporarily blinded my sensitive eyes.

Then they adjusted, and I realized I recognized the figure trying to break into my bar.

"Damn it, Bishop," I said as I threw back the bolt and opened the door. "What the hell are you doing here?"

"Trying not to sober up." He said it as if it should have been obvious.

"We're closed."

"So's the liquor store. That's why I'm here."

"How did you…?" I looked past him, and my gaze found the 4Runner parked sideways in the gravel lot. "You drove here? Drunk?"

"Yes, but *very slowly*," he said, each word exaggerated.

"Goddamn it. Give me your keys."

"No. If you're not going to serve me, I'll—"

"Give me your fucking keys," I snapped as I pulled him inside. "In half an hour, you'll be sober, and I'm going to kick your ass. And I'm only waiting that long because it won't be a fair fight while one of us is drunk."

"*One* of us?" Bishop snorted. "I can smell the twelve-pack you just drank."

"It was a six-pack." I bolted the door behind him and held one hand out, palm up. "Keys."

"Let's make a trade," he said, sliding one hand into his pocket, where the keys in question made a muffled clinking sound. "I'll give you my keys, and you give me a bottle of Crown. Not as a gift. I'll pay."

I exhaled, staring up at him. "It would be illegal for me to serve you right now, Bishop. You're already drunk, and it's well after last call. You can't order in a bar after last call."

"Yet somehow, you've clearly been drinking." His gaze seemed more focused. I could practically see him sobering up in front of me, even as that same blistering clarity began to surface through my own buzz.

Damn it.

"I wasn't drinking in the bar. I was drinking in my apartment," I informed him. "Which is perfectly fine."

"Shit, that's better than fine. Lead the way, Marshal." Yet Bishop pushed past me through the bar flap, where he grabbed an unopened bottle on his way through the swinging doors into the kitchen.

"Get back here!" I shouted as I followed him. "Do *not* open—" But I heard the seal crack just as I scented the bloom of whiskey—*good* whiskey—in the air.

"You are one brazen motherfucker, Bishop," I growled.

"Said the pot to the kettle," he mumbled as he jogged up the steps toward my apartment. "Marshal, the only way to stop me from drinking this whole bottle in the next half hour is to pour some of it for yourself."

"So, why exactly are we binge drinking at one in the morning, like college kids?" I asked as I tipped the bottle over my glass for the third time in fifteen minutes.

It was a juice glass, not a shot glass. No shifter trying to get drunk could afford to waste time with shot glasses.

Bishop huffed at me from the couch, across from where I sat in my favorite armchair. "Because extreme tolerance to alcohol is the worst part about being a shifter, and binge drinking is the only solution." He drained his fifth glass and set it on the coffee table between us with a thunk.

"Use a coaster, asshole. What are we, animals?"

Bishop blinked at me for a moment, his eyes freshly re-glazed with intoxication. "Animals! Ha!" Then he burst into laughter. "We *are* animals. That's the whole damn problem." His smile faded as he poured another.

We were already two-thirds through the bottle.

"Seriously. What the hell are you doing here?"

He took a drink. More than a sip, but less than a gulp. "Austin kicked me out."

"Bullshit." I sipped from my own glass, frowning at him over the rim. "He wouldn't do that."

"Not in so many words," Bishop admitted. "But I got the message."

"Which was what?"

He threw the rest of the glass back, and this time he set it on a rubber coaster. "That I am good at nothing more than getting in his way." He shrugged as he poured another. "He's not wrong."

"Yes he—"

"I don't know how to…detect. I can Google shit with the best of them—I'm not *old*—but I don't know what I should be looking for. Everyone else on our little task force has a purpose. Something they're good at. Something to contribute. But I…" Bishop shrugged, staring down into his glass.

"I'm sure you're good at…something." But after nine drinks in less than an hour, I was riding more of a buzz than I'd managed to tie on in at least a year and a half, and it felt like too much work to figure out exactly what Bishop Mattheson might be good at.

Other than drinking.

"I am," he insisted. "I fucking excel at kicking ass. Breaking skulls. I'm even better at that now than I was as a human."

"Yeah. We all are." *Comes with the claws.*

"But you just released the skull I came here to break. Took away my purpose, Marshal," he half slurred.

"Quit calling me that."

"Why? You're the Marshal, aren't you?"

I nodded. Then I turned up my glass. "But I'm off duty at the moment." At least for the hour it would take me to sober up. If I stopped drinking right...*now.*

Instead, I poured another.

"But my point," Bishop said, as if he'd just re-boarded his own train of thought. "Is that all these people are involved now, all trying to do the right thing. To catch this killer. To avenge my wife's death. *My* wife. I'm the one who failed her. The worthless motherfucker who couldn't keep her safe. I'm the one who lost her. And here I am twiddling my fucking thumbs, while everyone else seems to know what to do. I'm as useless now as I was when she was alive, and—"

"You know it wasn't your fault, right?"

He sighed, meeting my gaze with a wounded look. With more raw, unflinching honesty—unclouded by rage—than I'd seen from him since the moment we met. "I know it wasn't my fault in the same way you know it wasn't your fault. I understand that that's technically true. I didn't kill Yvette any more than you killed her, or any of the others. But we didn't save her either."

His words—his goddamn fucking *truth*—sucked all the air from the room. Right out of my lungs. I tried to breathe, but nothing happened. My airway just gulped at the painful vacuum his brutal honesty had left in its wake.

"You're right," I whispered when I could finally breathe

again. And by then he'd downed another glass. "We failed them. We both *suck*."

"Yeah. Well, at least you know how to find the fucker who pulled the trigger. Figuratively speaking. I'm totally useless until you give me someone to punch."

Numb, I drained my glass.

Everyone else was more interested in comforting and reassuring me than in acknowledging the painful truth. Were they worried it would break me? Send me hurtling into an abyss of trauma?

Bishop didn't seem concerned about that possibility. Because he thought I was stronger than that? Or because he was drunk?

"What about you?" he asked as I set my glass on a coaster. "What were you trying forget, before I got here?" His gaze settled on the six-pack carton full of empties on my kitchen counter.

"I was…um…coming to terms with some shit."

"Something to do with Silas?" He poured me another, and I realized we'd launched into some kind of bizarre role-reversal, where he was my bartender. Asking me about my troubles.

"Yeah. Just getting ready to mine my own trauma for clues."

"Oh yeah. Because you were, like kidnapped. Tied up, and shit." He shook his head. "That's fucked up."

I picked up the glass and drained it.

"I'm sorry." He leaned forward on the couch, his elbows resting on his knees. Holding his glass cradled in both hands. Staring down into it. "I know you probably don't want to talk about any of that. But I…well, that's kind of the other reason I came here. And I had to be drunk to get up the nerve to ask."

"To ask what?" Had he already said? Had I missed a question?

I was starting to remember what it felt like to be *truly* drunk. Back before I was infected.

"How did she feel? I mean, you went through that. You thought you were dying, right? You *could* have died. So... how scared were you? How scared—" Bishop's voice broke, and his hands clenched around his glass, his knuckles going white. "How scared was *she*?" He looked up, and the pain in his gaze felt like a punch aimed straight at my soul. "Did she... Did she die in terror?"

The ache in my heart swelled to take up my entire chest, bruising me from the inside out. The truth was that he would know much better than I would how Yvette felt before she died. He'd been there. But the deeper truth was that information wasn't what he really wanted from me. He wanted comfort. Reassurance.

I stood and rounded the coffee table to sit next to him on the couch. "Bishop." I plucked the glass from his grip and set it down, then I took his hand and held it. "I don't know what Yvette went through before she died. I have no idea what she was thinking or feeling. No more than you do, anyway. What I am absolutely certain of is that you and Austin did the best you could for her. To take care of her and make her comfortable. And I am just as certain that she knew that. I..." I cleared my throat, swallowing the lump that seemed determined to choke me. "I wish I'd had someone like you there with me, when I was sick. When I was confused, and afraid, and all alone." When I'd thought I was dying. "And I'm beyond grateful, on Yvette's behalf, that she had you both."

Bishop nodded, slowly. Then he nodded again. He let go of my hand and drained his glass, and because my options at that point seemed to be drink more or cry, I threw back my own.

When I stood, the world spun around me. For one blissful second, I thought I might pass out. But then Bishop was there steadying me, one hand on my waist. "Whoa…" he said, his breath stirring my hair, above my ear. "I think you've overcome your tolerance to alcohol, Marshal."

"Thank god," I whispered, my focus snagged on his throat, just inches from my face. "I'm so fucking tired of thinking."

"Me too."

I dragged my gaze up and found him staring down at me. My next breath caught in my throat, and suddenly I realized how good he smelled. Like whiskey and leather. Like hunger, and rage, and power. Like all the best, of both man and beast.

Bishop blinked. Then his mouth crashed down on mine like a gust of wind blowing the front door wide open. It was startling and electrifying for one white-hot second, but then, when I didn't pull away, that kiss…changed.

I could feel his loss. I could taste his rage. It all came spilling out of him and into me, but he must have been getting something in return, because his groan, the eager way he clutched at my hips…that was all hunger. Need.

It was a soul-deep ache for something too complex for me to process in that moment.

All I really understood, as the room blurred around me and I clutched at his shirt, as he lifted me and my legs wrapped around his waist, was that whatever this need was… I had it too.

The stubble on his chin scratched as he kissed his way down my neck, and I clutched at him when he eased the burn with his tongue. The first time his teeth grazed my throat, my legs clenched around him, pinning him to me with no conscious thought.

He growled, and the sound rolled through me, half anger, half urgent demand. By the time he set me down again, we were both breathing hard. His eyes had started to shift, though I doubt he realized it, and my entire apartment smelled like fury and lust.

My body was ablaze with a fire that had everything and nothing to do with the man standing in front of me.

He pulled his shirt over his head as I unbuttoned my jeans, shoving them down with my underwear still inside them, and by the time I had my top off, he stood naked before me, every bulging ripple of a fucking *flawless* physique high-lighted by the pendulum light fixtures hanging over my short breakfast bar.

Bishop was big. He was power given human form and shifter strength. And I realized, vaguely, that if he'd wanted to kill Nolan Blake in the parking lot, he could have done it with one blow.

Growling again, he kissed me, the hard, hot length of him trapped between us. His lips trailed down my neck, over my collarbone, then his mouth closed over my left nipple. I gasped when he sucked, hard, and moisture began to gather between my legs. Bishop groaned at the scent, and his hand slid down my stomach, his fingers prying my thighs apart.

He slid one finger inside me, groaning again, then with-drew to make a circle around my clit.

"Oh my god," I moaned into his hair, clutching at both of his shoulders.

His teeth grazed my nipple, and I yipped, surprised by the bolt of pain.

"Sorry." Bishop stood and took a step back, leaving me gasping. "I'm sorry. You taste so good, and I got carried—"

I grabbed his face, squeezing his chin. Making him look at me. "I don't want sweet. I don't want gentle."

His brows rose. His nostrils flared, as if scenting out the truth of my claim. Then his eyes dilated. "You sure?"

"I'm fucking positive."

Snarling softly, Bishop spun me around and bent me over the end of the kitchen counter, one hand in the center of my back to hold me in place. The tile was cold against my over-heated face and breasts. He kicked my feet wide apart, and I squirmed in anticipation. It all felt very primal. Satisfying in a way I'd never wanted before. Never even really considered.

I *liked* being in charge. I liked making the rules and enforcing them.

But this—

He slid one finger into me again, testing, and he groaned when my body clenched around him. His hand disappeared, and an instant later it clutched at my hip, steadying me. Holding me where he wanted me.

I felt his tip prod at me for just a second, then he shoved himself all the way in, slamming me into the counter. "Fuck," I moaned as he pulled out, only to drive into me again. I tried to lift myself onto my elbows, to gain some control over the angle, to thrust against him, but he held me pinned there, his hand hot against my back, a blistering counterpoint to the still-cool tile.

Unable to truly move, I could only...feel. Acknowledge that I'd given up control and enjoy the ride as he pounded into me, drawing hungry little grunts from me with each thrust. Rubbing just the right spot inside me, over and over.

Pressure began to build in a delicious, intimate spiral, and my breaths came faster. I started to squirm again, trying to push back against him. Trying to take what I wanted. "Faster," I panted.

"Soon," he growled, maintaining the pace he'd set as his hand clenched around my hip.

"Now," I snarled, trying to glare over my shoulder at him, but Bishop only laughed.

"Patience, Marshal," he whispered. And gradually, he began to fuck me faster. Harder. Drawing out my climb toward climax until I whimpered, frantically shoving my hips back at him as best I could. Chasing the bliss teasing me from *just* beyond reach.

Begging him for it with every desperate moan.

Finally, he groaned, and I felt him tense inside me. "Now," he grunted, slamming into me rapidly, again and again, rubbing that spot inside as his hand snaked beneath me, stroking my clit ruthlessly.

Exquisitely.

I snarled as I came with him buried deep inside me, shuddering under the power of his own release, rocking into me with the last of the aftershocks.

As I lay limp against the counter, Bishop stepped back, withdrawing, but when I tried to push myself upright, I found his hand still in the center of my back, holding me in place.

"Marshal, you are a little *hellcat*," he whispered. Then, chuckling, he gave my ass a sharp smack and let me go. "Fucking *snarling* at me…"

Gasping from the sudden sting, I pushed myself up and turned, relieved to see him removing a condom, though I have no idea when he put it on.

He smirked with one glance at my face. "Mind if I crash for a few minutes? Sleep it off?"

I shrugged on my way across the room. "You're not leaving until you're sober."

He smirked again, then flopped down face-first on my bed.

I closed the bathroom door and stared at myself in the mirror. At my flushed cheeks. At the red splotches on the points of my hips, where they'd slammed into the counter. Then I twisted to stare in shock—or amusement?—at the faint pink handprint on my right ass cheek.

Good god.

Well, at least I'd finally figured out what Bishop Mattheson was good at, *other* than drinking and breaking skulls.

I WOKE up less than an hour after I'd passed out, finally ready to do what needed to be done. What I hadn't been able to face two hours earlier.

Bishop snored softly beside me. Still nude and completely uncovered.

Shit.

What the hell was I thinking?

While he slept, I snuck—Snuck! In my own home!—into the bathroom for a shower, where I lathered up every single inch of my body, including my hair.

Shifters have great noses, and I could *not* walk around the bar smelling like the widower whose wife's murder I'd promised to solve and avenge. My customers would never let me live it down. Davey would never let me hear the end of it.

Austin would—

Bishop groaned from the bedroom. I tied my robe and raced across the room, praying that he wasn't about to puke in my boot.

"Shit," he said with one look at me. "I was hoping that was just a really hot dream."

"It was a hot *something*," I conceded. Hot fuck. Hot mess. The jury was still out...

"That's not funny. That shouldn't have happened." He stood, stone-cold sober, and began scanning the room for his clothes.

"Kitchen floor," I reminded him, and he groaned again at the memory.

"I'm sorry, Charley," he said on his way out of my room. "That was wrong. We shouldn't have. I mean, Yvette…"

I sprinted into the kitchen after him and put one hand on his arm, forcing him to make eye contact as he clutched his clothes to his broad, hard chest. "No. Don't do that. We didn't do anything wrong."

"But I *love* my wife. I miss her every fucking day. I would never have cheated on her—"

"And you still haven't. That wasn't a betrayal of your wife, Bishop. That was an expression of your grief. Of your anger. What happened wasn't about either you or me. Not together, and not separately. Sometimes passions get all mixed up. Anger feels like lust. Pain feels like pleasure. The human brain is a fucked-up merry-go-round of emotion and you clearly needed that as badly as I did. You needed a release of *some* kind, and if it wasn't that, it would have been something else. Possibly something violent involving Nolan Blake, when you were too drunk to remember why he doesn't deserve to die.

"The truth is that I needed that too. I've got some shit hanging over me, and… Well, it doesn't have to ever mean anything more than that. Both of us being in a *really* rough place and needing what the other had to offer."

Bishop blinked down at me. "You won't tell anyone?"

"Cross my heart." I drew an X over one robe-draped breast, and I swear I saw his eyes dilate, just for a second.

"Don't do that, Marshal," he growled. "I swear to god, I'm a good man, but I'm *only* a man."

I laughed, pleased to be back in control. "If you don't want everyone to sniff it out on their own, I suggest a shower. Lock the door when you head out, though, because I've got to go."

"Where? It's two-thirty in the morning."

"Men who wash my scent off, then sneak out into the night don't get to ask where I'm going."

Bishop snorted. "How many of those men are there?"

"Fuck off," I said as I bent to retrieve my newly cracked phone from the floor. But I said it with a smile.

FOURTEEN

"Hey Titus," I said into my phone, holding it slightly away from my face to keep from getting a glass splinter embedded in my cheek. "I know you're asleep, and this isn't an emergency, which is why I'm leaving you a rare voicemail instead of calling you back immediately." I slid a bottle of water into the light nylon drawstring pack on my way through the kitchen. "Two things, real quick. First, I broke my phone, and seeing as that's a business expense, I'll be charging a new one to my business card, along with rush shipping to get it here tomorrow. I apologize again for my temper. Also, thanks for the upgrade.

"Second, I spoke to Eamon. Turns out Silas had a kid. Boy named Denny, last name unknown. I'm headed out to that old cabin right now to see if I can dig anything up or jar anything loose. Eamon thinks the boy would be twenty-two or so now. I'm not sure this is the guy we're looking for. I don't know anyone named Denny, which means he isn't a regular, so he probably wouldn't know my actual regulars well enough to have heard them talk about their sisters and daughters. But I'm looking into him just in case.

"Oh, wait, I was wrong. There's a third thing. Turns out Vance knew we were going to search his—"

The phone beeped in my ear, cutting off the voice mail. Damn it. But I'd said most of what needed to be said. No need to call back, because if I called a second time, he'd answer, assuming it was an emergency. Then he'd order me not to go out to the cabin alone.

Since that order would be in consideration of my mental health, rather than of any physical threat, and considering that he hadn't actually given that order, I felt entirely justified in ignoring it.

The bar was quiet when I went downstairs. The lights were off, the doors locked. It was nearly three in the morning. Technically, Friday had begun, but it still felt like Thursday night, because I had yet to go to really sleep.

I slung my small drawstring pack over one shoulder and headed out the back door, locking it behind me.

In my truck, I slid an old CD into the player, then set track nine to play on repeat. I spent the entire half-hour drive singing "Save a Horse (Ride a Cowboy)." It was my brother's favorite song, when we were kids. Before either of us was old enough to know what that line even meant.

I sang at the top of my lungs, every word, because that way I wouldn't have to think about anything other than my own off-key melody and the memory of my brother trying to hit Big Kenny's low notes, before his voice dropped. Of little Davey dancing around us in the kitchen with her mop-stick pony, neighing on the chorus.

I sang it over and over, louder every time, until I saw a familiar tree on the side of the road. The cedar was broken in the middle. The dead top half was still kind of attached, forming a triangle with the ground as its third side, while the bottom half was still green and cedar-fat. I'd only seen that tree a few times in my life, but I would never forget it, or the narrow dirt road fifty feet beyond it, to the right.

My truck bounced as it rolled off the country highway onto the dirt road, then it bounced again and again, over potholes, tree branches and pinecones.

The road ended just like it had begun: out of nowhere. Like someone just got tired of cutting a road into thick forest, and quit.

I killed my engine and got out of the truck, then I stripped down to my birthday suit standing there in the dirt. In the dark. I shoved my clothes into the little nylon bag, along with my keys and my phone, then I threaded my arms through the straps that also formed the drawstring closure. I slammed the truck door and dropped into the dirt, where I shifted as fast as I could, breathing deeply through the pain. Through the pops, cracks, and groans of a body being forced into an entirely new shape.

Minutes later, I rose again on four legs that itched to run. I gave into that urge, racing so hard and fast that the little nylon bag stayed centered on my narrow feline back due to little more than my forward momentum.

My body knew the way. Or maybe my rage knew the way. Regardless, I wound up exactly where I'd intended to go with little conscious effort, and when I skidded to a stop on a patch of mossy soil, that pack slid down to hang against the right side of my rib cage.

I stood for a moment, staring at the cabin, huffing into the cold, dark night. I didn't want to shift back. My cat form was powerful. It was fast, and nearly silent, and more than capable of ripping through flesh and into organs. Of leaving its mark in bone. Compared to my vulnerable human form, my cat-self felt largely indestructible.

But my human self could open doors.

I shifted back in the woods, then I hurriedly pulled my clothes and shoes on to fight back the cold, as I stared at the cabin.

When it was built, the little one-room shack might have sat in a clearing. Now, though, it just kind of stood there in the woods, one with the trees and underbrush. Exactly the same as the last time I saw it, except for a big hole in the roof, where a fallen limb had punctured it.

I couldn't tell that a single soul had been here since Titus, Jace, Eamon and I left this place three years ago. I wasn't sure there was anything left to find here, but the truth was that we hadn't exactly lingered. I hadn't even gone inside; my job was just to get them here.

With the drawstring bag hanging nearly empty at my back, I approached the door. It hung ajar, which meant the interior of the cabin had been exposed to the elements, possibly for the past three years. I honestly had no idea whether or not we'd closed it when we left, last time. I pushed the door open, and the hinges squealed, the sound thrust like a dagger into the softer, ambient forest sounds. An instant after that, the top hinge pulled free from the wood with a sudden *crack*, and the outer corner of the door slammed into the ground.

Startled, I leapt back, my heart pounding. Then I scolded myself for being skittish. There was no one here; I could tell that with every breath I took. The forest had claimed this place long ago.

I shoved the door back, wincing as it scraped against the floor, cutting an arc into the buildup of dirt and moss. Moonlight shone through the doorway, and when I pulled down vines that had grown over the open window, there was enough light for my shifter eyes to see by, even without my flashlight app.

Turning slowly, I took in the small space. The bucket still sat next to the bed, the sheets still draped over the edge where I'd tossed them. Handcuffs still dangled from one corner rail, though now they were grimy and rusted. Everything was grimy from years of dirt being blown in through the cracked-open door.

Not that anything had been clean, exactly, even back then.

There were bird nests in every corner and rodent droppings all over the floor. Spiderwebs stretched from bedposts to the edges of the other furniture: a dresser missing two drawers, a nightstand on three legs, and the old wood-burning stove.

A stack of old newspapers stood in the corner next to the stove, probably intended as tinder, and a couple of hardback novels lay on the edge of the nightstand. They were the old, leather-bound kind, with no paper cover or images, and they were all so badly moldered that the titles could no longer be read.

I brushed away the cobwebs on my way across the room, to keep from walking face-first into them.

The nightstand drawer creaked when I pulled it open. It was the old-fashioned kind with dovetailed joints and no rollers. The drawer held several wadded-up receipts too faded to read, a half-empty matchbook, a brittle roll of duct tape, and a yellowed bit of fabric.

I slammed the drawer shut and backed away, my heart thudding.

Two of the six dresser drawers were missing. Two others were empty. But the left-hand center drawer held several old articles of clothing. They'd possibly been folded at one time, but had long since become a nest for rats, which had left their markings—and their droppings—everywhere.

The bottom right-hand drawer looked much the same,

except that there, the rats had found a pile not of clothes, but of papers, once nominally protected by several school-style cardstock folders. The colors had faded to pale pink, very, very pale yellow, and what was once either blue or green, and rats had nibbled on the papers themselves, which appeared to be little more than printouts of old emails addressed to Silas, from a woman named Becky.

Not Connie. Becky.

They were about her son, a little boy named Denny.

My heart pounded as I read short messages that seemed to confirm at least some of what Eamon had said about Silas's son.

Fifteen years ago, Denny got chickenpox, despite being vaccinated as a child. The doctor cost money, so Becky would be needing a little more this month.

Twelve years ago, Denny had unexpectedly outgrown all of his clothes over the span of a single summer, so in addition to the already late child support payment, she would be needing enough to cover several shirts and pairs of jeans bought at Walmart.

Ten years ago, Denny had decided to play Junior League baseball, and the fees and uniform costs were more than Becky could afford on her own, so she'd be needing extra in that month's child support as well. There were more printouts. A lot more. Becky obviously kept Silas well updated on his son's progress in life, at least as it related to her financial needs. But the rest of it was largely unreadable, after so long in the drawer.

And that was it. There were no pictures on the walls. No photo albums. No lockbox that might contain birth certificates, safety deposit keys, or someone's hand-written last will and testament. There was nothing else in the entire room, other than the bed where I'd been restrained, except for—

I crossed the room one more time and picked up the top book from a stack of three, still sitting on the nightstand. Desperate, I flipped through brittle pages, some of which disintegrated beneath my fingers. There was nothing in the book. Not even a name scribbled inside the front corner, advising how one could return the novel to its owner.

The same was true of the second book, which was in slightly better condition, having been shielded from the elements by the top one.

The book on bottom was the sturdiest of the three, and I could make out the title on the copyright page.

Treasure Island.

I started to flip through, but the book opened on its own to a section near the middle, where something had been shoved between the pages. It was a note, or a card, or something printed on thick paper.

I plucked it free and turned it over, and—

I gasped, nearly choking on dust. My hand fumbled at my back pocket and finally freed my phone, but it took me several more seconds to remember how to use the camera flash as a flashlight.

The sudden bright light was harsh in the ambient darkness, and I squinted while my eyes adjusted. Then I aimed the circle of light at the rectangle of thick paper in my other hand. Silas stared out at me from the faded photo, younger in this frozen image than he'd been when I met him. He was smiling, and the crooked teeth I remembered as menacing seemed almost charming, reflecting legitimate joy.

But it wasn't his face that had made me gasp, despite the shiver it sent through my spine. Despite the trauma it recalled.

In the photo, Silas had his left arm around a boy, no more

than twelve or thirteen years old. Faded with age though it was, I recognized that boy's face.

I knew the man he would become.

I slid the photo into my nylon pack, turned off my light, and called Vance as I trekked back through the woods toward my truck.

He answered on the second ring. "Charley?" He cleared his throat, and his next words were less gruff from sleep. "What's wrong? Where are you?"

"*Everything* is wrong. I'm leaving the cabin, and—"

"What cabin?"

"Silas's old place. I found—"

"What the living *fuck* are you doing out there in the middle of the night? Are you alone?"

"Yeah, but no one's been here for years."

"Yet I'm guessing you didn't know that for sure, when you went out there?"

"I had a hunch. Anyone carrying on in Silas's honor would have been an idiot to stay out here."

"And yet, idiots *do* commit crimes. Why didn't you call me?"

I shoved aside the voluminous branches from a cedar tree instead of answering.

"Charley?"

"I didn't call you because you cleaned your apartment."

"What? What are you talking—" His mouth snapped shut with the click of his front teeth colliding. "You still think I'm guilty. You think I cleaned to cover up my involvement."

"Not anymore, I don't. That's why I'm calling. I just found actual evidence."

"Awesome. But what am I supposed to think about you believing I could ever be involved in something like this?"

"That I was doing my fucking job, Vance. When there's

a murderer on the loose, you practice caution with people who're acting suspicious. That's, like, hour one of Marshal training. At least until you have reason to exclude them from suspicion. Such as a more likely suspect. Which brings me back to the reason I'm calling you from deep in the woods, in the middle of the night. I mean, if you're interested."

"Your sarcasm is noted, but not necessary." Springs groaned over the line as he sat up in bed. "Tell me. I'm putting you on speaker, so I can get dressed," he added, as the quality of his voice changed, and a soft thump told me that he'd set his phone down.

"I spoke to Eamon, and—"

"*You called Eamon?*"

"He knew Silas. Did you really expect me to ignore our only resource because of a personal grudge?"

"Hell of a personal grudge," Vance muttered over the line, his voice fading as he walked away from the phone.

"Anyway, he told me Silas has a son named Denny, who'd be around twenty-two now."

"And he never thought to mention that before?"

"He said he didn't think Denny was involved, because I only mentioned one kidnapper."

"So he's blaming *you* for—"

"I'm not defending him. I'm just telling you what he said. Which is that he didn't want to unfairly prejudice us against the kid because of what his father did, considering there was no evidence the kid was involved."

"I take it there is evidence of that, now?"

"Maybe? I mean, he fits the profile, which makes him the best suspect we have so far. Unless you want me to put you back on the list."

"Funny. But how does he fit the profile? I've never heard

of this kid, so the probability of him knowing any of our regulars is slim."

"That's what I thought." Finally, I could see moonlight glinting off the grille on my truck, up ahead. "But then I found a bunch of emails from his mother—Becky something or other—to Silas, mostly asking for money. I also found a picture of Silas standing next to the kid, when he was a young teenager."

"Becky? I thought Silas's ex was named Connie, or something."

I shrugged into the dark as I swung my nylon bag over my shoulder and began digging in it one-handed for my keys. "I'm guessing Connie was the one he lived with, but Becky was the kid's mother. Either way, the emails are from a woman named Becky."

I pressed the button on the key fob to unlock my truck, then I pulled the door open and slid into place behind the wheel. "Anyway, the photo is old, but the boy's face is still recognizable. And the reason none of us know any Denny Morelock is because he's been going by another name for years. Probably part of Eamon's attempt to keep him from being associated with the sins of his father."

"And I assume I'm going to recognize this name?"

"Yeah." I started the engine and twisted to look out the rear windshield while I backed rapidly down the dirt road and onto the narrow country highway. "You and I, and just about everyone else in the zone know Denny as Billy Bullen. My fucking short order cook."

FIFTEEN

There were three vehicles in the lot when I parked behind the Fat Cat Bar and Grille. One of them was Bishop's 4Runner, but the fact that it was lined up neatly between the other two told me he'd gone home after his shower, and that he'd been there, with Austin, when Vance called them both in.

"What the *hell*, Charley!" Davey demanded when I shoved my way through the swinging doors from the kitchen into the front of the bar. "It's four o'clock in the morning."

I arched both brows at her as I grabbed the nearest coffee pot and ran water into it at the bar sink. "I thought you wanted to be involved."

"I also want to sleep," she snapped. "Why am I here?"

"Because I need all hands on deck, and I couldn't leave you alone."

"In my home? Where I live? Alone?" she demanded.

"Extraordinary circumstances," I mumbled as I poured the pot of water into the reservoir on the coffee pot.

"That's for decaf." Davey grabbed the orange-rimmed

pitcher from me and exchanged it for the regular one. "Move out of the way."

As she took over, I lifted the bar flap, and—

"Charley," Davey called, and I turned back to see her staring at a conspicuous gap on the top shelf. "We're missing a bottle of Johnny Walker. Gold Label."

"It's not missing," I said with a glance into the dining area, where Tucker, Vance, Austin, and Bishop were gathered around a table in the center of the space—the only one that didn't still have chairs stacked on top of it. "I applied it to Bishop's tab."

Davey shrugged. "If nothing else, the man's good for business."

On my way into the dining room, I shrugged the nylon pack from my right shoulder and pulled apart the drawstrings. "For those who haven't heard, it turns out that Silas Morelock had a son named Denny. Not sure what his surname is yet, but I've found a picture of the two of them together."

I pulled the photo from my pack and slammed it down on the table. "Anyone recognize that boy?"

As the coffee pot hissed and dripped from behind the bar, all four men leaned in to look at the old picture.

"I mean, he looks really young there, but isn't that your fry cook?" Bishop asked.

"Technically, he's a short order cook. But yes," I said. "That's Billy."

"Wait, *what*?" Davey's steps tripped rapidly toward us. She shoved her way into the huddle, where she snatched the picture and held it up to the light. "Billy Bullen? Billy the Kid? No way. How can you be sure?" She squinted at the faded photo. "*Are* you sure?"

Heads all around us nodded. Our eyes were sharper than hers.

"Good god," Tucker swore. "How can Eamon *possibly* justify this?"

"Eamon?" Davey turned on me. "You spoke to Eamon? Do you tell me *nothing* anymore?"

It took all of my self-discipline not to glance at Bishop.

"Who's Eamon?" Bishop plucked the photo from my sister's hand before she could accidentally wad it up.

"The previous Marshal," I said, just as Davey blurted, "Charley's ex."

"Okay, that sounds like a story I would definitely like to hear." Bishop's focus lingered on me just a *little* too long. "But what does this Eamon have to do with Billy?"

"He's the reason Billy works here." Davey took the picture back from him and stared at it as she spoke. "We knew Eamon and Billy before Charley was infected. Before this was a shifter bar. Eamon was a regular back when our parents ran the place, and he talked them—or Charley, I guess —into hiring Billy. But..." She turned back to me. "Billy's just a kid. That's why they *call* him Billy the *kid*."

"Wait, so Eamon knew?" Vance demanded as the coffee machine sputtered with the last drops of the pot. "All this time? He knew who Billy was, and he got you to *hire* him?"

"Billy wasn't the son of a serial killer back then," Davey said as she headed back behind the bar and began setting out mugs, sugar, and creamer. "He couldn't have been. Eamon got him hired before Silas kidnapped Charley. Before there were any 'sins of the father' to hide from us." She folded a bar rag and set the coffee pot on it. "I'm not serving you assholes at four in the morning, so come help yourselves. But don't set the pot directly on the bar; it'll scorch the wood."

"Thanks." Vance was the first to cross the dining room and fill a mug. "So, we're supposed to believe it's just coincidence that Billy was working here when his dad kidnapped you from the parking lot?" he said as he handed me the mug he'd filled, then poured another for himself.

Austin scowled. "You know my feelings on coincidence in a murder investigation. Those two things are almost certainly related." He filled a mug for himself, then he dumped a good quarter of the sugar canister into it. "Either Silas found you through Billy, or Billy helped him kidnap you." He shrugged, the mug halfway to his mouth. "Or Billy hit you over the head himself."

"No. No way," Davey insisted as she pulled a six-pound bag of dry roasted peanuts from beneath the bar.

I shrugged. "All we know for sure is that Billy isn't the one who infected me." If he had been, they all would have known that with their first whiff of me, post-infection.

Instead, I carried a thread of Silas's scent. Fortunately for my sanity, much like bad breath, that wasn't something I could actually smell on myself.

"Billy loves us. He's one of the family. He would never do that," Davey insisted.

"He might, if he were following orders from the only parent he had left." Austin glanced at me over his mug. "His mother's dead, right? And you didn't know Silas was his dad?"

"I had no idea."

"None of us did," Tucker confirmed.

"So, what did Billy tell you about his dad?" Austin asked. "What did Eamon say about him?"

"Nothing," Davey said. "Billy's never mentioned his dad."

"When Eamon asked me to hire him, all he said was that Billy's mom had died and school wasn't his thing. He kind of implied that there was no father in the picture, and I never pressed for more information, because that seemed like none of my business. He said he thought it would do the kid good to have some responsibility. A job. And I agreed." I shrugged. "Davey and I bussed tables, mopped floors, and flipped burgers long before we could drive."

"He had a birth certificate, right?" Tucker said, clicking away at his laptop, at the other end of the bar. "He'd have to, if you're reporting his wages."

"Yeah." I set a steaming mug in front of him. "And of *course* I'm reporting his pay." The last thing a shifter-run business needed was a government audit. "I have a copy of his birth certificate on file in the office. I can get it if you want. Or you can just trust me that it says his name is William Bullen, and the date of birth confirms that he just turned twenty. Though he wasn't quite seventeen when we hired him."

"I do trust you," Tucker said. "But I still need to see the birth certificate."

"I got it," Davey said before I could even set my mug down.

"Thanks!" I called after her.

"Birth certificates are easily faked," Austin said, with one look at the irritation on my face.

"And I can't confirm that Billy's is real—that William Bullen actually exists—without driving down to the Vital Records office in Nashville or waiting two weeks for one to be shipped," Tucker said. "But I *can* try to confirm that Billy Bullen and Denny Morelock are the same person."

"If you can't confirm it's real, why do you want to see it?" I asked.

"Because the most convincing lies usually have at least a grain of truth to them, to make them easier to remember and stick to. Which means there's a possibility that some of the information on the fake birth certificate is real.

Including the name of his mother and the county where he was born."

"Okay, I got it." Davey emerged from the kitchen with a piece of paper in one hand. "And it's as boring as you might expect. But can you guess whose birth certificate is *not* boring?" She aimed a grin at Vance.

He groaned. "*Why* were you looking at my birth certificate?"

Davey shrugged. "I glanced at all of the ones on file." She turned to the rest of us. "Did you guys know that Vance's middle name is Purvis? *Purvis*! He is Vance *Purvis* Cooper!" Her gaze landed on him while I stifled a smile. "Your name is basically Perv, and that's never going to not be funny!"

Bishop whistled. "Ouch. Sorry, man."

"Can we get back on topic?" Tucker held his hand out for Billy's birth certificate. "I'm working on under three hours sleep, which is likely three more than Charley's had."

"We're all exhausted." I grabbed the paper and handed it to Tucker, who went back to his keyboard, and I got the impression he was basically tuning the rest of us out.

"I just can't see Billy doing this." Davey grabbed a handful of peanuts and crunched into several. "He's never so much as looked at me weird. And he's practically still a kid now, but he was *literally* a kid when this all started."

Austin shrugged. "Kids do what their parents tell them."

Davey snorted. "You *clearly* have no children. If I'd been on fire and my dad had told me to jump in the lake to put out the flames, I'd have rolled around in lighter fluid just to avoid doing what I was told."

"She is not exaggerating," I assured him. "And that point-less rebellion has been conferred upon me, in our parents' absence."

"False," Davey snapped back at me. "I'm an adult, and

you are not my boss, so there is nothing for me to rebel against. But my point stands. I can't see Billy being behind all this."

"He knows the zone members, right?" The firm dip in Bishop's brow worried me, as did the clench of his fists. "And they trust him?"

"Because he's harmless," Davey insisted. "And he didn't know either you or Austin, right? So then how would he know about Yvette?"

"She has a point," Austin said.

"On the bright side, since we set his schedule, we'll be able to confirm whether or not he has work as an alibi for the days the women were infected," I said. "At least for the cases where we have that information. Including Yvette's. Davey, grab your laptop and you and Bishop start matching up Billy's schedule with the infection dates we know about. Don't forget to verify that Billy actually worked on those days. That he didn't call in sick, even though he was scheduled."

She lit up with excitement at being included, and I mentally crossed my fingers that neither she nor Bishop would realize I was trying to keep her safe and him occupied until Billy could be brought in.

If Bishop got to Billy before we did, he would break that poor kid in half before we could verify that he was even involved.

"Can't Tucker do that?" Bishop asked. "We're about to go get this 'Billy the Kid,' right? I want in on that."

Shit.

"Tucker's busy confirming Billy's identity," I said. "And I'm just going to be straight with you. You cannot be on the team that brings Billy in, because I can't trust you not to kill him before we're sure he's guilty. Until we've questioned him and checked out his alibis, he's just a person of interest."

"Fine," Bishop said. "But you *are* about to bring him in?"

"Yeah." I drained my coffee mug and snatched my keys from the bar. "Vance? Austin? You ready?"

"Fuck that." Bishop stood. "I'm going."

"Bish…" Austin said, but I held up a hand to stop him.

"Mattheson," I snapped. "May I see you in the kitchen please?"

Davey's eyebrows shot up. Vance and Austin exchanged a glance. Tucker didn't even look up from his laptop.

Bishop growled softly as he followed me into the kitchen. "You know they can still hear us in here, right?" he said as the door swung shut behind him.

"Of course. But I thought you might enjoy at least a semblance of privacy while I hand you your ass."

"While *you*—?"

"You do understand that I'm in charge here, right?"

"Out here?" He glanced around at the kitchen, one arm extended to include the rest of the bar, and I *prayed* he wasn't about to mention what situations *not* out here might include. "Yeah. I got that. And I'm not looking to make an issue of it. But I already told you, there's only one thing I'm good at, and—"

"That's certainly not true," I whispered, fighting the flush I could feel settling into my cheeks.

"—I can be useful out there."

"And maybe someday you will be, if you decide to stay here after this is all over and work with us. But for now, I can't trust you, so—"

"You can't *trust* me?" He had the nerve to look offended.

"I know how badly you want Yvette's killer dead, so yes,

right now I can't trust you to follow orders you don't agree with. That's the kind of trust you'll have to earn."

"How?" he growled.

"By proving you *can* follow orders. Like the one I just gave you, to stay here and work with Davey."

His mouth opened, and I could see the argument coming. So I turned and marched back through the swinging doors, where I found all four of them watching me. Not even pretending they weren't listening.

"What?" Davey demanded, glancing from Vance to Austin. "What were they saying?"

"Nothing," I told her. "Just laying down the law."

"Loud and clear, *Marshal*," Bishop muttered from behind me, as the swinging doors creaked open.

"Ready?" I asked without looking back at him.

Austin nodded as he stood. "This feels more like a wild west posse than any arrest I ever made with the police."

He was not far off.

"Where does Billy live, anyway?"

I glanced at Vance, who answered, his voice dipping into a deep, grim growl. "Eamon took him in years ago. Kind of our version of a ward of the state. And I believe he's still living in Eamon's trailer, on the far side of the lake."

"Wait." Austin turned to look at all of us, his brows drawn low. "The former Marshal of the northern zone *took in* the son of the man who later kidnapped and infected the future— now current—Marshal? And is *still* letting that kid live on his property? Without telling anyone of his connection to all this?"

I nodded as I mentally sorted through his summary. "And Eamon *will* answer for that."

But as we headed out to the parking lot, the case fact eating at me was not what part Eamon had played in all of this. It was the role *I'd* played. I'd had multiple opportunities to protect the men of this zone and their unsuspecting human relatives. None of this would have happened if I'd realized sooner that Silas wasn't working alone. Or that Billy's background didn't add up. If I had even once in the three years he'd worked for me thought to verify his birth certificate. Or even to ask him about his family.

I'd failed the citizens of the northern zone over and over, and people had died. Ultimately, the blame for that could rest on only one set of shoulders.

Mine.

I RODE with Vance because it would be easier to get Billy to the bar in the back of his SUV than in the bed of my truck, for several obvious reasons. Austin drove separately, mostly to keep Bishop from following us in the 4Runner.

On the way around the lake, I called Eamon. Again. I'd called him twice on my way back from the cabin, but he wasn't answering.

"How suspicious do we consider that?" Vance asked when I dropped my phone onto my lap in disgust. "Does he usually answer when you call?"

"I don't usually call." In fact, before this, I'd only phoned Eamon three times since I took over as Marshal, and those calls were all attempts to sort out zone records he'd kept. Poorly. "As for suspicious… I don't think he had any idea that Billy could have been involved in anything like what Silas did. Did Eamon fuck up as Marshal? No doubt. But I can't believe he would intentionally put the zone in that kind of danger."

Vance nodded without taking his focus from the road. "If

he had, why tell you about Denny in the first place? Why draw attention to his own failures?"

"Exactly. That said, I *am* interested in what he could *possibly* have to say for himself. He knew about Billy's paternity. He *must* have. Even if he didn't suspect Billy of being involved, there is no excuse for him not to have told me about the connection between Silas and Billy after I was infected. After we had to execute Billy's *father*."

"Agreed," Vance said. "On all counts."

We parked nearly a mile from Eamon's trailer, and Austin's 4Runner pulled to a stop on the side of the road behind us. Any closer, and Billy might have been able to hear the engine. And he *would* recognize the sound of Vance's SUV.

"Sunrise is at six forty-nine this morning," I said, reading from an app on my phone. That gives us about an hour until twilight, which is when the human eye will begin to register daylight. We need to have him in custody and out of sight before then."

Because we could not risk anyone seeing us shove a boy who could pass for a teenager into the back of Vance's SUV.

Fortunately, this side of the lake was pretty sparsely populated. But as always, it was better to be safe than sorry.

"Vance, you'll go on foot." That was standard procedure. We always worked with one enforcer in human form, so someone could open doors, tie knots, and speak actual words on short notice. "This is your head start. Go on. We'll catch up."

Vance took off into the woods, in the direction of Eamon's trailer, at a quick jog, gently pacing his human-form legs and lungs, with a small backpack bouncing against his spine.

"The goal is to corner him." I pulled my shirt over my

head and shoved it into my nylon bag. Suddenly I really wished I'd had time for a burger. My body was not going to like shifting twice without sustenance. "Vance will do the talking, obviously. If Billy's in human form, he'll be cuffed. If he's on four legs, we'll basically hog-tie him."

"Then how do we get him back here?"

I gave him a look as I stripped out of my pants. "Vance will throw him over one shoulder and carry him to the car. If we're running short on time, I'll race back here and drive the SUV back to him, to speed things up."

Suddenly I wondered whether Austin had ever *really* put his shifter strength to the test. It was entirely possible that choosing to isolate himself from the rest of the Pride had kept him from understanding his true capabilities.

Though I highly doubted his best friend had fallen into that same trap.

"Charley."

I turned to find Austin watching me with a quietly intense expression I couldn't quite interpret. Despite our nudity, his gaze stayed focused on my eyes. "I just wanted to apologize for last night. For...Bishop."

My heart pounded so hard I was sure he could hear it. "For Bishop?"

"I know he showed up at the bar after I got tired of his pacing, and I know it was after hours. I just wanted to thank you for your patience with him. He's...reactionary. I mean, I can't say either of us is dealing very well with losing Yvette, if I'm being honest, but he tends to act first and think later, and I've never been able to pull him past that impulse. But whatever you said to him last night...well, he's clearly willing to listen to you." Austin shrugged. "He listened to Yvie too—they were really good for each other—but without her here to balance him out, he's sort of...well, he's been difficult."

"He's certainly...aggressive," I agreed, choosing my words carefully. "But sometimes controlled aggression is... useful." I cleared my throat, fighting to maintain the steady beat of my pulse. "We all grieve in our own way. We all deal with trauma in our own way. Just...please just try to keep that in mind."

"I do." Austin inhaled, and his gaze seemed to intensify. "He and I want the same thing. We just go about it differently. Which you've obviously noticed."

"Justice," I said, on a release of the breath I'd been holding. "You both want justice for Yvette." That's all he was talking about. He had no idea that Bishop and I had discovered a rather effective form of mutual therapy. And he was *not* saying he wanted the same thing.

"Yes, but...you have something good going on out here. This community is more isolated than I thought I'd want, but I'm finding that I like it. Murder investigation aside. I can't speak for Bishop, but I'm considering staying. If you'll have me."

"Yes, of course. I'd love to have you both."

Good god. What had I just said?

I felt like we were having two conversations at once, and I couldn't tell whether he meant for that to be the case. Whether or not he was aware of the double entendre in nearly every word we'd both spoken.

"I mean, you'd both—each of you—be an asset to the northern zone. If you feel like sticking around, once we get all this...sorted out."

Austin nodded, his blue eyes sparkling in the moonlight. "Thanks. It's good to know we might actually belong somewhere. It's kind of felt like we were floating out there all alone, after Yvette…"

"I can imagine." I shivered, and Austin frowned.

"You're freezing. Sorry. I've kept you standing here… naked." His gaze started to drop, but then it popped back up as he arrested the impulse. I couldn't resist a small smile.

The man *was* human.

"Yes, we should get going." I shoved the rest of my clothes into the bag, then I headed into the woods, where I knelt in a bed of moss and leaves. Despite the pain of each stretch and pop, despite the vicious itch of fur sprouting over every inch of my skin, I was acutely aware of Austin dropping to the ground on my right. I heard every grunt and moan of pain, and I internalized them, letting the swiftness of his shift spur on my own.

A solitary run is nice, but there's nothing like racing through the woods with someone.

I beat him into cat form, but just barely. When I stood, I spared a moment to stretch my new formation of muscles and tendons. Then I huffed playfully at him, choosing to see the joy in this moment, rather than the dark nature of our mission.

For a moment, anyway.

As he finally stood, strong and lithe on four powerful legs, I took off into the woods at a bound, leaping over brush and racing around trees. I leapt a small stream, and as I was airborne, enjoying the ripple of the breeze over my fur, I heard him right behind me, huffing with each deep, efficient breath.

His paws hit the ground a second after mine, and I forced another burst of speed from my legs, digging into the ground when it seemed to slide around beneath me. Launching myself off logs and trunks, when that seemed more fun than simply running.

FAT CAT

I should have been exhausted. I'd already run once, just hours before. But there was something about running with a partner that kept my adrenaline flowing. My heart pumping. And when I was truly focused, Austin, for all his stealth and power, was no match for my speed.

I beat him to the edge of the woods by a full body-length.

He pulled up short next to me, huffing, and I swear I could hear amusement in each short little pant. I could see it in the gleam of his round, greenish cat eyes. He'd enjoyed that just as much as I had.

"Glad you both had some fun," Vance said, appearing from around the corner of Eamon's old single-wide. The fact that he wasn't whispering set off my internal alarm. "And I hope you've got more in you, because we missed him. The bed's still warm, though, so I'm guessing Billy left less than ten minutes ago. Paw prints on the back porch say he went out in cat form. And that's not all I found."

SIXTEEN

I n human form again, Austin lifted the glass pipe—the shape and color of a pickle with a little green human face —from a dent carved into Eamon's wooden back porch rail. In the bowl of the pipe lay the charred remains of a weed roach.

He shrugged. "Waste not, want not. That's what my grandmother always said."

"Somehow, I doubt she was talking about pot," Vance said.

Austin snorted. "Clearly you never met my Nana."

"So, Billy's high," I said as Austin returned the pipe to its spot on the railing. "And on a run, in cat form. At five-thirty in the morning."

Vance nodded. "Insomnia does strange things."

When a brief search of the woods around the trailer had shown no sign of Billy, Austin and I had shifted back into human form. If we'd heard him, we could have followed the sound of his footsteps, or even the huff of his breath as he ran, but cats cannot track by scent. Alas.

Austin and I followed Vance inside, and stepping over

that threshold felt eerily like stepping into my own past. Much of the previous week had felt like that—like a tour of bygone traumas.

None of the furniture had changed, which was no real surprise. Billy couldn't have afforded to replace it if Eamon had taken it with him, and Eamon couldn't have gotten permission from multiple Alphas to drive a moving van through their territories even if he'd wanted to. So, he'd had to leave all his stuff here when he flew to Montana, where he'd had to buy or rent new stuff at his new place. Once he found a job.

Yet another of the hurdles thrown up in front of strays at every turn. There were only two free zones left in the US, and there was no such thing as unrestricted travel between them. Not by car, anyway.

Eamon's trailer no longer smelled much like him at all, and on one level, that was a huge relief. It meant that if he *had* been sneaking back into the Mississippi Valley Territory, he hadn't been staying here. Which meant he likely hadn't been seeing Billy.

Which lowered the chances that he was involved in any of this.

By contrast, Billy's scent was everywhere.

"Find anything?" I asked Vance as he came in from the bedroom.

"Not a goddamn thing," he swore, brows deeply furrowed. "There isn't one scrap of evidence in this entire trailer that Billy has ever been in contact with Yvette, or with any of the other victims."

"Other than you," Austin added, with a glance in my direction.

"He left his phone," I noted, pointing out where it lay on the charger, on one scuffed end table. "Which means he's either ditched it for good because he knew we were coming, or he had no idea we were on the way, and he left it because he went for a normal run without pockets."

And there was no evidence that he'd cleaned recently. Which made me think that the latter scenario was the most likely.

"Unfortunately, if he *is* coming back, he'll know we were here the second he walks in."

"He may not think anything of that," Vance pointed out. "He knows you searched my place and Tucker's. He may believe this is standard procedure for employees of the bar."

Austin's brows rose. "Maybe it should be."

"Shh!" Vance hissed before I could reply. He swung toward the front window, and I was suddenly glad we hadn't bothered to turn on any of the lights; we didn't need to, considering how well even our human-form eyes worked in the dark.

Austin and I each dropped into a squat, putting us below the level of the window, listening. After a second, I heard it— the snap of a twig, easily audible through a window left open two inches. A few seconds later, I heard the soft crackle of dry leaves, which continued instead of repeating, as it would have with footsteps.

"He's shifting," Vance said just as I drew the same conclusion; we all knew the sound a body makes as it writhes on the forest floor. Which either meant that Billy had no idea we were there, or he didn't think he had any reason to fear us while he was at his most vulnerable, mid-shift.

I pointed toward the back door, and Vance took off in that direction while Austin followed me out the front. We moved nearly silently on human feet, even though hiking boots were nowhere near as stealthy as a cat's paws, and converged upon

Billy from two sides, not twenty feet from the trailer. Just inside the tree line.

He had human arms, and his muzzle had nearly receded into a round human head, already forming a familiar squarish jaw as the last of his fur seemed to melt back into his follicles.

Billy's eyes rolled up at an awkward angle when Vance stood over him, as he convulsed with the last of his shift. For several seconds afterward, he lay panting on the ground, naked and evidently completely unafraid.

"Hey," he said as he finally sat up, tucking his knees to his chest. "What's going on?" The first diffuse rays of sunlight were just starting to bleed through the forest canopy.

For a second, I could only blink at him. Considering the circumstances, his complete lack of anxiety—confirmed by the calm pace of his pulse—seemed beyond preposterous.

"Was I supposed to come in early today?"

"We're taking you into custody," I said. "We've just finished searching your trailer. *Eamon's* trailer," I corrected myself.

Billy blinked up at me. "Seriously?" His pulse spiked, but just once. "Why?"

Austin glanced at me, but Vance never looked away from Billy, who still sat on the ground. Naked.

"For now, we just want to ask you some questions." I reached down and offered him a hand up.

"Okay." Billy shrugged. "My shift starts at nine today anyway." He frowned from me to Vance, then back. "Can I get dressed first?"

I nodded. "We're going to need to see your phone."

"You'll have to unlock it," Austin added.

Another shrug from Billy. "Okay. It's on the charger."

"Go get the SUV," I said to Austin, and Vance tossed him

the keys. Austin headed back through the woods on foot, at a jog, while Vance and I escorted Billy to his trailer.

Billy marched into the living room without a hint of modesty. He plucked his phone from the charger and unlocked it, then dropped it in my open palm on his way past me into the master bedroom. A room I'd spent considerable time in, two years ago.

Vance followed him and left the door open.

While Billy got dressed—Vance told him to pack a small bag—I scrolled through his texts and emails. Through the open windows in his browser, hitting the back button ad nauseam. Then through his cached history. There was nothing on his phone that referenced any of the victims, the most recent of which was Yvette Graham-Mattheson, and nothing in any of his map searches that indicated he'd ever been to Covington, where Yvette, Bishop, and Austin lived. In fact, his most recent map search was nearly eight months old, which seemed to indicate that unless he had another phone or a separate GPS unit somewhere, he hadn't left town in at least that long, unless he'd gone somewhere he was familiar enough with that he wouldn't need directions.

His ancient truck did not have built-in GPS capabilities.

Austin pulled up in Vance's SUV as I was securing Billy's hands at his back with a zip tie. He got into the back without complaint.

We drove Austin to his 4Runner, and he followed us back to the Fat Cat, where Vance and Tucker had Billy locked up in the basement a full two hours before he was due to show up for his shift.

With any luck, the lunch crowd would never even know he was there.

"Well?" Tucker said as he closed the basement door.

Davey held up one finger, telling us to wait as she pushed

through the swinging doors into the dining room. She was on the phone, trying to cover Billy's shift.

She came back in as I was pulling a stack of burger patties from the walk-in fridge. "Okay, Mitch will be here at nine to prep and open for lunch. We'll need someone else to start cooking at five, though, when he goes home."

I shrugged. "I still remember how to sling burgers." Assuming I could catch a nap before then.

"Debrief?" Tucker asked as Bishop came in from the front room.

Another shrug, as beef sizzled on the hot griddle. "No smoking gun. He didn't resist arrest. We found him shifting back into human form outside the trailer."

"Seriously?" Bishop sounded incredulous, and that was understandable. A shifter was never more vulnerable, in any single moment of life, than when he was defenseless in mid-shift. Which meant that Billy had not only chosen not to run from us, but he had intentionally put himself at our mercy.

I nodded. "We haven't questioned him yet, because he's high, but that won't last long." It was as hard for a shifter to stay high as it was to stay drunk. "So far, he seems to have no idea why we were at his home, or that we could have been any threat to him whatsoever."

"So, what's the plan?" Davey asked.

"Well, Billy needs to sober up, and I owe Eamon another phone call. And if he doesn't answer the goddamn phone this time, I'm going to fly to Montana and rip the information out of him in person." I flipped all six burgers, then turned to the row of plated buns Vance had set out on the prep station. "Where are we with Billy's alibi?"

"Still working it," Davey said as she sliced tomatoes on a chopping block. "It's taking us a while to narrow down the dates, considering that Yvette is the only one we have good information for."

"Fine." I dropped an onion into the industrial slicer and turned the crank, while Vance slapped slices of cheddar onto the buns. "Tucker, where are we on verifying Billy's identity?"

"Nowhere. But it turns out that if Billy Bullen *is* an alias, he hasn't entirely stopped using his real name, including his father's surname. Denny Morelock still has at least one social media account, which was last active two days ago."

I divided the stack of sliced onions among the waiting buns. "Do we know that it's *our* Denny Morelock?"

Tucker shrugged. "The publicly accessible data says he's from Tennessee, and Billy Bullen is listed as one of his friends, so there's a good chance. All of his photos are friend-locked, though, so I created a fake account and sent him a friend request. If he accepts it, I should be able to see at least some of his photos."

"You think Billy has an account under both of his names?" And would be stupid enough to friend his own alias?

Another shrug from Tucker, as I began slathering top buns in mayo and mustard. "If he does, we may be able to link him to some of the victims through that other account. I'll let you know when I know more."

"Thanks." I handed him the plate holding the first finished burger and dismissed him to return to his laptop. "Everyone else help yourselves. I have to make a phone call. And Bishop, stay the hell out of the basement!"

"*Pick. Up. The phone,*" I mumbled around a big bite of my burger as the phone rang in my ear. And rang. And rang. Yes, it was an hour earlier in Montana, but—

The phone went to voicemail again, so I hung up and redialed. And chewed. Then redialed. And chewed. Then redialed. And—

"Goddamn it, Charley," Eamon grumbled into my ear. Intimate memories tumbled over me at the sound of his morning-gruff voice, and I hated the power of that emotional wallop, despite everything I'd done to put it all behind me. "I haven't heard from you in more than a year, and now you're blowing up my phone at seven in the morning. Does this mean you miss me?"

"This is *not* a joke." I chewed rapidly, rushing through the bite I'd taken when I'd thought he wasn't going to answer. "Why the hell didn't you tell me about Billy? And why haven't you been answering your phone?"

"I was asleep. My phone was in 'do not disturb' mode. And what is it that I didn't tell you about Billy?"

As Marshal, he'd never put his phone on do not disturb. A Marshal was always on call.

Civilian life must be nice.

"I'm talking about his father, Eamon. How could you not tell me about Billy's father? How the hell could you let him live with you, after all that?" And why on earth didn't I bring a drink to wash down my burger?

"I honestly have no idea what you're talking about. I have no clue who Billy's dad is," Eamon insisted. "As far as I know, he doesn't either. Why are we talking about Billy, anyway. Has something happened? Should I call him?"

I shoved my plate back in disgust. "You could try, but his phone is sitting right here on my desk, so you're just going to wind up in another *infuriating* conversation with me."

"Charley, *what* is going on?" A familiar whisper of skin on skin told me he was scrubbing one hand over his face, a frustrated gesture he made every time he was woken up too early. "What happened to Billy?"

"Nothing happened *to* him. We took him into custody an hour ago, and he didn't resist. He didn't even ask why we were there. It was fucking weird. I've known him for years, yet I feel like I'm somehow just now meeting him, and I really need to know what's going on with him, Eamon. I need to know everything you know about Billy and his dad."

"Okay, let's start over," he said, and I heard a squealing sound like chair legs skidding across the floor. "Pretend I have no idea what you're talking about and start from the beginning. Why the hell have you arrested Billy?"

"For killing Yvette Graham-Mattheson! And possibly all the others!"

"Wait." That skittering sound echoed over the line again, and then I heard footsteps. Eamon was pacing. "Wait. You think *Billy Bullen* is your serial killer? He's a kid, Char! He was barely eighteen when you were infected, and—"

"Human kids kill people all the time. Why would that be different for shifters?"

"But *Billy*? He's—"

"I went back to Silas's cabin."

Silence echoed at me from the other end of the line. "Wow. Well, that couldn't have been easy."

"Don't—" I stood, pushing my chair back, and now *I* was pacing. "Just…don't be nice to me right now, okay? This isn't about me or how I feel. This is about the fact that we have a serial killer infecting and killing human women, and you basically unleashed him on us when you talked me into hiring Billy. When you failed to tell me that his dad was Silas fucking Morelock!"

I was shouting by then, and which meant they could definitely hear me in the dining room. If not for the extra insulation in the basement, Billy would be able to hear me as well. "I know he's Billy's dad. I found the photo."

"He's not— Why would you think that? What photo?"

My eyes narrowed at nothing. "You really expect me to believe you didn't know?"

"I expect you to believe it isn't true!" And suddenly he was shouting too. "But now I understand why you're so mad; that's one hell of a misunderstanding."

"There was a photo of them together in the cabin, Eamon, from when Billy was a child. It was stuck between the pages of an old book on the nightstand, and it was probably there the day he took me. If I'd opened that book while I was cuffed to that goddamn bed, I'd have seen Billy's face staring out at me, and none of the rest of this would have happened. I would have known. I could have stopped *all* of this."

"You saw a picture of Billy and Silas together? You're sure it was Billy, and not Denny?"

"Oh my god, just give it up!" I was practically stomping now, wearing grooves into the hardwood behind my desk. "I *know* that Denny and Billy are the same person. Tucker's online proving that right this minute. I know that *you* know that. That you covered it up. That you, like… You must have given Denny a new name, to keep us from associating him with what his dad did. I get that you probably had no idea he'd strike off down the same path. That you thought you were protecting an innocent kid. But how you could not tell me? *Me*, Eamon?"

"Okay, wait. Just slow down a second and think this through, Charley. What you're saying doesn't make any—"

"Don't fucking patronize me. I'm holding you account-able for this."

"Yes. Okay, hold me accountable." The very slight wiggle in his voice told me he was nodding compulsively.

That he understood just how much of a threat the larger shifter community was about to become to him. "I knew about Billy's connection to Silas, and when I found out that Silas was the one who attacked you, I should have told you. But that connection isn't what you think. He isn't Silas's son. Billy and Denny are *not* the same person, and if they were, that timeline would make no sense. You hired Billy— under the name William Bullen, his real, true name—a full year before you were infected. A full year before I would have had any reason to change Billy's name to protect him. So—"

My office door flew open, just as my printer whirred to life from on top of a filing cabinet in one corner. Tucker burst into the room and marched around me. "It's not him, Charley," he said. "Denny Morelock is not Billy Bullen."

"See?" Eamon said into my ear, clearly having heard him.

"Mute him," Tucker said as he grabbed the image he'd just sent to my printer.

"No, don't—"

I muted Eamon, cursing beneath my breath, then I set my phone on my desk, where we could both see the screen with that line crossing through the volume icon. Assuring us that even though Eamon was still shouting at me for information, he couldn't hear us. "What did you find?"

"Denny accepted my fake friend request," Tucker said. "Probably because I used a stock photo of a hot college girl as my profile pic. I can see his photos now, but there are no recent ones of him. At all. So I scrolled all the way back to the beginning, where I found this one, from several years ago." He slapped the picture onto my desk, and I stared down at it. It was almost identical to the one I'd found in Silas's cabin, only this photo included a third figure. Another boy, not much older than Billy. "That..." Tucker tapped on the third figure's face. "*That* is Denny. Silas's son. Look closely, Charley."

I blinked at the photo for a second.

"Fucking hell. That's Cam Senet." He'd been a regular for more than a year. In fact, we'd played 'Another One Bites The Dust' for him just last week, when his girlfriend had dumped him. The *very day* Austin and Bishop had showed up at the bar. "Hell, he was here last night." I swore as I picked up my phone, still staring at the photo. "Cam is short for Camden..." I said, thinking aloud.

"As is Denny," Tucker noted, completing my thought. "Which means his alias is really more of an alternate nickname."

I exhaled. "You think Billy's innocent?"

He shrugged. "No idea."

"It can't be coincidence that both Cam and Billy have a connection to Silas, can it?" I asked. "They could be working together. Right?"

Another shrug. "I guess it's time to talk to Billy again."

"And to find Cam." I unmuted Eamon and put him on speaker. "Have you actually met Denny?"

"Yeah. It's been years, but—"

"Was he a regular at the bar, when you were Marshal?"

"No, he was too young to drink, and he left town after his dad—"

"Do you know of any aliases he might have gone by? Nicknames? Mother's maiden name? Family names?" Anything that might help verify that Cam Senet was, in fact, the Denny in question.

"No. I don't know his mother's name. Billy might, though. He—"

"Thanks for the help. I gotta go. And the next time I call you, you better *damn* well answer your phone." I hung up and dropped my broken cell on my desk as I sank into my chair with my head cradled in both of my hands.

"Charley?" Tucker's footsteps echoed toward me, but they stopped at least a foot away. "Why'd you hang up on him? He still has infor—"

"We don't need him anymore; we have Billy, and frankly, even if Billy is a suspect, I'd rather talk to him than spend one more second on the phone with Eamon fucking McLane." I shoved my chair back and stood. "Come on."

"Have you seen the picture?" I asked as I shoved my way through the swinging doors into the dining area.

Davey, Vance, Bishop, and Austin all looked up from half-empty plates and laptop or phone screens, where they'd huddled to work in the corner booth. They all nodded.

"It's Cam Senet," Davey said. "Mr. Unlucky-In-Love, himself."

"Yup. Okay. Tucker, get us an address for Cam Senet, then Austin, you go scout it out. Keep an eye on him. Observation only. Do not engage. Don't let him see you. We aren't going to make a move until we've spoken to Billy and we have a better idea of what's going on."

I turned to Vance. "You're with me. Let's go talk to Billy the Kid."

SEVENTEEN

"Hey, Billy. I brought you some breakfast," I said as I opened the door at the bottom of the steps. "It's probably not as good as what you'd make, but I do my best."

It was a six-egg western scramble, and it was damn good.

Billy sat up on the cot Nolan Blake had occupied until yesterday, rubbing sleep from his eyes. His face was creased from the pillow. He'd been sleeping.

While we were upstairs trying to figure out what part he'd played in the deaths of six women, he'd been down here asleep. Evidently completely unfazed.

I took a deep breath to slow my pulse. To hide my anger and frustration from him. The hardest part about interrogating a fellow shifter was controlling my temper. Not just the external expression of it. The internal tells, too.

I folded down the tray slot and slid his breakfast into his cell on a paper plate, with a plastic fork.

"Thanks. That smells great, and I'm starving."

"I bet." *I hear weed does that.*

"I...um..." He stared down at the plate, as if he weren't sure where else to look. "I don't really know what to say. I'm sorry for the trouble. So…" He finally looked up, meeting my gaze with his brows furrowed in a sheepish expression that made him look about twelve years old. "So, how much trouble am I in, exactly?"

"That's what we're here to assess."

"But for the record…" Vance pushed the basement door shut as he came in behind me. "Lying only digs that hole deeper. Any chance you have of catching a break depends *entirely* upon you answering every question we ask honestly, and as thoroughly as possible."

"Jesus." Billy blinked, his focus shifting from Vance to me. "I mean, I know it's illegal in Tennessee, but I didn't think the Pride really cared about human laws."

"I—" I frowned as Vance set two folding chairs on the floor behind me. "Billy…" I sank into one of the chairs. "Do you know why you're here?"

"Because of the pot, right? It was just one joint. I didn't think you guys would really care about that, and it helps me relax. It also mutes the pain of shifting. And if you haven't gone for a run while you're high, you've never really lived…" He grinned, evidently trying to lighten the mood, and when that went over like a lead balloon, his brows dipped even further. "But this all seems like overkill for one blunt."

"I don't care about your pot, Billy. Unless smoking gets you arrested and brings you—and potentially us—to the attention of the human police. So make sure it doesn't get to that point."

"Yeah. Of course. I only smoke at home, and I never—" He sank onto the edge of the cot, his breakfast untouched. "So, wait, why am I here, then? Why were you guys out at the trailer?"

"We have some questions for you." I leaned forward in

my chair, but Vance only stood behind his, kind of hovering over it.

"Okay." Billy nodded, a lock of dark hair falling across his forehead. His right hand clenched the edge of his paper plate, crumpling it. His pulse was steady, but a little faster than normal. Which meant he was nervous, but not truly scared yet.

He seemed to *truly* have no idea what this was about.

Vance opened the voice recorder on his phone and turned it on. "Just so you know, we're recording this, and a copy of the recording will be sent to Titus Alexander, Alpha of the Mississippi Valley Pride."

"Yeah. Okay. So, this is serious, huh?" Billy set his plate on the cot next to him, still untouched.

"As serious as it gets," I said. "Are you high right now?"

"No. I wish—" Billy shook his head. "I mean, no. Stone cold. It never lasts long."

"Okay. That's good. Tell us how you know Denny Morelock."

His gaze narrowed, and I could practically feel his shields go up. "He's my brother. I mean, not by blood." Billy shrugged. "But we basically grew up together."

"As neighbors?" I asked. "Friends? What was the connection?"

"I told you. We were family. His dad and my mom were married. Common law, she called it."

Tennessee has never been a common law marriage state, so unless Denny's dad and Billy's mom were married according to the common law in some other state, he was wrong, whether he knew it or not. But the legality of their "marriage" wasn't the point.

"So, they lived together? Your mom and Silas?" Was Billy's mother the live-in girlfriend Eamon had mentioned?

"Yeah."

"Was your mom's name Connie, by any chance?"

"Yeah. Constance Bullen. I never met my dad, and she didn't seem to think I needed to, so…" Billy shrugged. "After what happened to you, Eamon said it would be best not to tell you about my connection to Silas. He said you were traumatized and had every right to heal in peace, and you wouldn't be able to do that if you knew he was my stepdad. But that since I hadn't done anything wrong, I didn't deserve to be run out of the community for the sake of your healing either, and that this way, we could both stay. You and I," he clarified, just in case.

"So, you're saying you had nothing to do with Silas kidnapping and infecting me? You knew nothing about it?"

"That's right. I hadn't lived with him for more than a year, by then. Not since my mom died. But Eamon was worried you wouldn't believe that. That you'd fire me and run me off."

I wanted to tell him that Eamon had been wrong about that. That I would never have punished him for what Silas did. But considering that we hadn't yet cleared him of involvement in several more murders, it seemed premature to assume he was telling me the truth about what happened three years ago. "How long were your mom and Silas involved with each other?" I said instead.

"From the time I was in middle school. Denny didn't live with us that whole time, though. He lived with his mom, Rebecca, until he got into some trouble, and she handed him off to his dad. To live with us. I think I was thirteen, then."

The year before he was infected. At least, according to the story he'd told us at Davey's request.

"And were Silas and Denny already shifters when you met them? When he and your mom…married?"

"No." Billy scooted back on the cot, tucking his legs beneath him with his back pressed to the cinderblock wall. "No, we were all three infected at the same time. On that fishing trip I told you about."

My gaze narrowed on him. "Silas and Denny went on that trip with you?"

Billy's pulse spiked for just a second. Not enough to necessarily indicate a lie, but enough to suggest that he was nervous about this line of questioning. "Yeah. Silas took us both out to the lake after school got out, that first year Denny lived with us. He said we were celebrating, because we both passed. But really, I think my mom was just ready to have us out of the house for a while. She said that even though Denny was just one more boy, he had this way of feeling like several."

"So, Silas took you camping?" Vance prodded.

"Yeah. We didn't go very far. Just out in the woods, a few miles from home. We had a tent, and sleeping bags, and this old camp stove. S'mores supplies, canned beans, and our fishing poles. And Silas, he had his rifle. Just in case we saw a deer."

"Did you see a deer?" I asked.

"No, but we caught several fish. We cleaned them right there on the lakeshore, then we took them back to the tent to cook them, but when we got there, there was this giant black cat in our tent, kind of...rifling through our stuff. We didn't know it was a shifter. We didn't know there *were* shifters. Silas had his rifle, but by the time he dropped all our gear and got the gun aimed, the cat had heard us. It tried to leave the tent, but we were kinda in its path, and everything was *crazy*. Silas was just standing there, aiming the rifle, shouting that he wanted to mount the cat's head on the wall, and it was like the cat could *understand* him.

"I mean, of course it could, but back then, we didn't know that was even possible, so anyway... The cat pounced. Silas fired the gun, but it wasn't a kill shot. The cat was wounded and scared, and it lashed out, while Silas was yelling at us to corner it, while he reloaded."

I blinked at him. "Your stepfather told you to corner an injured wildcat?" *Father of the year...*

"Yeah. We all wound up scratched—Denny's wound barely bled—and the cat ran off into the woods. Silas wanted to follow it. To get his trophy. But he was hurt pretty good. The cat shredded his shirt and gored him right here." Billy spread his right hand over the left side of his rib cage. "So, we packed up and went home."

"Where your mom sewed you up?"

"Yeah. Denny didn't need much more than a bandage, but Silas and I got stitches. That night, we were both burning up, but by the time my mom realized that ice baths weren't going to do the trick, Silas was already shifting. It happened to me right after that. She was *freaked* out." He shrugged. "But like I said, she'd heard rumors. And we'd told her about the cat in the woods."

"That was when you were fourteen?" Six years ago. Two years or so before the Pride was established. Three years before I was infected.

"Yeah," Billy said.

The poor kid never had a chance.

"So, tell us about Silas," Vance said. "How did he adjust to being a shifter?"

"He loved it." Billy frowned. "Can I get some juice? Or some water? I'm really thirsty."

Vance handed me his phone, which was still recording, and turned to grab a bottle of water from the case under the card table.

"Thanks," Billy said as Vance slid the bottle between the bars. "So, yeah, Silas loved it." He cracked open the bottle and drained half of it in a few gulps. "We all three did. We felt powerful. Fast and strong. We felt like we had this amazing secret. We saw really well in the dark, and we could lift really heavy things, and we could hear... Shit, we could hear people talk like we were fuckin' spies. But without the equipment. We felt like superheroes."

"And your mother?"

"She was paranoid, like I said. She thought that if anyone found out about us, they'd take us away from her and do experiments on us."

"So, you kept your secret."

"Yeah. For a long time. Then one day Silas came home and said he'd met another guy like us. He said the man smelled him in a crowd on the street and followed him to introduce himself." Billy's gaze found me, and suddenly I knew.

"Eamon," I whispered.

"Yeah. Silas invited him over, and Mom cooked for him. And he told us about everything. How we were strays, and how there are rules, and how the 'natural-born' cats will leave us alone if we follow the rules. How you can't tell anyone, and but you can still have fun, as long as that fun doesn't bring you to the attention of human law enforcement. Because if the 'council'"— He used air quotes.— "has a reason to hear about you, they'll come after you."

I glanced at Vance, who shrugged. Billy was not wrong. Back then, there had been no Mississippi Valley Pride. No Alpha, Marshalls, or enforcers to inform and protect the local shifter residents. And Pride cats preferred that strays remain out of sight and out of mind. Silent, obedient, and invisible.

"And he said there were no girl cats," Billy added. "Well,

no girl *strays*. He said there was a rumor that a girl survived being infected once, way down south, but that he'd never met one, so he wasn't even sure that was true. But Silas…well." He shrugged. "If you tell him he can't do something…"

My hand tensed around the edge of my seat, which I'd been clutching without even realizing it.

"So, he talked my mom into it."

Breath burst from my body on a surprised exclamation. "What?" I'd thought he was leading up to me. To my infection.

"Denny was only barely scratched, that day in the woods, so he didn't get sick when Silas and I did. We thought he wasn't going to, and he was pretty pissed about that. Then, a couple of days after Silas and I recovered from the fever, his scratch started looking puffy and infected. A day later, he had a fever. But his wasn't as bad as ours. He didn't get as sick as we did. Silas remembered that. So, he thought that if he just scratched my mom a *little* bit, she'd probably be fine."

"He knew that was illegal, right?" Vance interrupted, while I stared, transfixed, at Billy. Equally fascinated and repulsed by his story. By the history of the psychosis that had basically created me.

"He knew it was against the rules. But he said those were *their* rules, not ours. That if we weren't Pride cats, we didn't have to follow Pride cat law. And that my mom should get to make her own choice."

"Did she?" I asked. "Did she want to be infected?"

Billy shrugged. His pulse spiked again, just for a second. "I didn't see it happen. I just got up one morning, and she was making flapjacks and bacon, but she looked pale and kind of sweaty. When I asked if she was okay, she smiled and said she was going to be a shifter, just like me." He stared down at his fingers as they plucked at the thin sheet beneath him. "She didn't, though. She got really sick that night, and Silas wouldn't take her to the doctor. He said we couldn't, because they'd run tests. He said we had to take care of her, like she'd taken care of us. But nothing helped her. Not even the ice baths. She died before the sun came up."

"Oh my god." It took me a moment to realize I was the one speaking. I heard the words, but I couldn't really feel them. I hadn't meant to say them.

Silas killed his "wife." He'd experimented on her, heedless of the risk.

"Did Eamon know?" Vance asked.

Billy shook his head. "I don't think so. We buried her in the woods. I thought someone would come looking for her, but no one ever did. I don't think she had many friends, by then. Silas didn't like her to leave the house. She always said we were all she needed, anyway."

Billy drained the rest of his bottle and set it on the floor. "Things got bad after that. No body cleaned. No body cooked, or really shopped. Silas was mad all the time, and he had a hard time getting drunk, which just pissed him off. I stayed out of the house as much as I could, and one day I walked into town to look for a job. I thought I could flip burgers at that diner on Third, and they might let me bring home food no one wanted. But before I got there, I ran into Eamon. I hadn't seen him in a while, and he could tell something was wrong. I told him my mom had died and I didn't want to live with Silas anymore. That I was going to get a job and find some place to live on my own. And he said I could sleep on his couch for a while. 'Cause shifters in the community had to help each other out." Billy shrugged. "So, I did. And that's when I met you." He found my gaze again, and in that moment, he looked sadder than I'd ever seen him.

"So, you weren't with Silas after that?" Vance asked, when I couldn't seem to find the words.

"No. I was living with Eamon, working here. Then Eamon became the Marshal, and things started changing. And then one day, Charley was just gone."

"And you're saying you had no idea *why* I was gone?" There was a hard edge to my voice, despite my best effort to stay soft. To be friendly and receptive to whatever information he could give us. To be the person Billy would want to keep talking to.

I couldn't help it.

"No! I had no idea until you came back to work, and you smelled different. I could tell, then."

"And you could tell who infected me? You could smell him?"

"Yeah." Billy's pulse sped up a little, and it maintained that slightly elevated speed—a sign of ongoing stress. But I still couldn't tell that he'd told a single lie. "That's when Eamon took me aside and told me what had happened. By then, it was all over. Silas was dead. He said you'd executed him, and that was therapeutic. That now you could start to get better. And you *did* get better. Not just better than when you were first infected, but better than *before* you were infected. You'd been so upset before. Because of your brother."

"*No.*" I stood, and in the blink of an eye, I'd paced across half of the room. "This has nothing to do with Ben."

"It does, though." Vance's voice was calm and smooth, and I couldn't tell whether that was for my benefit or for Billy's. "Charley, can I see you outside, please?"

"No." I squared my shoulders and turned back to face him. Was it fair that I had to interrogate the suspect in a crime I was a victim of? No. And that would never have happened in the human justice system. This brutally unfair aspect of werecat law and order was the flip side of the same coin that had given me the right to execute Silas on my own behalf.

If I was willing to accept the benefits, I'd have to accept the costs.

"No," I repeated. "Let's keep going." I walked past Vance, headed toward the cell, but this time I didn't sit. "Was I targeted because of Ben? Because my brother was a shifter? Did you target me, Billy? Did you tell Silas about me?"

"No!" Billy's pulse spiked drastically before settling back into that elevated pace. "No. Charley, I swear, I didn't speak to Silas at all after I moved out. Not once since the day I moved in with Eamon."

"So, it's coincidence that I hired you, and a year later I was targeted by your stepfather? Kidnapped and infected against my will?"

Billy shrugged miserably. "I don't know about *coincidence*. It was probably Denny."

"By which you mean Camden Senet?"

Billy blinked. He glanced from me to Vance, then back, and I could practically see him assessing us. Trying to figure out how much we already knew.

"If you're innocent—if you had nothing to do with what Silas did—why have you failed to mention for at least the past year that one of our regulars—whom you saw here all the time—was Silas's son?" Vance demanded softly, as I paced back and forth in front of Billy's cell.

"Because I couldn't tell you who he is without telling you who I am!" Billy's frustrated shrug ended with his hands tossed into the air, like the flap of a crane's wings, only less graceful. "Are you...are you saying he killed Austin's sister? Bishop's wife? Is that why I'm here?" His focus volleyed between us again, faster. Panicked. "Is that why you were at the trailer this morning, before dawn? You thought *I* killed her?"

"Did you?" I sank into my chair again, staring straight at him, eye level.

"No! I never even met her!"

"Did Denny know her?"

"I have no idea! It's not like we hang out anymore. I haven't spoken to him since Charley was infected. I try not to even go out front, when I know he's out there, because—" His mouth snapped shut, his cheeks flushing slightly.

"Because you worried *he* would tell us who *you* are?"

"No, not really. I figured that if he got me fired, you'd toss him out, too. And I figured he thinks the same thing. Mutually assured destruction, or whatever. Only Cam and I aren't really enemies. Well, we weren't, anyway. Because I didn't know about Yvette. Charley, I swear. I was avoiding him because I was afraid that if we suddenly seemed to be old friends, you'd ask us how we knew each other, and if our answers weren't good enough, or if mine didn't match up with his, you'd keep digging, because that's what you do, and that meant that even being friendly with Denny felt kind of dangerous." Another shrug. "So, I just tried to steer clear of him. And he seemed fine with that."

"When was the last time you spoke to him?"

"Right after Charley was infected." Billy swallowed thickly. "Before that, though, I was trying to help him. Eamon had taught me all this stuff. About support systems, and how important it is for us to be there for each other. About how Titus was trying to form a community. About being resources for each other. And Denny didn't have any of that. So, I called him, and we started getting together on my days off. For…coffee."

Wherein coffee was actually weed, no doubt.

"And you told him about Charley?" Vance asked.

Billy shrugged. "I told him about everything. About everyone and everything I knew in the shifter community. I was trying to…show him a place he could belong. I'd found a new family, and I wanted him to have that too. And Ben had just died, so I told him how the community—what there was of it, back then—was coming together to mourn him and try to move forward together."

I had no doubt that he'd heard that—the exact phrasing—from Eamon.

"I told Denny how frustrated I was that there was nothing we could do for you and your family, because you were human. I told him how much I missed your dad, since your parents had moved, and—" Billy shrugged, looking helpless. "How much I thought you missed them too."

I had. I'd *really* missed my parents. Ben's death had been too much for them. They'd already been thinking about retiring, but after the funeral, they saw no reason to put it off. They were hurt. They couldn't stand to live in the house where we'd grown up—where Ben had grown up—anymore. So they'd signed the bar over to me and Davey and sold the house. And they'd moved to Florida. All within three months of Ben's death.

"So, Denny knew my brother was a shifter?" I asked, my voice low and as devoid of emotion as I could make it. "Before 'Cam' became a regular?"

"Yeah. But I didn't know what he was thinking. I didn't know what Silas had figured out. I didn't find out about any of that until afterward."

"Find out about what?"

Billy shrugged miserably. "That I wasn't the only one making friends. Learning stuff. Denny told me later—the last time I talked to him—that his dad had been trying to figure out what went wrong with my mom. Why she'd died, when we survived. He'd heard from some guy he met—a shifter—that some werecat scientist out west had discovered this gene. Or set of genes, or something. That you can't survive infection without them. He figured that he and Denny must have them, and I must too. But that I could have gotten those genes from my dad, instead of from my mom, and that's why she died, when we lived."

"And that gave Silas an idea…" I finished for him.

"Yeah. I didn't know it at the time, but Silas thought it could be done. That there could be female strays. And he thought the best bet would be to pick a woman he knew had that gene. I didn't realize I was giving him your name. I didn't know what he was planning until after you were already back at work, and he was dead. Until Eamon told me that you were still processing everything, and that might take a while, and I should just not tell you that I knew Silas, because you were still in a fragile state, and you might take that out on me, if you knew.

"So, I didn't tell you. But I did call Denny, because I didn't think it could be coincidence that I'd mentioned you and your family to him, and then his dad had kidnapped you. And infected you."

"And he admitted that?" Vance asked. "That he'd targeted Charley?"

"No. He didn't say he had anything to do with it, and I could tell from Charley's scent that he wasn't the one who bit her. But that's when he told me all that stuff. About genes, and Silas's idea. He said his dad had started talking about it like it was a mission. Some great deed he could do for the whole shifter community. To bring balance and ensure the survival of the species."

"That's fucking *nuts*," Vince swore, while I tried to stop my skin from crawling right off my body.

"Yeah," Billy agreed. "But by the time he told me, it was all over. Silas was dead. It was too late for me to…tell anyone. To stop it."

"So, for the record…" I cleared my throat, struggling to keep my voice steady. "Denny told you what his dad had 'figured out,' but he did not admit to taking part in my kidnapping and infection?"

"That's right," Billy said.

"Did you actually ask him if he was involved?" Vance demanded softly.

Billy sighed, staring at the hands clenched in his lap. "No. I should have. I *know* I should have. But the God's Honest is that I didn't want to know."

"Because he was your brother?" I had to admit, I might not want to know something like that about Davey.

"No." Billy looked up at me, his forehead furrowed, his brows drawn low. "Because I couldn't change anything. Because I felt guilty, and I knew you'd hate me if you found out, and I couldn't do a *goddamn* thing to undo it."

EIGHTEEN

"Seriously?" Tucker demanded as he pushed my office door closed, shutting my two enforcers and me off from the rest of the bar, where the day's first customers had just arrived. "Silas thought he was doing some kind of *good deed*?"

"According to Denny," I said.

"As related to us by Billy, anyway," Vance added.

"Hey," Bishop snapped from the hallway, as the doorknob turned. "Let us in."

With a sigh, I nodded, and Tucker let Bishop and Austin into the room, then closed the door behind them. My office suddenly felt crowded, but that was less about the number of bodies packed into the small space than about the fact that there were parts of this debrief that weren't going to be easy for the grieving brother and widower to hear. Or for me to say.

But they had just as much right to that information as I had.

"So, he admitted it?" Austin said as he sank into one of my guest chairs. He looked exhausted.

"Not exactly. He admitted that he found out, after the fact, that Denny was at least aware of Silas's plan for me, as it was…happening."

"And that Denny and Silas thought it was justified," Vance added, filling them in. "Silas felt 'driven' to start providing the shifter community with women of their own species. As if he were doing us all some great service."

"*What?*" Austin twisted in his seat, his gaze following Vance as he circled my desk.

"It's fucked up," I said as I sank into my own chair. "That wasn't so much an interrogation as the verbal equivalent of projectile vomit. Billy seemed eager to get the guilt of what he knew off his chest. But he couldn't verify for us that Denny was actually involved with my infection, beyond 'probably' giving my name to Silas. Which Denny got from Billy—inadvertently, Billy claims."

"And what did he know about Yvette?" Austin asked.

"Nothing that he admitted to. He seems to have no idea there were any victims between me and Yvette, though he admits that Denny seems a likely suspect in her case, based solely on the fact that he knew about the genetic factor and about Silas's 'mission.'"

Vince huffed. "And the fact that he's been going by a fake name—or at least a strategic nickname—since he inserted himself into the community."

"You've got to be *fucking kidding* me," Bishop growled, leaning forward with his elbows propped on his knees, his head in both hands. "Are we seriously saying that little shit didn't do it either?" He pointed at the floor, in the general direction of the basement staircase.

"I'm not prepared to say that Billy played no part in what Silas did," I said slowly, thinking each word through. "But I also see no indication that he was deliberately providing intelligence. And he doesn't know you or Austin. As far as any of us know, he didn't know Yvette either. And once Denny started coming around here as Cam Senet—a regular in his own right—he wouldn't have needed information from Billy."

"And you believe Billy's claim about why he never told us about Cam?" Tucker asked.

I shrugged. "I'm honestly not sure what to believe. Nothing in his physiological response to being questioned indicated a lie. Unless he's psychotic, and thus exhibits none of the normal physiological reactions to lying."

"I don't think that's the case," Vance said. "He was definitely nervous, but he seemed more concerned with preserving his position in the Pride—in the only family he has—than in hiding anything he knew, or the fact that he told Denny about Charley."

"So, you're saying he just wants to *fit in*?" Austin demanded softly.

"I'm saying that his biggest fear seemed not to be that we'd find out who he is and what part he did or didn't play in any of this, but that we'd hate him for it. Which Eamon seems to have led him to believe would be the case, justified or not."

"What about Denny?" Bishop said. "Why the hell would he carry on Silas's 'work?' Assuming he's the one we're actually looking for?"

"That's difficult to say, since we haven't spoken to him yet. But it's not beyond the realm of possibility that he actually bought into Silas's 'mission.'" I sighed as I leaned back in my chair. "According to Titus, they're not the first idiots to suffer that particular delusion of grandeur—a personal mandate to 'fix' our species gender imbalance. But based the numbers, I'd guess that Denny now qualifies as the most dedicated to the cause, historically."

"Is this a Frankenstein's Bride kind of scenario?" Tucker asked. "Were he and Silas trying to, like, make shifter girlfriends for themselves? Because I'm starting to think that most psychos are straight men. And that maybe that's their problem."

I rolled my eyes at him, but I didn't have the energy at the moment to argue his point.

"He didn't *say* they were trying to make girlfriends," Vance said. "But I don't think we can rule that out as Denny's real motive, considering how many failed human relationships he's had this year alone."

"Some girl named Tracy dumped him just last week. The night you guys first showed up in the bar," I added.

"So maybe he really is trying to make himself a 'bride,'" Austin said.

"For the record, we're calling that the Weird Science scenario," I added. "Because I'd much rather picture myself as a model sucked off the pages of a magazine than as a patchwork corpse brought to life by a bolt of lightning."

Austin shrugged. "Either way, it's disturbing that that's a common theme in some men's fantasy lives."

"Here, here." I lifted my empty shot glass and mimed a toast.

"My *wife*," Bishop growled, and the lack of focus in his gaze told me he'd tuned us out. "Yvette was the goddamn love of my life, and he thought, what? That he could just infect her and *take* her for himself?" He glanced at Austin. "Did he think she'd just leave us for the asshole who bit her?"

"We're not going to know what he was thinking until we can interrogate him. Where do we stand on that?" I asked, turning to Tucker. "I assume, since Austin is here, rather than staking out Cam Senet, that he wasn't home?"

"We don't actually have an address for him yet," Tucker admitted.

"Why? Is he not registered with the census?"

"He is, but there's no record of him ever actually living at the address he provided. Because it's a laundromat, attached to a Greek restaurant in downtown Buford."

"God*damn* it," I swore. "No one checked that address, when he registered it?"

"No, because that's never been the policy." Vance's voice was low and calm in response to my anger. "We've never had reason to verify addresses for voluntary registrants before."

"Okay, does anyone here think it's coincidence that he used a fake name and a fake address?" Bishop demanded. "Or can we please all agree that this Denny—Cam Senet—needs to be buried out in the woods somewhere? Assuming there's enough of him left to put in the ground, when I'm done with him."

"I agree that the case against him is pretty damning, at least circumstantially. Our top priority right now is finding him and bringing him in. *Alive*," I added with a sharp look at Bishop.

"Have you filled Titus in yet?" Tucker asked.

"No, but I left a message for him to call me. I feel like this isn't the kind of thing you say over voice mail. Or email."

"How did he know about Yvette?" Bishop glanced at each of us, silently demanding an answer. "Denny, I mean. I get that he found his other victims right here in the bar, from talking to the regulars?"

Ouch. True, but...I flinched at the reminder that Denny had likely been operating under our noses the whole time.

"But Austin and I aren't regulars. I'd never laid eyes on the bastard before we got here. So how the *fuck* did he even know my wife existed?"

I had no answer for him. Not even a theory.

"The only other shifter she even knew was Nolan Blake." Bishop stood, aggression pouring off him like fog rolling in from the ocean. "He must have said something about her. To Billy. Or even to Denny. Do we know if Nolan knows Denny? Are they friends? Drinking buddies at the bar?"

"All of the regulars know each other," Vance said. "I've seen you drinking with half a dozen of them in the past week."

"So, they *do* know each other?" Bishop persisted. "Nolan and Cam?"

"Sit down," I said.

Bishop spun to glare at me, fists clenched, and the tension in my office was suddenly too thick to breathe through, as Vance and Tucker seemed to swell up behind him. Taking up more than their fair share of space in my defense.

"*Sit,*" I growled without leaving my chair. Without even leaning forward. "Unless you want me to have you removed."

Bishop's gaze narrowed on me, and I could practically see him assessing the situation. Trying to decide how far he could push me.

Finally, he sat.

"It is entirely possible that Cam got Yvette's name from Nolan Blake," I admitted. "But that doesn't mean that Nolan intended to be providing him with a victim. Considering how difficult it is for most of the regulars to maintain a relationship, he could very well have been talking about the ones he knew to be successful. Trying to spread hope."

"You don't know that's true," Bishop growled.

"And you don't know it isn't. The fact that Nolan knew

your wife existed doesn't make him complicit in her death. Even if he happened to mention her to a man he had no idea was a serial killer." I leaned forward in my chair, folding my arms on top of my desk. "*Stay away* from Nolan Blake."

Bishop's eyes narrowed even further, but he didn't argue.

"I'm going to need you to verbally acknowledge that order," I added.

Bishop's nostrils flared. His brows dipped, and Tucker stepped closer to his chair. Which Bishop clearly either heard or felt. "Acknowledged," he finally growled. And I tried not to let my relief show.

"Does Billy know where Denny lives?" Austin asked, obviously trying to move us past the tension and steer the discussion back on track.

"He says he doesn't, and a cursory glance through his phone supports that. They don't seem to be in touch." Vance pulled the device in question from his hip pocket and tossed it to Tucker. "Feel free to do a deeper dive into that. It's unlocked."

Austin huffed. "Must be nice not to need a warrant."

"Helps make up for the fact that we lack the technological resources of even the most rural police department," I told him.

"Okay." Bishop glanced around at each of us. "So, now what?"

"Now, we find Cam and bring him in. Though, if he doesn't know we're looking for him, there's every chance in the world he'll come in on his own for a beer." I shrugged. "He was here last night. But we're not just going to wait for that," I assured Bishop, before he could start yelling. "I'm going to go back downstairs and find out every single thing Billy can remember about Denny, in hopes that'll give us some idea of where to look. And while I'm down there, Tucker will continue to search for an address online."

"You need to rest," Austin said. "You can't go down there compromised by exhaustion."

Vance eyed me with one eyebrow raised. "I'm sure Titus would agree," he said softly. Gently threatening to go over my head.

I rolled my eyes at them both. "Fine."

Austin shrugged. "I'd talk to him, but he doesn't know or trust me."

"Which means you and Bishop can get some sleep too," I told him. "Vance can prod Billy for more information."

Vance nodded. "I'll meet you back here in…" He glanced at the clock on his lock screen. "Four hours."

"Deal. And no one other than Vance goes into the basement during those four hours. Got it? Billy's been fed and he has everything he needs. Understood?"

Heads nodded all around the room. "Four hours," Vance repeated to me as he opened the office door. "Get some sleep."

NINETEEN

Despite my exhaustion, I lay in bed with the blinds drawn for half an hour, my thoughts racing, before I finally got up and swallowed six Tylenol PM tablets. Before I was infected, one would knock me out for a good eight hours.

These days it took half a dozen to make me drowsy, and my body metabolized them way too fast for me to get the full effect. Or duration.

I did finally doze off, but I'd been awake again and staring at the ceiling for twelve minutes before my alarm went off.

Ten minutes later, I headed downstairs, my hair still damp from the shower. I was exhausted, but clean and wearing fresh clothes, and on days like today, that was about the best I could hope for.

I plodded through the kitchen like a zombie with barely a glance at Mitch, who was slicing veggies in the mid-afternoon lull. Out front, I smiled and greeted a couple of regulars at the bar as I headed straight for the coffee pot.

"Sit." Vance turned me by both shoulders to face the bar.

"What? Why?"

"Eat," he said, and I found myself staring at a huge plate of chicken nachos with black beans and pickled jalapeños, served with sour cream and roasted salsa. "Mitch is no celebrity chef, but he makes a damn good plate of nachos."

"Thanks. They smell great. But we need to—"

"Titus said he'd ground you and put me in charge if you tried to work without at least four hours of sleep, two cups of coffee, and a good meal. Did you get four hours?"

"Four and a half," I lied with a straight face.

Vance rolled his eyes. "Eat. I'll fill you in when you're done, and you'll be thinking much clearer on a full stomach."

"He's not wrong," Davey whispered. Just in case either of our two customers was listening. "But if you wanted to eat this in your office, with the door closed…" Her brows rose. "Where you could safely fill me in on—"

"Sorry." I stuffed an overloaded chip into my mouth and spoke around it. "Can't possibly talk. Under orders to eat." And I must have looked ridiculous with my cheeks puffed out like a chipmunk, because she actually laughed instead of getting mad.

"You do owe me an update, though," she said as she moved down the bar to continue slicing limes. Which meant that none of the others had filled her in either, probably because Bishop was the most likely to do that without my permission, and he and Austin were still at their apartment, hopefully sleeping. "Also, this came for you." She set my new cell phone, still in the box, on the bar in front of me."

"Thanks."

I lifted the bar flap and carried my plate, mug, and new phone to the corner booth, where I stuffed my face in peace for the next ten minutes, while my new phone "cloned" my old one.

But I was only two-thirds of the way through my huge

meal and half-way through the data transfer when the front door flew open, ringing the bell dangling above it. I looked up as, to my speechless surprise, a toddler ran into the bar.

A *toddler*.

I popped up from my seat, coughing to dislodge the chunk of chicken I'd nearly aspirated as the dark-haired little boy wobbled across the room, squealing in delight. He darted between two unoccupied bar stools and planted both chubby palms against the front of the bar, then let out a gleeful squeal of triumph, as if he'd just crossed some sort of finish line.

"Wilder!" A female voice called in equal parts amusement and censure, and I turned as a woman followed him inside. "Sorry, everyone." She aimed a smile at the entire room. "He doesn't get out much, and at this age, they think everything is an adventure."

She tossed long, dark waves over one shoulder, and just as I realized I recognized her—those defined cheekbones and piercing green eyes—another, equally startling understanding fell into place.

Her child wasn't human.

That little boy—that *toddler*—was a shifter. I'd caught his scent as he'd raced past me, but I hadn't had a chance to process either it or the shock that had accompanied that understanding until I realized that the woman who'd come in after him was none other than Faythe Sanders.

Faythe motherfucking Sanders. The only female Alpha in the world.

I stared at her with my mouth hanging open, as did every single man in the bar. She was goddamn glorious, with that hair and those black boots. Snug maroon slacks and a beige silk blouse with a long bow at the throat, and a slim leather bag that could have held either diapers or a revolver, or both.

No, wait, Pride cats don't carry guns. That's kind of a point of pride with them. No pun intended.

Before I could gather my thoughts or think of a single intelligent thing to say, Davey dashed around the bar and scooped the little boy—Faythe Sanders's son—up into her arms, cooing at him as if he were a puppy she'd just found on the side of the road.

"Hi." Faythe smiled at the entire room, her gaze lingering for a moment on her son in my sister's arms. "I'm looking for —" Her focus found me, and her smile widened. "Charley." She took two steps forward, holding one hand out for me to shake.

I made my mouth snap shut. "Yes. Charlene Studebaker. Marshal of the northern zone."

"Faythe Sanders." Her handshake was firm, her skin soft and warm. She smelled like a complex combination of *cat* and *woman* yet somehow different than either Robyn or Kaci, both of whom had been born human. And beneath those strong main scents were subtly woven threads of both *power* and *mother*. And also *strength*. As distinct from power.

Faythe was clearly many things. And those were just the ones I could observe over the course of one handshake.

God, she was cool.

Davey gave me a weird look. Which was when I remembered to let go of the Alpha's hand.

"This place is *great*," she said, her gaze roaming the neon lettering and the backlit bottles. The patched booths, worn barstools, and the polished wooden bar itself, the centerpiece of the large front space. "It's yours?"

"Yeah, it's—"

"*Ours*," Davey finished for me. "Our parents left it to both of us."

"Oh, I'm so sorry!" Faythe said. "I didn't realize…"

"They're not dead," I told her. "They just moved to Florida."

"Not that there's a whole lot of difference!" Davey quipped, her voice high-pitched and sugary sweet with baby talk as she twirled her finger around one of the little boy's curls.

"This is my sister, Davey. I swear she doesn't usually manhandle other people's children."

"That's not true!" Davey cooed to the boy. "I pick up every child I see!"

"Nice to meet you, Davey." Faythe crossed the room toward them, though she seemed in no hurry to reclaim her son. She clearly knew my sister was no threat. "This is Wilder. My youngest. And let me tell you, he lives up to his name."

"Hi, Wilder!" Davey smoothed one hand down his back. "How old are you?"

The boy held up two fingers.

Faythe smiled. "Not quite. He'll be two next month."

"He's adorable," Davey told her.

"He certainly is." But I was less comfortable than my sister was having him in the bar. This was the infant son of not just one, but *two* Alphas. Including the only female Alpha in history. *She* was a goddamn national treasure. So what did that make her child?

I was not set up to protect and defend Faythe Sanders and her baby. If something happened to her on my watch, I would never forgive myself.

Neither would anyone else.

I made eye contact with Vance and nodded toward the kitchen, silently telling him to go secure the rear exit. Which was when I realized there was a large—*large*—man dressed all in black standing in front of the swinging doors.

The back, clearly, was already secure.

"I was hoping we could have a little chat," Faythe said, and her voice was now hyper smooth. The kind of calm that can only be deliberate. Rehearsed. It was a subtle display of vast strength—*no need to worry, I am in* total *control*—and I was both impressed and a little threatened.

I couldn't be sure which of those was her intent, but I was no longer worried about protecting Faythe Sanders or her kid. She did *not* need my help.

"A chat. Yeah, sure."

Faythe turned to address the entire room. "Gentlemen, could you please excuse us?"

When no one moved—I think our two customers were in shock over her scent alone—she cleared her throat and tried a rephrase. "The bar is going to close for about an hour." This time her voice held a hint of a growl, and chills rolled across my skin at just the sound. There was no question that she would be obeyed.

Both of the regulars drained their glasses and headed toward the door, staring at her as they passed. Faythe eyed Vance expectantly, one brow raised.

"Oh, Vance works for me. He stays," I added, and I felt like a bit of a badass for insisting.

One corner of Faythe's mouth quirked up. "Of course. Nice to meet you, Vance. This is Vic."

The guy blocking the way to my kitchen nodded without a word. He was in his mid-thirties and graying at the temples, but solidly built and no-doubt still super-fucking deadly.

"Wilder, do you want to play with Davey while Charley and I talk?" Faythe asked, smoothing the child's hair while he still sat on my sister's hip.

The little boy nodded, blinking big green eyes.

"Oh, we don't have any toys," Davey said. "We don't usually have kids in the bar."

Faythe threw her head back as she laughed, long hair swaying. She opened the leather bag and showed its contents to Davey. "If he gets bored with those, just give him a wooden spoon and a plastic bowl, and he'll be thrilled—and loud—for hours.

Toys. Her stylish leather bag held toddler toys.

Davey settled onto the floor with the little boy, in the cleanest spot she could find, and set several toys from the bag in front of him, while Faythe marched across the room and twisted the deadbolt on the front door.

Vance took up a position near Davey and Wilder, acting as backup in case anyone got past Vic.

"Let's sit." Faythe headed toward the booth where the remainder of my lunch was growing cold. "Please. Finish your meal," she said. "It smells good."

"Can I get you anything?" Davey asked.

"Maybe just a glass of ice water," she said, and before Davey could stand, Vance waved one hand at her, gesturing that he would get it. "Thank you."

As I slid into the booth, I noticed, through the front windows, that though our two regulars had left the bar, they were still waiting in the parking lot, in their cars.

Not that I could really blame them. I was literally the only female werecat they'd ever seen. They'd no doubt heard of Faythe Sanders but had probably never in their lives hoped to meet her.

There was another car in the lot. A black SUV. Through the tinted windows, I could see the outlines of three heads and three sets of very broad shoulders.

"Your men?" I asked, nodding at the vehicle. "Your husband? Marc? Would he like to come in?"

She smiled. "Marc stayed in Jackson at the party, with my two older sons."

The party. For Kaci's birthday.

"How is Kaci?"

Faythe shrugged. "You probably hear from her more than I do, these days."

"No, not really. Just that she's doing well in school. From Titus."

Faythe frowned. "You never see her? Ole Miss is only an hour and a half from here."

"If traffic is kind, yeah. But that's Jace's zone, and I have my hands full here. I don't get down there much, and Jace and Justus don't let Kaci out of their sight, basically...ever."

Faythe's frown deepened. "When she finishes school, I'd like that to change." She exhaled heavily. "I'd like a *lot* to change, actually. You and I need to become less of a proto-type and more of a...type. A ubiquity."

"Women...in power?" I guessed. *No complaint here.*

The corner of her mouth quirked up again. "Women with claws. Who use them."

"And Kaci doesn't?" I'd only met her a few times, but I'd gotten the impression that she wasn't exactly...tame.

"Oh, she does. When she graduates, Titus will hire her. She'll get some experience under her belt, just like I did. But we're gonna need more like her. More like *you.*"

"Okay, I have to be honest," I said as I leaned back against the booth. "I'm not sure what we're talking about. Or—"

"What the hell I'm doing here?" Faythe's head tilted slightly to the right. "Without a word of warning?"

"Well...yes."

Her smile widened, and for the first moment since she'd walked into the bar, Faythe felt...approachable. "The truth is that I've been meaning to come see you for quite a while. But things haven't exactly gone as planned for me over the past couple of years." She aimed an open-handed gesture at the toddler. "See exhibit A."

I couldn't resist a grin. "Wilder was a surprise?"

"Yes. A welcome one, but a very, very unexpected one. Who came very close to his brother." She shrugged. "Which kept me close to home much longer than expected."

"I can imagine." Though I could really *only* imagine. I did intend to have kids someday. But "someday" felt about a decade away.

"So anyway, I thought that while I was in the territory, I should make time to come up here and launch a hopefully ongoing discussion of our mutual interests."

"I'm glad you have, but I wish you'd told me! I would have come to you, to save you the trip." Not that this was a good time for me to leave the zone, exactly.

"Well, the truth is that I wanted you to myself for a little while. *Mostly* to myself," she amended, tossing a smile at Davey. Vance and Vic evidently didn't count. "And I wanted to see the famous Fat Cat! I wish we had a place like this in Texas. Not that we really have a shifter population dense enough to keep it afloat."

"Okay…" My nerves were back. What on earth could Faythe Sanders want to discuss with me? Without Titus or her husband and co-Alpha present?

"Titus has filled me in on the situation you guys are dealing with up here. I believe you have a suspect in custody?"

"Yes, but he's not looking entirely culpable, at the moment. We've identified what we believe to be the true culprit, though, and we hope to have him in custody very, very soon. Later today, in fact." I mentally crossed my fingers as I injected as much confidence into my tone and bearing as I could.

Faythe nodded, holding my gaze. "And you believe that this is all related to your own infection? What, three years ago?"

"Yes. Our primary suspect is the son of the man who infected me, and he might have been involved in my infection as well. Though we didn't realize that at the time."

"I assume Titus has told you that there's a somewhat long and rather inglorious history of men in our community trying to increase the number of women of our species, on their own terms? Invariably through violent and involuntary means?"

"Yes, he mentioned that." I sipped from the glass of water standing in front of me, which was when I noticed that Vance had brought me one too.

"I have an idea for how to stop that." Faythe hesitated, her eyes slightly narrowing. "For how to remove the 'need' these men think they're fulfilling. For how to put the power—the *decision*—into the hands of women themselves. Where it always should have been." She shrugged, but the gesture looked anything but casual and impulsive.

She knew exactly what she was saying.

Her trip to see me had not been spontaneous, and neither were her words. Every single bit of this had been planned out. I could see that, even if I had no idea what she was about to say.

"When men of our species start talking about needing more shifter women, they're not being honest about what they actually want," Faythe said. "They *say* they want to ensure the survival of the species, but you and I both know the shifter population isn't in decline. The density of your zone illustrates that pretty clearly."

I nodded. She was not wrong.

"What *natural-born* shifter men actually want isn't more members of our community in general, but more 'purebred' members, like themselves. Which can only be conceived by shifter women. And what *most* shifter men—both stray and natural-born—want is women they don't have to keep their species secret from. Women they don't have to worry about infecting."

"I mean…" Davey shrugged as she made a toy dance for Wilder. "That last one doesn't sound totally unreasonable."

"It isn't an unreasonable thing to want," Faythe conceded. "But it's a very difficult thing to *get*, for most shifter men. And no male shifter is entitled to his wants at the expense of a woman's choice in the matter. The choice to marry and/or have shifter babies, or the choice to become a shifter in the first place."

Davey nodded, clearly still thinking through all the implications.

Faythe turned back to me. "The problem is multi-faceted, obviously. The requirement for secrecy usually prevents shifter men from having true intimacy with a human woman."

Emotional unavailability: a problem we were all well-acquainted with, in the "stray" Pride.

"And those men who *are* in relationships with human women run the risk of accidentally infecting them," I added, tugging on the thread of her logic. "It's a low risk for casual relationships, but I'm guessing that risk increases the longer the relationship lasts, because of the frequency of intimate contact." Which was why I kept Davey strictly off limits to the men in the zone. *All* of them

"Exactly." Faythe nodded. "Infecting someone—even accidentally—is a capital offense, and men aren't allowed to disclose the possibility of infection. Which means long-term relationships put them at risk of execution, and human women can't make an informed choice for themselves about whether or not to accept the risk of infection and death."

"And occasionally, a problematic few of those frustrated men decide to try to *make* shifter women for themselves— even if women die in that effort."

Femicide, in the quest for a more convenient, satisfying relationship.

Faythe nodded again. "And while that crime itself has been rare up to now, the mindset that inspires it isn't. And when what's happening here in your zone becomes public, I'm worried that more men will be inspired to try it. Probably out in the free zones, where they're less likely to get caught by us, but more likely to expose our species to the public. Which is why I'm here." She leaned toward me over the table. "I have an idea that might stop shifter men from infecting human women illegally, against their will. Both intentionally and accidentally."

"Wow. Okay. May I ask how?"

Her green eyes practically glowed. "By making infection legal. Carefully regulated and *entirely* above board. And by taking volunteers."

TWENTY

"Wait, what?" I blinked at Faythe from across the table, trying to process what she'd just said. "You want to make it *legal* to infect women?"

"I want to establish an official process. But only in very limited, specific cases. Only for women who *qualify*, and who *volunteer*. I am absolutely *not* talking about a free-for-all 'infect the woman of your choice' -palooza. I'm not talking about individual werecats scratching or biting people *at all*. I'm talking about an official, approved, controlled, medically regulated process. A *volunteer* process."

"Okay, wait." My head spun. Davey was staring at us like her brain had just exploded. "How can they volunteer if they don't know shifters even exist? And *why* would they volunteer if scratch fever kills more than ninety-nine percent of the women infected?"

"That's two questions. I'll take them in order." Faythe sipped from her glass, her eyes sparkling with excitement. Which was when I realized—*really* realized—she was serious. She was *dead fucking serious*. "They would have to know. Obviously. And the truth is that some women already know. They aren't supposed to, but you know better than anyone that that system is untenable. My understanding is that one of the victims you're fighting for...she knew her husband was a shifter?"

"And her brother," I said.

Faythe nodded. "My brother's wife, Holly, she knows too. It's virtually impossible, in some cases, to keep our species a secret, and that's only going to get harder as time goes by. So, my idea is that we start with those women. The ones who already know. The ones who *want* to belong to the same world as their brothers and husbands. As their fathers and friends."

I could still feel Davey staring at me. At Faythe. She'd stopped breathing. She was *holding her breath*, listening to us.

"But—again—why would they risk it?" I asked. "Knowing they'd almost certainly die?"

"The women we're talking about, at least initially, are already taking that risk, just by being in long-term relationships with shifters. Our goal would be to lower the danger. Mitigate the risk. And we're not ready to start this yet, obviously. But a friend of mine is a doctor, and his brother is a geneticist, and they've been working on this problem for years. They're the ones who discovered the genetic element to surviving infection. And they've learned even more in the time since then. They believe that under the right circumstances—in the right environment—we could change those numbers dramatically."

I blinked at her. "The survival rates? You can change—presumably improve—the survival rates?"

"Yes. The Carvers believe that if these volunteer women were screened to make sure they were viable candidates and were infected in a controlled environment, constantly monitored by doctors administering IV fluids and a special antibiotic they've developed specifically for this purpose... And that if we can control the dose of the infection itself—"

"Wait, what does that mean?" The *dose* of the infection?

"So, when someone is scratched or bitten, there's no way to control how much of the infecting cat's genetic material is transferred from infector to infectee, for lack of a better term. But under the ideal environment, that infection could be controlled. Testing could determine exactly how much to administer, likely by injection, along with an initial dose of that antibiotic to preemptively fight the accompanying infection. Scratch fever. The Doctors Carver think there might actually be a safe way for women who're genetically eligible and want to be a part of our world to be given that opportunity."

"Oh my god." I couldn't think of what else to say. The images floating behind my eyes were of an old bed in a rickety cabin with a single filthy window. Handcuffs restraining me to the bed frame. A feverish sweat. Hours and hours of pain and nausea.

And she was saying it didn't have to be that way? That it could be like any normal medical procedure, in a controlled hospital or clinic environment? Under constant medical supervision?

That it could be a *choice*?

"Oh my god."

"And it goes beyond just the survival rate." Her eyes were shining again. *Glowing* with the possibilities. "I understand that I'm preaching to the choir here, so forgive me for telling you something you already know, but strays are typically initiated into our world in trauma. Their first exposure to their new existence is fear and pain, and a complete incomprehension of their new abilities, limitations, and responsibilities.

And I can only assume that trauma is even more intense for women, when they discover how very alone they are in this world. Am I right? How they've been set up as potential victims, right from the start?"

More so than I could ever hope to explain to her. So I only nodded.

"We could fix that too. Volunteers would know what they were getting into. They could be educated and counseled in advance. They could be psychologically screened. They could have an 'ambassador' of their choice present—along with their Alpha, of course—to shepherd them through both scratch fever and the initial shift. They would *never* be alone or vulnerable.

"Titus has a pilot program along those lines in place now, for male strays in Jackson, and he's had great success with it." She took another quick sip of her water, then barreled forward. "We have the opportunity to offer the very best parts of the shifter life to interested and qualified women, while mitigating—in some cases eliminating—the worst parts. We have an opportunity to change things. To shape our world for the better, in ways our society has never even dreamed of."

"Sounds like it." I nodded slowly. "But I have to ask… why? I mean, why would we do that? You just said that we don't really need more female shifters, so…why?"

"To fix the imbalance."

I opened my mouth to object, but she spoke over me.

"Not *that* imbalance. I don't care about the ratio of men to women. What I care about is that there are already women in our world who are not *of* our world but want to be, and they're being denied that option. Excluded and held apart from people they love. And there are women who don't even know our world exists, who're being dragged into it against their will, violently and traumatically. Like you were. *That* imbalance is fucked up. And if we admit into our world the women who want to be here, it will look to the men who still mostly run things like we're fixing the problem *they* believe exists."

"How big a problem do they believe that is, exactly? I mean, I get that there's a gender imbalance and they want more girls to be born, but is it really that big a deal?"

Faythe stared at me for a moment as if she were trying to figure something out. Finally, she tilted her head slightly to one side, and long dark hair fell over her shoulder. "Charley, are you aware that the Territorial Council doesn't know you exist?"

"What do you mean? Titus told them I survived infection, and I spoke to them on a video conference. Nearly three years ago."

Faythe smiled. "If I recall, you told them you would not be marrying any of their sons."

"Yeah. And Titus had to inform you all when he fired Eamon and hired me, and—"

"Yes, but he just said the new Marshal's name is Charley. They have no idea that Char*lene* Studebaker is the Charley running the northern zone. They think the Marshal is Charlie-with-an-I-E. Most have inferred that that's short for Charles. They don't know you're in innie, rather than an outie, and if they *had* known, they would never have let Titus hire you."

"You're fucking kidding," Davey swore.

Faythe turned to her with both brows arched. "I wish I were. And on another note, I know you're not a shifter, but just so you're aware, cursing in front of an Alpha is typically not permitted. And in human society, I believe the same goes for toddlers." She nodded with a grin at her son.

"Oh, shit. *Shit!*" Davey slapped her hand over her mouth.

"I'm so f-ing sorry. Damn. I mean *dang*! That's going to take some work."

Faythe laughed. "Yeah, it really does. I accidentally taught my three-year-old to say 'fuck me!'—" she mouthed the words "—when he stubbed his toe, and my mother didn't speak to me for a week." She shrugged. "It helps to think of being around an Alpha—and possibly a Marshal—like being around your parents. Same rules apply."

"Yeah, that might help," I said. "If we hadn't grown up in a bar. I was correcting the spelling of *shitweasel*—" I whispered the word. "—on the men's room walls before I was old enough for my first spelling bee."

Faythe frowned, trying to decide whether or not I was joking. Then she burst into more laughter. "I like you."

I liked her too. It was really, unexpectedly good to talk to another female shifter.

"So, you're serious? The council thinks I'm a man?"

"Yes, and they have no idea Davey exists."

Which I'd already known.

"Why wouldn't they have let Titus hire me?" I asked. "*You're* an Alpha."

"I'm *co*-Alpha. Which allows certain members of the council to believe that's a title I hold in name only, and that my husband makes all of the actual decisions. Not that they like that much better, considering that Marc is a stray, and they wanted me to marry one of their natural-born sons."

"Seriously?"

Faythe nodded. "When I was Davey's age, there were a lot of political machinations afoot, with my marriage being the ultimate goal. Those sitting on the Territorial Council back then, several of whom have since passed, were willing to destroy the South-Central Pride to get what they wanted."

She took a deep breath. "They killed my father in the process."

"Jesus. Now I see why your alliance with Titus is so strong."

Her smile was small, but genuine. "The Mississippi Valley and the South-Central Prides have several mutual interests. Also, we just really like Titus. And Jace. And *you*."

I bit my tongue before I could ask about the old rumors about her and Jace.

"But my point with all this is that some men—both council members and lone wolf crackpots—have always believed it is not only their right but their *duty* to preserve the shifter species through whatever means they deem necessary. The council has spent decades trying to breed tabbies, while individual psychos try to infect human women, and neither of them have given *us* any real choice in that matter. But if there were more of us—if women came into this world strong and unified, instead of scared and cowed, and isolated—we could…"

"We could what?" There was something I couldn't see. Something I still couldn't understand.

"We could be a force in the shifter community."

I could only frown at her. "Aren't you already a force?" A fucking *legend*?

"On a good day, I am a thorn in the sides of some very powerful men, and proud of it. But I want to be much more than that. I want *you* to be much more than that."

A tingle started at the base of my spine. "You're definitely speaking my language," I told her. "But…Titus is the Alpha, so…"

"And he's a great Alpha," Faythe said, reassuring me of her support for him. "But Alphas aren't the only ones capable of making a true impact in our world. And the leader these women are going to need isn't an Alpha. Not really. They're going to need more than that. They're going to need someone who understands where they've been and where they're going. Someone who understands the specific challenges they're going to be facing.

"*We* are what they need, Charley. We can bring them together and support them. We can help mold them into a unified force able and willing to stand up for itself." Faythe looked at me with those intense green eyes, and I couldn't understand how anyone in the world had ever told her no. How anyone had ever wanted to. In that moment I believed in everything she was saying. That I was there in that time and place for a *reason* and that everything that had happened to me had a purpose. That my trauma could be someone else's power. That it could be *my* power. That I could own it and turn it into something *amazing*. And that she could help me do that.

That I could help *her* do that.

So when she asked me the question I knew was coming— "Charley, are you in?"—there was only one possible answer.

"Yes. Of course. Just tell me what you need."

"It's early days, obviously." She leaned against the back of the booth, evidently more relaxed, now that she had my answer. "But with you in, we can move forward. I'll let Dr. Carver know, and we'll keep you apprised. I think we should move slowly in public; big changes tend to scare people. But that doesn't mean things won't be happening quickly behind the scenes."

My heart seemed to beat with a new rhythm. An urgency inspired by this new purpose. Somehow, despite the killer on the loose—a traitor still literally in my midst—the world seemed brighter.

I felt…focused.

"Does Titus know about this?"

"Yes, of course, and he's in total support. As are Jace, Robyn, Abby, and Kaci, which is why they were all on board with me taking this little mid-party detour. But no one else needs to know until further notice, so I'm trusting everyone else in this room to please keep this in strict confidence. It's my understanding that your sister is good at keeping secrets."

"I am *made* of secrets," Davey said from the floor, where Wilder was crawling over her left thigh to reach for a toy he'd dropped. "Vance is too."

Vance nodded, his protective gaze still glued to Davey and the toddler.

"What do you think the first steps will be?" I asked, turning back to Faythe at our booth.

"Well, I know the Carvers are still fine-tuning the design of their antibiotic compound, and I don't think they've yet started testing amounts of genetic material for infection. But I suspect they will be ready to start making lists of potential volunteers."

I could practically feel Davey's ears perk up, and I avoided looking at her. She wouldn't understand, because she didn't *want* to understand, that this was still in very early stages. They were nowhere near ready for actually injecting those volunteers. This wasn't safe yet. Faythe's plan was likely *years* from actually being put into action.

All of that would have to be a private conversation between me and my sister after, Faythe had left.

"I think he's, um, *poopy*," Davey called from across the room.

"Oh, here." Faythe popped up from the booth and was halfway across the floor before I'd even rotated my legs toward the open end of the booth. "Let me—"

"Oh, no, I got it." Davey stood, holding the toddler and leather bag.

Faythe glanced at her in surprise. "Have you ever changed a diaper?"

Davey shrugged. "How hard can it be? This girl in my high school got pregnant at fourteen, and she managed."

Faythe laughed. "Well, I'm not gonna turn that down. There are diapers and wipes in the inner pocket," she added, waving one hand at the bag already looped over my sister's shoulder.

"You can use my office," I said. "*Not* the kitchen." I was pretty sure there was some county health ordinance about diapers in food prep areas.

Vance took the bag from Davey. "I'll give you a hand." They disappeared through the swinging doors into the kitchen, and Vic went with them, no doubt to keep a protective eye on the inexperienced babysitters.

Faythe smiled as she turned to me. "They make such a cute couple."

"Who?" I blinked at her, confused as she stared at the swinging kitchen door. My focus had already returned to the possibilities for the future of women in the Pride. For *my place* in that world.

"Your sister and your enforcer," she said.

"Davey and Vance?" I laughed. "Oh, no, they're not—" A screeching sound echoed in my ears, like a siren going off from far away, and distantly, I realized no one else could hear it. "I mean they're not a—"

My head shook, back and forth, back and forth, and I couldn't make it stop.

I would *know* if they were—

"He looks out for her because I asked him to. I moved

Davey into the apartment next to his, specifically for that purpose. But they're not—"

Vance lived in the apartment next to my sister's. Where *I* had put her. An apartment he'd cleaned from top to bottom with bleach, the very day he knew I would be searching it.

Bleach, which could kill any trace of my sister's scent.

Oh my God. How had I never seen it?

If their connection was obvious enough for Faythe to notice the moment she saw them together, how had I *not* known? How long had it been going on?

"I hope I didn't step in something." Faythe stood, tugging her blouse into place. Straightening her slacks. "I didn't realize you didn't know. Vance seems like a good guy."

"The best," I confirmed, my voice hollow with shock.

"Like someone you trust."

"More than anything. With my life. With my sister's life." My words sounded like they were coming from the other end of a long tunnel.

The kitchen door swung open. Davey reappeared with the toddler on her hip, and Vance came in behind her carrying Faythe's bag. My sister returned the toddler to his mother, then she scooped up all the toys from the floor and dropped them into the bag.

"Charley, it's been such a pleasure," Faythe said as Wilder tugged at her hair, chanting what sounded like a nursery rhyme into her ear. "You'll be hearing from me very soon, and likely fairly often. I have your phone number. I'll text you so you'll have mine."

"That sounds good. Thank you so much for bringing this to me. I'm very excited for what this is going to do for the Pride." But the words felt like mush in my mouth. Tasteless. Formless. I wasn't even truly aware of what I was saying. As absorbed as I'd been moments ago by this new mission, suddenly I could think of nothing but my sister and my best friend. The two people I had trusted most in the world.

Until that moment.

Vic opened the door and helped Faythe and Wilder to the car, where several other enforcers got out to help buckle the child into his car seat. But rather than re-opening the bar for business, I locked the door behind them and turned to my sister and my most trusted enforcer and friend. Stealing a moment of privacy from the workday.

"Well, she seems *awesome*," Davey said, her eyes alight with excitement. I knew what she wanted to discuss, but that was not going to happen.

"Yeah, she is." I could hear the anger resonating in my voice. "And she says you two make an *adorable* couple." With that I marched past them toward the bar.

For a moment, silence reigned at my back. Then Davey's footsteps raced after me, quick and light. "Charley!" she called out.

"*Shit*," Vance breathed.

"Charley, wait!" Davey cried. "Please!"

I spun to face them instead of pushing through the kitchen doors. "I guess that's all the confirmation I need." My focus shifted from her to Vance, anxiety—betrayal—crawling over the surface of my skin. "You're fired. And expelled from the zone. Pack your shit. Drive straight to Jackson. Titus will be expecting you in four hours."

"Charley *please*," Davey begged.

"Let me explain," Vance added.

"No need," I practically growled. "I asked you to keep an eye on my sister. To protect her. You *knew* she was off-limits. You gave me your word, and you broke it. You—my *top* enforcer—you flouted the rules and undercut my authority. You broke my trust. You broke my heart. You put my sister at risk." I sucked in a deep breath, but that only fed the fire burning inside me. "You can*not* be here anymore. If Titus wants to hire you, so be it, but you're done in the northern zone. *Get. Out.*"

"*Charley!*" Davey shouted, her voice hoarse and half broken. Her pain tore at me like claws caught in my flesh, but I stood my ground, because I had no other choice. I wasn't just being mean, and that rule had not been made at random. "You're totally overreacting!"

"I assure you, I am not."

"You don't get to say who I go out with!" Tears stood in her eyes. "You are not the boss of me."

"But I am the boss of *him*." And of every other shifter in the zone.

"Bosses don't get to tell their employees who to date! There are laws about that! Probably even in the shifter world, and if there aren't, there should be. I think even Faythe would agree with me on that."

"This isn't about his personal life," I growled, and Davey backed away from me, her eyes wide at the deep, angry tone of my voice. At the animalistic quality that— like it or not—she could not truly understand. "This isn't about who he dates. This is about the order he disobeyed and about keeping you safe. It's *dangerous* for you to be in an intense relationship with a shifter who could lose control—"

"I would *never*—" Vance began.

"He hasn't lost control!" Davey practically shouted. "Not that that's any of your business!"

I took a deep breath, fighting for control of my temper. She wouldn't be able to understand the complicated relationship between my fear for her safety and my obligation, as Marshal, to discipline a zone member who'd disobeyed a direct order. Who'd lied to me not once, but for who knew how long.

That could not be allowed to stand. My authority could not survive blatant disregard of my rules. Especially by those I'd trusted most. Those to whom I'd delegated authority.

"I don't want his personal life to be my business, but that doesn't mean it isn't," I said. "It's my job to keep you safe. It's my job to keep *every* human woman in this territory safe from shifter men, and I cannot say I've done my job if I can't protect my own sister. And Vance, as an enforcer of this zone, must be held to an even higher standard than the average member. Your safety depends upon the men in this is zone believing that I will enforce the rule that you are off-limits. How can I make them believe that, once they find out that you've been sleeping with my top enforcer and most trusted friend? How can I possibly keep you safe now?"

"Maybe your premise is flawed! Maybe it isn't up to *you* to keep me safe!" Her face was flushed, her fists clenched. And while I sympathized with her indignation and frustration, her concerns were not the only ones I had to think about.

A zone that could not depend upon the unquestioned authority of its leader would descend into chaos and anarchy. Into violence. If I could not control my zone, Titus would have to.

He would replace me.

If I were not Marshal of the northern zone, both Davey and I would cease to enjoy the freedoms and safety we'd grown accustomed to among the male shifter population.

The way I ran things was the only way things *could* be run. The only way they would work.

"It *is* up to me," I insisted. "Whether or not you're able to understand that right now."

"She's right," Vance said. And I could see from the

complicated mix of emotions churning behind his eyes that he, at least, understood. That he'd *always* understood. He'd always known he was taking a risk, and he'd taken it anyway, because—

Because he loved her.

I was tearing them apart. I was shredding my sister's heart, not to mention Vance's, because I had no choice.

Because if I didn't, she could die.

"As careful as we—as *I*—always am, it's still careless." He took her hand, and I took a step back, staring at them, because suddenly I saw what Faythe had seen. Suddenly it was so obvious. At least, it should have been.

Did everyone else know?

No. If they did, I would have heard about it. There would have been gossip. Teasing. There would have been more rules broken, if this one was common knowledge.

Did *Tucker* know?

"Accidents happen, in the heat of the moment. That's why they're called accidents." Vance's thumb stroked my sister's knuckles, and I struggled to hold onto my anger in the face of their pain and heartbreak. "And the truth is that Faythe knows that better than anyone. She stood trial for that very thing when she was your age."

She… *What?*

Davey frowned. "Faythe was on *trial?* Like, in a *courtroom?*"

"Of the shifter variety." Vance nodded. "Titus said she accidentally infected her human boyfriend when her teeth shifted during a moment of passion. *Just* her teeth. Just a *little.* She didn't even know it had happened. But that was enough to change his life forever. And I would never forgive myself if that happened to you."

"I would never forgive you either," I said.

"I know." He let go of my sister's hand and backed slowly away from her. "I'll leave."

"No!" Davey shouted, grasping for his hand. Forcing him to back even farther away.

"I am so, so sorry," Vance said, and I could not tell which of us he was talking to. "The report from my interview with Billy is in your inbox." He headed through the swinging doors into the kitchen, and Davey turned on me, pain and fury both magnified by the tears still standing in her eyes.

"If you let him leave, I will *never ever* forgive you," she said, her chin quivering.

I wasn't sure I would forgive myself.

"I'm sorry." I had to force the words past a throat tight with my own pain and frustration. "I tried to save you from this heartbreak, Davey. I tried to stop it from ever starting. I know what you're feeling. I've been there. All I can do now is promise to help you through it."

Her tears fell and she glared at me through them. "Fuck your empathy and understanding." She grabbed her keys from the hook behind the bar, then she unlocked the front door and marched right through it, leaving me alone in the Fat Cat Bar and Grille with a short order cook in the kitchen and a prisoner in the basement.

TWENTY-ONE

"Charley?"

"Hey Titus." I exhaled in relief as I closed my office door, speaking into my shiny new phone. "Thank god you answered."

"Well, you called three times in the span of a minute and a half. During a birthday party." A door clicked shut over the line, and background laughter ended abruptly. "I assume this is an emergency involving a serial killer."

"Not exactly. Though I have an update on that for you too, now that you mention it."

"Now that I mention it?" I could practically hear the frown in his voice as he sank into his office chair with the groan of familiar springs. "Did that not warrant its own call?"

"It's been a long day."

Titus snorted. "Do they make any other kind?"

Valid. "So, I just fired Vance."

His silence was...thick. "May I ask why?"

"Because Faythe mentioned, completely offhand, what a cute couple he and Davey make. Which was when I realized that his apartment didn't smell like bleach the other day just because he's a good housekeeper."

Titus sighed. "He was purging her scent."

"Yeah." I sank into my own desk chair and fought the urge to reach for the bottle of tequila. It was running pretty low, which was probably a good sign that I should abstain, even if it was more of a mental crutch than anything, with a shifter's metabolism. "I told him to be at your place in four hours. Hire him if you want. He's a good enforcer. But he can't stay here. Not to work, and not to live."

"You sure?" he asked after a long pause. A *very* long pause. The kind designed to give me time to rethink what I had just said.

"We have rules for a reason, Titus. Please tell me I don't have to explain to you how dangerous—"

"No, I know exactly how difficult it will be for you to maintain law and order if those you're in charge of don't believe you'll enforce your word. And I support your decision one hundred percent...if you're sure that's your decision."

"So then, why are you tacitly questioning my decision?"

"Because I know how close you and Vance are. How much he means to you. And I wonder if there might not be another way to make your point?"

"Such as?"

"What?" Titus huffed, and the sound was not without a certain bitter amusement. "I have to think of everything?"

"Cute. But he's already on the way." At least, I hoped he was. "And I'm going to need a replacement. Someone who knows what's been going on here with Silas." I exhaled heavily. "Someone who *doesn't* look like Lochlan. Seriously send me the least attractive enforcer you have. My sister has a type. It's men."

269

"Charley, all of my enforcers are men."

"So then, you understand my problem."

He laughed.

"It's not funny. It's *really really* not funny."

"Maybe it would help if you tried to see the humor in the situation."

I growled over the line, and Titus sighed.

"I'll shuffle things around, and you'll have someone new by morning. Can you manage until then?"

"Yeah, thanks." I gave up the battle for willpower and pulled the nearly empty bottle of very expensive tequila from my drawer. It's not like I was gonna get drunk off one shot anyway. "I'll call in one of the guys from Memphis if I need to." One of my other, non-local enforcers.

"Good. So, what's the update on the case?"

"Do you remember Billy, my short order cook?"

"Vaguely. He's just a kid right? Davey's age?"

"A little younger. Turns out he was Silas's stepson. In a weird, backwoods common law kind of situation."

I filled him in on the case, and Titus was quiet for a moment, evidently processing the new information while I poured myself a shot, one handed. Without spilling a single drop on my desk blotter.

"Do you have Billy in custody?" he asked at last.

"Locked up in the basement as we speak. I'm not convinced he was involved, but I'm not prepared to let him go yet either."

"And Denny?"

"Still tracking him down. Vance did a second interview with Billy this morning and he left me a list of every place he and Denny hung out as kids, every place he ever worked, and every single friend and relative he ever heard Denny mention. Tucker is on internet duty, with Austin and Bishop standing by to do leg work as possibilities come up. When we find him, we'll bring him in."

Titus exhaled. "Do not under any circumstances go after this Denny alone. I know you're down a man now, but you take Tucker with you. Or Austin and Bishop, if you trust them. Do you understand, Charley?"

"Yes, of course."

Titus hesitated for a second, and I could almost hear his mental gears turning. "So, what did you think of Faythe?"

"She's a legend." I wanted to stuff the words back into my mouth the moment I'd said them, but it was too late.

He burst into laughter. "Don't let her hear you say that."

I hadn't meant to let *him* hear it.

"She doesn't seem to think much of her own influence," I said.

"That's because she's played the role of Sisyphus most of her life. As have I, at least in the shifter world. Eventually, that shit gets to you. If you don't know that yet on a personal level, you will."

"I think that's what she's trying to save me from. I think that's what she's trying to save *all* female shifters from. And I'm damn well going to help her."

Also, I was going to look up who the hell Sisyphus was.

"That's my girl."

I huffed. "If you think I'm anyone's girl you have not been listening."

Titus's laughter made me smile even as I hung up on him.

"ON YOUR OWN TONIGHT, CHARLEY?" Doug Myers asked as he sank onto the third barstool from the left—his favorite.

"Looks like it." I slid a basket of snack mix toward him. "Whiskey?"

"I'll start with a double. And a burger. That fancy one with fried onions on it."

"Sorry. Kitchen's closed tonight." Mitch had gone home at five, and I wasn't free to take over for him with no one else to man the bar. Figuratively speaking.

Tucker was stationed in my office, still looking for a lead on Cam Senet's whereabouts with one ear turned my way, in case there was any trouble.

"Where's Billy?" Doug asked. "And Davey? And...Vance?"

"They're all busy," Austin said as he pushed his way in from the kitchen through the swinging doors, surprising us both. "You'll have to make do with me tonight."

I'd been too busy to notice his car pulling up or hear him come in.

Austin assumed what looked like a practiced "bartender" pose at my side, bar cloth in hand. He looked thoughtful and ready. And pretty fucking adorable, with those blue eyes practically glowing at me.

Doug frowned up at him. "You work here now?"

"Just helping out in a pinch," Austin said. I arched both brows at him, and he shrugged. "No cocktails, right?"

I snorted. "This is a simple cont'ry bar, sir. We pour shots and pull pints."

"How hard could it be?" With that, Austin headed toward the other end of the bar to take an order.

"Just keep up with open tabs for tonight," I called as he walked away. "Keep good records." That'd be easier than showing him how to work the cash register or run a credit card.

Twenty minutes later, we hit a lull and I tugged Austin into the kitchen.

"What are you doing here?" I whispered.

"Tucker texted. He said you'd fired Vance and needed a hand."

"With bartending?"

Austin shrugged. "In general. What happened with Vance?"

"Caught him sleeping with my sister. Well, I didn't *catch* them, thank god. But they *are* caught."

He blinked at me for a second. Then he smiled. "Told 'ya."

"I'm sorry, what?"

"The harder I tried to keep Yvette and Bishop apart, the more futile that endeavor became."

But Austin hadn't been truly worried about his sister's safety, because he hadn't known there was any possibility Bishop could accidentally partially-shift during a moment of...passion.

But I knew. *Vance* knew.

"I take it Davey's mad at you?"

"If her refusal to answer her phone is any indication, she's nuclear-level pissed off." She and I were on the same cell plan, and usually I could track her phone. But she'd disabled her location.

I had *no* idea where my sister was, for the first time in years. And I'd fired the man I'd trusted to help keep her safe.

"Bishop is driving around aimlessly, looking for Cam Senet's car. Want me to see if he can keep an eye out for Davey too?"

"No!" The last thing I needed was for his violently passionate grief to meet her anger and need for rebellion. I didn't truly believe she'd cheat on Vance, but I wasn't about to start throwing attractive shifter men in her direction.

Never again.

Austin's brows rose at my reaction. "Okay. He's promised

to call me if he sees Cam's car, and *not* to act on impulse. But I'm not sure he actually has a wait-for-backup mode."

"Or a think-it-through mode," I added, and Austin laughed.

"Thanks for coming in. It's really nice of you," I said as I heard the bell on the front door ring.

He shrugged. "I figured you'd be happy for the company, even if I broke a few glasses."

"I am. But don't break my glasses."

He laughed again as we headed back out front.

An hour later, headlights flashed through the front window, and I recognized the sound of Davey's engine as she drove around to the employee parking lot. I left Austin taking orders and darted into the kitchen to intercept her just as she walked through the back door.

"Hey," I said, and she jumped, startled by my appearance. "I didn't think you'd come in tonight."

She glared at me, repositioning her canvas bag over her shoulder. "It's my bar too."

"I know."

"I'm not going to let you run me out of my own life, Charley."

"That is in *no* way what I'm trying to do. Will you come upstairs for a minute? I think we should talk."

"Who's watching the bar?"

"Austin."

She frowned. "Does he even know how to pull a proper pint?"

I shrugged. "He'll be fine for fifteen minutes. The guys all like him."

She heaved an exaggerated sigh and trudged up the stairs.

"Davey, I just want you to understand that I'm not trying to run your life," I said as I closed my apartment door behind her. "Sleep with any human you want. I promise I don't care, and even if I did—even if I hated your choice—I wouldn't say a word because it's none of my business, and I know that. As long as you stick to humans."

Her frown became a scowl. "I was really hoping you brought me up here so you could apologize and tell me you'd called Vance home."

I exhaled slowly. "I am sorry. I'm very, very sorry that you're hurt. That you're in this position at all. But no, I'm not bringing Vance back. I fired him for a reason, and I can't just go back on my word."

"You are such a hypocrite!" she shouted, and I flinched, hoping the noise from the bar would keep everyone downstairs from hearing her.

"How, exactly, am I a hypocrite? I'm not sleeping with a human."

"Okay, you're not being *directly* hypocritical, in, like, a literal sense," she amended. "But you let every asshole in that bar date human girls. We play "Another One Bites The Dust" and hand out a free shot every time one of them gets dumped. If you aren't trying to control their lives, why are you trying to control *mine*?"

"I'm not trying to control anyone's life. Not yours, and not Vance's. What I'm trying to do is keep you safe and uphold the rules I set for the members of this zone, both of which are *vitally* important to me. And one of those rules— one of the most important—is that you are off limits to the shifters in the zone. *All* of them. If I go back on my word, I'll be eroding my own authority. They won't believe there are any real consequences if Vance is able to ignore the rules. And this isn't just *a* rule, it's *the* rule."

"But it's a rule you had no right to make! I get that Faythe accidentally infected that guy years ago, but that sounds like a random anomaly. I mean, guys around here sleep with human girls all the time, and that has never happened to any of them. Right?"

I could only nod. We would definitely know if a woman one of them had slept with had been infected. Especially considering our recent scouring of local hospital records. But...

"That's a different situation. Their random hookups and short-term relationship disasters are one thing, but you and Vance...that looked serious. And not new or recent. Which means you're taking that risk over and over, while most of those other girls out there—" I waved my arm in the general direction of Buford. "—will dump their shifter boyfriend fairly quickly and never be in harm's way again." I sighed, silently begging her to understand, even if she wasn't happy about it. "And Vance knows that. He agrees with me. But he broke the rule anyway."

"*And what does that tell you?*" she demanded, still clutching her bag. Determined not to settle in or make herself at home. "We both knew how you felt, and we both broke the rule anyway. For the past *eight* months."

Eight months. Two-thirds of a year. Nearly half my time as Marshal.

"How is that possible? How did Tucker not know?" And despite the fact that his apartment was directly below Vance's, he hadn't known. That had been clear in his reaction.

Davey shrugged. "Tucker usually works the early shift at the bar, and he goes out of town a lot. I think he has a guy up north. We worked around his schedule."

That could not have been easy. And I understood her point: this was not a casual relationship. But that only empha-sized *my* point: they were taking that risk far too often.

"I want in," Davey said.

I crossed my arms over my chest. "In—?"

"I want to volunteer for Faythe's program."

"No." Pain shot through my chest at the thought, though I'd known it was coming. "No. Absolutely not."

"I'm exactly what she's looking for. A female family member of multiple known shifters, who already knows about your world. Who's in it, even if I'm not of it. And I want to be *of* it, Charley. I don't care if you'd actually be my boss then. I'll follow orders, I swear to god. I'll do everything right. And then you wouldn't have to worry about me, because I'd be able to take care of myself!"

"No! It isn't safe! They haven't even started testing the procedure yet, and even once they do, it'll take a long time to perfect. And even then, it won't be risk-free."

She threw her hands in the air, her bag bobbing on her shoulder. "Nothing is risk-free!"

No argument there. "Some of those women will still die, Davey. They're not all going to make it." Faythe hadn't said that aloud, but she knew it. "The only difference, in those cases, is that the women will be choosing to take that risk." Though I couldn't personally understand why they would.

"Exactly! Yes, my choice comes with risks, but it also comes with benefits. It'll let me into a world I've been stuck on the outside of for three years. It'll let me *belong* with the people I already know and love."

"No."

Storm clouds rolled across her eyes, and she looked for all the world like Ben. So determined. So strong. "I *am* going to volunteer, and you can't stop me."

"Of course, I can." Every word I said bruised me deep inside, but I said them anyway, through teeth I couldn't quite unclench. I'd rather be bruised from hurting her feelings than destroyed from losing her. "I'll be running the program with Faythe. I can exclude you."

"*Now* you're being a literal hypocrite. You just promised to help Faythe do the very thing you won't let me do." Davey crossed her arms over her chest, pinning the bag to her side. Mirroring my stance. "But I don't think she'll let you exclude me. I'm the sister of a woman who actually survived infection —the most genetically similar to you of anyone in the world. I'm their single best chance at making that happen again. At least at the beginning of the program. And I'm *going* to be first in line."

She marched past me, and I darted in front of her to block the door, my pulse racing. Terror burning in my veins. "The first women will be the least likely to survive. The doctors will still be working on the technique and the medications, and—"

"No, the first women will be the *most* likely to survive, because there will be fewer of them, and all the attention will be on them, and the program will have all this pressure to succeed, so the council won't shut it down. And they'll be testing that new antibiotic compound in the lab before they ever inject it into a human. By the time—"

"Davey, we can readdress this after the program is up and running. When Faythe and her doctors have proven it can be done. Consistently."

She shook her head. "I'm going to help them prove it."

"No—"

"And then you won't be able to keep me and Vance apart."

"My goal isn't to keep you apart. It's to keep you—"

"Safe. I heard. Get out of my way, Char. Unless you're planning to lock me up next to Billy."

I exhaled. Then I stepped aside.

Davey marched toward the door—then she stopped cold as she passed my coffee table. Staring at the empty Johnny Walker bottle.

Shit.

"I thought you said Bishop bought that bottle of Gold Label." She frowned as her gaze skimmed both glasses, only one of which was standing on a coaster. "Oh my god."

"Davey—"

"You're making a federal case out of me and Vance, and the whole time you're up here fucking the *grieving widower*? In the middle of his wife's murder investigation?"

"It's not... You don't understand what happened."

"Oh, I understand. You're a fucking hypocrite. In spirit, if not in actual deed."

"Okay, that's enough," I snapped. "This has nothing to do with you and Vance or with Faythe's pilot program. And it's still none of your business, or anyone else's."

"Meaning...you don't want me to tell Austin."

"Meaning you don't have the right to tell *anyone*. And not just for my sake. For Bishop's. It's not for you to judge how he copes with grief. And he *is* grieving. Believe that, even if you believe nothing else."

"I do." Davey sighed, her expression softening for just a moment, not on my behalf, but on Bishop's. "And I get it."

"And I haven't told anyone about you and Vance. Because that's your business."

She rolled her eyes. "And because you think it'd make you look like a weak leader, if people knew your second in command broke your rule."

"No, I think it'd make me look like a woman of my word, if people knew why I fired him. I'm not telling because it's none of their business. But people *will* start asking questions, once they find out he's gone."

Davey shrugged. "Fine. Answer any questions you want. You're the only reason we were keeping that secret in the first place, and now that you know, there's no real point in hiding it." She glanced at the empty whiskey bottle on her way past me to the door. "Also, if you haven't even washed the dishes yet, I know damn well you haven't changed the sheets. Just because I can't smell Bishop in here doesn't mean no one else will."

TWENTY-TWO

I stripped the bed and threw my sheets in the washer, and by the time I made it back downstairs, Davey was long gone.

"She said hi to everyone, then announced that she was taking a mental health day," Austin said when I joined him behind the bar.

"I don't suppose she said where she was going?" I whispered as I cut limes.

He gave me a sidelong grin. "No, but she had a couple of colorful suggestions about where *you* should go."

I sighed. This wasn't the first time one of our arguments had spilled over into the bar, and with any luck, none of the regulars had connected our sibling spat with Vance's absence.

"Yvette and I fought all the time," Austin whispered as he began emptying a crate of glasses, still steaming from the dishwasher. "I mean, we were close, but sometimes that proximity can chafe."

"Did she..." I hesitated, trying to figure out how to phrase my question without revealing anything about Faythe's secret project. "Did Yvette feel like she was on the outside looking in? As the only human in your household?"

"No, I don't think so. I mean, we didn't live in a very shifter-dense area, so if anything, I think Bishop and I probably felt more like outsiders in her world. Personally, I felt like a bull in a China shop. Took me forever to figure out how to…moderate my new strength. Once, I broke the door handle off a department car and had to pretend it just fell off in my hand. Manufacturer defect." He shrugged. "After that, I was always afraid I'd break something in the house. Or scare her."

"Yeah, I went through a similar phase. My understanding is that that's not a thing, for those who grew up as shifters."

He huffed. "Must be nice to know where you belong."

I wanted Davey to feel like she belonged. I'd done everything I could to make that happen here in the bar—*our* bar— because I already felt like making it a shifter haven was basically taking it over for myself. I wanted her in my life, and I wanted to be in hers.

But I couldn't risk losing her. I couldn't have her hurt because of her proximity to me and my job, or my problems.

Still, she had a legitimate grievance. In an attempt to protect her, I'd shoved her and Vance together. Could I really claim total shock that they'd taken it beyond friendship? Beyond the surrogate sibling relationship I'd hoped for?

Maybe I hadn't seen what was happening because I hadn't *wanted* to see. Because I'd known, deep down, that if I acknowledged that they'd broken the rules, I'd have to address the violation.

Or…maybe I was just plain blind.

Tucker left around ten pm, but he promised to continue working from the comfort of his home. He was already halfway through the list of contacts and places Billy had given us as possibilities, searching social media feeds for tags or pictures of Cam and searching public records for any property in his name. Either of them.

He was making a list of non-shifter friends who might know where to find Cam—under either of his identities—and places where he might be found.

I thanked him profusely for his efforts and asked him to keep me posted. Clearly, we were not going to find Cam/Denny tonight, but I still had high hopes for tomorrow.

And if we didn't find him in the next twenty-four hours, we were going to have to start officially interviewing my regulars about their contact with him. Which I'd been hoping to avoid.

Some of them would panic at the thought of the council taking over our investigation and potentially digging into their lives. Others would take it upon themselves to go hunting for Cam, and our attempts to stop them would take time away from the official manhunt. As would any potential leak of information to Cam himself.

It would be better for everyone involved if the rest of the zone knew nothing about what was happening until it was all over.

I closed the Fat Cat early again, because Austin and I were both tired and the bar was short-handed. By midnight, we'd cleaned everything and locked the front door. As I walked Austin out through the kitchen, I gifted him a full bottle as thanks for his help.

"Not necessary," he said, but I insisted, tucking the bottle into his arm like a baby. Or a football.

"I really appreciate tonight," I told him. "You tending my bar for free was above and beyond."

"Happy to help out anywhere I can," he said, lingering in the doorway. Staring down at me with those glittering blue eyes. "Charley, everything's a bit complicated right now, but when this is all over, I'd really like to take you to dinner. If you're at all interested."

For a second, I couldn't breathe. My chest felt like one big bruise.

A week ago, my life was simple:

Serve the drinks. Keep the peace. Solve the shifter crimes.

But now…

"Your heart's racing." Austin's focus on me intensified. "I can't tell if that means you wanted me to ask you out, or you were dreading that, and now I've put you in an awkward position. And I'm sorry if it's the latter. But I had to give it a shot."

"Why?"

He frowned. "What do you mean?"

"Sorry." I propped my hands on my hips, feeling more awkward than I had since the one middle school dance I'd attended. "I didn't intend for that to come out as rude as it clearly did. I just mean…why do you want to take me out? Is it because I'm a shifter?"

While my regulars were put off by my authority, there was no shortage of shifter men out there who'd never met a woman who smelled like me. Whose biology was evidently telling them to lay claim, as quickly as they could, to a very, very rare resource.

Yes, that was several steps more innocent than making one's own female shifter companion. Still…not what I was looking for.

Not that I was looking for anything. Not really.

"No," he said. "I mean, not directly anyway. Though I suspect you being a shifter has, at least in part, made you into the woman you are, and…I like that woman." The admission seemed almost bizarrely easy for him. He wasn't nervous, nor was he naively unaware of his own appeal. And he definitely lacked no confidence.

"I apologize again. I swear I'm not fishing for compliments. But…what is it you like about me?" I was pretty well aware of what I had to offer and what I did not. I was bossy—occupational hazard—and often too direct. I was grouchy, regularly sleep-deprived, and frequently moody. I could more accurately be described as a skeptic than an optimist. And my backlist of trauma…well, it ran deep.

Yet Austin grinned. "Frankly, I like that you handle your shit. You're in charge, and you're good at it. You make tough calls every day, and no matter how hard the wind blows, you may bow, but you never break." He cleared his throat and glanced at the floor, for just a second. Then he met my gaze with a boldness that stole my breath. "I think you're amazing. And I have since the moment you first marched me into your office like a boy in trouble with the principal."

My face flushed so hot I could practically see the glow at the bottom of my field of vision.

So much for not fishing for compliments.

"I'm not…I'm not everything you just said. I mean, that was really nice, but I'm not… I mean, sometimes I fuck up." I cleared my throat. Then I said the most truthful thing I could think of, as fast as I could. Even though he had no idea what I was talking about. "Sometimes I fuck up a little bit…on purpose. Not on the job. Just…in life."

Austin blinked at me. Then he burst into laughter. "That was refreshingly honest."

"Okay, you have to take off those rose-tinted glasses. I'm trying to tell you that I'm a little messed up."

"Oh, I know you are." He leaned down and stole a kiss—a delicious little nibble of my lower lip, which sparked a tiny flame deep inside me. "And like I said, I know things are complicated right now." Another kiss, and his next words barely skimmed my cheek on their way to my ear. "But they will calm down. And I've made up my mind. I'm not going anywhere."

"You're not—?" I stepped back, staring up at him.

"I want to be a part of what you're building out here. So I applied to the Buford police department this afternoon."

My pulse leapt into my throat. "You applied? You're... moving? Here?" A coup for the zone, to be sure, and a not-unwelcome development for me personally. Still...he was right. Things were complicated.

He nodded slowly, holding my gaze. "If there's a place for me."

With me, or in the Buford PD? Or both? More double entendre...

"Anyway, you don't have to answer now. In fact, don't. Take some time. Just...know that I'm here." Then Austin turned and walked across the gravel parking lot toward the white 4Runner.

Where Bishop sat in the driver's seat waiting for him.

Watching us.

HALF AN HOUR LATER, I lay in bed staring at the ceiling. Blinking into the dark, struggling to make my thoughts stop racing.

Failing. Miserably.

I'd failed to catch Yvette's killer. Fired my best friend. Alienated my sister. And locked up my short order cook, who may or may not have played a knowing role in my infection, but definitely would not be flipping burgers for me any time soon.

With a sigh, I sat up and turned on my lamp. There was no sense just lying there awake.

I was halfway to the bathroom in search of a handful of sleeping pills when the creak of a familiar floorboard stopped me cold.

Someone was downstairs.

A handful of people had keys, but Titus and Vance were both hours away, Tucker wouldn't come in without calling, and Davey...

Well, it had to be my sister. Except that the footsteps creeping softly up the stairs toward my apartment sounded nothing like hers.

I raced barefoot through the living room and pulled the baseball bat from the front closet, wishing for only the second time in the past two years that I kept a gun in the apartment.

My pulse pounding, I stood to the left of the door, listening as the loose third step creaked. Footsteps crossed the small landing and stopped just outside my door.

The knob began to turn, and I realized I hadn't locked it. Because I was in my own damn building, and I was a goddamn mythical creature, armed with fucking claws! I should have been safe!

A growl rumbled up from my throat as the door creaked open. I choked up on the bat, and as I swung, that growl swelled into a flat-out snarl.

Bishop caught the fat part of the bat in one hand, flinching as it smacked *hard* against his palm. Driving his arm back several inches.

"Ouch, Marshal. Swinging for the stands, I see. Good for you. There're a lot of creeps out there."

"There's one in here!" I snatched the bat from his grip and propped it in the nearest corner. "How the hell did you get in here? This is breaking and entering."

He held up a familiar key, dangling from an even more familiar keychain: a pewter skull wearing a cowboy hat. "Nah, it's only entering. And while we're on the subject…" He grabbed me by both hips, keychain digging into my skin, and his eyes widened when he realized my legs were bare. "Good," he growled, his eyes dilating as his nostrils flared. "Saves time."

"Let go!" I shoved him back and snatched the key from his fist. "This is Davey's. How the hell did you get it?"

"She gave it to Austin when he offered to open the bar for you in the morning."

"And you just *took* it? You have *no* boundaries."

Bishop shrugged as he pushed my front door shut. "Never really needed any. Austin said you had a rough day. I did too. And this really seemed to help us both last time, so…" Another shrug, as he pulled his shirt over his head.

"Stop! Don't take anything else off."

"Okay. That's a weird kink. Religious overtones. But I'm into it, if that's what you—"

"No, I— I thought you felt guilty last time, after we… helped each other." That's what that was, right? Mutual therapy? Mutual *naked* therapy…and nothing more.

This wasn't supposed to happen again.

"I did. But I've been thinking—"

"God help us all."

"—about what you said. Afterward. About that fucked-up merry-go-round of emotion. And about release. I *need* a fucking release right now." Something dark peered out at me from behind his eyes, his inner cat pacing. Menacing. Claws extended and ready to draw blood.

"Why? What happened?"

"Talking doesn't always make things better, Marshal." His voice deepened and that darkness swelled from within him, threatening to swallow any light. All of his hope and good humor. Leaving nothing but that stalking, ravenous beast. "It doesn't have to be this." Bishop's gaze raked over me, and heat burst from the pit of my stomach, throbbing as it spread throughout my body. "But it's gonna be something." The words rolled from deep in his chest on a low, savage growl, and I could *feel* his rage boiling beneath the surface. "I…I'm near my limit, Charley."

Charley. My actual name.

"And when I hit my limit, bad things tend to happen."

Jesus.

"I just thought maybe we could let something good happen again, instead. If you need a release, too."

I mean… It's not like I was sleeping.

"This is a bad idea," I whispered, my gaze caught on his chest. On the chords of muscle standing out in his arms.

"Then tell me you don't want it. Say that, and I'll go."

"There's no way this is going to end well," I said instead, so softly I could hardly hear my own words. "You know that, right?"

Bishop grunted. "No sense worrying about the end of something that never really began. This is what it is, right? We're just grindin' it out to feel better. Nothing more than that."

"Nothing more." But it was nothing less, either. "As long as we understand each other."

"Marshal, I understand more about you than I ever intended to." The space between us disappeared. Bishop's mouth crushed against mine, demanding as much as it gave. His teeth sank into my lower lip, tugging gently as his hands wandered beneath my tee shirt, dragging the material up slowly. He licked my lip, but didn't release it, and when I whimpered from the sting, he growled softly into my mouth.

He would release me when he damn well felt like it.

I groaned, throbbing in low, warm places.

Bishop sucked on my lower lip for a second, then let it go as he dragged my shirt over my head. I shivered from the chill, but he grabbed my arms before I could cover myself. "You want it like last time?"

I hesitated for a second, my throat tight. My heart racing. Then I nodded.

He took my chin and tilted my head up. "You're gonna have to say it, so there's no misunderstanding."

I blinked up at him defiantly. I didn't have to say a damn thing. He wanted this as badly as I did, and he wasn't going to walk away, even if I didn't play by his rules.

"We like what we like, Marshal. No shame in it. So tell me what you want."

I jerked my chin from his grasp and stared up at him. "I want it rough."

"You're the boss," he growled.

"Not for the next half hour."

His groan sank through every inch of my skin, warming it. Lighting me on fire. "You just remember that."

Bishop lifted me and my legs wound around his waist. The rough denim from his jeans chafed my most intimate parts, and when I tried to pull away from it, he clutched me closer, grinding up into me as he carried me across the living room.

I hissed at the abrasive sensation, and he growled, his grip tightening around my hips until I gave in and rode out the rough sparks of pleasure. A second later, his grip shifted, my only hint of a warning before I was suddenly airborne. Falling.

My brief shriek ended as the bed caught me and my mouth snapped shut.

"Don't move," Bishop ordered as he unbuttoned his jeans. So I watched as he shoved them down, followed by his underwear, and suddenly he was standing naked in front of me, in unparalleled shifter glory.

No human man could possibly attain such physical perfection. Not for long. Not without grueling work and a careful diet. But most shifters were hot, and Bishop…well… If the standard shifter hotness scale began at "bonfire," he was a goddamn nuclear explosion.

When he bent to dig into the pocket of the pants he'd just shed, I pushed myself backward, reaching for the lamp to turn it off. I could see him just fine in the dark, and no one driving by needed to catch his silhouette in my window.

But I only made it a couple of inches before a hand closed around my ankle. "I said, *don't move*," Bishop growled. He hauled me to the edge of the bed, and I hissed at the friction between my back and the sheet. When my butt hit the edge of the mattress, he pulled my underwear off, then he crawled over me, dropping blistering kisses in a line up my torso and neck until his face appeared, the heat from his body radiating against mine, though he held himself a couple of inches above me. "You don't listen very well."

"Says the man with impulse control issues."

Bishop chuckled, and the gravely sound echoed through me, triggering sparks in unexpected places. "Hey pot, kettle calling."

That time I laughed, but the sound ended in a soft gasp as he lowered himself, closing the scant distance between our bodies, and his warm breath brushed my ear. "Be good, and my impulse control won't become an issue."

I squirmed as his mouth closed over my earlobe, sucking gently. His mouth captured mine again, teasing, his tongue stroking against mine so smoothly, with such intensity that I hardly noticed him sliding my arms, first one, then the other, across the rumpled sheet. Until they met over my head.

"Stay," he growled, his chest rumbling against my breasts. Teasing my nipples. Then he kissed his way down my body again, stroking every inch of me as I arched into each touch, silently begging for more. But his contact was tormentingly light. A taste, when I wanted a feast.

Bishop's tongue dipped into my navel as his hands slid beneath my hips, cradling my ass. Repositioning me. I gasped when his teeth grazed the point of my left hip, briefly digging into my flesh. Claiming the spot, just for a second. Before he settled onto his knees on the floor.

I wriggled as he nibbled my inner thigh, soothing tiny bites with quick licks, as if he weren't sure whether he'd rather taste me or consume me entirely. I arched into him as his tongue trailed up my thigh, ending tantalizingly close to where I wanted him.

Yet still shy of the mark.

Bishop growled. The sound hummed against my skin, rumbling into my very soul. Echoing with a desire for something I couldn't quite bring into focus.

Something aggressive and primal. An emotion so fundamental—so centered in who he was and how that man came to exist—that it couldn't be put into words or stuffed into a category.

It was as sharp as a blade, hot as flame, and as hard as that bolder he called a skull. It was both sword and shield. Offering and command. The driving force that dominated every moment of his life.

That need *was* Bishop Mattheson, and in that moment, I was nothing more than a raft riding the current of his passion. Surging with each wave. At the mercy of the tide.

He licked my thigh again, and the sensation felt suddenly

raspy. Not actually painful, but...intense. I could feel each individual, tiny bump on his tongue.

No, those weren't bumps. They were hooks.

His tongue had shifted, at least a little.

Before I had time to consider the ramifications of that development, or to even think about pushing him away, he hooked a hand beneath each of my knees and spread them wide, pressing my legs flat against the mattress. Exposing me fully.

I started to sit up, and he snarled. His head popped up, his fierce gaze warning me not to move. To keep my arms over my head, where my fists clenched handfuls of my own sheets.

My heart leapt into my throat and every muscle in my body tensed. "Tongue," I whimpered, unable to resist the caution, despite his warning growl. What if he didn't know his tongue had shifted? A cat could literally strip the flesh from its prey's bones, and he was very near a very sensitive part of my body.

Bishop growled again, and his grip tightened on my legs. Then his head disappeared.

A strangled cry ripped free from my throat at the first touch of his tongue between my legs, and for a second, I couldn't tell whether the sensation was pleasure or pain. All I could be sure of was that it was rough.

Just like I'd asked for.

Hot and wet, he stroked the entire length of my exposed sex, teasing my clit with the tip of his tongue at the very end. My cry ended in a strangled groan.

That wasn't a human tongue, but it wasn't entirely feline either. He wasn't trying to hurt me, but he *was* pushing my limits. And his tight grip on my legs demanded that I trust him.

That was the name of this filthy game, after all. Half an

hour when I wasn't the boss. When I didn't have to think. I could just…feel.

He licked me again and again, long and slow, and my groan became a guttural, inarticulate moan of pleasure. The sensation was strange, like nothing I'd ever felt. Not pain, but definitely sharper than any human tongue. I could feel every pronounced bump, and the sensation was overwhelming. All-consuming. It was familiar, yet strange, like he was speaking a new language full of beautifully sharp syllables I didn't quite understand, and he was goddamn *fluent*.

His tongue circled my clit, each softly formed little hook teasing, and I tried to arch up toward him, begging for more, but he held me in place. Content to give only at his leisure. Unconcerned by my impatience.

My pleasure built slowly, and I whimpered, frantic for more, but every time I tried to express my frustration, he growled softly. The one time I moved my arm, reaching for his head in a moment of desperation, he stopped licking me entirely, leaving my swollen sex throbbing, abandoned.

I swear, I nearly cried.

"Please," I begged, returning my hand to its position.

He rewarded me with the return of his tongue, but no faster than before. No harder. I could only wait, grasping desperately at each sensation as he slowly, slowly pushed me toward a blistering crest of pleasure.

Finally, he let go of one of my legs, and I gasped when two of his fingers slid inside me, searching for that slightly rough spot inside. He groaned when he found it, and the soft curses spilling from my own lips echoed the sentiment.

"Please," I moaned again, and he began to stroke inside me with both fingers, while his tongue worked in beautiful harmony, and somehow, that rough sensation that had shocked me minutes before was suddenly not enough.

"Oh, god," I moaned as my body tightened around him, pleasure surging toward a peak.

Then it all stopped, and I cursed the very hell that had spawned him.

Bishop chuckled as he lifted me, then laid me down in the center of the bed, my head on my favorite pillow. "Pa—"

"I will gut you where you stand if you tell me to have patience," I snarled at him.

His laugh deepened until I couldn't be sure, despite the heated mirth shining down at me in his eyes, that there wasn't a hint of a growl threaded through the sound. "Does that mean you're close?"

"A nice breeze would push me over the edge."

"Well then, that'll make this fun. For me," he added with a wicked grin. Bishop leaned over me and lifted my arms until my fingers brushed the wooden slats of my headboard. "Hold on," he ordered, and I was irritated at how eagerly my hands complied, gripping the wood as if it would save me from this torturous delay in my gratification.

Evidently satisfied with my position, he ran both hands over me, his work-roughened palms skimming my nipples, drawing another obscene groan from me. One hand slid lower, over my stomach then lower still, until his fingers stroked over my still swollen sex, teasing me mercilessly.

I moaned, gripping the headboard hard enough to make it creak as my hips arched up.

"Bishop…" I groaned when his fingers disappeared.

"Don't worry, Marshal," he whispered as he settled himself between my legs, lifting his hips out of reach when I arched toward him. "You're going to get what you want. But you're going to wait for me." He finally lowered himself and rubbed the entire length of his erection against me.

"Why the hell would I do that?" I snarled, writhing to

demand more contact. I'd tried delaying my release once years ago, as a doe-eyed girlfriend convinced that the best orgasm had to be a simultaneous orgasm. That peaking together would somehow magically bind me to the twenty-two-year-old idiot I thought I loved that month.

The reality was that I cooled down just as he was revving up, and he was much less willing to wait for me than I was for him. Which left me to finish the job on my own an hour after he left.

Lesson learned.

"You're going to do it because I fucking told you to," Bishop growled as he slammed fully into me, and I was reminded, as my body throbbed around him, desperately trying to keep him in place, that he was *nothing* like that clueless kid from years ago.

Cooling down with Bishop inside me was not going to be a problem. It wasn't even going to be a possibility.

I clung to the headboard as he pounded into me, and there was nothing slow or gentle about it. Which was when I remembered that he needed this too.

He scraped against my clit at the crest of every stroke, as he rubbed that spot inside me relentlessly. In seconds, I was panting, writhing beneath him, unable to control the twitch of my hips. The clench of my legs around him. Even as I mentally fought the spiral of pleasure rapidly swelling within me.

"I can't wait," I moaned.

"*Wait*," he snarled, pounding into me even harder. His command came with no mercy. No compassionate slowing of his pace.

"Agggh, *god*," I pleaded, desperately fighting the inevitable.

"Don't you dare," he groaned into my ear, but I could tell

he was close. He grabbed my leg, pinning my knee to the bed, driving himself even deeper. Pounding against me mercilessly. And that was all I could take.

I shuddered as euphoria crashed over me, my body clenching around him over and over as I thrust my hips up with each wave, grinding out my release against him.

On the tail end of my crest, as waves of aftershock lapped over me, Bishop groaned and slammed into me with a mad frenzy, driving me toward an instant, blistering peak as the top of my headboard beat against the wall.

Through my own scream, I heard the sheetrock give as I came for the second time.

TWENTY-THREE

"Good god," Bishop exhaled as he rolled over, one hand on my hip to roll me with him, draping my leg over his thigh. Still buried deep inside me. "Fucking insatiable," he murmured against my lips between kisses that were more like ravenous little demands. "But you're *terrible* at following directions."

"That's not fair," I said as he finally rolled away. "You basically set me on the edge of a cliff, told me not to jump, then stood behind me and pushed."

"It wouldn't be a challenge if it weren't challenging, Marshal." He sat up and grinned at me over one shoulder, then he headed into the bathroom. When I heard the condom hit the trash can, I made a mental note to actually take out the trash. Or burn it. And to wash my sheets. And bleach every molecule of his scent from my apartment.

"I'm familiar with the concept of a challenge, but your expectations are unreasonable," I insisted as I pulled my tee over my head.

"Eh. You'll get there." He grinned as he stepped back into my bedroom, still completely nude. "I have faith."

Questions tumbled through my mind at the implication that I would have a chance to perfect delayed gratification under his...tutelage. Was he planning to stay in Buford too? With Austin?

This was growing rapidly, unsettlingly complicated.

"I can fix that," he said as he tugged his pants up. I thought he was talking about the complicated nature of our arrangement—or maybe the impatient nature of my orgasm—until I followed his gaze to the gash in the sheetrock peeking from behind my headboard.

Bishop pulled the bed several inches from the wall to better assess the damage. "Ten minutes with some drywall compound and a trowel. You have more of this paint?" he asked, running one hand over an undamaged stretch of wall.

"I have no idea."

He shrugged. "They can match it at the hardware store. I'll fix that divot in your bathroom wall while I'm at it. You should really put a doorstop in there. That'll prevent your knob from hitting the wall."

"That sounds dirty."

He grinned. "That was intentional. But my point stands."

"Okay, this is weird."

Bishop snorted. "Me talking home repair is the most mundane thing I've ever done in your bedroom."

Fair point. And I wasn't going to argue, if he wanted to fix the damage he'd caused. But... "Are you sure you know how to do all that?"

"I work in construction, Charley." His smile grew distant. "Yvette used to ask me the same thing, though. She had every confidence that I could build whatever my day job required, but she wasn't entirely sure I had the skills to assemble a shed in the backyard." His gaze found mine, and it was distinctly...soft. "She'd have liked you."

"Your *wife* would have liked me?" The woman screwing her husband? Not that I'd be doing that, if Yvette were still alive.

"Yeah. You have a lot in common."

She liked it rough?

I swallowed the question before it could come out. I wasn't going to cross that line. If screwing me, then talking about his wife helped him process his loss, I wasn't going to get in the way of that by prying for intimate details.

"It's entirely possible that you're some kind of self-destructive phase I'm going through," I said. "That deep down, I don't feel worthy of sweet and gentle, at the moment. That all I really deserve, while I'm failing basically everyone I know, is…"

"Me?" Bishop finished.

I sighed. "I didn't mean that the way it sounded."

"No offense taken. And I might actually believe your crackpot amateur psychology, if I couldn't tell how much you like it…hard. And you *do* like it. This isn't about punishing yourself, Marshal. This is about giving in to what you really want." He shrugged. "Or maybe you're dealing with some shit, just like I am."

"Maybe it's both," I admitted. "But that doesn't mean it isn't a phase."

"Duly noted. Speaking of which," he said on his way into the living room. "I assume you're aware that Austin has a schoolboy crush on you."

"That's not exactly how I'd describe it." Austin was a grown-ass man, and while he might not be as aggressive as Bishop, he certainly hadn't been shy about his interest. "But yes, I'm aware."

He came back into the room pulling his shirt over his head. "So, do you like him?"

"Are you seriously asking me that? Before I even have my pants on?"

"Yeah. Do you?"

"Yes, actually. He's pretty great. He worked at the bar tonight, just to help me out. Unasked. But I'm not really sure what to do about that, because I wasn't looking for *this* to happen," I said, arms wide to indicate our latest hookup. "And I'm pretty sure he'll hate us both when he finds out."

When. Not if.

Austin deserved to know about this…complication. Even if I had no idea how to tell him.

I headed into the living room, where I snatched my jeans from the floor and stepped into them.

Bishop followed me. "Oh, he knows, and he doesn't hate either of us."

My fingers stilled, my button only halfway through the hole. "He— *What*?"

Another shrug. "I don't keep secrets from Austin. Not since Yvette and I tried to sneak around behind his back. After that, he made me promise."

"Wait, you and I are…banging it out. And your best friend, who has a 'schoolboy crush' on me *knows* about it?"

He shrugged. "We discussed it."

"You discussed it? *This*?" I gestured between the two of us. "Does that not seem *incredibly* awkward to you?"

His brows arched. "It seems more honest than awkward. He's a good guy, Charley. A much better man than I am. If what we're doing means you can't give him a chance, I'll step aside. Don't get me wrong. I'll miss it. Especially on days when I either need to kill someone or fuck *really* fuckin' hard. But Austin's… He's my best friend. You're awesome, and he's awesome, and I'm not going to stand in the way of that."

I sank onto the edge of my coffee table, trying to understand what I was hearing. *Austin knows*. And Bishop, who was *made* of hard edges and sharp corners, thought I should give him a chance. "I thought you didn't want anyone to know about this. About us."

"I don't want any of *those* assholes to know." He waved a hand at the floor, and by extension, the first-floor bar. "They don't know me, and they didn't know Yvette, and they wouldn't understand how much I still love her—how much I fucking *miss* her—if they knew about this. But Austin understands."

I exhaled slowly. Austin knew I was sleeping with his best friend, and he didn't hate me. He still came to the bar to help out. He still asked me out. To *dinner*.

"You two have *nothing* in common, do you?"

Bishop snorted. "If you're asking me what he's like in bed, you're barking up the wrong tree. He's not my type."

"No, that's not what I…"

I mean, I wasn't *not* asking that. I guess.

"I'm going to need to think about this." I plucked Davey's keys from the coffee table and tossed them to Bishop, who caught them one-handed. "Give those back to him, please. If he was serious about opening with me in the morning, he'll need them." And I'd need the next eight hours to figure out how the hell I was going to face him.

But Bishop tossed the keys back to me. "Can't. We have to go bring in Cam Senet. And as badly as I hate to cover those up," he added with a glance at my still-bare breasts. "You should probably put a shirt on."

I snatched my tee from the floor near the front door, where he'd dropped it. "Trust me; if we knew where to find Cam, we'd already be on it."

Bishop sat on my couch and stuffed his foot into one hiking book. "Oh, I found him. Well, not him, but his place."

"You *what*?" I did *not* sit. "You found Cam Senet's house—"

"It's really more of a trailer."

"—and you didn't tell anyone?"

"That's why I'm here. And this *is* me telling you."

"Bishop, I asked you what happened tonight, and—"

"And I told you I was trying not to do a bad thing." He met my gaze as he loosened the strings on his second boot. "That was the bad thing. I came here to keep from killing him, because I know *you* have your heart set on some kind of official proceeding."

"I—" *Damn it!* "Okay, that's a *step* in the right direction, but you can't just withhold information like that! We could have been out there catching him, instead of..." I trailed off, jabbing one arm in the direction of my bedroom. "How the hell am I going to explain that delay to Titus?"

Bishop snorted. "I seriously doubt you're going to have to, but if you do, I'd *really* like to be there to hear it."

"No. You would not. Where is Cam now?"

"No idea. But I found his place, and if he has no clue we're onto him, he has no reason not to go back there at some point. So, my options were to wait there, thinking about Yvette's last hours, getting angrier and angrier by the moment, until I ripped his throat out the second I saw him, or..." He mimicked my gesture toward the bedroom. "Thanks for that, by the way. That shit? The two of us? That's not normal. Is it always like that, for two shifters?"

"No." Not with Eamon and me, anyway. "Can you please focus? How can you be sure Cam lives in whatever trailer you found, if he wasn't there?"

"The whole place smells like a shifter. Front doorknob. Folding chairs on the back deck."

"Tell me you did not go inside."

"Of course not. Didn't touch a goddamn thing. I know how scent transfer works, Charley. "Speaking of which…" His gaze trailed down my body.

"Shit!" I stood and pulled my shirt off again. "Strip and get your ass in the shower." Before I was even sure he was following orders, I raced into the bathroom, where I turned the shower to full-hot, then stripped out of my own clothes and twisted my hair up into a knot.

The water was still ice cold when I stepped beneath it, and I squealed as chill bumps popped up all over my body.

"I'll keep you warm," Bishop said as he wedged himself in with me. There was *not* room for two in my tiny stall, but there was also no time to spare for two separate showers.

"Don't keep me warm," I said through chattering teeth. "Don't even touch me. The whole point of this is to wash your scent off." As I reached for the soap, I couldn't help but notice that he was fully erect again. "Really? Already?"

"Like you're not interested," he said, sniffing the air in my direction. "I can smell your arousal, Marshal."

"Fuck off. And *wash*."

The water warmed up as I handed him a plain soap bar and grabbed my body wash. "How did you find Cam Senet's trailer?" I asked as I lathered my arms and torso. "There's no way you just stumbled into it."

"No. I spent most of the night waiting for Tucker to text me an address to check out, as he found them. But mostly I was just driving around, waiting. Then I got an idea of my own."

"I'm all ears," I said as I struggled to wash my legs without bending toward him or soaking my hair.

"Oh, you're much more than that," he assured me, running soapy hands over his chest way too slowly not to be deliberate. "But anyway, I was scrolling through Senet's social media pictures, and I realized I recognized that one selfie he took in a bar that wasn't the Fat Cat. And I thought, why would a shifter go to a non-shifter bar?"

"You tell me." I shoved him over so I could rinse. "You clearly did the same thing, if you recognized it."

"Austin and I went to several bars looking for Nolan Blake before we found this one. We just knew the shifter bar was around here, but we didn't know where it was or what it was called. Anyway, I figured that the only reason Cam Senet would have to go to a human bar was to find a human woman. So, I went back to that bar."

"And he was there?"

"No. Again, I have no idea where he was tonight. But when I started asking about him, I met this woman named Tracy."

"Oh my god." I stared up at him, only vaguely aware that a fine mist from the shower was hitting my hair knot. "She's his ex."

"I know. You told us she dumped him the night Austin and I came to town. As it turns out, she was still feeling hurt about his 'emotional unavailability,' especially considering how much of a catch she considers herself...for a man who lives in the, and I quote, 'goddamn Hideaway trailer park.'"

"Oh my *god*! Bishop, that's fucking brilliant!" I launched myself up onto my toes and planted a kiss right on his mouth. But what I'd intended as a brief, triumph-fueled gesture lingered much longer than that, because he dropped the soap, lifted me with slick hands, and pressed me against the wall of my own shower while he plundered my mouth with a resurgence of our earlier heat.

"Damn it," I swore as I shoved him back.

He laughed as he set me down. "You started that."

"I— Give me the godddamn soap." I lathered up again quickly, rinsed off, then wrapped a towel around myself while I brushed my teeth at the mirror. "There's a new toothbrush under the sink," I told him. "Brush well, then throw it away. And don't fucking touch me again until we're both dressed."

"YES. HIDEAWAY," I said as I clicked my seatbelt into place in the passenger's seat of Bishop's 4Runner.

"That trailer park off the highway?" Tucker said, over the phone.

"Yeah. He lives, like ten minutes from the bar. This whole fucking time."

"How sure are we? I haven't found an address yet, and—"

"Abso-fucking-lutely sure," Bishop said as he pulled out of the parking lot. "I could smell the fucker everywhere."

Tucker hesitated. Then he lowered his voice. "He went there? Alone?"

"Yes, but Cam wasn't home, and he swears he didn't touch anything."

"Okay, stay where you are and wait for me," Tucker said. "You need backup."

"She *has* backup," Bishop growled.

"Charley—"

"We're short-handed, Tucker," I said. "And Austin has no car here in town. I need you to take him to the bar and set up the other cell for Cam. I don't love putting him down there with Billy, where they could get their stories straight, but I haven't come up with anything else yet, so for now, we're just not going to leave them alone."

"You can't use Bishop in the field," Tucker insisted.

"He's had no training. I'll grab Austin and bring him, but we're coming to you, not the bar."

"I need the cell prepared, Tucker, and I'm your—"

"Boss. I know. But Titus is yours, and he told me *not* to let you go after Cam alone."

"She's not alone," Bishop growled.

"*Wait for us*." Tucker insisted. Then he hung up.

"I'm getting really tired of people telling me to wait," I grumbled as I leaned forward to shove my phone into my pocket.

Bishop snorted. "I may not have 'training,' but I'm the one who found this asshole," he said.

"And that was awesome. But Tucker's not wrong. If you're going to be out here with us, you *have* to follow orders. I believe you're familiar with the concept."

Another snort.

"Promise me. Promise me this like you promised Austin you wouldn't keep any more secrets from him." I wanted him to mean it.

Bishop glanced at me before turning back to the road. "Fine. I promise. Out here, you're the boss."

"Damn right."

"But in the bedroom—"

"I'm the boss in there too, unless I decide to take the night off."

Bishop laughed out loud. "Fair enough. Though I'm pretty fond of your nights off."

I squirmed in my seat at the memory, but then a familiar sign on the side of the road pulled my focus back where it belonged. "That's it. Pull in across the street. Behind that auto body shop." It had been closed for hours, and a tiny family-owned place like that had no exterior lights and no cameras.

While he parked, I texted Tucker with our updated location. I had yet to speak to Austin since I'd found out he knew about Bishop and me, and I wasn't entirely sure how that was going to go. Fortunately, we had more pressing matters to deal with.

"Which unit is his?" I asked, staring at what I could see of the trailer park around the back of the body shop.

"It's one of the big lots in the back. A quarter acre or more. He's got a double-wide, bricked up to the windows, with a custom front porch and back deck. Pretty much the best-case scenario for a trailer park."

"What's behind it?" We were outside of town, and I couldn't see any lights, other than TVs glowing through the windows of a couple of trailers in the front of the park.

"Nothing. Woods. Hey, look. You can actually see Senet's place from here, if you squint. Through the trees. Back there on the left."

Thanks to the cloudless night, the bright three-quarter moon, and the fact that the trees were winter-bare, he was right. "There's a light on. Dim. Like it's behind a curtain."

"That wasn't on earlier. He's home." Bishop reached for the door handle, but I grabbed his arm.

"Watch and wait. That's all we're doing until they—"

"The light went out." His whole body tensed, his eyes narrowed as he stared through the windshield. "That's—" He leaned forward. "I think the front door is opening. We have to move. Now."

"No, we wait. If he drives off, we'll just follow him and text Tucker with an update."

Reluctantly, Bishop leaned back in his seat. "I'd rather be giving the orders."

I patted his shoulder. "You'll get there," I teased, throwing his own words back at him. "I have faith."

"Cute." He turned back to the windshield. "He's not

getting in the car. He's... I think he's heading into the woods. On two feet." Bishop turned to me, the desperation in his gaze a wordless plea. "If we don't go after him, we could lose him."

"You said yourself that he'll come back to his home."

"I said he'd probably come back if he doesn't know we're onto him. What if he does know? Or what if he finds out while he's out there? He might never come back. We could lose him, Charley."

I exhaled. Each second ticking by felt like sand slipping through my fingers. Like time running out. "Promise you won't kill him. *No* unnecessary force. We *need* to hear everything he has to say." We didn't even know for certain that he was guilty.

"I swear on my life. On Yvette's grave."

"Fine. But you *follow my lead*." I opened my door and climbed out, then closed it as softly as possible, while Bishop did the same. Then I jogged across the street and into the woods, with him at my heels.

We couldn't move at top speed and maintain total silence, which wouldn't have been an issue if we were following a human. But Cam's hearing was just as good as ours.

"You go right?" Bishop whispered when we reached the trailer, indicating that he'd take the opposite direction. But I was loathe to lose sight of him. I didn't think he'd intentionally disobey orders, but I couldn't be sure what kind of impulse control limitations he might have when he came face-to-face with his wife's suspected killer.

"We stay together," I insisted as softly as I could. He scowled—that would cut our chances of finding him virtually in half—but he didn't argue.

I let him veer about ten feet away, because I could cross that distance in a hurry if I needed to, and we moved as quickly and quietly through the woods as we could, alert for any sound that didn't belong in nature. Namely, the snap of a twig breaking beneath someone's foot.

For several minutes, we heard nothing, and I was convinced we'd lost Cam. That we'd have to rely on the hope that he really didn't know we were looking for him. But then—

"There," Bishop said, so softly I practically felt the words. He turned to the east, and I wished I had cat ears that could swivel to listen in a specific direction. But then I heard it: not the snap of a twig, but the rustle of a winter-bare branch as someone brushed it out of the way.

I motioned for him to *go* and we took off, curving away from each other to approach the sound from different angles. To surround Cam, as best we could with just the two of us.

In seconds, I saw the silhouette, backlit in what moonlight there was, only...there were two of them. Cam was not alone. He and his partner were moving quietly through the woods, taking care with every step, as if they knew we were here. Looking for them.

I couldn't see Bishop as I snuck closer, until suddenly a dark form burst into sight from the opposite side of the silhouettes. When I saw him coming, I lurched into action, tackling the nearest form.

I realized my mistake as soon as I got close enough to smell him, which was far too late to stop myself from driving Austin to the ground.

His startled *oof* blew hair back from my face, and I heard Tucker cursing softly on the ground a couple of feet away, as Bishop scrambled to his feet. "What the fuck are you two doing here?" I demanded in a fierce whisper.

"You called us!" Tucker returned. "And I knew damn well you weren't going to wait, so we snuck in from the back. We thought we heard something, but it must have been you."

"It wasn't," Bishop said as I helped Austin to his feet. "I saw him come out of his trailer. That's the only reason we didn't wait."

Tucker looked unconvinced. "Well, he's gone now. With any luck, he had no idea we were here."

"Should we check out the trailer?" Austin said. "Since we don't need a warrant, under shifter law?"

Tucker shook his head. "Not unless we want him to know we were here."

"He's right," I said. "But I'm going in."

"Charley—" Tucker began, but I cut him off with a look as I pulled a thin pair of gloves from my jacket pocket.

"I'm going in alone, and I won't touch anything. But if there's anything that can be learned without leaving a scent, I'm going to find it. You three keep watch. Out of sight." With that, I headed back through the woods toward the rear of Cam Senet's trailer.

The back door was unlocked, and I was starting to wonder if that was a shifter thing. Or a stray thing. We were just so arrogant about our newfound abilities that we considered ourselves invulnerable?

Gloves on, I opened the door and snuck inside, resisting the urge to turn on a light, when I didn't truly need one. Old habits die hard.

Cam's kitchen was about what I'd expect from a bachelor who hadn't had a girl over in at least a week. Two empty pizza boxes, trash can overflowing with takeout bags, and cereal bowls stacked up in the sink at odd angles, because of the spoons wedged between them. Nothing in the kitchen screamed "I'm a serial murderer," and the living room wasn't much better. Or neater.

I was about to turn around and sneak back out, without even bothering with the bedroom, when a familiar shape caught my eye, propped against one end of the couch.

My pulse thudded in my ears as I crossed the room and picked up the canvas shoulder bag. There were probably twenty just like it in Buford, Tennessee alone. It could belong to anyone. Maybe Tracy had left it here before she dumped Cam.

My hands shook as I opened the bag.

Davey's laptop was still inside.

TWENTY-FOUR

"This is my fault," I said, sipping from my third cup of coffee as I paced alongside the booths lining the west wall of the bar. Every nerve ending in my body was on fire from the caffeine overload, but I needed something in my hands.

Alcohol seemed unwise, and Cam's throat wasn't yet available, so…

"It's not your fault," Austin insisted, while Tucker's rapid-fire typing continued from across the room as he tried to oblige my command to *fucking find Cam Senet*.

He was worried too. Austin and Bishop understood exactly what it was like to fear for a loved one's life, but Tucker knew Davey personally, and I could tell from the hard line of his jaw and the deep set of his brow that he was in this with me.

Davey in danger was a zone-wide crisis, and if the regulars found out about it, we'd have a riot on our hands.

"It *is* my fault." Terror churned deep in my soul, its dark undertow threatening to drown me. For the first time since I'd become Marshal, I felt completely, terrifyingly helpless.

Useless. "I practically drove her away." And I had no real plan for how to get her back.

Austin sighed from his bar stool, clearly frustrated that I would not accept his comfort. "She left of her own volition."

"Because I pissed her off."

Bishop snorted. "Something tells me that wasn't the first time, and she's never marched into the arms of a killer before, has she?"

I stopped pacing to glare at him, and coffee sloshed over the edge of my mug. "She didn't march into the arms of a killer. She was kidnapped." That's the only way Davey would ever have wound up anywhere near Cam Senet's trailer.

Unless…

No. I shoved that possibility back as hard as I could, ignoring my spill. Davey would never be stupid enough to go looking for him. Trying to get infected on her own, because I'd sworn to stop her. Yes, she was determined, but she wasn't reckless.

"Regardless of what happened, I'm the reason she was out there alone in the first place." Anxiety wrapped around my chest like a huge rubber band, and I fought for a deep breath as I picked up my phone and texted my sister for at least the twentieth time in the past half hour.

 Pick up your goddamn phone!

I still couldn't track her, and she wasn't answering my calls or my texts, and—

My phone rang, startling me so badly I nearly dropped my mug. I set it on the nearest table and hit the "accept call" button before I'd truly processed that it wasn't my sister calling.

"Charley?" Titus said into my ear.

"Oh, thank god." I'd called him twice too, but it was past two in the morning. "He has Davey." I marched across the bar again and shoved my way through the swinging doors into the kitchen, desperately trying to calm my racing pulse. To arrest the tide of unbidden worst-case-scenarios threatening to wash me out into a sea of paralyzing grief.

I could not afford to be sidelined by fear. This was the time for clear thought and decisive action: the kind of crisis I'd spent the past year and a half preparing for. I just hadn't expected it to involve my sister.

"Who has Davey?" The slight creak of bedsprings whispered over the line, along with the rustle of fabric as he got out of bed.

"Cam Senet. We found where he lives—"

"*I* found it," Bishop called from out front, and Austin cleared his throat, scolding him without a word.

"—but he wasn't there. There's a possibility that we *just* missed him—that he knew we were there—but I'm not sure yet. Either way, her bag was in his living room."

And I took it.

I shouldn't have—if he goes back and sees it missing, he'll know someone was there—but I couldn't leave her things in that monster's house. It felt like I'd be abandoning what little I had left of her.

"She was *there*, Titus. He had her. He still has her. I *know* he does, because she would not have left her laptop behind."

"Were her keys in the bag?"

"Yes, but her car wasn't there. Neither was her phone, but obviously she's not answering."

"Okay." Titus sighed, and I could hear his footsteps moving softly through his massive house. He was awake and fully with me. "Let's assume for the time being that he has it.

That he's seeing your texts. Don't say anything to her that would clue him in."

"I haven't. Obviously, he can tell I'm worried that she's not answering her phone, but that's it."

"Is there anything in your previous texts to her that we should worry about?"

"No. I don't generally discuss zone business with my sister, and never via text." As per policy for non-Pride employees.

"Good." A soft click echoed over the line, and I heard the sharp hiss of his expensive and fully automatic espresso machine. "What do you need?"

"More hands. Eyes and ears." I paced back into the front of the bar. "We need someone watching his place twenty-four/seven until we find him, and we may need to canvass the whole damn town. Assuming he's even in town. Tucker's doing his best to track him down, but we're all working on very little sleep."

Practically a chronic deficit.

Tucker waved off my worry on his behalf.

"Well, I won't tell you to sleep, because I know you won't do it. But I will send you all the help I can spare." Titus paused. "Do you want Vance?"

"Yes." There was no hesitation on my part. "Yes, send Vance. But don't tell him why until he gets here. I don't want him to get himself killed speeding."

"He already knows, and he's on the way," Tucker said without looking up from his screen. "I texted him half an hour ago."

I glanced at him from across the room with a sigh. "Did you hear that?" I said into my phone.

"Of course." Titus sounded irritated, but probably not because of Tucker's text. He felt he should know—understandably—about any sudden traffic into and out of his zone. "I'll make some calls and send anyone else I can spare."

"Titus, we're going to need Spencer." I didn't bother spelling out for him why we would need a triage nurse, because I was sure he understood my gravest fear.

"He'll be on the road in less than an hour."

"Thank you."

"Keep me updated."

"You know I will." I hung up and turned to Tucker, who had the courtesy to stand and face my wrath. Only...there was no wrath.

"I'm sorry," he said. "But Vance belongs here. Especially now. And we need him."

"Yes, we do." I engulfed him in as tight a hug as I could manage, my cheek flat against his shoulder. "Thank you."

"You're not mad?" he said as his arms wrapped around my back.

"Of course, I'm mad. But I'm your boss, not your Alpha. I should have asked for your advice before firing him in the first place, because that affects your job and your safety too. Don't get me wrong. He's not getting off without consequences. But I'm glad he's on the way."

"I'm going back to stake out Cam's place," Bishop said as I stepped out of Tucker's embrace.

"No." I still didn't trust his rage impulse. Especially considering how badly *I* wanted to kill Cam Senet at the moment.

"I'll go with him." Austin stood and grabbed the jacket he'd draped over the back of his stool. "And while I'm at it, I'll show him how a stakeout works."

"Does that mean snacks?" Bishop asked. "I think we should maintain our energy level."

"Sure. Take whatever you want from the kitchen. But

nothing from the bar." I felt like that should have been obvious, but…

"I gotta run to the bathroom, then I'm good to go," Bishop said as he disappeared around the corner, opposite the kitchen.

Austin's gaze captured mine. "Can we talk for a second?"

I exhaled deeply. Then I nodded and led him into the kitchen.

"Listen, Bishop told me—" I began, but he cut me off with a shake of his head.

"That's your business. Nothing to do with me."

"Really?" I frowned up at him. "*Nothing* to do with you?"

"I mean, he's not *my* type, so I can't say I understand the appeal, physically, but you're the second very good woman who's found something worthy in Bishop, so…" Austin shrugged.

"That's not exactly what's happening here."

He grinned. "I know that too. And I hope you get what you need out of it. But if you decide you want something else…"

"Something other than sex?" Was that what he was offering me?

His brows rose. "Something more than *just* sex."

"Ah." I sighed, arms crossed over my chest as I leaned against the stainless steel counter. "This is so fucking awkward."

"Doesn't have to be. Bishop's rough around the edges, and god knows he's got issues. But he's not a bad guy, and I hate to see him hurting like he is. If you two are good for each other in that sense, who am I to get in the way?"

I could only stare at him. "You two are quite a pair."

He laughed. "I'm not sure what that means."

"It means I'm pretty sure you care about each other far

more than either of you cares about me. And that's not a criticism."

"He's my best friend. We're *just* friends, but yes, I love him. And I want to see him happy. And *healthy*. And…un-incarcerated."

I was starting to think I didn't deserve either of them. Especially considering that I'd *fired* my own best friend.

"So, what did you want to talk about, if it isn't…that?"

"I just wanted to make sure you understand that what happened to Davey isn't your fault. And we *are* going to get her back."

"Oh, I know we'll get her back. I'm just not sure we'll get her back alive."

"You can't afford to think like that."

I blinked up at him. "I can't afford not to. You know that. Or have all of your missing persons cases had happy endings?"

"I've only had one. Covington is not a large town. In fact, it's actually shrinking."

"And did you find your missing person?"

Austin held my gaze, but his forehead furrowed. "Yes. With a bullet through his skull."

"Then you understand why I can't afford blind optimism here. I need to prepare for the reality that's actually in front of me, and there's only one reason Cam Senet would take my sister." I frowned with a sudden new thought. "In fact…" I motioned for him to follow me as I headed back into the front of the building.

"Tucker," I said as I pushed my way through the swinging doors, and he looked up from his screen.

"Yeah?"

"Let's think this through before they head back to Hideaway."

"Never a bad idea," he said, lifting his mug for a sip.

"It makes no sense for Cam to go after my sister." It hadn't occurred to me before, in my near-blinding fear and rage. "There's no upside to that for him. If she survives, which is clearly his goal, we'll know who infected her. And if she dies, we'll never stop hunting him. So, there's zero chance he expects to get away with this. So why would he do it? Why take such a high-profile target?"

"Opportunity," Austin said, before Tucker could hazard a guess. "I've seen that before. Criminals make a stupid, risky move because when opportunity presents itself, they just can't resist."

"What opportunity are we talking about?" Bishop said, drying his hands with a paper towel as the men's room door swung shut behind him.

"The opportunity to take Davey, when that was not in his best interest," Tucker explained. "There's no quicker way to bring himself to our attention, even if we hadn't already been onto him, than by taking the Marshal's sister. The surrogate baby sister to every cat in the zone."

"You think we should call them in? All those 'big brothers?'" Bishop asked.

"I think that would be chaos," I said. "And it would dramatically lower the chances of us bringing him in alive, when we really need to question him."

"Also, it's against protocol," Tucker pointed out. "They're not employees of the zone or the Pride, and they're not trained, so they dramatically increase the chances of bringing this to human attention."

"I'm not trained either," Bishop pointed out.

"Yes, but you're already in the know, you're directly involved, and you're under close supervision," I reminded him.

"Yours, or his?" Bishop glanced from me to Austin.

"Both," we replied in unison.

"Okay," Tucker said, pulling us back on track as I settled in across the table from him. "So, we think that Cam took Davey because, what? He just ran across her, randomly? Doesn't he see her all the time, here? Why take her now?"

"I don't know," I admitted. "Maybe he knew we were onto him." I shrugged. "If he thought he was going to have to run anyway, why not make off with everything he could."

"Was he packed?" Austin asked. "When you were in his trailer, did you see suitcases, or empty drawers, or anything?"

"No." I'd glanced in his bedroom after I'd found my sister's bag, but nothing had stood out. "Maybe he didn't know he should be on the run until he spoke to Davey. Maybe she accidentally tipped him off."

"Maybe he could tell she was upset, after your fight," Tucker said.

"Maybe, but she wouldn't look to him for comfort. She knew he was our prime suspect."

"Is there any chance she went to him?" Austin asked as he slid into the booth next to me. "Any chance she was trying to prove herself? To you? By trying to bring him in on her own?"

"No. No way in hell. She's not stupid, and she isn't reckless." Even her relationship with Vance had been strategically and carefully handled, in order to keep it secret. "She wouldn't do that."

But there *was* that possibility I'd intentionally shoved aside. The idea that I'd not only driven her lover away and denied her the shifter existence she wanted, but had also pushed her into the arms of a killer because she knew he would be willing to infect her.

But no. Again, she wasn't reckless. She wanted a

controlled infection, with medication and support standing by. She wasn't stupid enough to risk her life with Cam, after he'd killed at least half a dozen other women who almost certainly also had the shifter gene.

She *wasn't*.

"Okay, well, however he got her, he has two options at this point," Tucker said.

Austin shrugged. "Run, or dig in and hide."

"I'm guessing that if he runs, we're fucked," Bishop said.

"Largely, yes," Austin agreed. "Though I could probably call in a favor and see if he's been ticketed anywhere or used any toll roads. Most of those have cameras that log license plate numbers."

"It doesn't make sense for him to run, though," I said, thinking aloud. "He's doing this for a reason. And he probably thinks that if he can successfully add a female shifter to our numbers, there are people high up in the community— council members—who'll want to know how he did it, and whether he can do it again. And he may not be entirely off-base there. He may be counting on an eventual success to save his life. Which means he *needs* to keep Davey alive. Which makes running less likely, considering how sick she'll be."

"He'll have taken her some place stable," Tucker said. "Some place he can treat her."

"Why?" Bishop said. "He didn't do that with any of the others, right? He certainly didn't play nurse with Yvette."

"We have no idea how any of it went down with Yvette or the other women," I admitted. "I still can't figure out how he managed to leave such a clean bite on her, or why he would let her go after that. And as far as we know about the others —" Based entirely on what Nolan Blake was able to tell us about his sister. "—they had no idea they'd been infected.

None of their hospital reports even mentioned an animal attack."

"Okay, so he changed his MO with Davey," Tucker said. "Because of that irresistible opportunity she presented, as the sister of the only successfully infected woman he's ever met."

"Whom his father infected," I added. "It makes sense, if you squint just right. A man in his family successfully infected a woman in Davey's. Maybe he thought he could replicate that."

"Or at least that he had to try," Austin said.

"Right. So, he wants to keep her alive." Bishop sank into a chair at a table several feet away. "But if he knows we're onto him, he's not going to keep her at his place, right? So there's no point in going back there?"

Austin shrugged. "Except to do a more thorough search."

"Yes. Will you two do that? I'm going down to talk to Billy again. There *has* to be more he can tell us."

"He's been interviewed twice," Tucker pointed out. "And Vance is very thorough."

"I know. But if Billy was holding anything back— anything at all—surely he'll give it up when he hears about Davey. He looks up to her. He likes her. He'd want to help, if he can."

Tucker closed his laptop. "I'm coming with you." I started to object but he kept talking. "I've exhausted all the online leads, unless he has something new to offer, anyway."

"Okay, then." I stood with him as Austin and Bishop shrugged into their jackets. "You two let us know if you find anything helpful at Cam's. Otherwise, we'll meet back here."

"I'm a little afraid I'm never going to sleep again," Bishop mumbled as he followed Austin toward the back door. "But it'll be worth it when that asshole is rotting in a shallow hole in the ground."

A minute later, we heard the 4Runner's engine start from out back, and Tucker turned to me. "So, you and Bishop Mattheson? Or you and Austin Graham?"

I flinched. "You overheard us?"

"Not on purpose." He shrugged. "But you had to know that secret wouldn't keep."

"Vance and Davey's did."

"Until it didn't."

"Well, whatever you're assuming, you're probably wrong. I'm not actually involved with either of them."

Tucker's brows rose. "Define 'involved.'"

I sighed as I backed toward the basement stairs. "I'd rather not."

He shrugged, a hint of a grin peeking out at me from the upturn of one side of his mouth. "Whatever's going on is none of my business. All I know is that you deserve better than Eamon, and I hope you get it."

I gave him a hug, blinking back surprised tears. Then I cleared my throat and headed down the stairs. "Let's do this."

"WHAT DO YOU MEAN, he took Davey?" Billy launched himself off the cot in his cell as if it had just sent a jolt of electricity through him. "Are you sure? How do you know?"

"I found her bag at his place, and she's not answering her phone. She's not at home." Which we'd confirmed on our way to the bar from Cam's trailer. "She's missing, Billy. He has her."

"You searched Denny's place? What place?"

"We're the ones asking questions," Tucker said, stationed behind me to my right, close enough that his shadow merged with mine. He could be quite intimidating when he wanted to be.

Evidently this was one of those moments.

"Yeah. Okay." Billy nodded several times, rapidly, his pulse racing. "What do you need, then?"

"Information. Anything you can give us," I said.

He sank onto the cot again. "I've told you everything I know."

"And yet you came up with more when Vance interviewed you yesterday. I'm asking you to try one more time. For Davey. Anything you can remember about any place Denny used to go. Any building he'd have access to. Some place he wouldn't be noticed. Or bothered. Some place he could take her while she—" I bit the rest off, not because he shouldn't hear it, but because I couldn't say it.

"You think he bit her."

"Or he's going to." *Please, please don't let us be too late.* "Why else would he take her?"

"*Where* would he take her?" Tucker stepped forward, even with me.

Billy shook his head, lank hair falling over his forehead. "I don't—"

"What about his mother?" Tucker demanded. She wasn't mentioned in any of his social media, the email address she'd written to Silas from was inactive, and without access to his birth certificate, we had nothing else to go on. No way to identify her.

"I told you, I never met her. All I know is her first name. Rebecca. Silas called her Becky. My mom did too. She didn't like Denny's mom. Said any woman who'd give her kid away over a 'behavioral incident' wasn't any good as a mother anyway."

That assessment hardly seemed fair to me, considering the severity of Denny's current *behavioral incident*, but that wasn't the point. "Did she say anything else about Becky?"

Billy shrugged. "I mean, yeah. She was Silas's ex, and my mom had opinions. She thought Becky gave Denny too much freedom, then blamed Silas when her approach backfired. She thought Becky was wrong to want money from Silas, but not his 'presence' in Denny's life. Until she got tired of him and gave him to us."

It was a one-sided debate without Becky's input, but all of that was beside the point. "Did your mother ever say anything about where Becky lived? Where Denny was before he came to live with you?" If his mother had left him any property, it could be exactly what we were looking for. Assuming she had passed.

"Um..." Billy closed his eyes, clearly searching his memory. "She said once that she thought Becky had really sent him to live with us because there wasn't room for a teenage boy in their place. 'Cause it only had one bedroom. She said Becky was probably tired of sleeping on the couch in her own home."

I could understand that, whether or not it was her reason for sending her son to his father.

"Did she say where that was?" Tucker asked. "Or what kind of place it was? A house? Apartment? Trailer?"

"Apartment?" I guessed, having never seen a one-bedroom house or trailer. But if it was an apartment, chances were slim that Cam would have taken Davey there. Both because his mother couldn't have left him a place she didn't own, and because there'd be too many neighbors as potential eye-witnesses.

"I don't know," Billy said.

"What town?" Tucker asked. "Do you know what school Billy went to, before he lived with you?"

"It was something small. Even smaller than my school. He said there were only, like, thirty kids in his class. I don't remember the town, but he did have this school shirt he used to wear, until he outgrew it. I remember that the mascot was a beaver, because Silas used to laugh every time Denny wore it. I didn't get why, at the time."

I turned to Tucker, who nodded, then practically raced from the room, armed with a new nugget—small though it was—of information.

As he closed the basement door, I sank into a folding chair several feet from Billy's cell. "Is there anything else you can think of? *Any*thing? Anything at all?"

He shook his head. "I would tell you, Charley. I swear to god, I would never do anything to put Davey in danger."

"Okay. Thank you." I stood again and handed him a bottle of water from the half-empty case under the card table. "We're not opening the bar today, but someone will be down with some breakfast in the morning."

"It isn't morning?"

"Sun won't be up for a few more hours," I said.

"And you haven't slept?"

"*No one*'s sleeping until Davey's home." One way or another.

"Charley," Billy called as I opened the basement door. "Do you think she's okay?"

"No," I said without turning around. "I really doubt she is."

TWENTY-FIVE

"Parker's Mill," Tucker said the second I came through the swinging doors into the front of the bar.

"What?"

"Parker's Mill," he repeated, clacking away at his keyboard. "Ever heard of it?"

"I mean, yeah. I grew up here. It's not far from Buford. Not really big enough to be a town. More like a...rural community."

"It's an unincorporated township about fifty miles from here. Their school system was absorbed by the county eight years ago, but before that Parker's Mill High school was home to Parker the Beaver." He spun his laptop around for me to see the results of his Google Image search for "Tennessee high school mascot beaver."

"Only one in the state," he said, presumably referring to the mascot.

"Hey!" Bishop called as the back door squealed open from the kitchen. "We found something!" A second later, he followed Austin into the front of the bar, waving a thin, hardbound book overhead. "You ever hear of a place called Parker's Mill?"

Tucker huffed.

"It's a forty-minute drive from here, if you follow the speed limit, and I've never heard of it," Austin said as Bishop set the smallest high school yearbook I'd ever seen on the bar top in front of me.

"Freshman class." Bishop flipped the book open to a page he'd marked with a utility bill sent to Cam Senet's trailer. "We figure that's the only year he attended before he went to live with Silas. Look familiar?" He set one finger down on a picture labeled "Denny Brewer."

"Brewer?" I squinted at the image, but it was definitely Cam. "His social media is under Denny Morelock."

"We're guessing he started using his dad's surname when he went to live with him," Austin said. Which meant he would have been going by his mother's last name until then.

Tucker was already typing, presumably searching for—

"Rebecca Brewer." He sat back with his arms crossed over his chest, a look of triumph spreading across his features. "Long-time resident of Parker's Mill, Tennessee, according to her obituary from two years ago. She left behind one son, Denny, and was preceded in death by her parents, James and Sylvia Brewer."

"Thank god," I whispered as I crossed the room toward him.

"Property search coming up," Tucker added as he leaned forward to fish his business card from his wallet. "Good thing Titus is generous with the budget."

Tucker typed, read, and typed some more, while I brewed a fresh pot of coffee.

"You're gonna drown in that shit," Bishop said as I

poured myself a fresh mug. "You should have some water. Stay hydrated."

"And you should mind your business," I said. With a small smile.

"Someone's here." Austin rose from his barstool an instant before I heard the unfamiliar engine, and he beat me into the kitchen because of the second and a half it took me to set my mug down without spilling it.

Bishop was on my heels, and by the time we got there, Austin stood in the open kitchen doorway, glaring out at the car shining its headlights into the back of the bar. He was growling softly, every muscle in his body tense and ready for a fight.

Bishop took one look at his best friend and assumed a similar aggressive stance, puffed up with testosterone. Or with some cat hormone I had no name for. He stepped in front of me, blocking my entire view of both Austin and the door.

"Okay, enough of that. Move over," I scolded as car door hinges squeaked from the parking lot.

Austin's growling intensified, which meant he didn't recognize whoever had just parked behind my business.

"Stand down, and tell Charley I'm here," a commanding voice called from the gravel lot, and my heart leapt into my throat. I darted around Bishop and shoved Austin aside, then raced out the door to throw my arms around Jace Hammond.

"Hey, Char," he said as he returned my hug. "I heard you might need an extra hand. Though it looks like you've added several recently." He nodded at the two men now standing shoulder-to-shoulder in the kitchen doorway, evidently satisfied that I was not in danger. "What's that about?"

"I have no idea. They're acting weird."

"They're acting *territorial*." Jace gave me a pointed look I chose not to analyze. "Who are they?"

"Hey, assholes!" I called toward the kitchen. "Come meet the other Marshal."

Austin stepped forward first, with his aggressive posture in full recession, and Bishop followed, his metaphorical hackles still raised.

"Jace Hammond, this is Austin Graham and Bishop Mattheson. Yvette was Austin's sister and Bishop's wife. Guys, Jace is the Marshal of the central zone of the Mississippi Valley Pride, and an Alpha in his own right. So behave."

"Nice to meet you." Austin offered Jace his hand to shake, and Bishop only followed suit when Austin elbowed him.

"You too," Jace said. "I'm so sorry about Yvette. And I'm here to help however I can."

"Titus didn't mention you were coming." I linked my arm through Jace's to escort him into the bar, relieved to have such trusted backup. He'd been working as either an enforcer or a Marshal for more than a decade and was more experienced than anyone else in the Pride. Including Titus.

"I volunteered," he said. "Abby says hi, by the way." Jace had been with Faythe's younger cousin for nearly four years. "She's hoping to get up here to see you soon. And Davey," he added. "I don't believe they've met."

"I certainly hope they get to." I let Jace go as one of the other guys closed the kitchen door behind us.

Out front, Tucker turned from his screen to greet Jace, while Bishop whispered to Austin.

"How'd he get here so fast?"

"He lives just a couple of hours away," I said. "And he clearly ignored the speed limit."

"Speaking of which, Vance is only an hour out," Tucker said.

"He better not get pulled over," I grumbled. "He won't do

Davey any good from a jail cell." I sighed. "Where are we on the property search?"

"I've only found one possibility." Tucker spun his laptop around so I could see a satellite image zoomed in to the point of pixilation. "Rebecca Brewer's mother passed away when she was in her forties, about a year and a half after her father, who was older. She had some kind of genetic heart condition that may also be why Rebecca died young. The Brewers owned a few acres of scrub brush on the outskirts of Parker's Mill, and the county property records say that a one-bedroom domicile was built there nearly fifty years ago. It does not appear to have been improved much since then, other than the addition of an outbuilding and a blacktop driveway."

"That's it. That *has* to be it," I breathed. "Does it say who owns it now?" Could Cam have sold it?

Tucker clicked on another tab at the top of his screen. "Camden Brewer."

"Brewer," Austin repeated. "That's why it didn't show up during previous property searches."

"I take it this Camden has another name?" Jace leaned with one hand on the back of the booth as he peered at the screen.

"Two of them," I said. "He went by his father's surname —as Denny Morelock—for most of the past decade, but around here, we know him as Cam Senet."

"He's led us on quite the virtual hunt," Tucker added. "Managing social media in two names, though not very active in one, with no personal details whatsoever. We all knew him, but it turns out none of us knew anything concrete or helpful, like his address or where he works."

"He mostly talks about girl troubles when he's in the bar," I added.

"Which set off no red flags, because *most* male shifters have girl troubles," Jace said.

Tucker nodded. "Exactly. Myself, excluded."

Jace gestured at the satellite image on Tucker's screen. "But you think this is where we'll find him?"

I shrugged. "He's not keeping her at his trailer, and the cabin where his father held me has fallen into *vast* disrepair. His mom's place is too strong a possibility to overlook."

"Okay then, let's go."

"I'm texting Vance the address," Tucker said as he closed his laptop. "It's between here and his current location, so he might actually be able to meet us there."

"Three cars," I said as everyone started shrugging into jackets and packing up electronics. "Tucker and Austin on four legs, everyone else on two. Shift on the way, please, to save time. I want us ready to go the moment we get there. And we take Denny *alive*, unless we have to go through him to get to Davey. Which is my call. Understood?"

Everyone nodded.

JACE DROVE WITH TUCKER, who shifted in the back of his SUV. Austin shifted in the 4Runner while Bishop drove, because I couldn't trust Bishop in cat form. Too much speed, power, and built-in weaponry, and too many instincts I'd never personally seen him navigate. He'd be slower and at least marginally easier to control on two human legs.

But I trusted Austin in the field, and I damn well trusted Tucker. And with any luck, two cats and four of us on foot, once Vance arrived, would be more than enough to handle Cam Senet. Assuming he was alone.

Assuming we hadn't missed *another* silent partner.

My GPS agreed with Austin that it was a 40-minute drive

down several backroads, but we made it in under 30. Fortunately for us, there was precisely zero police presence on the county roads, which would not have been the case on the highway.

Vance pulled up at our rendezvous point as we were all piling out of our cars.

"Where is she?" he demanded as his door flew open.

"We just got here," I told him. "But according to the satellite image, the building is half a mile that way." I pointed to the south. "We haven't verified that anyone is there yet, obviously."

He stared at the image I showed him on my phone, from the link Tucker had sent. "The building faces north. Can't be more than two entrances to a place that small. So we approach from both directions? Cover both entrances?"

"That's the plan," I confirmed. "You, Austin, and Bishop are with me. Tucker's going on four legs, with Jace."

Vance looked up and notice Jace for the first time. "Hey, man, thanks for coming."

"Wouldn't miss it," Jace assured him. "Titus says Spencer is less than an hour out. Though we're still hoping we won't need him. He can come straight here or pivot toward the bar. He's waiting to hear from us, when we determine which is preferable."

I nodded. "We'll call him as soon as we know for sure. You and Tucker go ahead. You'll need a head start to circle the cabin. We'll be right behind you, approaching from the north."

Tucker huffed through feline nostrils, his sleek fur practically glittering in the moonlight. Then he and Jace took off toward the south.

"First aid kits?" I asked, turning to Bishop.

"Two of them." Both of which we'd brought from the bar.

He tossed me one, and I tucked it into my backpack. "Jace has the other."

"Thanks. We bring Cam in alive, if at all possible," I reminded Vance.

"I know."

"I know you do, but I also know that this is personal for you, now."

"I can do my job, Charley." He hesitated, staring down at me in the dark, deep brown eyes shining. "If it's still my job."

"It is. For now." I propped both hands on my hips. "But I swear to god, Vance, that if you ever break the rules again—"

"I won't. I love her. Never doubt that. I'd give my goddamn life for either one of you. But this is all my fault, and if being with me puts her in danger... I'd rather have her alive than *have* her."

I sighed, guilt gnawing at me. "Okay, I'm only going to say this once. I was wrong to fire you. You were wrong to break my rules, and especially to keep a secret like that, but I didn't make it any better. And Davey's definitely safer with *both* of us at her back."

"Char—"

"I'm not finished," I said, and his mouth snapped shut. "This is not your fault, Vance."

"She wouldn't be out there if I'd been there."

"I fired you."

"And I left."

"Good god. Everyone made their own choices, Davey included," Bishop snapped. "But the only bad guy here is Cam Senet. Now let's deal with him and put all this to fucking rights, as best we can."

Austin gave a feline huff of agreement.

Vance shrugged. "He's not wrong. Davey's as stubborn as

you are, and she had every right to stomp off in anger without worrying about being kidnapped."

I pulled him aside and lowered my voice while Bishop dug in the back of his vehicle. "What did she say to you? Is there any possibility that she…sought Cam out?"

Vance frowned. "Why would she—" His mouth snapped shut as understanding dawned. "I truly don't think so. She told me she plans to volunteer for Faythe's program, and I tried to talk her out of it, but she seemed really determined. But she's too smart for this, Charley. She wants to be a shifter, but she doesn't want to die in the process."

"That was my thought too." Yet the possibility still nagged at me.

"Let's *go*," Bishop snapped. "They've had enough of a head-start."

I agreed, so we took off into the woods to the south, racing as fast as we could go until we got close enough to be heard, according to my GPS. My heart raced, pulse swooshing in my ears as I signaled the guys to stop. I smelled wood smoke, and there was light up head. Just a faint glow leaking between some cedars at the moment, and likely too faint for human eyes to detect. But it was in the right direction and approximately the right distance.

"I see it," Vance whispered.

Bishop nodded, and at his side, Austin huffed through feline nostrils.

My phone vibrated in my pocket, and I pulled it out to see a text from Jace. "They're in position," I whispered as I texted back. "They can see one male form through the window, and Tucker confirms that the silhouette is consistent with Cam Senet's build. They'll defend the rear exit, until they hear us come through the front. Let's go."

We moved as quietly as we could toward the small house,

sacrificing speed for silence. Ignoring the cold. The building came into focus, its outline emerging from the shadows as we carefully stepped over fallen branches and exposed roots, ducking beneath bare, low-hanging deciduous limbs and veering around fat, fragrant cedars.

The house was tiny and old, but in decent repair, smoke rising from what appeared to be a hand-stacked stone chimney. The blaze in the fireplace was part of the light source we'd seen, but not all of it. The main room was well lit, and as we approached, just yards away now, I saw a male silhouette cross in front of a sheer-covered window.

Bishop tapped my shoulder, and I turned to follow his gesture to a familiar vehicle parked to one side of the house, on a blacktop driveway cut in from the main road, which we'd avoided. I couldn't swear that it was Cam's car—I didn't know what each of my regulars drove—but I'd definitely seen it in the parking lot at the Fat Cat.

"It's packed," Bishop whispered, and when I squinted at the hatchback window, I could see squarish forms covered by a dark blanket.

Cam was ready to run.

Vance darted past me, moonlight glinting off something clenched in his fist, and seconds later, air hissed from both of the vehicle's rear tires, ending any possibility that Cam could escape by car.

I sighed, worried that Cam would hear that. And he certainly could, if he were paying attention. Fortunately, he seemed preoccupied with whatever was going on inside.

I saw no indication that he knew we were there.

We approached the front door, all three men at my back, careful not to step in front of either of the two visible windows. For a moment, I considered knocking. But it was the middle of the night, and there were no close neighbors, which mean there was virtually no chance we'd lure him to the door under a false, non-threatening pretext.

So instead of knocking, I kicked the front door in, relishing strength I hadn't had as a human woman, as the impact reverberated through my right leg.

Old hinges squealed and aged boards splinted. The solid wood panel swung open to crash against the wall.

Startled, Cam Senet spun toward me from the middle of the small front room, holding a damp cloth in one hand and a plastic bottle of water in the other. A trail of droplets led across the dusty floor through an arched doorway into the kitchen.

"Charley." He blinked at me and understanding surfaced behind his eyes. He looked startled, but not truly surprised.

"Where's Davey?"

"She's gonna be fine," he said, instead of answering. "You were."

Fear engulfed me like a brutal, body-wide bruise. "Don't move, Cam." I stepped aside, scanning the otherwise empty living room, and Austin leapt through the doorway on four legs, Bishop and Vance on his heels.

Panic flashed across Cam's features. He dropped the bottle and the cloth and spun toward the back door, just as Jace kicked it open.

Mistaking me as the lesser threat, Cam spun toward me again, grasping for something at the back of his waistband with his right hand.

"Gun!" Jace shouted.

Cam aimed a pistol at me. He fired three times, the blast of sound deafening in such a small space, especially for sensitive shifter ears. The muzzle flashed as something crashed into me from the right side, driving me across the room. I landed in a musty armchair, pinned by an enormous but familiar weight.

"Move!" I shouted as I shoved Bishop over, dimly noting a sharp, burning pain in my right arm. And the fact that my own voice was drastically muted in my ringing ears. By the time I regained my feet, Austin had Cam pinned to the ground, his muzzle biting into his prey's throat with enough pressure to break the skin and drip blood on the floor, but not to crush his throat.

Or rip it out.

Yet.

Jace grabbed the gun Cam had dropped, clicked the safety back on, then shoved it into his own waistband, as Tucker followed him into the small space, snarling.

"Hold him there," I said, and Austin growled softly without removing his teeth from Cam's throat.

"Charley!" Vance shouted as Jace pulled a set of metal handcuffs from a pouch at his waist.

"Where's Davey?" I demanded, nudging Cam with one foot.

"Charley!" Vance shouted again, and I glanced around the room, but didn't see him.

"Shift back." Jace tossed his backpack at Tucker's feet. "They need first aid." His focus slid from me to my left, and I turned to find Bishop sitting in the chair I'd just clawed my way out of, his left hand clutching his right shoulder. Where blood poured from a bullet wound.

"Shit!" My focus scanned him, looking for any other injuries. "Are you okay?"

"Fucking peachy," Bishop growled through clenched teeth. "You?"

I knelt next to him, trying to apply pressure to the wound,

but pain lanced my right arm. Which was when I managed to piece together the past minute and a half.

Cam had fucking *shot* me, and Bishop had caught a stray bullet when he'd tried to tackle me out of the way.

"Don't move until we can examine you," Jace said to me, tapping on his phone. Probably texting Spencer. "Just sit down, and I'll be right there." He pocketed his phone and turned to Austin, who still stood snarling at our handcuffed prisoner. "Don't let him move."

"Charley! Get the fuck in here!" Vance shouted again, appearing briefly in an open doorway across from the kitchen.

Pulse racing, I shoved myself to my feet, clutching my injured arm, and lurched across the small, crowded space, dodging human and feline forms on my way to the only bedroom. Where I found Vance sitting on the edge of a full-size bed, next to my sister's prone form.

"She's out cold," he said as I sank onto the other side of the bed, still struggling to hear him while my ears rang. "And burning the fuck up."

"God*damn* it." Horrified by my sister's bright red cheeks, I felt of her forehead, where I left a smear of my own blood.

Vance frowned at me, sniffing in my direction. "You're bleeding."

"Fucker shot me. Bishop too," I mumbled, pushing Davey's sweat-soaked hair back from her forehead. "My arm's useless. I need yours."

Vance nodded, his jaw tight, eyes narrowed with a calm but deep distress. "First aid kit?"

I swung my backpack onto the bed from my good shoulder, wincing at sharp pain caused by the motion. "In there. We'll need the scissors. And ice. Find every bit of ice in this shithole. Put in a bag or wrap it in a towel."

He disappeared into the living room, on a mission, and I began a frustratingly slow and methodical exam of my sister, looking for the bite. Or the scratch.

As the ringing in my ears began to fade, I heard the guys talking in the other room, along with Bishop's bitter hiss of pain, but I registered little of it until Vance returned to my side.

"She definitely didn't come willingly. Huge bump on the back of her head," I said as he sat on the other side of the bed. "Probably a concussion, but that's the least of her worries at the moment. There's a scratch mark in her inner elbow. It was probably tiny, until it swelled up." I lifted her left arm to show him a bright red, inflamed spot that smelled vaguely of an early-stage infection.

Vance unzipped the first aid kit and set it on the comforter next to a quart bag full of large, old-fashioned ice cubes. "That's all there is," he said. "One cracked plastic tray in the freezer."

"Okay. Run it slowly over her face and forehead, then up and down her arms. Keep her as cool as you can." That was all I could think of to bring her temperature down, until I could get some medication into her.

I dragged the first aid kit closer and dug in it one-handed until I found a half-full bottle of acetaminophen suspension. "Open that and pour an adult dose," I said, handing it to Vance.

"Baby Tylenol?"

"It's for the whole family. Says so right there on front." I set the ice bag on my sister's chest and patted her cheeks firmly, first one then the other. "Davey. Hon, I need you to wake up. Just for a minute." No response, so I patted a little harder. "Davey!"

She groaned, and her eyes fluttered.

"How is she?" Jace asked, and I looked up to see him standing in the doorway.

"Alive," I said. "For now. How far out is Spencer?"

"Twenty minutes. He's got IV antibiotics and assorted other goodies, which is why he got started later than Vance. Tucker's ready to look at your arm."

"It can wait," I said, turning back to Davey to see that Vance had poured the little plastic dosing cup full of a thick purple liquid.

"At the very least, you need a bandage and a tourniquet," Jace said. "You're too tired already to be losing that much blood."

"Then send Tucker in. I'm not leaving her side."

Jace nodded, then disappeared.

I took the dosing cup from Vance. "Sit her up for me."

He slid one arm behind Davey's shoulders and lifted her. Her eyes fluttered open again, and for a second, they almost came into focus. "Charley?"

"Yeah. I'm right here. And I need you to drink this. All of it. It's going to help bring your fever down." *I hope.*

She opened her mouth obligingly, like a small child, and I poured the acetaminophen into it, left-handed. "Swallow," I reminded her as her eyes began to flutter.

She swallowed, and Vance laid her back down.

"Rest now," I said, but she was already out. I knew from experience that she wouldn't remember any of this. "Okay, take the scissors and cut her shirt off. Then her pants," I added as Tucker came into the room. "Then run that bag of ice over her limbs to cool her down." That was the best we could do, without the resources for an ice bath.

"Scoot down here," Tucker said as he sank onto the end of the bed, clearly well aware that was as far as I could be dragged from my sister. "How's Bishop?" I said as he sliced up the side of my blood-soaked sleeve with a pair of scissors from our other first aid kit.

Vance mimicked him, cutting carefully up the center of Davey's shirt.

"Grouchy, in pain, and glaring daggers at Cam Senet," Austin said from the doorway, and I leaned around Tucker to see him standing, fully dressed and human, in the doorway.

"Mark me down for those first two, as well," I said.

"How bad is it?" He kept his distance so Tucker could work, but he looked concerned.

"Through-and-through," Tucker said. "She needs antibiotics, stitches, and once it starts to heal, a couple of good shifts." Because as my body put itself together in a new form, it would also begin piecing together torn muscle and skin. "How's the pain?"

"If Davey weren't sick, I'd ask you to hit me with a sledgehammer," I said through clenched teeth. "But for now, I'd chew on a Tylenol, if you have one."

Vance dug four pills from the first aid kit and gave them to me.

"Sixteen rounds accounted for," Austin said as I chewed the bitter tablets. "Thirteen still in the magazine. One hit the doorframe and one hit the wall, and that one smells like your blood. The last appears to be lodged in Bishop's shoulder."

"Once the bullet's out, that's probably nothing some time and a couple of shifts can't fix," I said, hoping I sounded confident. "We'll have Spencer check him out once he's seen to Davey."

"What's the plan?" Tucker said as he trimmed my bisected sleeve from the rest of my shirt. "How long are we staying?"

"Only until Spencer says we can move her," I assured him. "We'll put her in my apartment, so I can take care of her and question Cam." I glanced into the next room, over Austin's shoulder. "Jace!"

"Yeah?" he called.

"We need to sedate Cam," I said. "If he can shift his hands, those cuffs won't hold him." But a sedative could keep him from shifting.

"On it." Jace appeared behind Austin and showed me a pre-loaded syringe, also from our rather specialized first aid kit.

"Wait!" Bishop bellowed, accompanied by the creak of the ancient chair as he stood with a groan.

I launched myself from the bed and pushed past Austin, loathe to leave Davey, even with Vance at her side. "Bishop, stay away from him," I snapped as he knelt next to our prisoner, across from Jace who stood ready with the syringe.

Bishop scowled at me. "I just want to talk to him for a second before you sedate him. You owe me this, Charley."

I exhaled slowly. "Fine. But make it quick." Interrogation was my job, and I wasn't going to miss a damn thing Cam Senet had to say. But my sister's life was my top priority.

Bishop turned back to Cam, snarling at him from inches away. "Why did you kill my wife?"

Cam tried to squirm away, but Jace planted one foot against his hip. "Who's your wife?" Cam finally said, the first words I'd heard from him since he'd shot me.

"Yvette Graham-Mattheson," Bishop growled, as Austin stood over his shoulder, both fists clenched. "Tall, with long, curly dark hair and blue eyes. You bit her three months ago, in Covington, and she died right in fucking front of me."

Cam frowned. "Sorry, dude. I remember all of them, and I kept meticulous records. But I was never in Covington, and there was no Yvette anything in my project."

"Fucking liar!" Bishop's left fist flew as he snarled, and

Austin pulled him back, blunting a blow that should have shattered Cam Senet's face. Instead, it glanced off his jaw.

"Seriously, man. I'm proud of my work, and I'll tell you whatever you want to know. But I've never heard of your wife. And I never bit anyone. I just scratched them, casual-like. In passing. They never even saw the claw." He lifted his cuffed hands, showing off a single partially shifted finger on his right hand. "Davey's the first one I ever took, and that's only because I had no choice. And I never *bit* anyone."

TWENTY-SIX

"Hey." Vance came out of my bedroom as I was transferring my sheets from the washer into the dryer. One handed, thanks to a new sling and the sterile bandage wrapped around the top of my right arm, covering my painful, freshly stitched wound.

"Hey," I said. "How is she?"

"Still unconscious. Fever's 104.2, even with the meds. Spencer's got her covered in ice packs and hooked up to that IV."

"Can you keep an eye on her while I go back downstairs? Text me if anything changes."

He frowned. "You don't think the second interview can wait?"

Jace and I had interrogated Cam the moment we'd gotten Davey settled, but I'd been reluctant to leave her for long.

"I don't think *Bishop* can wait." He'd threatened to bust down the basement door, even with a bullet hole in one shoulder, if I didn't let him in to talk to Cam again. "And I need to stay busy."

Despite exhaustion and injury, I couldn't sit still. Something wasn't right. There was no reason for Cam to deny biting Yvette, when he'd admitted to everything else, unprompted.

We'd missed something.

"Speaking of Bishop…" Vance eyed my dryer as I closed the door and turned it on.

"Don't start."

"It's none of my business," he began.

"People keep saying that, then talking about it anyway."

Vance smiled. "And I'm only asking because people *are* going to talk, and you're the Marshal, which comes with a certain respect protocol. So, I kinda need to know how hard I should shut down the rumors."

I sighed. "There's no real point, anymore." Spencer had no doubt gotten a good whiff of my sheets as I'd stripped and remade the bed—one-handed—for Davey. Austin and Tucker already knew. And with Bishop in his current state of indignant rage, he seemed less and less concerned about what anyone thought of his grieving process or our special little brand of rage-aversion therapy. "So, I would say don't dignify the rumors with any real reaction, and just remind anyone you hear talking—about me and Bishop *or* you and Davey—that none of it is any of their business. Hopefully they'll get bored with it and move on."

"I think they're more likely to be distracted by Davey's infection and Cam's arrest. At least for the time being."

"As they should be. That's definitely the headline. Emphasis on the part where we caught the bad guy. Speaking of which, Titus is on his way, and I'd like to have some concrete information about Yvette before he gets here. But you text me if anything changes with Davey."

Vance nodded. "Of course. I won't leave her side."

I peeked into my bedroom, and my heart ached at the

sight of my sister lying so still on the bed, gel ice packs lining her legs and one arm, the other hooked to an IV hanging from a metal stand.

"I'm doing my best for her," Spencer assured me from the chair he'd pulled up to the mattress, where he was taking her pulse from one wrist.

"I know. Thank you. I'll be downstairs for a few minutes, but Vance has instructions to let me know if anything changes."

Spencer nodded. "Give him hell." Then he turned back to Davey, and I headed downstairs.

"I hear you," Bishop was saying as I pushed through the swinging doors into the dining area. "But what I don't understand is why we should believe a single goddamn world that motherfucker says. He's an admitted murderer."

"He hasn't actually admitted to murder," I said, as Jace and Austin twisted to face me from the booth opposite Bishop. Where their only real task for the past half-hour had been to keep him out of the basement. "During the first interview, he admitted to seven counts of intentionally infecting a human woman—one more than we even knew about—but his goal wasn't to kill them." Which Bishop knew.

"And his MO for each of them was the same," Austin added. "A single scratch on the hand or arm, delivered as he bumped into them on the street, after identifying and stalking them for days. He says most of them didn't even register the scratch at that moment, and none of them identified him as the source."

"And you believe him?" Bishop growled. "All of you?"

Jace sighed. "We're going to talk to him again, but so far, I see no reason not to."

"The records are right there in front of you, Bishop." I pointed at the notebook where Cam had kept fairly meticulous hand-written notes, including names, dates, places, and pictures printed from social media and paper-clipped to the pages. "Yvette is not there."

"He could have ripped out her page."

"Why just hers?" Austin's voice was so calm and steady I marveled at the effort. He'd lost Yvette too, but he didn't get to be the furious, vengeful one. Over the past week, I'd come to realize that was because he felt almost as obligated to protect Bishop from himself as to avenge Yvette's murder.

Which kept him on the steady and rational—though no less determined—end of their quest for justice.

"I don't know why he'd rip out Yvette's page! Why the hell would he keep such incriminating notes, anyway?" Bishop demanded, clearly frustrated that he had no way to refute our point.

"Because he didn't think of it as a crime," Austin explained for at least the third time. Not because Bishop couldn't understand, but because he didn't want to. He couldn't stomach the idea that the bad guy we'd caught might not be the one who'd murdered his wife. That all our effort could offer him no closure. "He considered his 'work' to be a medical experiment he was conducting for all of shifter-kind, and he kept notes like an official record. Or as close as he could get, considering his somewhat basic understanding of scientific principles."

"He wanted to be able to replicate any successes as closely as possible," I added.

"Which is why you're the first entry in this book?" Bishop flipped to the front, where my own picture stared out at me, clipped to a page just inside the cover. "It looks like he spent nearly three years trying do what his dad managed." He tapped the word "success" where it was written in capital red letters at the bottom of my "entry."

"Yes, that's why." I swallowed the mortifying discomfort I felt at the sight of myself—of my deepest trauma—documented in some psycho's demented journal, as if I were a lab rat in a cage. "And Yvette's not in that book," I repeated.

Personally, I was starting to think he should be grateful for that.

"Then why the living hell is she *dead*?" He pounded on the table, then flinched at the pain clearly shooting through his shoulder, even after Spencer had removed the bullet and sewed up the wound. And shot him full of antibiotics.

I'd gotten a similar treatment, minus the bullet removal. And it hurt a *lot* more now than it had an hour ago, since the shock had worn off. As had the painkillers.

"I don't know. And I'm sorry that I've failed you," I said as I settled onto a chair near their booth.

Bishop sighed. "You haven't—"

"But I'm working on it," I assured him. "We *will* catch Yvette's killer. I just don't think that's Cam. And I don't think you do either." We'd been over and over the evidence.

Bishop scowled. "I want to talk to him again."

"You can come down with me," I said. "But just to listen. I promise I'll ask everything we all want to know, but that's my job, not yours."

"Fine," he grumbled.

"You too," I said to Austin, who nodded. Then I turned to Jace. "May I see you outside?"

He arched one brow at me, but nodded.

"Take some more Tylenol and wait here," I said to Bishop. "I'll be right back."

"What's going on?" Jace asked once the back door of the bar had closed behind us, but I led him into the rear parking lot, shivering against the cold, before I answered.

"I hate to impose on you again, and I know you're probably as tired as I am."

"I doubt that," he said. "What can I do?"

"I need someone brought in, quietly, and I have no one else to ask at the moment."

His brows rose. "Happy to help. But I'll need a little more information…"

"YOU MOTHERFUCKING *ASSHOLE*!" Billy shouted as I descended the basement stairs with Austin and Bishop at my back.

"He's been like that since we locked Cam up," Tucker informed me when I opened the door. "I keep hoping he'll go hoarse."

"Davey? Really?" Billy yelled, trying his best to rattle the bars between his cell and Cam's. "You could have fucking killed her."

"He may have," I said, and Billy went silent, turning toward my voice. His hair was lank and needed a wash, and his clothes were hopelessly wrinkled. I couldn't help feeling a little sorry for him, even though he'd put himself there.

For his part, Cam appeared unruffled by the shouting. He sat on his bunk, leaning against the wall as if none of this truly bothered him. As if persecution were to be expected for a mission the rest of the world refused to accept as legitimate.

He'd adopted that affect the second we'd thrown him in the cell.

"How is she?" Cam said, and Billy turned to snap at him.

"You have no right to ask that!" He spun back to me. "Is she okay?"

"She's unconscious, and we're mitigating a high fever

while we pump her full of fluids and antibiotics. Only time will tell."

"You're going to execute him, right?" Billy demanded. "Fucking rip his head off."

"Here, here," Bishop snarled.

"I swear I had nothing to do with any of it," Billy insisted. "I would never hurt Davey, and I would have told you who *he* was from the start if I'd had any idea what he was doing. But even if you aren't going to let me go—even if you don't believe a word I'm saying—I'll gladly stay in here my whole fucking life if you'll just end his." Billy pled with another furious glance into Cam's cell. Where Cam sat silently on his empty bunk.

"The kid has more sense than I gave him credit for," Bishop said.

"He's an idiot, but he's telling the truth," Cam said. "Billy had nothing to do with any of it. So make sure he doesn't get any of the credit."

"Fucking *fuck off*," Billy shouted, spittle flying. "I hope you rot! There *is* no fucking credit."

"Let Billy out," I told Tucker. "Jace is waiting upstairs to take him home, then he needs your help with one more thing."

"What thing?" Austin asked.

"I'll explain when we're done here," I promised. "And this shouldn't take long." I turned to Billy, as Tucker escorted him out of his cell by one arm. "Thanks for your help. Sorry it took so long to clear you."

"Wish I could have done more." There were bags under his eyes, and he might have lost a couple of pounds, but it was nothing a good night's sleep and a big meal couldn't fix. And maybe a joint. "Can…can I still work here?" he asked, much softer.

"Of course." I put one hand on his shoulder. "I would never have cut you off just because of who your stepfather was. I hope you understand that. But you owe me and this entire community absolute honesty and transparency. I know you didn't do any of this, but you could have stopped it if you'd told me the truth from the beginning."

"I will from now on. I swear." There were tears in his eyes.

"You'd better. I don't hand out many second chances," I warned him.

He nodded. "Can I see Davey?"

"No." I glanced at Tucker. "Take him home. Billy, the bar's going to be closed for a few days, so take the opportunity to rest and do some serious self-reflection. I'll call you when we open up again."

"Okay. Thanks," he said as Tucker half-dragged him toward the stairs.

"We're sure he's innocent?" Bishop said. "On all counts?"

Austin nodded. "He's got problems, for sure, but he's no killer."

"I take issue with that characterization," Cam said, still seated on his cot. "I never set out to kill anyone."

"And yet, that's what you accomplished." I pulled the folding chair toward his cell and sank into it, well out of reach. "We've been through your 'notes,' but I have a few more questions to ask you, for the official record." I opened the recording app on my phone and tapped the red button.

"I've already told you everything I—"

"Were you there when your father kidnapped me?"

Cam looked surprised by the question. "No."

"Did you know he was going to do it?"

He hesitated, but finally shrugged. "Yeah. I gave him your name, after Billy told me about your brother. I figured that meant you had the gene, and that kind of became the corner-stone for our theory. But I wasn't there when he…did it."

I took a breath, fighting not to let him see how horrifying this whole line of questioning was for me. "So, your notes about me…?"

"They're based on what he told me, before you guys hunted him down. Before he even knew you were going to live. He died in triumph, you know," Cam said. "A fucking martyr for the cause. You were a victory for him."

"*Fuck off*," Bishop growled, and I ignored him, though I respected the sentiment.

"And you got the other names from the locals? The bar regulars?"

Cam nodded. "I already told you that."

"Were you working with anyone—"

"What about Yvette?" Bishop demanded, ignoring me when I turned to glare at him.

"I told you," Cam said. "I'd never heard of you or your wife until you showed up at the bar a week ago. I had nothing to do with whatever happened to her. Though I am sorry for your loss."

Bishop lunged at the cell, and Austin held him back, but he was snarling too, now.

"Were there any others?" I asked. "Any you didn't document?"

"No. I kept very clear records. Make sure you show those at my trial."

"This *is* your fucking trial," I snapped. "And *this* is the goddamn record." I held up my phone, which was still recording. "You've already confessed. And if you're under the delusion that this is going to somehow make you famous, let me disabuse you of that notion. You're no hero. No martyr. Even if my sister lives, you're not going down in history as some kind of champion for creating another female stray. I'm going to execute you, bury you, fill in the grave, when it starts to sink as your corpse rots, and I'm going to wipe your name from the annals of shifter history. No one outside of this zone will ever know what you did, and in a few years, even the locals will forget you ever existed. *There will be no glory for you.*"

Not at my expense. Not at my sister's expense. Not at the expense of the seven other women he'd murdered on some psychotic quest that might only gain traction and copycats, if the details were to get out.

"You will never leave this cell," I told him.

Cam sneered at me. "Maybe not. But you'll think of me every time you see your sister. Every time you get even a whiff of her scent."

I turned to Bishop and Austin, fighting to control the rage burning through me, a struggle they both clearly understood. "Satisfied?"

Austin nodded. "I'm done with him." He turned to Bishop. "He'd have taken credit for Yvette, if he had anything to do with it. Please tell me you see that."

Finally, Bishop nodded, his jaw clenched. Unshed tears shining in his eyes. "I'm done with this asshole."

"We all are." I turned back to the cell and pulled Cam's pistol from my waistband. Then I shot the motherfucker through his goddamn skull.

TWENTY-SEVEN

"Hey," Bishop said from the open doorway of my bedroom. He held up a bottle of top shelf whiskey. "I left an IOU downstairs. Care to join us out here?"

Austin nodded at me over his shoulder.

I glanced at Vance and Spencer. We'd been stationed in chairs at Davey's bedside for the past forty minutes, letting Cam's corpse drain onto the basement floor while I held my sister's limp hand.

"Go on," Spencer said. "She's stable for now, and I've got it under control."

I stood and pulled him into a hug. "Thank you again for coming. I can't tell you what this means."

"It's no problem, Charley. I'm sorry my services are needed." He patted me on the back before letting go. "Titus is an hour out."

"Okay, thanks."

Bishop, Austin, and I settled around the coffee table in my living room, while Vance grabbed glasses from my kitchen cabinet. He passed them out, then took a seat next to me on the couch.

"What now?" Bishop said as he poured himself half a glass, left-handed.

"Square one?" Austin took the bottle and poured himself a double. "After all this. Back to fucking square one."

"Maybe not," I said as Vance took the bottle. He poured for us both, and I tossed my drink back instead of answering the questioning looks aimed at me from all over the room.

"Where's Jace?" Austin asked. "What's going on? Where did you send him?"

I poured myself another as the sound of a familiar engine rumbled faintly from outside, spiking my pulse. "Give me ten minutes, and I'll tell you."

"Hell no." Bishop stood, and I stood with him, lurching between him and the front door.

"Stay," I said. "Just drink with us for a few minutes, and then, with any luck, this'll all be over."

"What the fuck did you do, Charley?" he growled, and Vance stepped toward us, even though Bishop's growl wasn't aggressive. And wasn't aimed at me. "What's happening?"

"I had a suspect brought in. And as soon as he's locked up, we'll go talk to—"

Bishop tried to lunge around me, and I shoved him back, hissing at the fresh pain in my arm. Austin grabbed Bishop's good arm, and Vance planted himself in front of the door.

"Five minutes," I said, in as calm a tone as I could muster. "Pour yourself another drink."

Austin let Bishop go, and we all poured another round and listened to several sets of footsteps crossing the floor of the bar beneath us. We tracked them, Bishop's foot tapping aggressively on my floor, while we sipped expensive whiskey, tension radiating throughout the room.

We listened as those footsteps descended the basement stairs. As the door opened. As a shocked gasp echoed softly toward us, my new suspect clearly reacting to the sight of Cam's corpse and the ruin that was his face.

"Oh my god," Bishop said, and I couldn't tell whether he'd recognized the owner of that gasp or he'd just figured out what conclusion I'd come to nearly an hour ago, when I sent Jace and Tucker on their mission. "Get out of the way, Charley."

I stepped away from the door and set my empty glass on the coffee table. Then I followed him down two flights of stairs with Vance and Austin right behind us, praying that I'd hear the cell door clink shut before we got to the basement.

I did. But it was close.

"Nolan fucking Blake," Bishop roared the second he made it through the basement door. "I fucking *knew* it."

"Wait. You don't understand." Nolan backed toward the rear of the cell Billy had just vacated and nearly tripped over his blanket in an attempt to get as far from Bishop as he could. "You don't know what really happened."

"Jace," I said, motioning toward Bishop, and he and Tucker stepped between Bishop and the cell, holding him back. I turned to Nolan. "He may not understand, but I think I do." I inhaled deeply. "She paid you, didn't she? Ten thousand dollars. The bulk of her savings. Yvette paid you to bite her."

"Bullshit!" Bishop roared.

"No," Austin whispered, shaking his head. Devastated by the sudden wave of guilt washing across his features.

But Nolan nodded. "She wanted to be like you two. She wanted to be truly *with* you. And she knew you wouldn't do it. I was the only other shifter she knew. So she offered me cash. She was desperate, and I needed the money." He shrugged. "And I figured it should be her choice. I didn't hurt her. I swear I barely broke the skin. She wasn't even scared.

She looked…relieved. It's what she wanted, and if it wasn't me, she'd have found someone else. You *have* to know that." Another shrug. "So I did it. She gave me the cash, and I shifted so I could bite her. Then I shifted back while she bandaged the wound, and we went our separate ways. That was it."

"You *motherfucker*," Bishop snarled.

"I'm sorry she didn't make it. Truly. But that's not on me. She made her choice. And the whole damn thing was her idea." Nolan exhaled, pain etching lines across his forehead. "Turns out that's more of a choice than my sister got."

"Oh my god," Austin whispered. "God*damn* it, Yvette."

"I worried that's what Davey had done," I told them. "It wasn't. Cam took her. But the idea stuck with me, because it felt…plausible. Like something my sister *might* have done, if she'd gotten desperate enough. And it seemed to fit with Yvette's cash withdrawal."

"We didn't find any money," Tucker said. "Nothing new in Nolan's accounts."

"I put it in my mother's account." Nolan aimed his words at the floor, shame threaded through them. "To replace what I borrowed from her and lost at a riverboat casino in Missouri."

"For the record…" I glanced at Vance, who held up his phone, where he'd been recording the whole thing. "Do you confess to biting Yvette Graham-Mattheson?"

"Yeah," Nolan said, and his voice sounded thick with fear. He knew what was coming. "But she asked me to. She *paid* me to. It was what she wanted."

"But you knew it was against shifter law?" I prompted, and he nodded. "And that it would likely lead to her death? Aloud, please."

"Yes, I knew. But shouldn't she get to make that choice for herself?"

"That's not at issue here," I said. Though it was certainly starting to feel like *an* issue. "The fact is that you took cash payment from a human woman in exchange for infecting her, when you knew that was against the law. Is that right?"

"Yes."

"And then you lied about that repeatedly during interrogation, and you took specific measures to hide your crime?"

"Yeah." Nolan shrugged. "What else was I supposed to do?"

"*You were supposed to not kill my fucking wife!*" Bishop roared.

"I think that's enough," Jace said, and Vance stopped the recording. "It's on tape, and we have six witnesses."

"So can I kill him now?" Bishop demanded, and I could practically feel the rage pouring out of him, like heat emanating from a blaze. "I don't want a gun. I want my hands around his goddamn throat. He fucking confessed."

"That's Titus's call," I said.

Bishop turned on me, gesturing angrily at Cam's corpse. "Why wasn't that Titus's call?"

"It was. We had authorization to execute, after we got a confession. But he doesn't know about Nolan yet. We have to do this right, Bishop. The council has…standards. And our methods *have* to stand up."

Nolan groaned, and I turned to see him curled into a ball, tucked into one corner of his cell, as far as he could get from the puddle of blood beneath Cam's corpse.

"Titus will be here soon. In the meantime, we have work to do."

⋅ ⋅ ⋅

By the time Titus arrived, we'd removed Cam's body and cleaned up the blood. When the sun went down, we would bury him next to his father.

This time, though, I had no urge to participate in that myself. I wasn't willing to leave Davey.

"It doesn't look good," Titus said, seated in one of the guest chairs across from my desk. Jace sat next to him, but everyone else was in the bar. Waiting. "Two killers in one territory, both infecting and killing human women."

"Only one was a serial," Jace pointed out.

"And we caught both of them," I added. "Doesn't that part look good?"

Titus sighed, running his hands down the front of his slacks. "That'll certainly help me put a positive spin on it. Have you sent the confessions?"

"Yeah. Both recordings, along with copies of all of the rest of the evidence." I exhaled. "Please tell me we don't have to turn over Nolan to the council."

"We should have handed over Cam," Titus admitted. "They'll be pissed that didn't get the chance to question him. To look for a way to blame us for this, and to fucking *learn* something from his efforts. Not that they'd openly admit that."

Which was why we'd executed Cam as soon as we were certain of his guilt and had collected all the evidence. This would all have to be presented very carefully, and I didn't envy Titus the job.

"Handing Nolan over would go a long way toward making up for that."

"But Austin and Bishop—"

"Have a claim. I know." Titus nodded. "They have a *right*."

I could only shrug, my hands folded on my desktop.

"Ending Silas helped me heal. I considered it closure, until I found out about Cam. They deserve the same opportunity."

"I agree," Jace said.

Titus exhaled again. "As do I. I'll deal with the council."

"Bury him somewhere else, though," Jace said. "I wish we had an industrial incinerator. That came in handy several times, back on the ranch."

The Lazy S, capital of Faythe's Pride, where he'd served as an enforcer for years.

"Since we don't, we'll have to spread out the graves and treat them with lime. Just in case."

"Like with Silas," I said.

Jace nodded. "Do you need help?"

"No. We'll handle it from here. I appreciate everything you've both done."

"Three zones, one Pride," Titus said. "Next time, it could be us calling on you."

We all let that thought hang in the air for a moment. And finally, Jace smiled. "So, the brother and the widower are staying?"

"Looks like it. Austin hasn't heard back about his job application yet, but I can't imagine the Buford PD turning him down. And Bishop swears he can do construction anywhere. He works in a pretty wide radius anyway."

Jace's brows arched. "They sound like handy men to have around."

I rolled my eyes at him, ignoring Titus's obvious amusement. "We're all handy, around here."

"Are we putting them on the payroll?" Titus asked?

"Austin, definitely. But part time, like Spencer. We need his police resources, so he'll need to *be* a cop. Bishop is…temperamental. He needs training before I can trust him in the field."

"He's definitely mercurial," Jace agreed. "But he's strong, fast, dedicated, and loyal to a fault, and those are very valuable qualities in an enforcer. If he'll follow orders. If you can handle him." Jace cleared his throat and his gaze narrowed on me. "Not to get into your personal business, but...*can* you handle him?"

Titus's brows rose, but he said nothing as he waited for my answer.

"Not going to lie; he's a challenge. We'll see," I said. And that was as much as I was willing to commit to, at the moment.

"Okay, file the paperwork and keep us updated," Titus said.

"Fucking paperwork," I grumbled.

"It can wait," he said. "For now, deal with Nolan Blake and take care of your sister. Keep us updated on that too. Spencer has volunteered to stay as long as you need him. And Faythe has requested updates as well. She sends her absolute best."

She'd texted me as much, as well, along with a clearly heartfelt offer to do anything she could to help.

"I'll thank her."

Jace jumped up from his chair, staring at his phone. "Looks like you're going to get that chance in person. She's pulling up right now."

"What? Here?" I stood, and my chair rolled across the floor behind me.

Titus looked surprise as well. "She goes where she wants, when she wants, and for security's sake, she rarely gives advanced notice." Because enemies can't lay a trap if they don't know where you'll be. "Keeps my life adventurous. Yours too, now. Evidently."

Shit. I'd barely slept in days and could use a shower. I was not at my best.

I led Titus and Jace out of my office and into the front of the bar, where Tucker, Austin, and Bishop were already on their feet, staring out the front window into the glaring morning sunlight. In the parking lot, Faythe and Vic, the enforcer I'd met a couple of days ago, were getting out of a shiny black SUV. A second enforcer remained behind the wheel.

Faythe carried a small cooler.

Today, she wore a praline-colored hip length blazer over a matching blouse and slim-cut jeans. More casual than last time, but still well-put-together and functional enough to make me seriously consider updating my own girl-boss wardrobe.

Would it be weird for me to dress like the world's only female Alpha? Or would that just be the shifter version of dressing for success? For the job I wanted?

She marched toward the front door with Vic at her back, and I raced forward to unlock it, whispering to the guys on the way. "Female Alpha, incoming. Be cool."

Titus chuckled.

I wasn't sure anyone else had processed what I'd said.

"Faythe," I said as I pulled open the door to let her in.

"Charley." She wrapped both arms around me, her little cooler bumping against my back. "How are you? How's Davey?"

"I'm fine. Davey's…well, we're doing everything we can for her," I said as I led Faythe and Vic inside. "It's so kind of you to come, but that really wasn't necessary."

"It was," she said. "For multiple reasons. The Doctors Carver send their best." She placed the cooler in my hands, but her small smile looked more apprehensive than hopeful.

I flipped back the top to find a medical vial nestled on an ice pack.

"It's only been tested in the lab," Faythe said. "Never on a patient. And you certainly don't have to use it. I'll understand if you don't want to use your sister as our guinea pig. But I wanted you to have the option."

"This is…?" I had a vague idea, but no words to put it into.

"The 'designer' antibiotic we've been working on. Not me, specifically. I know nothing about medicine," she said. "But the Carvers have been designing this specifically to fight scratch fever. It's pretty successful in the lab, but like I said…" She shrugged.

"Davey would be the guinea pig." I glanced around at the room full of men all watching us in silence. "Will it hurt her?"

"No. Absolutely not." She shook her head firmly. "The worst-case scenario is that it won't work. That it'll be ineffective."

"She'd be no worse off than she is now," Vic added.

"So then, there's no reason not to try it?"

"Assuming she's not allergic to any antibiotics," Faythe said. "But it's your call."

"It isn't, though. It's what she wanted. She told me, but I wouldn't listen."

Faythe took my arm as I clicked the little cooler closed. "May I see her?"

"Of course. If she were awake, she'd want to see you."

Faythe hugged both Titus and Jace on her way through the front room, then I introduced her to everyone else. She was gracious and professional, and though I'd heard stories about her fierce temper and a sailor's mouth that rivaled my own, and I had no doubt she'd be a formidable opponent to anyone dumb enough to face off against her, she'd clearly grown into her role.

I led her up the stairs, wishing for the millionth time as we stepped into my private space that I was a more consistent housekeeper. But she spared no glance for my laundry hamper or dirty dishes. She just marched across the living room and into my bedroom, where she greeted Spencer warmly and took Vance's hand briefly before leaning down to run the back of her fingers across Davey's forehead.

"Poor thing," she murmured. "I can't imagine how hard this must be for you." She stood, and her gaze slid from me to Vance. "For all of you."

"It's torture," Vance whispered, watching Davey while I gave Spencer the cooler.

"A gift from Dr. Danny Carver," Faythe explained. "He's included a note on dosage."

Spencer opened the cooler and removed both the vial and the note. "Is this what I think it is?"

Faythe nodded. "We weren't planning to start human trials quite this soon, but…" She shrugged. "Every cloud, right? With any luck, this is the silver lining."

Spencer turned to me. "You're the next of kin. Is this what you want?"

"I've been assured it won't hurt her. And this is what she wanted." I turned to pull Vance close. "Agreed?"

He nodded, linking his arm through mine.

"Dr. Carver has emailed some forms he needs filled out to the letter," Faythe told Spencer as he read the note. "I assume you understand how important that is, for the future of the program?"

Spencer nodded. "Of course." He exhaled. "I didn't expect to be involved in this." And I could see the weight of that on his features. On his shoulders.

I felt it, along with him.

"Are we ready?" he asked as he pulled a sealed sterile syringe from the bag of supplies he'd brought with him.

I nodded, then we all watched as he administered the first carefully measured dose through Davey's IV. She never even stirred.

"I'm not sure how long it will take to see any difference," Faythe admitted. "But please let us all know if and when that happens. And keep us updated...otherwise."

"We will," I said. "Thank you so much for this."

Faythe took my hand one more time and squeezed it. Then I walked her downstairs, where Jace and Vic were getting caught up over coffee in the worn corner booth.

Titus and Jace left with Faythe. Titus was headed home, but Jace insisted on escorting Faythe and her men to the border.

"We're about to head out too," Austin said, appearing next to me at the window as I watched the line of SUVs disappear down the country highway.

I turned to see Tucker and Bishop standing near the kitchen door.

"Tools are loaded." Bishop's voice was gruff. Deep with pain. "You sure you don't want in on this?"

I shook my head. "This is your moment," I told him, my gaze sliding toward Austin to include them both. "Your justice. I'm happy to come for moral support, if you want, but not until Davey's...better. If you're willing to wait."

Bishop sighed, and I could see what just the thought of another delay would cost him.

"It's okay," I said, pulling both him and Austin in for a hug. "Go on. Get your closure and her justice." *And say goodbye*.

Because that's what they'd really be doing. This was the

end of a long road for them both, and I understood that completely.

"Don't worry, boss," Tucker said as I let them go. "I got 'em."

"Thank you." I squeezed his shoulder. Then I went upstairs, where I insisted that Spencer crash on my couch for a nap.

I curled up on my bed next to Davey, threading my fingers through her warm, limp grip as I listened to the footsteps climbing the basement stairs. To Nolan's soft sobs and pointless apologies.

Tears formed in my eyes and dripped onto my pillow as the footsteps faded. As the back door closed.

Vance watched through my bedroom window as Bishop's 4Runner drove off, the growl of his engine fading with distance.

The whole thing was a fucking tragedy. If Yvette had waited another year, she could have been in Faythe's pilot program. She could have made her choice. But she had no way of knowing it would ever exist. And that didn't give Nolan the right to risk her life for any amount of cash. To break rules meant to save lives.

With any luck, things were changing. *Rules* would change. But until then...

"It's not your fault," Vance said. "He made his own choice. The wrong one. There's no better way to handle this."

"We all made choices. Most of them were wrong," I pointed out, glancing from him to Davey.

"I know. If you want my resignation, you've got it. Just don't ask me to leave. Not now."

"I want you on the job," I told him. "I want you at my back, and at hers, if she ever makes it out of this bed. But my rules stand, Vance."

"I know. I swear to god."

"I'm going to consider that a renewal of your enforcer oath."

"Fucking count on it." He sat in the chair on the other side of the bed and took Davey's other hand. "Starting now. Get some sleep, Charley. I got this."

TWENTY-EIGHT

I woke up around noon to find Spencer replacing the gel packs lining Davey's legs. "How is she?" I said as I sat up, pushing tangled hair back from my face.

"The fever spiked, and she had a small seizure," he said. "But it's been calm since then."

"And no one woke me up?"

"It was over as soon as it started," Vance insisted from the other side of the bed. "Or we would have."

"She gets a second dose of the new antibiotic in a couple of hours." Spencer frowned at me as I stood. "How are *you*?"

"Fine. More than accustomed to sleep deprivation."

"They're back," Vance said, and I turned to find him staring out my bedroom window. "Austin and Bishop, anyway. I told Tucker to go home and get some rest."

"Okay. Thanks." I ran one hand down Davey's too-warm arm on my way around the bed toward the bathroom, where I brushed my hair and teeth. When I emerged again, Austin and Bishop were waiting in my living room.

"How'd it go?" I asked as I started a pot of coffee in my tiny kitchen. I could tell nothing from their freshly scrubbed faces and damp, clean-smelling hair. Except that they'd had reason to shower before they came back.

"We want to stay," Bishop blurted out, staring at me from the other side of my breakfast bar.

"I...?" I set the coffee pot beneath the drip. "Okay. Yes, that's already been discussed." I shot a questioning look at Austin.

He sighed. "It's taken care of. We've logged the coordinates of the...disposal on the encrypted virtual drive Jace gave us, along with the rest of the evidence. He took all the originals with him. We have no way of accessing anything on that drive—it's a one-way system, unless you have download access—so there should be nothing incriminating here."

"Except the jail cells in the basement," I said, one corner of my mouth crooking up. "If the human police ever get that far, we're all fucked anyway. As a species." But that had always been the risk. The best we could do was mitigate anything beyond that. "And it went...okay?"

Austin nodded.

Bishop shook his head. Then he nodded. "Fucker got what he deserved. But I didn't get what I wanted."

I pulled several mugs down from the counter. "Which was...?"

"I wanted to end a cold-blooded murderer. A stone-cold killer. But that asshole just kept blubbering. And apologizing." Bishop exhaled. "It wasn't what I expected."

I nodded. "It usually isn't."

"It's over," Austin said. "That's all it ever needed to be. So...thank you."

"No need. You guys found him. If anything, I delayed your justice."

He shrugged. "You went where the investigation led.

That's all we can do. And it might never have led us back to Nolan, if not for you."

I didn't feel like I deserved that praise. But I was glad it was over.

"We want to stay," Bishop repeated. "I can't go back to Covington—to that house—again. Not without Yvette."

I nodded. I couldn't be sure yet whether he was avoiding grief or legitimately trying to move forward. But it was his choice, either way. "You can stay at Pine Cove, if you're happy there and want the community feel. There are a couple more empty units, if you want to spread out. Including the one next to where you are now, if you wanna be neighbors. You'll have to sign an official lease, though. And pay rent."

Austin nodded, then he turned to Bishop. "You want the one we're in, or the one next door?"

Bishop shrugged. "Who fucking cares? I just want a fresh start. Some place I can remember Yvette without feeling like she should be there. Like she *will* be there, when I round the corner."

"That actually sounds healthy," I said, as the last of the coffee dripped into the pot.

"It may take us a couple of weeks to break our lease and get moved," Austin said. "To sort all that out."

I nodded as I began filling mugs. "Take your time. And when you're ready, I have an offer for you from Titus. As an enforcer. If you're interested. Northern zone. Part time. Comes with the shifter version of a security clearance and more responsibility than I can truly say is fair."

"For both of us?" Bishop asked.

"Just Austin, for now. But your offer will be forthcoming, once you've been trained and have demonstrated that you can follow orders. If you're interested."

"Yes," Bishop said.

I set my mug down and held his gaze across the counter. "I want to be clear. This job is about more than busting skulls. This is a community. A family. We solve problems, but not all of those require force. There's a lot of listening. Patrolling. Bartending," I added with a smile. "And a fuck-ton of paperwork. But it's all or nothing. You can't just walk in here throwing punches."

He exhaled again. "I'm more than that. Swear to god."

I nodded. "You're going to get the chance to prove that." My gaze slid to Austin. "And you…welcome aboard. I'll forward you the paperwork, and Titus will be in touch."

Austin smiled. It was an exhausted smile—more relief than true happiness, which made sense under the circumstances—but I could almost feel it click, deep inside me. He was a good fit, for the job and for the zone. And with any luck, we'd be as good for him as he was for us.

Bishop wasn't the only one who needed a new start.

I slid a mug across the counter toward each of them, and I was turning toward the fridge, my fingers crossed that my half-gallon of milk was still good, when Vance burst in from my bedroom.

"She's awake!"

I raced across the apartment, milk forgotten, to find Davey pushing herself slowly upright in my bed. Her cheeks were still scarlet, her eyes still glazed with fever. "Hey!" I practically cooed as I sank onto the mattress next to her. "How do you feel?"

"Like I caught the flu, and it brought some friends." Davey turned her head slowly, and she smiled weakly when her gaze landed on Vance. "I knew she'd relent," she whispered. Then she saw Spencer and she frowned. "Who're you?"

"This is Spencer Cole," I said. "He's one of a couple of miracles keeping you alive right now."

"Are you thirsty?" he asked her.

"Yeah." She nodded, but the motion seemed to upset her balance.

"Take it easy," Spencer insisted. "I'll get you some water. Charley?" He motioned for me to follow him into the other room.

"What does this mean?" I asked as I filled a glass with ice water in the kitchen, while Austin and Bishop listened in. "Is she out of the woods?"

"Not yet," Spencer said. "But it's a good sign. I've never nursed an infected woman, but for the men, we consider them in the clear when the first shift begins. So, we'll just keep taking care of her until then—rest, fluids, and antibiotics— watching for those signs."

I nodded. "Thanks."

"—never even saw him. I just woke up in a strange bed, with this burning in the crook of my elbow." Davey lifted her arm as I returned to the room, staring at the still-inflamed scratch. "And a wicked pain at the back of my head. Cam was standing over me, and I tried to run, but then I passed out." She shrugged unevenly. "That's all I remember."

"That's okay." I held the glass for her, so she could sip steadily. "You may remember more later, but you may not. Doesn't really matter though. We got him. We got you back. And it's all over now. All you have to do is rest and get better."

"Am I...am I going to? Get better?" Fear shined in her eyes as I set the water glass on my nightstand. "This isn't how it was supposed to happen."

"You're going to be fine," I said, mustering every ounce of confidence I had. Desperately hoping I wasn't lying.

"Faythe paid you a visit, and as it turns out, you are, in fact, the very first subject in our little project. Earlier than expected, and before they could get the clinic set up. But your statistics will officially be the first on record."

Davey's brows rose. Her eyes widened. "I'm gonna be shifter-famous?"

Vance laughed. "That was kind of always your destiny, one way or another." He leaned in for a kiss. "With that face, it was always in the cards."

She rolled her eyes at him, still smiling. But then, in an instant, her entire expression collapsed into a grimace of clear pain. "Charley, something's wrong."

"What?" I sank onto the bed while Spencer crossed to the other side, where he lifted her wrist to take her pulse. "What's happening?"

"Everything hurts. Like...*everything*. And..." She jerked her arm from Spencer's grasp and began clawing at both of her legs. "I itch *all over*."

A smile spread across my face, and with it came a massive wave of relief. "Davey. Hon. I have good news and bad news." I captured her hands, to keep her from clawing herself open while Spencer began disconnecting her from the IV. "The next few minutes are going to be the worst pain you've ever felt, and there is absolutely nothing that can be done about that. Not a damn thing. But once it's over, you're going to be *just fine*.

"Even better, you're going to be one of us."

ALSO BY RACHEL VINCENT

SHIFTERS

Stray

Rogue

Pride

Prey

Shift

Alpha

WILDCATS

Lion's Share

Blind Tiger

Wild Card

UNBOUND

Blood Bound

Shadow Bound

Oath Bound

SOUL SCREAMERS (YA)

My Soul To Take

My Soul To Save

My Soul To Keep

My Soul To Steal

If I Die

Before I Wake

With All My Soul

MENAGERIE

Menagerie

Spectacle

Fury

LIVING DEAD GIRL

Living Dead Girl

THE STARS NEVER RISE (YA)

The Stars Never Rise

The Flame Never Dies

BRAVE NEW GIRL (YA)

Brave New Girl

Strange New World

100 HOURS (YA)

100 Hours

99 Lies

YA STANDALONE

Red Wolf

Every Single Lie

No One Is Alone

ABOUT THE AUTHOR

Rachel Vincent is a former English teacher and an eager champion of the Oxford comma. She shares her home in Oklahoma with two cats and her husband, who's been her # 1 fan from the start. Rachel is older than she looks and younger than she feels, and she remains convinced that writing about the things that scare her is the cheapest form of therapy—but social media is a close second.

For more information…
www.rachelvincent.com